THE CRASH WAS CATACLYSMIC . . .

The huge sedan hit his car alongside, knocking it from the road.

With his vehicle now totally out of control, Koesler could do nothing but hang on as the small Escort bounced and careened from one limestone shelf to another.

As it neared the bottom of the hillside, the car was virtually catapulted from a slab of limestone. Then, as if in slow motion, it nosed over. As Koesler saw the ground coming to meet him, his only thought was to wonder if, when he next opened his eyes, he would see his parents, departed friends, Jesus, or what. . . .

Also by William X. Kienzle
Published by Ballantine Books:

ASSAULT WITH INTENT

SHADOW OF DEATH

WILLIAM X. KIENZLE

BALLANTINE BOOKS • NEW YORK

Library of Congress Catalog Card Number: 82-25309

ISBN 0-345-31251-1

This edition published by arrangement with Andrews and McMeel, Inc.

Manufactured in the United States of America

First Ballantine Books Edition: April 1984

Gratitude for technical advice to:

DETROIT

Sergeant Roy Awe, Homicide, Detroit Police Department
Ramon Betanzos, Professor of Humanities, Wayne State University
Margaret Cronyn, Editor, *The Michigan Catholic*
Lucille Duquette, Promotion Department, WXYZ-TV
Jim Grace, Detective, Kalamazoo Police Department
Sister Bernadelle Grimm, R.S.M., Pastoral Care Department, Samaritan Health Center
Timothy Kenny, Principal Trial Attorney, Wayne County Prosecuting Attorney's Office
Orlin D. Lucksted, Special Agent, F.B.I.
Sergeant Daniel McCarty, Homicide, Detroit Police Department
Thomas Petinga, M.D., Director of Emergency, Mt. Carmel Mercy Hospital
Rudy Reinhard, World Wide Travel Bureau
Noreen Rooney, Editor, TV Listings, *Detroit Free Press*
Andrea Solak, Assistant Prosecutor, Wayne County Prosecuting Attorney's Office
Neal Shine, Senior Managing Editor, *Detroit Free Press*

ROME

Kathleen McNamara Betanzos, Tour guide

LONDON

Richard Cohen, Divisional Director, Hodder & Stoughton

IRELAND

Sean Gallwey, Superintendent, Garda Siochana, Dublin Castle
Thomas J. O'Reilly, Superintendent, Garda Siochana, Phoenix Park

With special thanks to Chris and Mary Murray, Tom Murray, Gerald and Patricia Murray, Dom Murray, Eileen Keirns, Margaret Gallagher, Gertie McDonagh, R.N., Sean Tansey, and the people of Gurteen, County Sligo.

Any technical error is the author's.

FOR FIONA, who is Javan, my wife

TORONTO

"You don't want to see your bishop go to jail, do you?"

"N—no, Eminence," Father Maurice Ouellet, the master of ceremonies, stammered. As usual, he had no notion of what his Cardinal-Archbishop had in mind.

"Then, Maury, go find a dime and put it in the parking meter, or my car will be towed away and I'll be hauled off to jail."

Father Ouellet's left hand found the pocket in his trousers through the slit in his cassock. He rummaged through a handful of coins in search of a dime. "Where is your car parked, Eminence?" Ouellet asked, stifling a smile. After all, this was Holy Thursday's Chrism Mass. It would not do for the Archbishop's secretary and master of ceremonies to break up in the sanctuary of crowded St. Michael's Cathedral.

"It's just out the door there on Church Street. Under the spreading chestnut tree, as luck would have it."

Ouellet briefly pondered the immediate future. The Mass had just begun. The choir was singing a vernacular version of the Kyrie, which would be followed by a choral rendition of the Gloria. He had plenty of time to safeguard his Archbishop's car. With that special grace shared by adroit emcees and maître d's, Ouellet made his departure from the sanctuary appear to be part of the ritual.

Adrian Cardinal Claret spoke softly out of the right corner of his mouth. It was a signal for Father Ed MacNeil, deacon of the Mass, seated to the right of the large upholstered red throne, to lean toward His Eminence.

"For some reason," said Claret, "the choir puts me in mind of the classical definition of clerical tact."

"What's that, Eminence?" MacNeil asked out of the left corner of his mouth.

"It happens at an old solemn high Mass," out of the right corner of his mouth. "The old pastor is the celebrant. The oldest assistant is the deacon, and a young priest, just ordained, is master of ceremonies.

"Well, they're all seated during the Creed. The pastor's arms are folded across his chest.

"The master of ceremonies leans over to the deacon and whispers, 'Tell Monsignor to put his hands on his knees.' After a moment, the deacon leans over to the pastor and says, 'The choir sounds pretty good today, doesn't it?' The old pastor nods. Then the deacon leans back to the master of ceremonies and says, 'The Monsignor says, go to hell!' "

MacNeil chuckled quietly. "The choir does sound good today, doesn't it?"

Claret smiled and nodded.

Holy Thursday is a special feast in the Catholic Church for many reasons. Catholics, in common with all other Christian denominations, commemorate the Last Supper that Jesus shared with His Apostles. But for priests, the feast holds a unique significance. It marks the event during which Jesus instituted the Eucharist and invited the Apostles to "do what I have done" —in effect, creating the cultic priesthood. Many priests considered Holy Thursday to be a sort of birthday of their priesthood. In recent years, a ceremony of "Renewal of Commitment to Priestly Service" had been added to the Holy Thursday liturgy.

In addition, during the Chrism Mass in Catholic dioceses throughout the world, bishops gathered with their priests and as many of the faithful as they could entice to the ceremony, to solemnly bless the oil that would be used to consecrate candidates for baptism and confirmation and to anoint the sick. Each year on Holy Thursday, the past year's unused blessed oil was disposed of and each parish was offered a new supply of freshly blessed oil at the Cathedral. There was, then, a practical reason why each parish was represented by at least one of its priests: Someone had to go to the Cathedral to pick up the new oil.

The choir was midway through the Gloria when Father Ouellet returned to the sanctuary. He and the Cardinal exchanged a knowing glance. The deed had been done; His Eminence's car was protected for another hour.

The Gloria concluded, the Archbishop rose to lead the congregation in prayer.

"Father, by the power of the Holy Spirit you anointed your only son Messiah and Lord of Creation; you have given us a share in His consecration to priestly service in your Church. Help us to be faithful witnesses in the world to the salvation Christ won for all mankind. We ask this through our Lord Jesus Christ, your Son, Who lives and reigns with you in the Holy Spirit, one God, forever and ever."

"Amen," the congregation affirmed loudly.

This was followed by two readings, one from the Old Testament, the other from one of Paul's Epistles.

During the readings, Cardinal Claret absently toyed with his pectoral cross. Father Ouellet, aware that many in the congregation were watching the Cardinal rather than the lectors, noticed the Cardinal fingering the gold cross suspended on a cord around his neck.

Ouellet leaned near the ear of Father MacNeil and whispered, "The Cardinal's hands should be resting on his knees."

MacNeil looked surprised. He then smiled, leaned toward the Archbishop, and whispered, "The choir sounds good today, doesn't it?"

Claret glanced at Ouellet, then, a smile tugging at the corners of his mouth, whispered to MacNeil, "Tell him to go to hell."

An eager young priest proclaimed the Gospel reading rather forcefully. Then he began preaching a homily playing on the functions of oil in everyday life.

Claret had heard it all before; many, many times. It was not long before he tuned out the young priest and pursued his own stream of consciousness.

Holy Thursday held a special significance for Claret because his priesthood was so precious to him.

Last year he had celebrated the fiftieth anniversary of his ordination. Just as Saint John, writing his gospel memoirs from exile on the island of Patmos, could remember not only the day but the hour he first met Christ, Claret could clearly remember his ordination as well as all the related minor and major events of the past fifty years.

He had been born, raised, and ordained for service in the diocese of Saskatoon. During his postgraduate studies in Rome, he used to kid his classmates that he owed his rugged constitution to his Saskatchewan heritage. He especially enjoyed telling priest-students from tropical countries about the frigid winters in his hometown, where, he would boast, only the hearty survived.

It got to be a game. The other doctoral students would periodically ask him how cold it was in his hometown. Claret would invariably reply that it was so cold that the Saskatoon flasher walked the streets describing his anatomy to innocent passersby. At least the first time around, he had to explain the special North American connotation of the term "flasher" to the many non-North Americans in Rome.

If Adrian Cardinal Claret had a single regret in all his clerical years it was that so few of those years had been spent as a parish priest. After obtaining his doctoral degree in theology, he had been assigned as a seminary professor.

Then a few years in the chancery. After which, he was appointed auxiliary bishop of Edmonton, and finally, made Archbishop of Toronto. For the past twelve years, he had been a Cardinal, a hierarchical position second only to that of the Pope.

There had even been talk in recent years that Claret was in the running for the Papacy. At seventy-six, he was by no means too old for the office. Besides, he was in vigorous good health—undoubtedly, he assured others, the result of his rigorous years in rugged Saskatchewan. He had established an outstanding record in Toronto. He was a brilliant and gifted writer. And, perhaps paramountly, he was a proven conciliator. The world, in special ways the Catholic world, was in deep need of conciliation. The Papacy would be an extremely appropriate platform from which to exercise an effective conciliatory role.

The rumor amused him. He was not convinced he was cut of papal cloth. He imagined himself standing on a balcony above St. Peter's Square, in white cassock and zucchetto, microphones bending toward him, the world eager to hear his first pontifical words, while he would be toying with the temptation to say something utterly ridiculous—just to get rid of the tension and to begin the demythologizing of the Papacy. No, it was not for him.

"The bishop rises."

"What?"

"The bishop rises." Father Ouellet seemed perturbed Claret had not heard the direction the first time.

The homily had concluded. It was time to proceed with the Chrism Mass. Claret had, indeed, been lost in thought.

Now for the Commitment Renewal. A small altar boy, bearing a large liturgical book opened to the appropriate page, approached the Cardinal. The boy seemed overwhelmed by the book. But, somehow, he managed.

The Cardinal adjusted his bifocals.

"My brothers, today we celebrate the memory of the first Eucharist, at which our Lord Jesus Christ shared with His Apostles and with us His call to the priestly service of His Church. Now, in the presence of your bishop and God's holy people, are you ready to renew your own dedication to Christ as priests of His new covenant?"

"I am," each responded simultaneously.

Claret led his priests through the ritual commitment. He then resumed the high-back throne, or cathedra, just as Father Ouellet was about to direct, "The bishop is seated." Ouellet's pursed lips betrayed frustration. Claret enjoyed these small games. Nothing hurtful. Merely playful.

Three deacons, each bearing a container of oil, approached the Cardinal. Each, respectively, loudly intoned his presentation.

"The oil for the holy chrism."

"The oil of the sick."

"The oil of the catechumens."

The oils were then set aside for later attention. The Mass proceeded.

As one familiar ritual blended into another, Claret felt a

rare sense of warmth for and unity with his priests—a good percentage of them gathered with him this day around the main altar of St. Michael's Cathedral. It was their special day, the liturgical anniversary of their priesthood. They had assembled this morning to renew that unique supper first celebrated almost twenty centuries before. They might have their differences from time to time, he and his priests, but for this moment they were united spiritually and emotionally in their common priesthood.

A deacon brought a vessel of oil to the altar. Father Ouellet indicated the proper prayer in the Missal. Claret prayed.

"Lord God, loving Father, you bring healing to the sick through your son, Jesus Christ. Hear us as we pray to you in faith, and send the Holy Spirit, man's Helper and Friend, upon this oil, which nature has provided to serve the needs of men. May your blessing come upon all who are anointed with this oil, that they may be freed from pain and illness and made well again in body, mind, and soul. Father, may this oil be blessed for our use in the name of our Lord Jesus Christ."

The Archdiocese of Toronto had just been provided with a year's supply of oil for the sick.

The greeting of peace was given and received with more than ordinary enthusiasm, as priests and bishops milled about the sanctuary and nave of the cathedral shaking hands or embracing. The effusive spirit of camaraderie spread to the lay portion of the congregation; many left their places to mingle in the aisles, greeting and wishing each other "the peace of Christ."

There would be no extraordinary ministers of the Eucharist to help distribute communion. The cathedral staff well knew the mind of Cardinal Claret on this point. Extraordinary ministers, a post-Vatican II creation, were lay people appointed to assist in the distribution of communion—when there was a shortage of priests. But they were just that: *extra*ordinary The priest was the ordinary minister of communion. And there certainly was no shortage of priests here.

Claret was appalled at the practice in so many churches of using extraordinary ministers while one or another of the parish priests lounged in the rectory. Some priests considered distribution of communion to be a proper function of the laity. But this clearly had not been the mind of the Church. Nor was it the thinking of Cardinal Claret.

Besides, Claret enjoyed distributing communion. He could not understand why some priests apparently did not enjoy it. Priests seldom got closer sacramentally to their flock than when presenting their people with spiritual food at communion. After all, hadn't that been the enjoinder of Jesus to Peter—if you love me, feed my sheep. As often as he had the opportunity, Claret distributed holy communion and always with great reverence.

And so, Cardinal Claret, ciborium in hand, stood front and center in the sanctuary, presenting a consecrated wafer to each approaching communicant. Next to the Cardinal stood Father Ouellet, extending a gold-plated paten beneath the chin of each communicant who chose to receive the host in the mouth rather than the hand.

The other priests present processed to the altar to communicate themselves. Some few took ciboria filled with wafers or chalices of consecrated wine, and assisted in the distribution.

"The body of Christ," Claret announced, proffering a wafer.

"Amen," a well-dressed young woman affirmed.

Undoubtedly, she was not a parishioner of the cathedral—at least not one who resided within its technical boundaries. The cathedral was situated near the center city, an area populated mostly by transients, the elderly, and the poor. Claret thought it gracious of such outsiders, as this woman obviously was, to attend the Chrism Mass. Thursday morning was a difficult time to clear one's calendar for a religious service.

"Body a'Christ."

Claret heard the formula elided by the priest standing nearby. It was one of the cathedral's assistants. The Cardinal glared at him. After Mass, Claret would lecture the elderly cleric on the reverence due this Sacrament as well as on the disedification of the laity.

"The body of Christ," said Claret.

"Amen," a youth responded, extending his cupped hands.

Claret smiled. A young lad, his life before him. A possible vocation to the priesthood. It was the Cardinal's invariable presumption. Though it was unlikely. Not that many years before, almost every Catholic boy, especially those attending parochial schools, at least considered entering the priesthood. Now, there were so few seminarians. Where was it all to end? Who would follow the present clergy?

"The body of Christ," said Claret.

"Amen." The black man extended his tongue. Ouellet positioned the paten beneath the chin as Claret placed the wafer on the tongue.

Something was wrong. Claret knew something was wrong, but he was so startled by the sudden feeling, he did not know what it was. He looked down. A crimson stain was spreading at an alarming rate over his white cotton outer vestment.

"Oh . . . oh, I've been hurt," a bewildered Claret stated loudly.

He staggered backward and collapsed.

"Call St. Michael's Hospital!"

"Call the police!"

"My God, the Cardinal's been assassinated!"

Pandemonium!

2

"Oh, my God! Oh, my God! This is terrible!" Father Ouellet buried his head in his hands.

"Get hold of yourself, Father," said Father MacNeil. "It's just a lucky thing that St. Michael's is only a few blocks from the cathedral. I do believe that was the shortest ambulance ride I've ever had."

The two priests sat side by side in the waiting room of the hospital's emergency department. It was not unlike corresponding rooms in almost all hospitals. An occasional statue or religious print established its Catholic character.

Small groups of people sat or stood in clusters throughout the room. Beyond the swinging doors were several trauma rooms outfitted to handle, at least initially, almost any medical emergency imaginable. But the waiting room held its own peculiar trauma. Friends or relatives of emergency patients generally were confused, bewildered, isolated, and helpless. They had delivered a loved one to this emergency facility or had arrived after the delivery and had joined the vigil. Something or nothing was being done for the patient, but the friends and relatives had no idea what, if anything, was happening. Periodic intercessions with the desk attendants more often than not proved fruitless. The patient was doing as well as could be expected. Or, doctor so-and-so was in attendance. Or, we're still trying to find out what's wrong.

Just questioning the attendants was made to seem such an imposition that the more meek simply sat, entwining their fingers and wondering. The more dauntless went right on asking for—even demanding—updated information, on the theory that their squeaking might win a little medical oil for the subject of their concern.

Slightly more than half an hour before, the relative tranquility of the emergency department had been shattered when a gurney bearing Adrian Cardinal Claret had been wheeled through in the company of several Toronto police officers and a couple of clergymen in liturgical vestments.

The Cardinal had been whisked through the waiting room so quickly that none of the visitors had recognized him, even though his picture had appeared often enough in newspapers and on television. All the visitors could surmise was that the new patient must be a very important person.

They were correct. St. Michael's top trauma team had been summoned. No sooner was the Cardinal wheeled in than they began working on him.

"I can't believe this actually has happened," said Father Ouellet. "I mean, who would want to harm the Cardinal?"

"It's the times," Father MacNeil reflected. "We live in violent times, Maurice. But the Cardinal . . ." He shook his head. "Why would anyone want to attack him? Such a good man!"

Two men with the same and similar questions on their minds approached the clergymen.

"Inspector Hughes, RCMP." One of the men proffered his identification in a manner which seemed to demand that each priest examine it carefully.

"You would be," Hughes consulted his notepad, "Fathers Ouellet" —Ouellet nodded— "and MacNeil."

"How did you know?"

"We were at the church."

"The cathedral."

"Yes." The Inspector accepted the correction impassively.

"Which of you was standing near the Cardinal when he was attacked?"

"I was," said Ouellet.

"I see." Both the Inspector and his associate were taking notes. "Can you describe the assailant?"

"Let's see. I think it was the third or fourth person to receive communion from the Cardinal . . ."

"Talk about a Judas," MacNeil interjected.

"Yes, it was the third." Ouellet was positive.

"Male or female?" This was one of those times, Hughes determined, when information would have to be pulled out piecemeal.

"Male." Ouellet was surprised by the question. It would never have occurred to him that a woman would be capable of such a wanton attack.

"Height?"

"Let's see. I was standing one step up and the man's head was about the same height as my shoulder. I would guess about six feet, give or take an inch."

"Weight?"

"I have no idea. Not fat. Not thin. Perhaps 190 pounds."

"Race?"

"I beg your pardon?"

"White, black, Oriental, Hispanic, dark, light?"

"Oh . . . black, very dark."

"Any distinguishing marks?"

"Marks? Uh . . . oh, yes; his hair, It was, uh, what do you call it, uh—"

"Natural?"

"Yes, I guess that's it." Ouellet could see the outside doors to the waiting room. A group of newcomers was entering hurriedly. They looked about as if searching for something or someone. "Are those the Metropolitan Toronto Police?"

Hughes glanced over his shoulder. "No, those are newspaper reporters. They will be followed shortly by the TV people."

He returned to his task. "How did the assailant strike?"

"I didn't see it."

"But you were standing right next to the Cardinal?"

"Yes, but . . . well, you see, I was holding the paten

under the man's chin, so I couldn't see what he was doing with his hands.''

''Neither could the Cardinal, then, eh?''

''That's right.''

A doctor emerged from the inner sanctum. Everyone looked at him expectantly, each hoping for information about his or her loved one.

The doctor looked around. Noticing the two clergymen, he started toward them. He reached them at about the same moment as the reporters.

''I'm sorry.'' The doctor shook his head. ''We did all that was possible. At first it didn't seem to be a major wound. It was an abdominal cut approximately an inch and a half long. There was minimal tenderness.''

The doctor was elaborating more than was necessary for the two priests. But the media people, as well as the RCMP representatives, were taking notes.

''We probed the wound. There was an upper angle toward the left shoulder. At that point, I ordered an X ray. We were looking specifically for air and shadows. Of course an IV was started as soon as the Cardinal was admitted.''

''Did the Cardinal regain consciousness at any time?'' a reporter asked.

''No, not really. At one point, he tried to sit up. We were struck by his grayish coloring and intense perspiration. But he said nothing.

''At about the time we discovered that the Cardinal's spleen had been ruptured, he slipped into deep shock. We immediately started closed chest massage, gave him blood, and attempted to restore his blood pressure. But we couldn't control his internal bleeding. Irreversible shock set in and at that point, he expired. I believe it was a combination of his age and the shock. I'm sorry.''

''I can't believe it.'' A most rare tear wound its way through the furrows of MacNeil's face. ''Adrian is gone. I was talking to him—joking with him just minutes ago.'' He paused. ''He was a good man.''

''Who could have done this to a man like Cardinal Claret?'' asked Ouellet of no one in particular. ''Why would anyone do it?''

''If we can discover the 'why,' Father,'' Inspector Hughes said, ''we may very well find the 'who.' ''

3

"Death to da Pope! Death to da Pope! Death to da Pope!"
He accompanied his chant by banging on a steel drum.

The noise was absorbed easily in the cacophony of Yonge Street outside.

The room in which the men had gathered was large and relatively bare. A table, a few chairs. Most of the men lounged on the floor or squatted against the wall. Several shuffled to the drum's rhythm. The room was not unlike a hall hired and furnished by neo-Nazis, except that where one might expect to find a picture of Adolf Hitler, there hung a portrait of Haile Selassie, the late Emperor of Ethiopia.

If one did not already know, it would have been almost impossible to make out whose likeness it was, due to the nearly impenetrable smoke that almost literally filled the room. Those who were not puffing their own massive spliff of marijuana—ganja—were passing a chillum pipe filled with the drug.

Most of the men—all of them black—wore their hair in long, tight ringlets.

Resting on a small stand, with several powerful lights focused on it, was a large menacing knife. The bloodstains had not been wiped from it.

"Death to da Pope! Death to da Pope!"

"Bredren!" An imposing figure of a man raised his arm.

The group fell silent. They continued to draw on their ganja as they looked at the standing man through half-closed eyes and thick smoke.

"Bredren!" he repeated. "Dis day, I and I go up to da church and do da job. I and I strike for Jah. Jah happy now. Da prince of Babylon been striked down. Dis day we do our job."

"Good Rasta man!" they responded.

"Everyting Irie. It be perfect. I and I strike down de son of Satan. We done done our job. Jah be pleased."

"Good Rasta man!"

The speaker took a long draw on his enormous, self-rolled spliff. Heavy smoke billowed from his nostrils. He held the spliff high in the air. "Ganja!" he announced.

"Jah be praised! Haile Selassie I be praised! Bless de Lion of Juda!"

The speaker leaned back against the wall and was silent for some moments. A smile played at his lips. Whatever his vision, he was enjoying it in the privacy of his imagination.

"Now, bredren," the speaker resumed, "it be up to Rastas in de udder parts of de world to take up de knife and strike down de bad satans of Babylon."

"Good dreads! Good Rastas!"

"Bredren, we be in dis togedder?" The question was rhetorical.

"We be in dis togedder!" They responded with fervor.

"Den pay mind to what I and I gonna do!"

The speaker unsheathed a knife only slightly less formidable than the one on the stand. He approached the stand and stood so near it his head and shoulders caught the full glare of the spotlights. The rest of his body was in shadow. Deliberately, he made a small incision in his wrist and mingled the ensuing blood with that already caked on the larger knife. One by one, each man in the room approached and silently followed suit.

When the ritual was complete, the speaker again raised his hand, although there was no sound to silence.

"Bredren," he said, "now it be time for de Rastas of de world to strike down Babylon one by one. And den we go home. And den we go wit de Lion of Juda!"

With that, the speaker approached the now blood-saturated stand and slowly turned the knife until it pointed in a southeasterly direction.

The drummer resumed his rhythmic chant. Some joined in the ensuing symbolic dance. All contributed to the dense ganja smoke.

The macabre ritual, at least in its Toronto phase, had been concluded. But, somewhere else, it would begin again.

4

"Some suite!"

"It's Canada!"

Don Louis Licata merely smiled. They had been waiting a long time. Too long for the limited patience of his two soldiers. "Now, now, boys," he said, "this is the Windsor Arms. One of the most prestigious hotels in Toronto. Why, Pierre Elliot Trudeau dines here when he is in town."

"Maybe we should try the food." One of the soldiers winked.

"And," Licata continued, "they say Marlene Dietrich stays here when she comes to Toronto."

"Now that would change things."

"What?"

"If a dame like Marlene Dietrich was in this suite."

"Ha!" The second soldier chortled. "That's what you need, a *villuta!*"

"Marlene Dietrich is no prostitute!"

"You don't need a certain woman. Any one will do." He laughed again.

"Boys, boys!" Licata raised a hand. "Hold it down. I want to think before the others get here."

The sitting room held six chairs. Just enough. Three with their backs to the window were occupied by the visitors from Detroit. The three near the door would be occupied by the Torontonians whose arrival was not scheduled for another half hour.

The silence was broken by a noise from the adjoining bedroom.

Each soldier drew a snubnosed revolver from his shoulder holster. Licata cautiously eased the bedroom door open, then stood back as the two men preceded him into the other room.

No one made a sound as the trio began checking behind the wall pictures, under the bed, through the dresser drawers, in the closet. The sound occurred again. It seemed to come from the wastebasket, across the top of which was lying a telephone directory. One of the men nudged the basket with his foot. The sound was repeated. Warily, he eased the directory off the basket. Weapons at the ready, both men leaned forward to peer into the receptacle.

"A mouse!"

Relieved laughter rang through the room.

"In the Windsor Arms!"

"So much for the prime minister and Dietrich!"

"Now, boys, this is an old hotel. And old hotels are entitled to their mice."

"What do you want us to do with it, boss?"

Licata shrugged. "It's not our problem. It's the hotel's problem. Call the desk."

There couldn't have been that many mice in the Windsor Arms' recent history. No one seemed proficient in the animal's removal. First came a maid, who took one look at the small creature, shrieked, and ran from the room to the laughter of the three men. Next came a porter, an Asian who spoke English haltingly. He tried several methods of entrapment before chancing upon a plastic laundry bag, which he pulled over the basket. He then inverted the basket and, with the triumphant visage of a successful lion tamer, exited the room with a large plastic bag containing a very small, frightened mouse.

"Think he'll kill it?"

"Naw. If he doesn't eat it, he'll probably let it out in the alley."

"Then if the mouse remembers how it got up here in the first place, it'll probably be back."

"Whaddya think, boss . . . if it comes back, we shoot it?"

"Let's hope we'll be gone by then."

There was a knock at the door.

One of the soldiers opened the door just enough to see who was in the hall. Instantly, he flung the door open. Three men, one in advance of the other two, entered.

"Don Vittorio!" Licata embraced the lead man.

"Don Louis!" The other returned the embrace.

The two pairs of soldiers appraised each other at a glance. Then all six seated themselves. The two dons sat close together facing each other. Their guards positioned themselves on either side and slightly to the rear of their respective dons.

"Our condolences on the recent loss to the Catholic community of Toronto," said Licata.

"It was a great loss. Cardinal Claret, while not *compatriota*, might have been Papa. There was talk . . ." Vittorio Gigante's voice trailed off, as though the others would understand what was left unspoken. "The *astutatu* was an eminent man in many ways."

"Is there any progress on the identity of the *astutaturi?*"

Gigante shook his head sadly. "Nothing more than was in the paper. Black. Probably from off the street. No motive.

Possibly high on dope. We've been on the streets, but . . . nothing."

"What will happen now?"

"We're considering putting out a contract."

"Ah, as in New York."

"Yes, with the poor nun. Raped, tortured, twenty-seven crosses carved into her flesh. Only thirty-one years old. The police could do nothing. But when our brothers put out the word, those bastards knew they were dead men. It didn't take them long to turn themselves in. They were safer in jail than they were on the streets."

Don Vittorio chuckled at the thought of all that power. He was echoed by the others.

"How much?" Licata inquired.

"Twenty-five Gs."

"Same as New York."

"Yes. Five times the usual."

"That is why we have come, Don Vittorio. And, it seems, just in time."

"You have news of the *astutaturi?*" For the first time, animation entered Don Vittorio's voice.

"We, too, have been on the streets. As you know, Don Vittorio, not much separates Toronto from Detroit."

"Sister cities."

"Yes. And we have been able to get some information. Not all. But some." Licata shifted in his chair and drew himself closer to Gigante. "We are certain it is not the work of one. It is a conspiracy."

"A conspiracy!" Now there was a concept Gigante found familiar.

"Yes. A conspiracy. And one that we in Detroit are most interested in. So, before you put out your contract, we would like you to consider what we have to propose."

Gigante spread his hands. "But of course. We are brothers. Your cause is our cause."

5

Peculiar to the Catholic priesthood of the Latin rite, as compared with any other vocation in Western civilization, is that upon death there are no direct descendants. Often there are not even immediate survivors. The priest leaves neither wife nor child. At most, a few parishioners or consanguines make up the mourners. Seldom does a mourner at a priest's funeral need to be assisted from the scene overcome by grief.

This is even more true in the case of a deceased bishop. Not only does the bishop rarely leave any close kin, but he has been buffered from the laity by layers of clerical bureaucracy.

The funeral of a bishop, then, as far as the laity is concerned, is usually marked by one-tenth sorrow and nine-tenths curiosity. On the part of the visiting, concelebrating clergy, it is largely a social function wherein old but seldom-visited confreres bring each other up to date.

Then, too, as far as the clergy are concerned, theirs is a strong and active faith in an eternal life after death. So it is quite natural, even supernatural, that a priest's funeral can truly be said to be celebrated.

In any case, there were no moist eyes as the faithful gathered for the Mass of Resurrection for His Eminence Adrian Cardinal Claret.

The laity—by invitation only—were already in their places in the cathedral. The congregation included most of the movers and shakers of Toronto, Catholic and non. But the clergy would occupy the majority of places in the cathedral. It was a notable cast of clerics.

The Apostolic Pro-Nuncio, Archbishop Tito Fulmo, would represent the Vatican. Canada's only other Cardinal, Andrew Audette of Quebec, would be principal concelebrant of the Mass. Ten of the thirteen American Cardinals were present to concelebrate, as well as hundreds of Canadian bishops and priests, along with a few from the United States. Of the latter, most would be from Buffalo and Detroit.

Bishops were vesting in the cathedral rectory, while the priests vested in the school across the street.

Detroit's Archbishop Mark Boyle found himself in a peculiar hierarchical position. His elevation to the Cardinalate had recently been announced. But he had not yet been to Rome for the ceremonies that would make him a Cardinal. So, while he vested with the other archbishops, several Cardinals stopped by to say a few words to their new brother in this extremely limited, exclusive, and august club.

"I believe," Boyle was saying to Archbishop Leo Bernard of Cincinnati, "that the vocation crisis in the Archdiocese of Detroit could correctly be described as catastrophic."

"Congratulations, Eminence," said a passing Cardinal.

"Thank you, Eminence."

"It's not much better in Cincinnati," Bernard replied. "I don't know what we're going to do for priests in the near future. I read an article the other day by some priest who claims the problem is rectory life. That you can't expect men of different ages, experiences, and tastes to live together without tension, friction, and eventually, a great deal of stress."

"I read that article too. It ran in our paper, the *Detroit Catholic*. If you ask me, it is nonsense. Priests need priests. Once you have priests living in apartments, alone, you have created a fraught situation—"

"*Ad multos'annos*, Eminence," said a passing Cardinal.

"Thank you, Eminence."

"As far back as any of us can remember, and more," Boyle continued, as he tied his cincture and adjusted the alb at his ankles, "rectory life has proven not only practical but desirable. Without rectory life, where would the priest be when the faithful need him in an emergency?"

"I fully agree, Mark. And in addition to what you noted, what could we possibly do with all those rectories? There are few families who would consider buying a building that had been built as a combination home and office. And, speaking of buildings, what are you doing with that huge minor seminary of yours? What is it . . . Sacred Heart?"

"Yes. Well, we have moved just about every small diocesan department we can think of into that building. Let's see, we have the Department of Formation, the Office of Pastoral Ministry, the Hispanic Office, the Black Secretariat, Senior Citizens—"

"When's the consistory, Mark?" a passing Cardinal inquired.

"The last week of April, Eminence."

"Good! We'll be there. Congratulations, Eminence."

"Thank you, Eminence."

"In any case," Boyle continued, as he adjusted his pectoral cross, which now hung outside the alb, "you can see what it is we are attempting. Keeping the building filled—at least as much as humanly possible—and useful. If it is difficult to put a rectory on the market, trying to sell a seminary complex simply is an almost impossible concept. And to think that not twenty years ago, we were considering building additions to the seminary.''

"Pope John, when he called the Second Vatican Council, couldn't have known how much 'fresh air' those open windows of his were going to let in.''

Archbishop Boyle shook his head. It was impossible to understand the workings of the Holy Spirit.

"Eminentissimi ac Reverendissimi," one of the masters of ceremony loudly enounced, *"procedamus in pace."*

"In nomine Christi, Amen," the bishops responded.

In the school hallway, one of the masters of ceremony called out, *"Reverendi, procedamus in pace."*

"In nomine Christi, Amen," the priests—at least those older priests who understood Latin—responded.

The procession into the cathedral had begun.

"Bob Koesler." The tall, trim, blond priest extended his right hand to the younger priest who had become his procession partner.

"Ouellet, Maurice Ouellet." The two shook hands. "Where're you from, Father?"

"Detroit." Koesler pondered momentarily. "Ouellet . . . weren't you Cardinal Claret's secretary . . . the one who was with him when he was attacked?"

The younger man looked pained. "So I was mentioned in the Detroit papers too. Yes, I'm the one. But I'm trying to forget it.''

"Sorry."

"Oh, that's all right. It's just that I've told the story to the police so many times I've grown tired of it. Besides, I've had nightmares practically every night since.''

"Sorry again." Intent on changing the subject, Koesler inclined his head toward a series of spires in the area. "I guess there's no mystery about why they call this Church Street.''

Ouellet's gaze followed in the direction of Koesler's nod. He smiled. "They also call it 'Redemption Street.' ''

"Oh? Because of all the churches?"

"No." Ouellet directed his companion's attention across

the street. Koesler laughed. Almost every other establishment was a pawnshop.

The clerical procession wound its serpentine way from Church Street, down Shuter to Bond along a tall, black, wrought-iron fence. The first segment of the procession was mainly in a black and white motif as the priests marched in their black cassocks, white surplices, and a white or golden stole over their shoulders. They were followed by the red uniforms of the monsignors. Then came the impressive purple of the bishops. Finally, there was the breathtaking crimson of the Cardinals.

Bystanders who had gathered outside the cathedral earlier and were now standing two and three deep on the sidewalks had anticipated a memorable pageant. They were not disappointed.

"By the way," Ouellet turned to Koesler after a pause in their conversation, "I suppose congratulations are in order on your archbishop's getting the red."

Koesler smiled. "Yes. We're very pleased and proud of him."

"It's about time!"

"What?" Koesler seemed nonplussed. "Why do you say that?"

"Anybody who can run the Archdiocese of Detroit can run anything—and ought to be a Cardinal."

"Oh, it's not as bad as all that. Rumors of Detroit's ungovernability have been greatly exaggerated. Of course," Koesler reflected, "it's not Philadelphia or Los Angeles."

"Philadelphia . . . is that bad?"

"I've heard they've just begun saying the rosary facing the people."

Ouellet laughed. "All kidding aside, there is some talk of the new Cardinal Boyle's being *papabile*."

"Yeah, I know. We've heard it too. I suppose there's some truth to it. But it's hard to get used to. I just can't get comfortable with the idea of actually knowing a Pope personally. I've never even *met* a Pope, let alone knowing one as well as I know Archbishop Boyle."

"All I can tell you," Ouellet sighed, "is that, given half a chance, the idea can grow on you. I used to feel the same way. Who, besides a few Vatican monsignors, gets to know a

Pope personally? But then the rumors started about our Cardinal Claret. And after a while, you get used to it. To paraphrase that Yank football coach, just remember: The Pope puts his pants on one leg at a time just like everybody else.''

''Yes, except the Pope usually changes his clothes in a phone booth.''

They both laughed, as they turned the corner of Shuter onto Bond Street.

Koesler noticed a historical marker set back from the iron fence, near the cathedral. He squinted, trying to read it.' ''Principal Church for Largest English Speaking Diocese in Canada.'' His lips silently formed the words. But something seemed out of place.

''I see you have vandalism problems even in Toronto . . . or is that supposed to be part of the marker?'' Koesler gestured at the clenched black hand painted at the base of the marker.

''Isn't that odd; I don't believe I've ever noticed that before. And I've seen that marker hundreds of times.'' Ouellet shook his head. ''Just goes to show how familiar things can get.''

With that, they entered the cathedral and joined in the hymn the choir had already begun.

''Keep in mind that Jesus Christ has died for us and is risen from the dead. He is our Saving Lord. He is joy for all ages.''

''There he is. That's the one.''

''No, it isn't; he's too tall.''

''No, that's how tall he is. I've seen his picture that many times. He's the one.''

Archbishop Boyle knew the bystanders were referring to him. He was aware that his photo had been in the papers a great deal lately, especially in the *Detroit Free Press* and the *News*, not to mention the *Detroit Catholic*. He had not been aware that he had been featured in the Toronto papers as well. But, then, one does not become a Cardinal every day.

Being elevated to the Sacred College would be the culmination of his ecclesiastical career, Boyle mused. It was not entirely an unexpected honor. He would not be Detroit's first Cardinal. The late Edward Mooney's red hat hung from the ceiling of Blessed Sacrament Cathedral. At least part of the naming of a Cardinal was precedent. And, several years ago, Boyle had been elected by his peers to a term as president of the United States Conference of Bishops.

But he had enemies, and he knew it. His reputation with Rome was that of a crashing liberal. Whereas nothing could be further from the truth. Mark Boyle was a churchman to his very marrow. And above all else, he was loyal to Rome and the Pope. But the Curia, viewing what it considered the uncontrolled liberal experimentation of Detroit, had fought against his elevation. It was a wonder that the Pope had been able to fight off his advisors and name Boyle a Cardinal.

He, of course, had heard the rumors concerning his possible accession to the Papacy. Those who believed or spread those rumors, Boyle was certain, must be unaware of the invisible but effective opposition he faced in the highest echelons of the Vatican.

But, in the end, it did not matter. All he had ever wanted to do was to serve his Church. He would be more than content to finish out his days serving as a Cardinal.

He turned the corner from Shuter to Bond. He did not notice the historical marker. As he entered the cathedral, the Twenty-third Psalm was being sung. It was Boyle's favorite. He joined in.

"Yea, though I walk through the valley of the shadow of death, I will fear no evil: for thou art with me; thy rod and thy staff they comfort me."

The procession ended when the last of the Cardinals took his place in the sanctuary.

"In the name of the Father and of the Son and of the Holy Spirit."

"Amen."

As the familiar liturgy began in this unfamiliar setting, Father Koesler's mind cruised off on a flight of distracted musing.

It truly was an impressive sight. Bright sunshine illumined the huge stained glass Gothic window above the substantial off-white marble altar. The green of the carpet, laid throughout the cathedral, contrasted nicely with the gold, red, purple, scarlet, and white vestments of the varying ranks present.

Koesler glanced over his shoulder. There were two confessional boxes tucked against either rear wall. How typical. The priest had a theory that nobody ever planned for confessionals. Each pastor, he surmised, had a church built, then as an afterthought, stuck confessionals in some out-of-the-way corner. The result was that the average confessional could qualify as a torture box. Cramped, dark, and cold in the winter; hot and airless in the summer. Even recent renovations of the compartments involving dismantling the barrier between priest and penitent, enabling them to confer face to face, hadn't done much to improve the situation.

"The Lord be with you," Cardinal Audette intoned.

"And also with you," everyone responded.

Ten Cardinals attended Cardinal Audette, five on each side. Koesler could not recall seeing so many Cardinals together at one time. At least not live and in color. And yet, when there would be need to elect a new Pope, no pundit ever mentioned any of these eleven as a possible candidate. Though one of the College of Cardinals undoubtedly would be elected. But one who soon would become a Cardinal *had* been mentioned with some frequency: Detroit's Archbishop Mark Boyle, now seated among the bishops and archbishops in attendance.

An American Pope! Koesler tried to recall the whimsical tale he had heard when in high school about the first American Pope. The story had been part of a fictional French Cardinal's nightmare. In this prelate's dream, the American who was elected Pope took the name Buster I. His first infallible pronouncement had concerned extramarital sex. Pope Buster had declared it to be good, not evil. In response, the entire French navy had sailed across the Mediterranean, firing salvos in honor of the new doctrine.

Koesler chuckled. Several of his neighbors glanced at him.

"The Church in Toronto has lost a universally respected leader and I have lost a very dear and beloved friend," Archbishop Tito Fulmo began his eulogy.

Archbishop Fulmo was renowned throughout Canada for speaking publicly at the drop of a hat or at any occasion whatsoever.

Which brought to mind Detroit's late Edward Cardinal Mooney, now gone more than a quarter of a century. He, too, had let no public occasion pass without a few words. Even when someone else had already delivered the principal address, Mooney would speak. Invariably, he would invoke the formula,

"I don't wish to add anything to what Father has already said, but . . ."

The specific occasion Koesler now recalled was the funeral Mass of an Orchard Lake Seminary professor. Orchard Lake was the only national Polish Seminary in the U.S. Not unexpectedly, the sermon was delivered entirely in Polish. At the conclusion of the Mass, to everyone's consternation, and without the slightest notion of what the preacher had said, Mooney stood and declared, "I don't wish to add anything to what Father has already said, but . . ."

Koesler smiled. Covertly, he tried to detect whether anyone had noticed his silent levity in the midst of a serious homily. Apparently, none had. He'd have to be careful about this sort of thing.

"Pray, brethren," Cardinal Audette proposed, "that our sacrifice may be acceptable to God, the almighty Father."

"May the Lord accept the sacrifice at your hands for the praise and glory of His name, for our good, and the good of all His Church," the congregation responded.

Here we are at the Canon of the Mass, thought Koesler, and nothing's happened yet.

He caught himself: What did he expect to happen?

Maybe it was a foreboding. Perhaps it was the incongruity of the setting. In this cathedral, less than a week ago, a man—a priest, a Cardinal—had been murdered. Now, in that same cathedral, a lot of nice, very civilized people had gathered to eulogize the old gentleman. Not an angry, protesting word had been uttered.

The police were investigating the crime, but, according to all accounts, had made precious little progress. The consensus seemed to be that one of the street crazies, with nothing better to do, had dropped into the cathedral, seen a defenseless victim, stabbed him, and fled. It could have been anyone. With that kind of distinct possibility, there was every chance that Cardinal Claret's murder would end in the unsolved crimes file.

This liturgy was moving along so smoothly, indeed, that Koesler's mind was free to wander to more cluttered liturgical experiences.

There was the master of ceremonies at a solemn pontifical Mass years ago, who, after the bishop was seated facing the congregation, had stepped forward and placed the miter on the bishop's head. Except that the miter was backward. As the priest released the miter and stepped back, the lappets, the two tails that ordinarily fall from the miter along the bishop's nape, fell in front of the bishop's face, covering his eyes. The priest gulped and moved to immediately set things right, but was halted by the bishop's upraised hand. "Leave it the way it is," the bishop snapped, "and let everyone see what a fool you are!"

That had been one interesting liturgy.

Another, although Koesler had not been an eyewitness, had occurred regularly at each pontifical Mass presided over by one particularly cantankerous bishop. As the ceremonies proceeded, the bishop would suspend, or dismiss, one priest after another. A priest would sing the epistle, come before the bishop for a blessing, the bishop would tell the unfortunate priest he had done a rotten job, and would dismiss him. Each discharged priest would repair to the sacristy and smoke a cigarette, not bothering to divest. When a sufficient number of suspended priests were absent from the altar so that it became impossible to continue the pontifical ceremonies, the bishop would be forced to reinstate them all. This maneuver took place so often that pontifical liturgies in that diocese became known as *liturgia reservata*.

Communion time. Koesler chided himself for not having paid better attention to the Mass. Routine had a way of dulling concentration.

When his turn came, Koesler shuffled down the aisle toward the center communion station.

"The body of Christ," proclaimed Cardinal Audette, holding the communion wafer aloft.

"Amen," Koesler responded.

Suddenly, it occurred to him that he was standing at the very spot that had been occupied by the assailant. And that Audette was standing where Cardinal Claret had stood when he was murdered. A shudder passed through the priest.

As he turned to return to his place, Koesler roughly computed the distance between where he now stood and the door through which the assailant had escaped. It was a considerable distance. If the killing had been deliberately planned, it would have to have been a suicide mission. No one could

have relied on the utter confusion that had actually followed
the stabbing as a cover for a getaway. Koesler was growing
more and more convinced that it had been a spur-of-the-
moment attack.

"The Mass is ended," Cardinal Audette intoned, "let us
go in peace."

"Thanks be to God," all responded.

The final recessional in the pamphlet that had been spe-
cially prepared for this Mass of Resurrection was "Let Hymns
of Joy." Koesler joined in the singing:

> Let hymns of joy to grief succeed.
> We know that Christ is ris'n indeed:
> Alleluia, alleluia!
> We hear his white-robed angel's voice.
> And in our risen Lord rejoice.
> Alleluia, alleluia, alleluia, alleluia!

Then Koesler noticed it. At the very bottom of the final
page of the pamphlet was the imprint of a black fist. It
appeared as if it had been, perhaps, stamped on the paper.
Hastily, he looked at the pamphlets being held by the priests
on either side of him. The identical mark at the identical
place. Suddenly, he recalled the black fist on the historical
marker outside the cathedral. As far as he could tell, it was
the same symbol.

Strange. Very, very odd. All the way out to St. Augustine
Seminary, where the mortal remains of Cardinal Claret would
be consigned to the earth, Father Koesler kept thinking about
the black fist.

DETROIT

"I might have known. I *should* have known," *Free Press* theater critic Larry Delaney edited himself. "When Joe Cox offers to buy lunch, it's not going to be at the London Chop House."

"That's right," *Free Press* travel writer George Singer agreed. "It's going to be at the old faithful Econ."

"And we are obliged to bring our own press kits for show-and-tell." Delaney riffled through a disarray of newspaper clippings on the cluttered restaurant table.

"Gentlemen," said *Free Press* staff writer Joe Cox, munching his Dandy Don, "there is no such thing as a free lunch."

"There he goes, coining another phrase." Delaney fingered a rigid fry.

The three were dining in an eatery located appropriately on the ground floor of the *Free Press* building. The location was appropriate in that the eatery was, from any vantage point, pedestrian.

Cox's hot dog was named in honor of Don Meredith, star of "Monday Night Football." Other sandwiches on the Econ's menu were dubbed for media personalities—some local, such as the Mort Crim or the Bill Bonds; others national, such as the Dan Rather or the Ted Koppel. All sandwiches were overwhelmed with Bermuda onion, sliced or diced, depending on the mood of the short order chef.

"I mean," Delaney continued, "management leaves me at sixes and sevens as to whether I cover the New York theater season. Yet they can send this worthy soul," he looked derisively at Cox, "off to Rome to cover a Cardinal's installation."

"Go easy on this worthy soul, Larry," said Singer. "It isn't every day somebody becomes a Cardinal . . . especially *Detroit's* Cardinal. Hell, Cardinals have only been around since—"

"About the sixth century." Cox wiped the corner of his mouth.

Singer smiled. "Already started your research, eh, Joe?"

"Well, as I said when we began this banquet, you're a lucky sonuvabitch, Joe." Delaney pushed his plate to one side. It contained most of its original french fries, about one-quarter of the Howard Cosell ham sandwich, and all of a significant slice of Bermuda onion. "The Roman Summer Festival is starting early this year. You can have your pick of grand opera, operetta, ballet, concerts, jazz, art exhibitions, circus-in-the-streets, and a whole collection of old and new movies."

"And all this," contributed Singer, "against an incomparable historical backdrop."

"Take *Aida*—please." Delaney found it impossible to pass up a comic line. "It's the open-air version staged at the Baths of Caracalla."

"Where's that?" Cox moved the map of Rome across the table toward Singer, who pushed aside his empty plate. Singer's stomach was not as aesthetically picky as Delaney's.

Singer located the Baths on the map just south of the Colosseum. Singer, who had been a sportswriter before moving to the travel desk, was being groomed for his own column, the dream of most journalists. One position he probably never would occupy was that of restaurant critic. An omnivore, he constantly fought a weight problem.

"This is the *Aida*," Delaney resumed, "with its armies of Egyptian warriors, its crowds of Ethiopian slaves, and herds of live animals."

"Elephants?" Cox swirled the coffee in his cup.

"Elephants," Delaney confirmed. "Then there's *Tosca.*"

"Ah, *Tosca!*" Cox clapped his hands and raised his eyes heavenward in mock rapture.

"You're really in luck, you turkey." Some manifestation of envy was beginning to creep through Delaney's usually bland demeanor. "This presentation is billed as an 'itinerant *Tosca.*' They stage the opera at the actual places where the libretto sets it. So, for Act I, Mario Cavaradossi will meet Floria Tosca in front of the Church of Sant'Andrea della Valle."

Cox leaned toward Singer, whose finger moved to the site of Sant'Andrea della Valle on the Corso Vittorio Emanuele.

Satisfied, Cox returned attention to Delaney.

"Then, in Act II, the singers, orchestra, and audience will have moved to the Farnese Palace, where, in the Piazza Farnese, Tosca will confront and kill Baron Scarpia while Mario is being tortured and imprisoned."

Cox inclined toward Singer, whose finger moved around the corner from Sant'Andrea della Valle to the nearby Piazza Farnese.

Back to Delaney.

"Finally, after another quick bus trip with perhaps a snack and a little vino, all will gather at the Castel Sant'Angelo where Mario is executed and Tosca leaps over the battlement to her tragic death." Delaney slumped slightly in empathy with Floria's fate.

Cox consulted Singer, who located the Castel Sant'Angelo near the bank of the twisting Tiber.

"What about the movies?" Cox probed hungrily.

"What else, you lucky dog, but a film festival!" said Delaney.

"A film festival!"

"Yes. Everything from about thirty American silents to *Last Tango*, the film that made Pauline Kael famous, to a collection of cinema verité, a clutch of contemporary classics, a Hugh Leonard retrospective—and a special showing of Abel Gance's *Napoleon.*"

"*Napoleon?*"

"Yes, with the final scenes shot à la Cinerama some

twenty-five years before Lowell Thomas commercialized the process.''

"Say, Joe . . ." Singer nibbled on a breadstick he had liberated from the basket before the waiter had cleared the table, "have you given any thought to *work* while you're in Rome?''

"Work?''

"Yeah," Delaney leaned forward for emphasis, "that for which the Freep is sending you to the Eternal City. I've given you more than enough entertainment material—and George has given you expert directions on where to find it—to keep you busy for your entire stay in Rome.''

Something was up. Cox sensed it. Something about his companions' expressions. Cox slowly turned in his seat. Suspicion confirmed. Standing directly behind their booth was Nelson Kane, city editor of the *Detroit Free Press,* and Joe's immediate superior.

"Uh," Cox cleared his throat, "hi, Nellie. How long you been here?''

"Long enough." Kane, in light raincoat and Irish slouch hat pulled low on his forehead, was obviously returning from lunch. "Stop by my desk when you get a chance, Joe. Like now." He turned and headed for the bank of elevators.

Cox turned to his now grinning companions. "Thanks. Thanks a lot. I needed that." He rose to leave.

"Don't forget this." Singer handed Cox the check.

"Didn't you forget something else?" asked Delaney, as Cox accepted the slip and turned to go.

"What?''

"The tip.''

Cox consulted the check, then grudgingly let a dollar flutter to the table. He could hear the others snickering as he headed for the register to settle accounts.

Joe Cox was the nonpareil of the *Free Press* city room. His resumé boasted a Pulitzer Prize. His work was uniformly workmanlike to excellent. He was the type of reporter who was a constant challenge to the *Detroit News.* Yet, possibly because he was so very good at what he did, and because he was very aware of that fact, there was a subtle touch of adolescence about him. From time to time, he required a figuratively short leash.

Usually found holding the other end of that leash was
Nelson Kane. Now in his mid-forties, tall, balding, heavyset
but not fat, Kane was that clichéd but authentic creature, a
newspaperman's newspaperman. He had spent his entire professional life with the *Free Press*, and was one of those rare
and fortunate people who loved his work.

Cox scooped his notepad from his desk and approached
Kane's desk in the center of the long, rectangular, white-
walled city room. As Cox took a seat at the side of the desk,
Kane marveled again at the reporter's physical resemblance to
the actor, Richard Dreyfuss.

Kane unwrapped a cigar, bit off an end, then inserted it
between his teeth. The bad news was that it was cheap. The
good news was that it would not be lit. "Cox," he said, "I'm
going to tell you a story."

"Oh, good!" Cox responded with clearly fraudulent
enthusiasm.

"Before you got here, we had a religion writer whose
name shall not be mentioned, but who was infamous nonetheless."

"I think I know the one you mean . . . the one who used to
phone people for a story and when they would tell him they
had no comment they could hear him typing up the comment
they hadn't made . . . and then they'd have to read the paper
to find out what they'd 'said.' "

"The very one.

"Well, one of the Popes died. I don't recall which one. It
doesn't matter. Anyway—and this happened at a time when
the brass were even more reluctant than they are now to send
a reporter on location—anyway, the decision was made to
send this religion writer to Rome to cover the election of the
new Pope.

"Well, the new Pope was elected. Radio and TV told us
that. But we were waiting for the personalized, on-the-scene
report of our own correspondent in Rome . . . our own man
in the Vatican. Our deadline got nearer and nearer . . . still
no word. With the deadline just minutes away, a goodly number of us were gathered around the teletype. Finally, it clicked.
Code letters, dateline Rome, our man's byline, then 'Exclusive
to the *Free Press*,' and finally: 'Today, amid the grandeur of
St. Peter's Basilica, puffs of white smoke appeared over the

Sistine Chapel as the Roman Catholic Church elected a new Supreme Pontiff.' That was followed by three dots, and then, 'Pick up wire service copy.'—''

Cox continued to smile, as he had throughout the account. "Very amusing. But what's that got to do with me?"

"Just this: I don't want to find myself standing in front of a teletype reading: 'Rome, April 19, by Joe Cox. Exclusive to the *Free Press*. Today, amid the grandeur of St. Peter's Basilica, twelve new Cardinals were created by the Roman Catholic Church . . . pick up wire service copy.' ''

"Nellie, you know me better than that!"

"I also know what can happen when you and Lennon cover the same story in the same town. In this case, it spells 'Roman Holiday.' ''

"Hey, that *is* neat, isn't it? A terrific serendipity when the *News* decided to send Pat to Rome. Should save you guys some money, too. You don't 'spose the *News* and the Freep would want to split the cost of our room?"

"Now that's exactly what I mean." Kane rolled the unlit cigar from one side of his mouth to the other. "Just because the two of you live together in Detroit without benefit of clergy doesn't mean that it'll work in this case. Especially when you're both covering the same story and especially when that story is in a foreign city."

"What do you mean?"

"What I mean, Cox, is, that for all practical purposes, your hotel room will be your office. You won't have any other office. You're working this assignment for us. What if you have to make phone calls? What if you have to talk to me or one of the other editors? What if someone phones you? Lennon can hear everything. And if she gets a lead from any of those phone calls or messages, she goddamn well is going to take advantage of it.

"And the same holds true for you. The *News* won't want such an arrangement any more than we do. This is not a vacation. It's not even a working vacation. You and Lennon may be 'significant others' for each other here. But in Rome you don't *know* Lennon. Except as a competing reporter. And a goddamn competent one at that."

Lennon had received much of her journalistic training at the *Free Press*. Kane still winced at the memory of her departure to the rival *News* . . . although he had to admit she'd had good reason at the time.

"O.K., O.K. But as long as we're both on this story, there is one thing I want to know."

"Yeah?"

"When does it end?"

"What?"

"After the ceremonies in Rome are completed," Cox consulted his notepad, "on May 4th, the Detroit contingent—or at least most of it—will move on to England and Ireland before returning to Detroit. So when does the assignment end? Rome? England? Ireland?"

"England and Ireland are courtesy visits . . . part of the entourage's package tour. The news angle is Boyle's becoming a Cardinal . . . which takes place in Rome. That answer your question?"

"Ordinarily, yes. And I could have figured that out. Except that I have a feeling . . . a sort of presentiment."

"Like what?"

"I don't quite know. Like all premonitions, it's hard to spell out—"

"Try."

"Well, a couple of things have happened and I don't know if they add up to a scenario."

"Go ahead."

"First, Boyle is named a Cardinal. Then the Cardinal in Toronto is killed—literally wasted. Cardinal Claret was an important figure in the Church. So is Boyle. What if—and I know this is going to sound farfetched—what if there proves to be a connection?

"What if precisely that important Canadian Cardinal was killed deliberately—for a specific reason? What if whoever killed Claret intends to attack another important Cardinal—of the United States? I just mean . . . what if . . ."

Normally, Kane would have dismissed this as a remote possibility. The Toronto police had pretty well concluded that the Claret killing was a fluke. Some hophead had simply struck at random and happened to hit a very important person.

But . . . if there was one thing he and Cox shared it was a keen news sense. A feeling not only for news that had happened, but a sense of the direction in which news was going to develop.

And the *Free Press* was still smarting from that fiasco wherein their erstwhile executive manager had arbitrarily pulled their leading sports columnist, despite his protests, home from the Olympics, saying that he'd been in Munich long enough . . . and that furious columnist, under threat of dismissal, had boarded the jet home, only to discover when he deplaned in Detroit that terrorists had captured the Israeli athletes, and the eyes of the world were now on Munich.

"Play it as it lies, Joe. I'll just rummage around in the exchequer in case—in the unlikely case—your hunch is right," sardonically, "for a change."

2

The atmosphere was tense. The result of an exchange of many angry words. The twenty people—three of them women—gathered in the small office were black. The stenciled sign on the outside of the closed door read: OFFICE OF BLACK CATHOLIC SERVICES, ARCHDIOCESE OF DETROIT.

"What it comes down to," Perry Brown was almost shouting, "is that he's abandoned us! That's the bottom line!"

"You're being simplistic," Ty Powers charged.

The argument, initially joined by nearly everyone in the room, now had narrowed to these two. They were the only ones still standing. Powers, tall, well-built, light-complexioned, was director of Black Catholic Services, appointed by Archbishop Boyle.

Brown, of medium height, pencil-thin, Afro-topped, was a physician whose patients included many in the black community who could afford neither medical treatment nor hospitalization insurance.

"How many Catholic schools in the core city has Archbishop Boyle closed?"

"Perry—"

"How many of our parishes has he closed?"

"Perry, it's not so much that the Archbishop is *closing* schools and parishes."

"No? Then what is it?"

"He's pronouncing them dead. They died. We didn't build them; white Catholics did. Then they moved away. There weren't enough black Catholics left to support them. So they died. There wasn't anything the Archbishop could do about it."

"He could keep them open and operating!"

"Be reasonable: How is he going to do that?"

"By making a commitment to the core city!" Brown looked around. Most of those present seemed to be in agreement with him.

"The Archbishop *has* that kind of commitment. The Inter Parish Sharing Program was *his* baby. It was *his* idea to have suburban parishes share with the inner-city parishes."

"Well," Brown placed his hand on the chair in front of him and leaned forward, "I've got news for you and for him: His baby died abornin'."

"That's what I've been trying to tell you: Archbishop Boyle wants to keep our parishes and schools open. And he's even tried to keep them open with programs like the IPSP, but his hands are tied. The whites who built these churches and schools have moved away. And," Powers emphasized, "they have made it very clear they are not going to continue to support them."

"Precisely why the Archbishop should not have made the sharing voluntary."

"Not voluntary!?"

"Not voluntary!" Brown converted Powers' shocked tone into one of triumph. "It does not require an MBA to know that all temporalities in this archdiocese are held in the name of the Catholic Archbishop of Detroit, whoever he may be."

"You mean . . ." Powers seemed unable to complete the thought.

"Take it! Take the money from the savings of the rich parishes and distribute it to the poor. If the 'have' parishes will not be Christian to the 'have-not' parishes, then *impose* Christianity on them."

There was a stunned silence.

"Why not?" someone finally asked, rhetorically.

"It makes sense," someone else commented.

"It makes damn good sense," another added.

Silence. They were awaiting Powers' response.

"Ridiculous. It's ridiculous. One move like that and he wouldn't have a diocese anymore. You may recall, in 1968, the year after the riots, when the Archbishop allocated a healthy chunk of the Archdiocesan Development Fund collection to the needs of the inner city. There was plenty of very audible griping from white Catholics about how all their money was going to be used by 'those niggers.' And the following year, the ADF collection plummeted.

"If he were to simply take money, even surplus money, from suburban parish savings and apply it to the inner city, why, in no time he would have a hundred percent of nuthin'! And, eventually, the aid the Archbishop is able to give us now would dry up. And we'd be left sharing with him a hundred percent of nuthin'!"

In the pause that followed, some mumbled agreement with Powers, others with Brown.

"Boyle would not be the first Irish martyr," Brown suggested.

"You're not talking martyrdom, Perry. You're talking fiscal insanity!"

"Christianity ought to have a little bit of insanity mixed in with it, the way I look at it," Brown responded. "Didn't St. Francis of Assisi call himself 'a fool for God'? Besides, now that our Archbishop is going to become a Cardinal, this would be heeded by just about everyone in the world.

"You're part of his official family, Tyrone; you're part of the bureaucracy . . . why don't *you* test the water? Why don't *you* propose the idea? You never know till you try. Maybe the new Cardinal Boyle would be willing to consider martyrdom."

"Let me put the shoe on the other foot, Doctor." Powers smiled. "You're going to Rome with the Detroit contingent. You'll be with us when the Archbishop becomes a Cardinal. Why don't you take it upon yourself to propose this 'martyrdom' to the Archbishop?"

Brown appeared lost in thought. Finally, he said, "You have a point, Tyrone. Perhaps it's time for me to make an unmistakable statement on this matter."

Brown once more retreated into his contemplation. He seemed troubled by what he found there.

3

In a separate wing of the building that housed the Office of Black Catholic Services, Mrs. Irene Casey, editor of the *Detroit Catholic,* was seated at her desk in her private office. She was talking on the phone.

"What's so different about your backyard shrine to the Blessed Mother?"

"What's so different?" the caller echoed.

"Yes, different—unusual, out-of-the-ordinary. You know, a lot of Catholic homes have backyard shrines. And as we enter spring, most of them get their shrines ready for summer. You must realize that it's simply impossible for us to run pictures of all these shrines. We just don't have the space."

"So?"

"So what is special or different about *your* shrine?"

"Well," the woman hesitated. Obviously, she had not anticipated any resistance to having a photo of her shrine placed in the archdiocesan newspaper.

"Well . . . if you drive up Lahser between, say Eleven and Thirteen Mile Roads, you'll see lots of statues of the Blessed Mother in the yards. But," her voice rose, "they're all Immaculate Conception statues."

Irene could not suppress a smile. She was grateful video-phones were not yet in general use.

"Now, *my* shrine," the woman continued triumphantly, "has the Pilgrim Statue of Fatima as the main attraction!" She paused to allow this revelation to have its effect.

Shifting papers on her desk, Irene said nothing.

"Well?" the woman snapped at length.

"Well, what?"

"Well, what do you say to that?"

"I can think of any number of backyard shrines that have the Pilgrim Statue of Fatima," Irene exaggerated. She won-dered if anyone had ever wasted time on a study of the subject.

"Now you listen here, Mrs. Casey: I'm a parishioner of St. Ives, and our pastor subscribes to the *Detroit Catholic* for all his parishioners. This is a parish the *Detroit Catholic* can ill afford to lose!"

"I understand. And I agree. But you must understand what

precious little space we have in the paper. If we ran a photo of one private shrine, I wouldn't be able to refuse anyone else who has a shrine. And very soon the paper would be filled with nothing but shrines. So you see, there just would have to be something unique before we could consider yours.''

"Well," Irene could tell from her altered tone that the woman was taking another tack, "my husband and I occasionally see a vision over the shrine . . . at least," in a slightly smaller voice, "it looks like a vision."

"Fine," Irene spotted light at the end of the tunnel, "you get a photo of the vision and we're in business."

"Oh, what is it with you people!" Obviously, the party was over. "Last year you refused to run a photo of my daughter twirling her baton!"

"You're the mother of the cheerleader!"

No way could Irene have forgotten: the woman, within the confines of the *Detroit Catholic*, was notorious.

"Yes, I am! And you haven't heard the last of me!"

The woman slammed down the receiver. Irene gently massaged her ear and prayed that her caller was mistaken and that this would indeed be their terminal connection.

The phone rang again. It was going to be one of those days.

"Mrs. Casey?" The familiar deep voice resonated with barely curbed fury. "This is Father Cavanaugh at Divine Child. I am just going to make a statement. I do not expect a response from you. It's about a story that appeared in the latest issue of the *Detroit Catholic* . . . about two former priests who are now employed by Wayne County as marriage counselors.

"Your story quoted them as saying that they were happy in their new work and that they felt completely fulfilled. One of them even compared what he was doing to what he did as a priest, stating that counseling was now his full-time ministry.

"I just want to say, Mrs. Casey, that this is not the sort of story one should find in a Catholic newspaper. When you have ex-priests who are out of work or who have found only distasteful employment, that is the sort of story you should print.

"That is all, Mrs. Casey. I just want you to know how I, and many others, feel.''

He broke the connection.

This type of call, though rare, was among the things Irene found most unpleasant about her position as editor of a Catholic newspaper. Even if she had been allowed to respond, there was little she could have said to a man like that. He was a priest and she was of the laity. She could not overlook his privileged position. Nor would he allow her to overlook it.

Furthermore, what could anyone say to someone like Father Cavanaugh, whose mind and heart were closed?

"You look as if you just lost your best friend, Irene." John Howe, gray-haired business manager of the *Detroit Catholic*, knocked pro forma on the open door as he entered her office.

"I feel like it. I just had a very depressing phone call."

"Nothing serious, I hope."

She shook her head.

"Well, then," he brightened, "I've got some good news: The archdiocese is going to pick up the whole tab for your trip to Rome!"

"Well, there's a break."

"You said it! In our present financial condition, it would have been pretty tight, to say the least. I was going to offer to pay half and see how the chancery would react. But Monsignor Iming called just a few minutes ago and said they would take care of all your travel and hotel costs. You're on your own for food and out-of-pocket expenses. But we can handle that with no problem."

"That's just great!" Irene beamed.

"Of course," he grew serious, "that covers just Detroit to Rome and back."

"No London or Ireland, eh?"

"I'm afraid not." He smiled. "You'll just have to wait for an Irish Catholic Press convention for a visit to your homeland.

"Unless," he shrugged lightheartedly, "unless you find something that needs reporting in addition to the Rome story."

"That's another definition of 'fat chance.' It's not as if a visit to England or Ireland per se constitutes a breaking news story. I mean, what can happen to an archbishop after becoming a Cardinal?"

"I guess you're right. Well, anyway, have a nice 'Roman Holiday.' "

4

Maybe this is what it had been like at the Tower of Babel—a confusion of tongues, Father Koesler mused.

He was standing near Gate Three in the Michael Berry International Terminal at Detroit's Metropolitan Airport. He was attempting to remain at the fringe of the crowd. But it seemed that if one was not part of one crowd, one was swallowed by another.

Koesler did not often utilize Metro's international terminal, so he was not familiar with its day-to-day operation. But, at this moment, it was clearly proving its cosmopolitan character. People of seemingly every known complexion, costume, and tongue milled in groups of varying sizes. Caftans and muumuus, prayer beads and rosaries, tilaks and beauty spots.

The group on the fringe of which Koesler was trying to stay was Detroit's Rome-bound contingent . . . two chartered planeloads.

The center and focal point of this group, quite naturally, was Archbishop Mark Boyle, on his way to becoming His Eminence Mark Cardinal Boyle. He was surrounded by representatives of the local news media, friends, well-wishers, and the merely Catholic curious. The Archbishop stood bathed in the unreal glare of the television lighting. Nearby and sharing in the periphery of the sungun, Koesler could identify many of the movers and shakers of the archdiocese as well as the city of Detroit. It was as if they constituted the *dramatis personae* of a play about to unfold.

Maynard Cobb, Detroit's mayor, was presiding at the battery of microphones. He was developing the theme of how proud the city was of its new Cardinal. He had already explained that the press of civic duties prevented him from accompanying the group to Rome. But, he affirmed, he hoped to be able to join them there before all the induction ceremonies were completed.

Maybe. But Koesler made a wager with himself that they would not see Cobb again until they returned to Detroit.

Although they had met only a few times, and very briefly at that, Koesler was convinced that Cobb was practically perfect for his job. In his early sixties, graying, with a vocabulary suited for a White House visit or, alternately, appropriate for the nadir of the black ghetto whence he had sprung, Cobb could feel Detroit coursing through his body, and he fought for his city every step of the way.

While not, to anyone's knowledge, a religious man, Cobb was well aware of the national and international publicity a new Cardinal would draw to Detroit. And Cobb was determined to milk that limelight for all it was worth.

Standing next to Cobb was Archbishop Boyle, with his characteristic bemused expression. He seemed quite content, even though theoretically he was the center of attraction at this affair, to stand aside for the mayor.

Those who knew Boyle—and their number was not legion—understood that Boyle did not take himself overly seriously. Above all, he was the epitome of a Christian gentleman. Shortly, the reporters would begin asking him questions. Then he would bloom. He had been an educator. No matter what else he became, he would always be an educator. And when he explained his answers to the reporters' questions he would be right at home.

Koesler recalled the photo story the *Detroit Catholic* had published the week after Boyle's nomination was announced. The photos spanned the time from Boyle's youth to the present. He had been an outstandingly handsome young man. Slightly more than six feet tall, he was still handsome, with thinning white hair, sooty eyebrows, piercing blue eyes, and attractive Irish features. It was not difficult for those associated with him to be very proud of him.

Nor was the Archbishop without a sense of humor. Though many might think of him as dry, the wit was there. Unlike some, Archbishop Boyle was sufficiently secure in himself and his position that he did not require that his face be ubiquitous in the archdiocesan newspaper. So that when he and several other Catholic functionaries were scheduled to fly to Rome for the first session of the Vatican Council, and Father Koesler, then editor of the *Detroit Catholic*, had sent a photographer to snap the Archbishop and his entourage boarding the plane at Metro, Boyle had commented that the *Detroit Catholic* should just take photos of him on the boarding ramp of each of the airlines that served Detroit, and then in the future they could run the appropriate photo automatically; no matter where he was bound, they would already have the correct shot in their files, he said.

It was impossible not to be aware of the man standing on the other side of Boyle in this impromptu tableau. Inches taller than the Archbishop, and large in every direction, Inspector Walter Koznicki, chief of the Homicide Division of the Detroit Police Department, seemed relatively uninterested in the proceedings. But then Inspector Koznicki seldom was what he seemed.

Over the past several years, a warm relationship had developed between Inspector Koznicki and Father Koesler. The priest had proven helpful in the solution of several homicide cases involving the Catholic community. The initial professional association of the two men had blossomed into a friendship based on mutual respect.

Inspector Koznicki was not in attendance today in his professional capacity. He was taking a vacation, and was a member of the delegation on its way to Rome. As a prominent Detroiter, and also a Catholic, Koznicki had been invited to join the other VIPs appearing with the Archbishop and the Mayor.

As the sungun played about the tight-knit group before the cameras, Koesler recognized some of the other important people, all of whom were familiar faces.

There was Liz Taylor look-alike Joan Blackford Hayes, director of the Office for Continuing Education for the archdiocese. She long had been the token female in the Boyle administration. However, as is so often the case with most women who have risen to a high bureaucratic level, she was far more qualified than any man in a comparable position.

Koesler recalled a meeting he had attended with, among many others, Mrs. Hayes. Attired in a striking red ensemble, she had raised her hand to ask a question. Archbishop Boyle, seeing the upraised hand and the red apparel out of the corner of his eye, had said, "Yes, Monsignor . . . uh . . . er . . . Mrs. Hayes." At that moment, Koesler had wondered whether a woman could become a monsignor because an archbishop, even mistakenly, had called her one. The question dissolved quickly when he remembered that only a Pope can make a monsignor.

Now that he recalled the incident, Koesler's peculiar stream-of-consciousness led him to wonder, if Boyle did indeed become a Pope, would that make Joan Blackford Hayes a monsignor retroactively?

Speaking of tokens, standing just to the rear of Mrs. Hayes was Ty Powers. Koesler could easily recall a time when there was no diocesan Office of Black Catholic Services and also a time when there were nearly no black Catholics for whom to have an office.

Actually, there were not that many more even now. But the "time" for blacks had come in a way that it had not yet for women. A few years ago, the consensus was that most blacks who converted were merely trying to become white, not necessarily Catholic. But now there was a better, if thinner, ministry for core city blacks. Most of today's inner-city priests still happened to be white. However, most of them no longer forced the white man's religious experience on their black parishioners. A few even blended the essence of the Catholic Mass with a healthy measure of free-wheeling Baptist worship.

Powers' expression puzzled Koesler. Here the man was about to embark on a trip—a free trip at that—to Rome. Most of his fellow travelers were ebullient if not downright euphoric. Yet Powers seemed preoccupied and troubled.

Mayor Cobb had completed his statement, but remained standing close to Archbishop Boyle. As long as the TV cameras would grind away, Cobb would linger on.

As was his wont, Boyle had a prepared statement, which he read carefully. It was a solemnly composed declaration asserting his unworthiness for the honor that was about to be accorded him in Rome. But he would accept the Cardinalate in the name of and to the honor of the good people of the Archdiocese of Detroit. He thanked all who had come to wish him well, as well as those who would be accompanying him.

He folded the statement and tucked it in the inside pocket of his black suit coat. The gold chain carrying his pectoral cross and appearing across his chest swayed gently.

He removed his eyeglasses and looked expectantly at the reporters. The questions were not long in coming.

FIRST REPORTER: Archbishop, you're considered to be a liberal as far as the Church hierarchy is concerned. Do you see this recognition on the part of the Pope as an endorsement of your policies in Detroit?

BOYLE: Oh, no, my dear young man. "Liberal" and "conservative" are labels attached to people for the sake of convenience. But in reality, most people are liberal, if you must, about some issues, and conservative about others.

FIRST REPORTER (determinedly): But, compared with other dioceses, especially in this country, there seems to be a lot of freedom. Some priests say if you can't get away with it in Detroit, you can't get away with it anywhere. Care to comment?

BOYLE (smiling tightly): I suppose you would have to ask the priests whom you are quoting about that.

SECOND REPORTER: Will any of your policies change in the diocese once you've been made a Cardinal?

BOYLE: No, my dear young lady. I have no plans to change anything in the archdiocese. Things change, of course. That is only part of life. But such changes will not spring from the honor that has come to me.

THIRD REPORTER: What's the purpose of your stopovers in England and Ireland?

BOYLE: In England I will visit my dear old friend Cardinal Whealan, the Archbishop of London. And in Ireland — he permitted himself a smile — well, my parents, may the Lord rest them, were born in County Dublin. My visit there will be a touching of roots and a bit of a vacation for me before getting back to Detroit.

Something wasn't quite right. Koesler couldn't put his finger on it. But something was definitely amiss.

THIRD REPORTER: How long have you known you were going to be made a Cardinal?

BOYLE (after a pause): It was, I believe, March 27th that the Apostolic Delegate to this country phoned me.

SECOND REPORTER (consulting her notes): But it was released to the media on the 28th.

BOYLE (smiling): You seem surprised.

SECOND REPORTER: Yes. I thought you'd have to keep the secret longer!

BOYLE (chuckling): Our motto is not *secretum gratia secreti.*

Mixed sounds of incomprehension and laughter.

Koesler was still trying to detect what was wrong. There was some movement in the crowd immediately in front of

Cobb and Boyle that seemed inappropriate, even problematical.
But though he was taller than most of those standing nearby,
Koesler was unable to isolate it.

FOURTH REPORTER: Archbishop, this may be a bit premature,
but there is talk of the Papacy . . .

Boyle, with what might almost be classified as a frown,
began shaking his head.

FOURTH REPORTER: . . . as a Cardinal, you will be in
the running to become Pope. Some pundits have said—

It was unreal. Koesler could only think of similar episodes
he'd seen in the past. But it had always been on TV, never in
person. A sungun was knocked over and several cameramen
and reporters near the front seemed to collapse in a heap.
Several people were shouting. A woman screamed.

It was over as quickly as it had begun.

The square peg Koesler had sensed in the crowd was a
young black man who was now prostrate on the floor by
virtue of his being knelt on very decisively by Inspector
Koznicki.

The Inspector had worked the man's right arm behind him
and was prying a large knife from his fingers. Everyone else
seemed stunned into inactivity.

A phalanx of Mayor Cobb's bodyguards, airport security
officers, and members of the Wayne Country Sheriff's Department converged on the two men and assisted Inspector Koznicki
as they swept up the captive and hustled him into a nearby
room, into which a seemingly incredible number of people
immediately crowded. The door then closed.

One minute there was mass confusion. The next, all was
peaceful and quiet. There were now far fewer people in the
waiting area. The missing were all in the room with the
would-be assailant.

The media people pulled themselves and their equipment
back together and crowded around the closed door.

Whatever was going on, the next news would emerge from
that room.

5

"Good evening, ladies and gentlemen, and welcome aboard Trans World Airlines charter flight 1302 to Rome . . ."

"I wonder why it is," Father Koesler asked his seat partner, Inspector Koznicki, "all stewardesses sound alike?"

"I suppose it is their training." Koznicki wedged his way deeper into the narrow seat in a futile attempt to find comfort.

"At this time, please give your attention to the flight attendant at the front of your cabin . . ."

"Maybe," Koesler suggested, "if we get out of our suit coats . . ." He was experiencing almost as much discomfort as Koznicki.

The two wrestled out of their jackets.

"The laminated instruction card in the seat pocket in front of you explains and illustrates the important safety features of this aircraft. The card should be read carefully before takeoff . . ."

"That feels better." Koesler let out a sigh. "Now, what'll we do with them?"

"Let me take your jacket, Father. Wanda can hold them until we are airborne. Then we can put them in the overhead compartment." Koznicki was referring to his wife, in the aisle seat. She was accompanying her husband on this, their first vacation together in years that would be unencumbered by any of their children.

"The emergency exits in the 707 aircraft are the forward left door, the forward right door, the rear left door, and the rear right door. In addition to the four cabin doors, there are four over-the-wing window exits . . ."

Koesler fixed on the nearest exit, then returned his gaze to the attendant at the front of the cabin.

She continued explaining emergency procedures.

The plane taxied to its final ground turn onto the far end of the runway. The pilot braked; the hum of the engines rose to a whine, then a full-throated roar as the plane gathered momentum, raced down the runway, and pulled itself upward.

"I'm glad that's over!" The color began returning to Koesler's white knuckles.

"Yes," said Koznicki, "they do say that takeoffs and landings are the most dangerous times in flying."

"No, dear," a smiling Wanda Koznicki corrected, "the most dangerous time in flying is the automobile trip to the airport."

All three smiled.

A steward passed by, pushing a cart filled with small bottles containing a vast variety of potables.

"Isn't it a little early for that?" Koesler asked. "I mean, we're still climbing!"

"Well, Father," said Koznicki, "this is a charter flight. It may prove to be more of a party than your usual flight."

The prophesy was correct. Archbishop Boyle's Irish-blooded relatives were the principal reason the liquor cart was not put to rest until the very early hours of the following morning.

"And you're sure," said Koesler, pursuing the conversation they had begun earlier, "that the young man who attacked Archbishop Boyle was acting alone?"

"As sure as we could be in an initial investigation. If it proves otherwise as the investigation continues, my people will notify me."

"And he wasn't attacking Mayor Cobb? The Mayor and the Archbishop were standing very close to one another."

"Oh, no, Father. I, too, was standing close by, as you will remember. I saw him inching through the crowd and I followed his progress until he was standing directly in front of the Archbishop. When he arrived at that point, I was fortunate enough to prevent him from causing any harm."

"I'll say you prevented him. I don't think the kid knew what hit him!"

Koznicki smiled. "No, he did not attack the Mayor, but he certainly got his attention."

Wanda was served a chablis, Koznicki a Stroh's, and Koesler a bourbon Manhattan. He was slightly surprised—and pleased—that the mobile bar stocked bourbon.

"Were you able to come up with any motive? I mean, if the guy was acting alone, if he wasn't part of a conspiracy, what possible motive could he have for attacking the Archbishop? He'd have to be insane!"

"No, I think not, Father. It is a phenomenon we are seeing more and more in America: Somebody who is nobody trying to become somebody by attacking somebody who is important. The people who made attempts on the lives of Presidents Ford and Reagan, the one who shot and killed John Lennon, were all people who wanted to be recognized. An act of violence gave them their moment of recognition. They are not in the same category with the assassins of President Kennedy or Martin Luther King, Jr.—people who killed with a purpose and after their attack tried desperately to escape.

"No, Father; I am quite sure that that young man saw Archbishop Boyle on the TV news. The TV exposure made it obvious that this man was important, that he was leaving for Rome, and that there would be a press conference at the airport. At that point, the young man decided it was time for the world to know his name."

Koznicki paused. "You know, it is funny, but I cannot recall his name." He shook his head. "No matter; with the publicity that will be given him, the world will shortly know who he is. Except that he will have to forfeit a great many years of freedom for his moment of recognition."

"Probably. But only after batteries of lawyers and psychiatrists get done arguing over his sanity," said Koesler, his tone betraying a tinge of cynicism. "Personally, I think the time has come to enact new standards. If the law can differentiate between first-, second-, and third-degree murder, why can't they establish similarly relative degrees of insanity?

"First-degree insanity would mean that the defendant was insane at the time of the crime, did not know right from wrong, and was incapable of standing trial for the crime charged.

"Second-degree insanity would mean that the defendant was insane, but capable of distinguishing right from wrong, and was capable of standing trial.

"Third-degree insanity would mean the defendant was temporarily insane at the time of the crime."

"An interesting suggestion," commented the Inspector. "I wonder what our forensic psychiatrist, Dr. Fritz Heinsohn, would have to say about that."

"Probably a lot, and probably all of it gobbledygook," replied Koesler with a grin.

Dinner was served.

Delmonico steaks, each done medium, sculptured baked potatoes, french beans, spinach and mushroom salad, a lemon tart. Each tray held a small bottle of California cabernet sauvignon. Not bad, for an airline; but then, a party had been predicted.

After a perfunctory, but nonetheless heartfelt, unspoken grace, Koesler fell to with gusto; the afternoon's events had given him more of an appetite than he had been aware of. He was left with his thoughts of those events, as the Koznickis conversed in low tones throughout the meal. Later, after the steward had replenished their wine supply, Koznicki turned to Father Koesler. "By the way, Father, what was it that made you raise the possibility of a conspiracy?"

"Oh," Koesler sipped his wine reflectively, "it was mostly that incident in Toronto. You know, the murder of Cardinal Claret."

"Yes?"

"I suppose it was just the coincidence. Cardinal Claret was attacked suddenly and unexpectedly, at a time when the public could approach him freely and unrestrainedly. And he was killed by a young black wielding a knife.

"Plus, if I remember the newspaper account correctly, Father Ouellet, who was standing alongside Cardinal Claret at the time, described the young man as wearing his hair in a natural or Afro. And . . . well, those same conditions were present this afternoon when Archbishop Boyle was attacked. So, naturally . . ." Koesler allowed the sentence to remain uncompleted.

"Even if your hypothesis does not prove true in this case, it is a good analysis, Father. It never ceases to amaze me that you react to such situations in much the same manner as a police officer. Are you sure you did not miss your vocation?" It was not the first time the Inspector had kidded his friend with such a question.

"Oh, no." Koesler laughed. "I'm where I ought to be. If, by some stretch of the imagination, I ceased being a priest, and someone asked me what else I was qualified for, I fear I would be forced to answer, 'Nothing.' "

"Good evening, ladies and gentlemen. This is Captain Kamego. We are presently flying at an altitude of 42,000 feet, and are right on schedule. We should land at Leonardo da Vinci airport at 9:00 A.M. Rome time, which would be 3:00 A.M. Eastern Daylight Time.

"Now, for your entertainment, we will be showing a movie in just a few minutes. The name of it is . . ."

A slight pause.

"The name of it is, *Assault with Intent*. Have a good flight, and if there is anything we can do to make your trip more comfortable, please let us know."

"*Assault with Intent!* Isn't that . . . yes, it is! Good grief, that's the movie they filmed in Detroit last year!" Koesler was caught between excitement and incredulity. "That's that film about those attacks on our seminary professors. I was in that movie! Or, rather, someone portrayed me in that movie . . ."

Both Koznickis were smiling at their animated friend.

"The last I heard of that film, all the major TV networks and distributors had turned it down. It was a throwaway— dead on the shelf. I wonder whose idea it was to resurrect it for this flight?"

"Would you like another Manhattan, Father?" an attendant interrupted.

"No, thank you. I want to be cold sober to see *this* movie!"

It was undoubtedly a testimonial to the wretchedness of the film that by halfway through its showing, all in the cabin were either gathered around the mobile bar or asleep.

Father Koesler was snoring.

SAN FRANCISCO

A massive black fist closed around the pole as the man swung himself easily onto the cable car. As long as he had lived in San Francisco he had delighted in riding the cable cars. The openness, the sense of being at one with the rolling city, the sardinelike closeness of his fellow passengers—all contributed to the atmosphere of conviviality, or at least camaraderie one usually found on board.

And he desperately needed something cheerful. He had just attended a conclave that had deeply depressed him.

He did not belong to the group whose meeting he had attended. But he was able to transcend many disparate groups. He had the irritating feeling he should do something about what he had heard at the session. But what? The matter did not directly involve him. And if he did react, how far was he prepared to go?

The flow of his thoughts was interrupted by a sweet little blue-haired lady seated next to him.

"I beg your pardon . . ." She touched the sleeve of his black suit coat.

"Yes?" He looked up, startled.

"Are you a Father? I mean, are you a priest?"

"No, madam, I am not." He resembled and indeed sounded like James Earl Jones. Or possibly Robert Earl Jones. Somewhere between junior and senior. His accent was that of a highly cultured Haitian.

"No? Well, I didn't think so, even though you're dressed like one. But, then, you never can tell these days. The people who look like priests *aren't*, and the ones who don't look like priests *are*. Land a' Goshen, how's a body to tell? Though the good Lord knows there aren't very many . . . uh . . . uh . . ."

"Black priests?"

"Exactly. Well, then, if you don't mind my asking, just what are you? A Baptist minister? No, they don't wear roman collars, do they? How about Anglican? Episcopalian?"

"I am a Roman Catholic deacon, madam."

"Oh, really? I don't think I ever met one of those before. Well, then, how are you addressed? I mean, what do I call you?"

"You may call me 'Reverend' if you feel comfortable with that."

"Oh. Reverend. Reverend! Oh, I like that! You don't get to call many people 'Reverend' anymore. All your priests want to be called Bill or Bob or Harry. Oh, I like 'Reverend'! And what is your name, Reverend?"

"Toussaint. Ramon Toussaint."

"Reverend Ramon Toussaint. Oh, I like that! It has a fine ring to it. Is that French?"

"More or less. It means 'all saints.' "

"All saints! Oh, I like that! That's a feast day, isn't it? I mean, a holy day of obligation, that is. There aren't that many people pay any attention to holy days of obligation anymore. Go to church on a holy day of obligation nowadays and you could fire off a cannon in the middle aisle and never hit a soul.

"What do you think, Reverend Toussaint? Do you think there's the respect for holy days of obligation that there used to be? Or haven't you been a Catholic all that long?"

"I would be forced to agree with you, madam. But, now, if you will excuse me, I would like to read from my book."

"Oh," she noted for the first time the small black leatherbound book Toussaint held, "the holy office! Oh, I like that! Used to be you could see the priests walking up and down, up and down, hours on end, reading from their little holy office. Don't see that anymore. Why, you take your average new priest and put the holy office in his hands and I'll just bet he wouldn't know what to do with it. Well, I'm all for that, Reverend Toussaint; you just go right ahead and read your holy office!''

Toussaint nodded and opened his commonplace book. He would not discard the reprieve just to correct a mistaken impression.

It was, he thought, fortunate. God does indeed move in mysterious ways His wonders to perform. If it had not been for the bluehaired lady's incessant prattle, he would not have tried to escape behind his commonplace book. And if he hadn't opened his book he would have completely forgotten the shopping list Emerenciana had given him. But, here he was, looking at the list. A marvelous coincidence!

Toussaint rose and nodded pleasantly to the blue-haired lady, who smiled sweetly in return. He swung down from the cable car and walked toward the grocery. The neighborhood was most familiar to him. It had been his community for the past several years since he left Detroit for an assignment in Our Lady of Guadalupe parish here in San Francisco.

As he walked, he was greeted by nearly everyone he encountered. Shortly after his arrival, he had become the acknowledged leader of what had once been a Chicano barrio but was now simply another mixed neighborhood. He was respected as much by Hispanics as by blacks, Catholic as well as non-Catholic.

He addressed each person by name. But he offered no more than that. He was still disquieted by what he had learned at the meeting he had attended earlier.

He completed the marketing and returned home directly.

During dinner, there was little conversation, and what there was was awkward. Very unusual.

"What is it, Ramon? What is wrong?" His wife clutched her coffee cup with both hands as if for needed warmth . . . or reassurance.

Toussaint placed his fork on the plate and stared at it for a few seconds. "I must leave, 'Ciane . . . for a short while."

"For where? Why?"

"I must go to Rome. That is all I can tell you."

"Rome! But you just came back from Canada!"

"Yes. But something has happened. I must not tell you what. But the situation requires my presence."

She sipped her coffee. "Is there danger?"

He shrugged, then smiled. "To me? No, I think not. To others? Possibly." Then, after a moment's thought, "Very possibly."

"Does it have to do with those who will be inducted into the College of Cardinals?" She caught his suddenly pained expression. "Does it have to do with Archbishop Boyle?"

Back in Detroit, Boyle had been close to being a friend. Indeed, it was Boyle who had ordained Toussaint a deacon. The Toussaints would have unreservedly considered him their friend had it not been for the fact that the Archbishop was ordinarily so reserved that almost no one but a few peers considered him in the category of a friend.

Toussaint smiled again. "Now, I have told you I cannot explain the reason I must go to Rome. Only that I must go and that I will return as quickly as I can. In a matter of days. Two weeks at the maximum."

"You will see Archbishop Boyle?"

"Of course."

"Then give him my greetings."

"Of course."

"When will you leave?"

"Time is of great importance. I will leave tomorrow morning."

"Then come. We will make one of our prayers for this journey."

Emerenciana Toussaint was a *mambo*, a voodoo priestess. This was known to almost no one outside the Haitian community. Among the few who knew was Father Robert Koesler. And he had told no one.

ROME

"Ladies and gentlemen, we will shortly be starting our descent into Rome. The local time is 8:45 A.M."

Father Koesler stirred in the narrow seat. He glanced at his watch. No, it isn't, he thought; it's 2:45 A.M. by my metabolism's time. He seldom slept in his clothing and didn't much care for the experience. On top of that, he was convinced he had, as the advertisement so euphemistically phrased it, the worst breath of the day.

"Did you watch the movie?" Koesler turned toward Inspector Koznicki, but not enough so that he would actually breathe in his direction.

"No, I must confess I fell asleep." Every cell in Koznicki's body felt constricted.

"Did you see any of it?"

"About the first half-hour. Then, since I could not leave the plane, I fell asleep."

"Wasn't it awful?" In an attempt to render his breath acceptable, Koesler swirled orange juice around his mouth.

"If there is an award that is the antithesis of the Oscar, that movie deserves it."

"You're absolutely right. We were both actually portrayed

in that movie and neither of us could stay awake long enough to see how we did.''

The 707 touched down smoothly and began taxiing toward the terminal.

"For your safety, Captain Kamego requests that you remain seated with your seat belt fastened until he has turned off the seat belt sign. That will be your signal that we have arrived at the gate and that it is safe to move about.''

Koesler peeked around Koznicki. "Yes, I know, Wanda: Now that we're on the ground we start the most dangerous part of our journey.''

The three chuckled.

"Ladies and gentlemen; our aircraft has now parked at the gate and we will be deplaning through the forward cabin door.''

Koesler lifted himself partially out of his seat. He could see into the first class compartment. Archbishop Boyle was standing, putting on his suit coat. Boyle, his close relatives and some of the more important diocesan personages had enjoyed the precious extra space provided in first class. Koesler envied them their unrumpled clothing and limber limbs.

Everyone passed through the passport check and customs uneventfully.

"By the way, Father, speaking of the 'dangerous' drive ahead, would you care to accompany Wanda and me? We are going to take a taxi to the hotel.''

Koesler gave the invitation a few moments' thought. "Thanks just the same, Inspector, but I'd better take the chartered bus. I told Father Brandon I'd ride into Rome with him and I think he's already aboard. I'll see you later at the hotel.''

Brandon, head of the Archdiocesan Department of Education, was, indeed, on the bus. His short fuse was already burning. His furrowed brow resembled lowering clouds.

"Hey, why so glum?'' Koesler lowered himself into the seat next to Brandon. "Look at all this sunshine! It's just a beautiful spring day in sunny Italy.''

Brandon did not reply. He merely and significantly tapped his watch, making sure Koesler could see the dial. It read 3:25. Apparently, Brandon figured it should be self-evident that 3:25 in the morning was no time for banter, no matter how brightly the sun was shining.

Actually, Koesler felt no better about his compressed night than Brandon. Neither had slept well or long. Both wanted nothing more than to reach their hotel and relieve their jet lag with at least a nap.

After the luggage had been stowed aboard, the driver swung into his seat and the bus chugged off reluctantly. The driver said nothing, so it remained unclear whether he spoke English.

Koesler felt Brandon's body began to slump in the next seat. He glanced over. Brandon's chin neared his chest. He was falling asleep.

The bus came to a fork in the road. One signboard, pointing left, read Roma. The other, pointing right, read Castel Gondolfo. The bus turned right.

Koesler nudged Brandon.

"Huh?" Brandon mumbled, head slowly coming erect.

"Hey, Stew, this is interesting. We just turned down the road to Castel Gondolfo, the Pope's summer residence. Isn't that interesting?"

"Mmmmpf . . ."

Brandon had returned to sleep. Koesler, interest aroused, rubbernecked from his bus seat.

There it was: The entrance to Castel Gondolfo loomed just ahead.

"Hey, Stew, we're here. It's Castel Gondolfo!"

"Huh?" Brandon shook his head and peered through the window. If it was important enough to be awakened twice, he might just as well look at it.

"Hey, look at all those armed guards!" Koesler reached across Brandon, pointing.

"Security."

"Security?"

"Yeah," Brandon explained. "You know, it was after those attempts on the Pope's life last year. They beefed up security. You must have heard about it."

"Well, of course I did. But I had no idea the security was so intense. He must be in residence now. That's a small army outside the gate. And armed to the teeth! Nobody could get through that."

"That's the idea." Brandon slumped again and tugged the brim of his hat down, trying to shut out the sun.

Because he was napping, Brandon missed the next questionable turn. The bus circled Lake Albano and began transversing the paved layers of roadbed slowly ascending Monte Cavo on the opposite shore from Castel Gondolfo.

Koesler watched mesmerized as the bus drove back and forth, even higher up the mountain. He was convinced he was viewing Castel Gondolfo from every possible vantage. He was also convinced that he was seeing more of the palace than he cared to see. Especially since with each passing moment he longed more and more for a toothbrush, a shower, and a bed.

The bus finally left the mountain and the Castel and drove off. Despite his exhaustion, Koesler was enjoying the beautiful rural scenery and the tree-shaded roads.

Another fork in the road. Another signboard pointing left to Roma; another signboard pointing right to Marino. The bus turned right.

Koesler looked around the bus. No one else seemed to have noticed that while they were theoretically headed for Rome, they were consistently turning away from it. He decided, for the common good, that action was called for.

He rose and approached the driver. It was not an easy jaunt. The bus was swaying like a camel. "Excuse me." Koesler tapped the driver's shoulder. The man gave no indication he was aware of Koesler's presence. "Excuse me, but aren't we going the wrong way? I mean, every time we see a road sign pointing toward Rome, we turn in the opposite direction. You see? Aren't we going the wrong way?"

"No spika."

"What?"

"No spika."

"Oh."

Feeling ineffectual, Koesler returned to his seat. He could not help thinking of the Koznickis' offer of a taxi into Rome. They probably were comfortably asleep by now. He, too, could have been. But no, he had to accompany Father Brandon—who, like the Koznickis, was off in dreamland.

Up ahead was another fork. Koesler wondered if he dared hope for an end to this odyssey.

The sign pointing left read, Roma. The sign pointing right read, Grottaferrata. The bus turned right.

If he had not known better, Koesler would have sworn they were being shanghaied. Although recent news events made it not inconceivable that the Red Brigade—no, he shook his head; it couldn't be. In any event, they might just as well be being shanghaied. They were captives on a bus in a foreign land traveling in the opposite direction from their destination, with a driver who could not—or would not—speak English.

The bus rolled slowly into a village so picturesque it almost seemed to be a picture postcard come to life.

They circled the town's piazza, then slowly jolted to a stop near a curb. The driver turned off the engine, pulled on the emergency brake, opened the doors, stood, walked down the steps, halted outside the door, and lit a cigarette.

"What? What?" Father Brandon adjusted his hat and rubbed his eyes. "Where are we? Are we here?"

"In a manner of speaking, I guess you could say so," Koesler replied.

"Where are we?" A sense of panic began intruding on Brandon's consciousness. "This isn't Rome!"

"No. If I had a free guess, I would say this is the lovely village of Grottaferrata. At least that's what the latest road sign indicated."

"Grottawhat? What's the meaning of this? We're supposed to be in Rome! What's going on?"

"I haven't a clue."

Brandon rose and started for the front of the bus. "Well, I'll find out pretty damn soon."

"I wouldn't bet on that."

Brandon had to get in line to interview the driver, who, in response to all questions, passively repeated, "No spika."

Brandon finally reached the head of the line. "What's going on here? Why aren't we in Rome?"

"No spika."

"Get on this bus immediately and take us to Rome!"

"No spika."

"Roma!" Brandon said, trying his hand at Italian.

"No spika."

"It's no use, Stew," said Koesler. "For whatever reason, we are on a sightseeing expedition and I don't think he's going to take us to Rome till he's good and ready."

"I'll get to the bottom of this! I'm going to call Monsignor Iming!"

"The Archbishop's secretary? What can he do?"

"For one thing, he can speak Italian. I'll get the bus driver on that phone and Joe can damn well tell him to get us the hell into Rome!"

Koesler decided to accompany Brandon. There wasn't likely to be a better show in Grottaferrata.

It was, indeed, Koesler who located the public phones. The entire small storefront was given over to public phones. There were nine separate booths along one wall, and one control panel behind a counter near the front of the building.

Behind the counter stood one of the most pleasant-appearing women Koesler had ever seen. Pasta had made her round, but pleasantly so. Her face was beautiful and her smile beatific. She was obviously pleased to see two priests in her establishment.

"I want to make a phone call." Brandon mimed holding a phone and speaking into it. "I want to call Villa Stritch."

"Si." She smiled.

"Where do I make the call? Where?" He tried Latin: "*Ubi?*"

"*Numero sette.*" She smiled and pointed.

That seemed clear enough. Brandon walked to the seventh booth, stepped in, and disappeared.

A few moments later, his scowling face reappeared. He was holding the receiver to his ear. "There's no dial tone," he complained.

"Si." She smiled.

"No dial tone! There's no dial tone!" He pointed at the receiver.

She nodded. She comprehended. She clarified. "*Non como a Novo York . . .*" then she made a high-pitched, prolonged humming sound.

Even Brandon understood. Unlike New York, there was no dial tone. One simply dialed. On faith.

Brandon disappeared again. After some time he emerged. The call had not removed his scowl. He offered the operator a handful of American coins. She checked the amount of time he'd used, and removed several coins from his outstretched hand.

"Gratia." She smiled.

"Prego," Koesler tried.

She smiled even more broadly.

Koesler turned to Brandon. "What happened?"

"Nothing. Not a damn thing. No answer. Probably discon-
nected the phone and enjoying a nice long nap."

"Or shower."

They, as well as their fellow passengers, proceeded to mill
about the streets of Grottaferrata for the better part of an hour.
It was beginning to feel like home. Finally, their driver called
out something that could have been *"Andiamo!"* and entered
the bus, followed quickly by his passengers.

Now, Koesler happily concluded, they were on the right
track and following the signs toward Rome. Finally they did
indeed enter the Eternal City. They drove, haltingly due to
heavy midday traffic, down the Corso Vittorio Emanuele.
Just before they crossed the bridge over the Tiber, Koesler
looked to his right and, down the wide Via della Conciliazione,
he caught his first sight of St. Peter's Basilica, the world's
largest church. Oddly, he wasn't as impressed as he had
expected to be.

It was nearly noon when they arrived at the Garibaldi. As a
group, there were few things in life they had wanted more
than to reach this hotel.

As they walked into the hotel, Koesler spotted the Koznickis
seated in large upholstered chairs in the lobby, surrounded by
their luggage.

He hurried to them. "What happened? Why aren't you in
your room?"

"The rooms were not ready for occupancy until after noon,"
Koznicki wearily replied.

The dawn came up like thunder. Koesler clapped a hand to
his head. "That explains it!"

"Explains what?"

"Our sightseeing tour of the countryside. We've been on
the bus or in a small village since we left you."

Koznicki smiled ruefully. "Perhaps you had the better of it
after all. At least you saw some scenery. We have been
confined to people-watching. And mostly Americans, at that."

"And we recognized only one person in this lobby all
morning," added Wanda. "That was Cardinal Gattari."

"The Secretary of State?" Koesler whistled. "You were involved in Very Important People-watching. I wonder what the next Pope was doing in the lobby of the Garibaldi?"

"I do not know," said Koznicki, "but he surely is an imposing figure of a man."

An announcement was made that the rooms were now ready. Everyone converged on the registration desk. ·

As he stood in line, Koesler could not help but overhear a conversation emanating from behind a nearby pillar.

"I don't care what they do to me," the voice was saying, "I'm never going to take on another contract like that. It's too dangerous. For a while, I didn't know: It could have been them or me. I mean, toward the end they were getting pretty ugly. I tell you, I'm through with it. Finito. Never again."

The voice spoke in heavily accented English. Koesler peered around the pillar. The voice belonged to their bus driver.

2

The technical process of making a Cardinal comprises three steps.

On April 28, Pope Leo XIV presided over a secret consistory involving all the Cardinals then present in Rome. During this consistory, the Pope read off the names of his candidates for the Cardinalate. At each name, each Cardinal raised his biretta and bowed his head, indicating his assent to the nominee. A gesture that is the closest thing there is to a rubber stamp.

On April 29, the candidates assembled at prearranged locations in Rome. The three American candidates gathered at a crowded Roman Chancery building. A monsignor from the Vatican Secretary of State's office, accompanied by one of the laymen attached to the papal household, presented each candidate with the official *biglietto*—the letter informing him of his elevation. As Archbishop Boyle accepted his *biglietto*, he became His Eminence Mark Cardinal Boyle.

Tonight, April 30, the final ceremony in the process of becoming a Cardinal was scheduled. In one of the great halls adjoining the papal residence, the Pope would receive in audience all the new Cardinals. During the ceremony, he would place on each Cardinal's head a scarlet biretta, the sign of their office, and he would reveal the name of the individual Roman parish each Cardinal would become titular bishop of.

For tonight's ceremony, Father Koesler had been given a blue ticket. A quick study of others' tickets revealed there were also gold and red tickets to this event. He was unable to determine the exact import of a blue ticket. Apparently, there was no way of knowing where one's ticket would lead until one got there.

As Koesler began climbing the seemingly endless staircase, he realized Detroit reporters Joe Cox and Pat Lennon were only a step behind him. He dropped back to join them.

"Evening, Father." Lennon greeted him brightly. "We haven't seen much of you since we got to Rome."

"Are you kidding?" said Cox. "The good Father wouldn't be traveling in the same low-life circles we move in."

"Oh, I don't know about that." Koesler winced. Among many appellations applied to him, he most despised "the good Father." Like most epithets, the user gave little thought to it. "By the way," Koesler continued, "may I inquire as to the color of your tickets for this event?"

Cox searched his pockets.

"Blue," said Lennon.

"Yeah," Cox located his ticket, "blue."

"Mine too," said Koesler. "Would you happen to know what that entitles us to?"

"Haven't a clue, Father," Lennon replied. "We won't know till we get there."

Somehow, Koesler now felt more confident of a good seat. He knew he personally was relatively unimportant in the scheme of things. But he was sure reporters for major American newspapers would not receive short shrift.

Cox and Lennon were just ahead of Koesler as they reached the tuxedoed master of ceremonies at the top of the stairs. He waved them behind two sawhorses to the left. Koesler was thus surprised when, after displaying his blue ticket, he was directed behind the sawhorses on the right.

Koesler looked about, trying to comprehend what was going on.

He was in a huge vaulted chamber. The only furnishings were sets of sawhorses arranged to create an aisle down the middle of the room and across the back. Behind these sawhorses milled a growing throng. One thing was certain: This was a way station; whatever was going to happen was not going to happen in this anteroom.

Koesler was not alone in reaching this conclusion. After a brief conference, Cox and Lennon agreed they had no chance of covering the ceremony from this room. But where was *the* room, and how could they get to it?

The desired direction was soon made evident. An ecclesial procession was filing through the door at the left rear of the room, proceeding along the rear wall, and heading through the door at the right rear.

Koesler angled as close as he could to the path of the procession. There were several rows of people in front of him. However, his height made it possible for him to see at least the upper half of the procession. The crossbearer was followed by acolytes, then bishops, then Cardinals, then the new Cardinals—among them Cardinal Boyle—and finally, the Pope.

Applause rang out along the length of the procession, swelling when segments of the crowd recognized a favorite son. For the Pope, the applause was near-deafening.

Koesler was surprised. And a little disappointed. He was surprised that up this close the Pope lost much of his mystique. He was merely a wizened little old man. Koesler was disappointed that the Pope was so surrounded by Swiss Guards that it was difficult to catch sight of him. It must be the increased security.

It was incredible. Where else would one be given a special ticket just to stand in an unfurnished hall and look at other ticket holders for two to three hours while the ceremony you had come to see was going on somewhere else?

The only extraordinary item in the hall worth studying was the tall, imposing Swiss Guard securing the entrance to what was presumably the ceremonial room. Interesting history. Their uniform was said to have been designed by no less than Michelangelo, who was said to have modified it from a 1496 battle uniform. And, if memory served, during the sack of Rome in the sixteenth century, all but twelve of the Swiss Guard had died defending the Vatican Palace. One wondered what had been wrong with those twelve.

The present stance of this particular guardsman seemed to

be what passed for "at ease." Koesler recalled the ritual which demanded that each guardsman snap to attention each time a bishop or similar high ecclesiastic passed before him. What would happen, he wondered, if a bishop were to walk back and forth repeatedly in front of a guardsman, just to get him to salute. How long would the guardman's patience last? But then, one probably wouldn't be able to find a bishop with that peculiar a sense of humor.

Koesler glanced at his watch. 8:15. Theoretically, fifteen minutes into the ceremony. How long was one expected to stand in one place and study a Swiss Guard? It's 8:15; do you know where your Swiss Guard is?

Then, something out of the ordinary took place. Joe Cox and Pat Lennon coolly stepped out from behind the barrier, walked purposefully to the guardsman, spoke to him briefly, displayed something in their wallets and walked past him into the ceremonial room.

Koesler pondered their maneuver a moment and decided, why not? It was unlikely the guardsman would run a poor priest through with his halberd.

He stepped into the aisle, walked up to the guard, opened his wallet, and displayed his supermarket check-cashing card, pointed toward the ceremonial room and said, "I'm with them."

The guardsman, who seemed to neither recognize the card, nor understand English, simply shrugged.

Koesler, bracing himself, despite his earlier mental bravado, for a poke from the halberd, walked past him through the doorway. When nothing happened, he relaxed.

An opulent kaleidoscope unfurled before him.

Heads of state were glowing in their resplendent uniforms and brilliant sashes. The hierarchical vestments were, as always, magnificently impressive. And withal, there was that distinctive color known as cardinal red. The vivid meld of vermilion and orange was perhaps the most eye-boggling shade in the spectrum.

Even so, it was not as sumptuous as it had been before Pope Paul VI had simplified the Cardinal's garb in 1969. Gone were the voluminous *capa magna*, the train of scarlet moire, the ermine cape, the golden tassels, the red leather slippers with gold or silver buckles.

But most of all, gone was The Red Hat.

It had been a purely ceremonial *galero*. With a normal crown but an overlarge brim and two strings of fifteen tassels each hanging from it. Of course, it was never actually worn. But heretofore, in the installation of a Cardinal, the hat, borne by two monsignors, had been touched symbolically to his head. It was then shipped home with the Cardinal and held in limbo until, at his death, it was hung fron the ceiling of his cathedral.

Till recent years, it had been so distinctive a symbol that being named a Cardinal was more popularly referred to as receiving the red hat.

It was at this ceremony that the new Cardinals would have received the red hat. But now, the Pope would merely place on each Cardinal's head a simple scarlet biretta.

The Pope had been speaking for a very long time. Every three or four paragraphs, he would switch to a different language. Koesler had lost count of the number of languages in which the Pope was proving himself fluent.

The time had come. As each Cardinal knelt before him, the Pope placed a biretta on the head of the new Prince of the Church, intoning, "For the praise of the omnipotent God and for the honor of the Apostolic See, receive the red hat, symbol of the great dignity of the Cardinalate, which means that you must show yourself to be fearless even to the shedding of blood for the exaltation of the Holy Faith, for the peace and tranquility of the Christian people, and for the liberty and expansion of the Holy Roman Church."

At the words, "the shedding of blood," Koesler was arrested by the memory of the slain Cardinal Claret and the airport attack on Cardinal Boyle. Clearly, the Pope's words were not empty ones. For whatever reason, the Cardinal Archbishop of Toronto had shed his blood in violent death. And, if not for the alertness and swift action of Inspector Koznicki just a few days ago, Cardinal Boyle might not have lived to hear those words. Koesler wondered what thoughts were going through Boyle's mind at this minute.

The attacks were incomprehensible to Koesler. The phenomenon of a deeply insecure person seeking instant fame by assaulting someone famous was, as Koznicki had sadly noted, becoming all too increasingly common. But Koesler, while accepting the explanation, could not understand it. And Cardinal Claret? Was his murder the same manifestation of a modern phenomenon, or was there something deeper, more sinister involved?

Ceremony completed, the exit recessional had begun. Now each Cardinal wore his new biretta. Again the applause. Again the cordon of Swiss Guards surrounding the Pope. Anyone determined to make the pontiff shed blood would have to smash his way through a phalanx of tall stalwart young men.

Koesler made his way out of the hall and down the seemingly infinite steps. Clearly, it was lots easier going down than coming up. He continued across St. Peter's Square to the far section where the buses huddled like a herd of elephants.

As he was walking along the row of vehicles, Koesler heard his name called. Turning quickly, he struck his head against an outside rearview mirror on one of the buses. Feeling blood running down his face, he quickly put a handkerchief to the wound.

"Hey, Bob; sorry!" It was Father Brandon. "I wouldn't have called to you if I had thought this would happen."

"That's all right; my own stupid fault . . . how bad is it?"

Brandon examined the wound in the bright glow of the bus' headlight. "Not bad. Little more than a scratch. But you know how head wounds bleed."

"Lucky I didn't break my glasses." Koesler applied as much pressure as he could to the cut. If it was as small as Brandon had described, it should clot in a matter of minutes. Meanwhile, with the blood that had already splotched the right side of his face, he looked as if he had been in a street fight.

"Just like a Cardinal," Brandon commented.

"How's that?"

"They get a commission to go out and shed their blood and they send some poor priest to do it for them."

3

" 'Venus of Cnidus—Roman Copy after Praxiteles.' Hmmm."

They walked on.

" *'Sleeping Ariadne*—Imperial Roman Art.' Hmmm."
And on.

" *'Bathing Venus*—Roman Copy after a Bronze Original by the Bithynian Artist Doidalses.' Hmmm." Joe Cox turned to his companion. "So what do you think it is; do you suppose women were built differently back then?"

Pat Lennon smiled. "Large ladies, aren't they?"

Lennon and Cox were in the middle of the Pio-Clementino Museum on a route they hoped would lead them to the famed Sistine Chapel. There were no affiliated ceremonies scheduled for today, so, as was the case with most of the entourage associated with the new Cardinals, they had gone sightseeing.

"It's not just that they're large," said Cox, "it's that each and every one of these statues depicts a very zaftig lady. And I've got to assume the artists were not doing posters for Weight Watchers."

"You've got to admit they're shapely."

"Oh, yes. Hourglass figures. Except that their hours look more like days."

"This is a good lesson for you, Joe. It's all relative. Until comparatively recently, only large, fleshy females were considered beautiful. Today's slender models would have been considered unattractive. Men wanted their women amply endowed all over. Today, 'amply endowed' is Jayne Mansfield or Dolly Parton. It's all a matter of taste . . . and tastes change."

"The more there is of you, the more there is for me to love, eh?"

Lennon smiled again. "Feel cheated?"

Cox moved close and slid an arm around her waist. Far from feeling cheated, he was always proud to be in her company. She resembled a slightly taller, younger Brenda Vaccaro with that actress' husky, sexy voice. And she was a first-class journalist to boot.

"Watch it, Cox!" She laughed. "This is the Vatican. You want to create bad thoughts for some Swiss Guard?"

They wandered on through the museums, gazing at figures of statuesque women and superbly muscled men.

"Hey," Cox called from several feet away, reading from a small sign attached to a windowsill, "there's hope. Here's a sign that gives directions for the Sistine Chapel."

"Really? Which way is it?"

"These are not directions for *finding* it. They are directions on the decorum expected in it if you find it."

"Oh . . . and what do they suggest?"

"These are not suggestions. They read more like instructions."

"Like what?"

"Well, it points out that the Sistine Chapel is a sacred place. You've got to wear modest clothing, and you're expected to observe a reverential silence."

"That makes sense, I guess."

It was not long afterward that they found the steps leading to that structure distinct in so many ways from all others.

"Modest clothing!" warned Cox.

"Reverential silence!" affirmed Lennon.

Actually, they heard the Sistine Chapel before they saw it. And when they did see it, the scene brought to mind the Tower of Babel. Throughout the chapel, clusters of tourists gathered about their guides. That which differentiated one group from another was language. Here a German bunch, there a French, here a Polish, there an English, and so on. Many members of each group, in the age-old tourist custom, were chatting with their fellows. Thus the guides had to deliver their spiels at nearly peak volume.

It took Cox and Lennon several minutes to adjust their hearing as well as their psychological sensitivities to this cacophony. Once adjusted, they decided to explore together the marvels of Michelangelo and friends.

Father Koesler had found the chapel about half an hour earlier and had attached himself to the fringe of a tour being conducted in English. From a distance of only a few feet, he found it a definite challenge to hear and understand the guide, who was speaking very loudly, if not distinctly.

"This building," the guide was saying, "is a bit more than five hundred years old. It was built in the reign of Pope Sixtus IV by Giovannino de' Dolci, based on plans by Baccio Pontelli. The Sistine is the Pope's official private chapel. In addition to many liturgical functions, the conclaves for the papal elections are held here."

Koesler's gaze was fixed on the famed ceiling. Michelangelo's ceiling art was so busy the priest couldn't decide what to focus on first. There was the renowned creation of man wherein God reaches out to touch the finger of a flaccid Adam. Human life is about to begin.

"The pavement is a prominent example of fifteenth century Roman mosaic artistry," the guide went on. "The two groups of six frescoes each on the main walls depict events in the life of Moses, the 'liberator of Israel,' over there," she pointed to the left, "and events in the life of Christ, the 'liberator of all mankind,' over there," she indicated the group to the right.

Or, thought Koesler, still examining the ceiling, there is the scene of the expulsion of Adam and Eve from Paradise. How many times had he seen these celebrated paintings reproduced in framed prints, in textbooks, magazines, seemingly everywhere. He was deeply moved that he was actually in the presence of Michelangelo's original work.

"After discarding his initial design," the guide had now caught up to Koesler and was explaining the ceiling, "which involved the depiction of the twelve Apostles, Michelangelo decided to relate his work to that already existing on the walls, where the history of mankind is depicted. His subjects were the Biblical stories of the Creation, Adam and Eve, the Flood, and the resumption of life on dry land by Noah and his family."

Ah, yes, there was the drunken Noah and his naughty children over in the corner of the ceiling, near the top of the entrance to the chapel. Head tilted back, Koesler had been looking at the ceiling so long he was finding it difficult to breathe. He dropped his gaze to the crowd and massaged his neck. One problem with looking at the ceiling for an extended period was that it hurt.

There was something different about that man. What was he doing? He seemed to be contemplating his hand, which he held at belt level, palm upright. Curious. He just stood there, studying his palm. Then Koesler was able to see that the man was holding a thin, flat object in his open hand. It was a mirror. The clever fellow was looking at the Sistine ceiling as reflected in the mirror he was holding! Koesler marveled at the simplicity of it. There was one person who would suffer no crick in his neck. It was too late for Koesler, but he would be telling others of this marvelous discovery.

"That is Somebody," said Pat Lennon.

"Undoubtedly," Joe Cox acknowledged.

"No, not him. *Him* . . . the guy in the simple black cassock. He just came into the chapel. I caught a glimpse of him as he entered. I thought I recognized him, but I wasn't sure. I can't place him, but I think he's somebody important."

"Want me to go ask him? 'Excuse-a me, sir, but are you somebody important?' "

"Joe!"

"He's probably a humble Italian parish priest, just come in to join the crowd. In a little while, we'll know."

"How?"

"If I'm right, he'll take up a collection."

The unimposing clergyman in the plain black cassock stood, hands locked behind his back, before the Rosselli panel, *Moses Receives the Tables of the Law*. Cardinal Giulanio Gattari visited the Sistine Chapel each Thursday morning as faithfully as possible. He knew the Sistine as a lover knows his beloved. At each visit, the Cardinal, wearing a simple black cassock for anonymity's sake, would select an appropriate painting as a source for meditation. It was a tribute to his power of concentration as well as to his familiarity with the chapel that he was capable of meditating amid its constant turmoil and hubbub.

The painting before which he now stood was a montage of Moses receiving the Law, descending from the mountain, and breaking the tablets, as well as a depiction of the unfaithful Israelites worshiping their golden calf.

Everyone breaking the law, Gattari mused. The Israelites breaking the First Commandment. Moses breaking all ten.

Ah, Moses, he thought; what a thankless task was yours! You wanted no part of the whole thing. But you were called to confront the Pharaoh and announce God's message to let His people go. Then you led them through the desert. Never did they have faith in you. They argued with you and questioned you at every turn. They treated their God no better. Even you were led to call them a stiff-necked people.

And what of me? Gattari continued in reverie. What if Providence does, indeed, place me in the Chair of Peter? It would be no accident. It would be a combination of a smiling fate and my own ambition. But there is no doubt: I am in the favored position. No one stands between me and the Papacy but Leo XIV. And he is an old man. No matter how carefully they guard him, he cannot live forever. He cannot live much longer. Then nothing will stand between me and my destiny but a sacred consistory.

Now, I must torture myself with the unending question: What am I to do with it once I gain it? Why do I want it? Why should anyone? Like Moses, I would gain leadership over a stiff-necked people. Some demand more progress. Others insist on a return to a day that can never be recaptured. I can anticipate no more respect, obedience, or fealty than has been accorded Leo. Why do I want it? At this point, what could I do to avoid it? Must I pray *ad multos annos* for Leo, that doddering old fool!

"In the Last Judgment, on the altar wall," the guide intoned, "the central figure is Christ as Judge, right hand raised in a violent gesture of condemnation. At his right, in the shadow of his uplifted arm, is the Blessed Mother. To his left is St. Peter, holding the Keys to the Kingdom, one in each hand."

Koesler was grateful for no longer having his attention called to the ceiling. He studied the wall. It was a terrifying vision of Judgment. As usual, going to heaven seemed relatively uninteresting compared with the terror of being dragged into hell.

"Down below," the guide continued, "is the entrance to hell, with the boat of Charon, in accordance with Dante's description, overflowing with the souls of the damned, and Minos, king of the nether world, whom Michelangelo—adding the ears of an ass—characterized as Monsignor Biagio Martinelli, Pope Paul II's master of ceremonies, who had criticized Michelangelo's work."

Koesler was staring at what appeared to be an enormous patch of black paint. He wondered why Michelangelo would simply waste so much valuable space. Then he saw it. Just the hint of a contorted face, six white teeth in a shrieking mouth, and eyes that long for what they can never possess. It was the head of a damned soul in the cave of hell. Terrifying!

His sense of horror was amplified and intensified at that instant as a scream came from the rear of the chapel.

"Oh! No! No!" It was a scream as much of dread as of surprise.

"Joe! Joe! Look!" Pat Lennon pointed.

Cox, following her gesture, saw the black-cassocked priest they had previously noted crumble to the floor. A knife was buried in his chest. His blood was flowing freely.

A large black man bent over the writhing figure. In an instant, he straightened, turned, and ran from the chapel. Cox dashed after him. Screams and shouts filled the chapel as tourists shrank from the wounded cleric. The first to move to him were Pat Lennon and Father Koesler.

Cox pursued the younger, stronger, faster man down library corridors, through museum settings, past coin collections. Whereinhell was the Swiss Guard now that he needed them! Added to Cox's handicaps was the fact that the assailant had a knack of running through and over people and obstacles, while Cox had to go around them. Although, truth to tell, in a straightaway race, Cox would never have been able to catch up with, let alone head the man.

At long last—although it really hadn't been that long—Cox gave up—or rather gave out. Chest heaving, he stood in the middle of a long corridor, as a group of tourists stared wide-eyed at him.

Slowly, gasping and panting, he made his way back to the chapel. Most of the people who had been there were still there. A small group was clustered around the victim. In that group were Lennon and Koesler. Several of what seemed to be paramedics had placed the victim on a stretcher and were taking him away.

Cox noticed that the sheet covering the cleric had not been pulled over his face. Cox hoped that signified in Italy what it did in the United States, that the victim was still alive.

Cox then noted an evergrowing number of *carabinieri* spreading through the chapel. They were questioning everyone, searching for eyewitnesses. One was interviewing Lennon, another was questioning Koesler. Since it would inevitably become Cox's turn, he decided to join Lennon.

"Oh, here he is," said Lennon as Cox came to her side. "This is the man I told you about . . . the one who chased the assailant."

The Italian officer got Cox's full identification. "So," he said in barely accented English, "it was very brave of you, signore. But you could not catch him?"

"No. As a matter of fact, about halfway through the chase, it occurred to me that I wouldn't know what to do with him if I did catch him."

"Please?"

"He was almost twice my size!"

"Doubly brave of you."

"Who was the victim, anyway?" Cox's question was directed to the officer, but Lennon answered.

"You know, I said I thought he was important, Joe. Well, I was right. I realized who he was when I saw him on the floor. It's Cardinal Giulanio Gattari!"

Cox whistled softly, then caught himself. He felt as if he might be the only person ever to whistle in the Sistine Chapel. "The Secretary of State! We should have recognized him!"

"I think we were thrown off by the simple black cassock. You just don't expect to see a Cardinal dressed so plainly."

Koesler, who had finished his interview, was now listening in.

"The Cardinal," commented the officer, "was in the habit of walking about Vatican City dressed without ostentation. But, tell me, Signore Cox, since you chased the assailant, can you describe him for me?" The officer's pen was poised over his pad.

"Well, he was maybe six-foot-two or three; he wasn't wearing a suit . . . let's see, it was an unmatched jacket and pants and a blue shirt open at the neck; no tie. He weighed maybe 240-250. Black, very dark complexion. And there was something funny about his hair . . . it was in a natural." He thought a minute. "No . . . no, I'll take that back. It was done up in those—oh, you know—like long wriggly corn rows."

"Oh—" That was as far as Koesler got before Lennon hastily led him away, as the officer looked after them quizzically.

"Father," she said, "you got a look at that man . . . and you know what that hairstyle is called, don't you?"

"Well, yes. It's not corn rows. It's dreadlocks. It's what happens when some blacks wash their hair, if it happens to be very long, and they just let it dry out without any additional treatment."

"Very good, Father." Lennon sounded like an elementary

school teacher. "And I suppose you also know who wears their hair that way as a matter of conviction?"

"Well, yes . . ." Koesler was beginning to feel like a pupil who was doing very well in school. "They call themselves Rastafarians."

"Right. It's just as I suspected. You know all this and I know all this and in a matter of an hour or so at most I will make sure the Italian authorities know all this.

"But, for the moment, Joe Cox doesn't know all this. Now in just a few minutes, Joe and I will be filing our stories to Detroit. Joe will write—modestly—of his brave participation in the event. But he will not know of the possible connection with Rastafarians. And I will. Are you getting the picture?"

"Yes, of course. After all, I used to be actively involved in journalism. Even if it was with the weekly *Detroit Catholic* and not a daily. You want your scoop. But what about the police investigation?"

"Father, it's a matter of minutes—an hour at most. Just as soon as Joe files his story—and, if his track record holds, that will be even faster than I file mine—I will go to the police and fill out the picture. It won't impede their investigation and I'll still have my scoop. Then, we'll just sit back and let Joe wait till his angry editor cables him before he gets the picture."

"I see. But I thought you were . . . uh . . . friends!"

There might have been some Detroiters who were confused over whom Henry Ford II was married to, but almost everyone knew that Cox and Lennon shared almost everything but their scoops.

"Everything, Father, is fair in love, war, and journalism."

4

The two men strolled along the Via di San Gregorio. They walked slowly, deliberately, only peripherally aware of the Forum ruins they were passing, so absorbed in conversation were they.

"It all happened so quickly—so unexpectedly, I should say," Father Koesler was explaining, "that we were all pretty dumbfounded. All of us, that is, except Joe Cox, who chased after the guy."

"Yes," Inspector Koznicki nodded, "and from the description he gave of the man, Mr. Cox is fortunate not to have caught up with him."

"I think he probably wanted more to interview him than apprehend him!" Koesler, smiling, shook his head at the memory, and then his face grew solemn: Cardinal Gattari had survived the immediate attack, only to die shortly thereafter en route to the hospital.

Koznicki, hoping to hearten his companion, spoke again. "I must say, Father, your phone call to Father Ouellet in Toronto was an inspired bit of detection."

"More a lucky coincidence. While I was talking with Pat Lennon about how the assailant wore his hair in dreadlocks, I recalled that Father Ouellet had described Cardinal Claret's killer as a black man with his hair in a 'natural.' As a matter of fact, that was the word Joe Cox used to describe the man he chased. He said the man had a 'natural,' then corrected himself."

"But not perfectly accurately."

"By now he's been enlightened. Anyway, when I phoned Father Ouellet after lunch—he was just about to go over to the cathedral for the early morning Mass—I asked him to describe the man's hair, and, sure enough, it was dreadlocks—although Father Ouellet had never heard of that term."

"I am sure that added information will be a help to the Toronto and Rome police who are investigating their respective homicides."

Koesler wondered whether his friend's statement meant that the murders of two Cardinals were the purview of the Canadian and Italian police and none of his or Koesler's business. Koesler hoped that was not the case.

"I think there's more to it than that, Inspector—oh, look over there!" He pointed to where, evidently just a few minutes before, two automobiles, a Fiat and a Volkswagen, had collided. There did not appear to be much damage to either vehicle. But an unwonted crowd of men had gathered at the scene. Only a small percentage could have actually witnessed the collision. Yet, here were all these men, arguing angrily. Some were even becoming physical, pushing and shoving.

The only explanation for this precipitate brouhaha was that apparently one of the cars had been driven by a woman. And what a woman! Blonde, taller than any of the men, and busty enough to be fairly popping from her light dress. She paid little heed to the commotion about and because of her, but appeared to be waiting for the hubbub to die down so she could drive away.

Koznicki laughed heartily. "I have always thought that to make an Italian movie, all one had to do was walk down a street in Italy with a camera on one's shoulder. I believe the cinéma verité was conceived with Italy in mind.

"But, Father, you were saying—?"

"Maybe I'm being an alarmist, but how many times have there been attempts on the lives of Cardinals? Oh, perhaps in the Middle Ages, but not now . . . not today. Cardinals grow old and slip away quietly in their sleep. Yet in the past few weeks, two Cardinals have been murdered, and another attacked. Are these events connected? Will there be more?"

Koznicki grew reflective. He had learned to trust his clerical friend's deductive powers as well as his intuition. But there seemed little if any connection between these attacks. And, even if there were a link, technically, as a foreigner in this country it was none of his concern, even though he was a homicide detective.

"I really cannot find any connection here, Father," he said, at length. "It is more than likely that the attack on Cardinal Claret was, as the Canadian police suspect, the random act of a young hoodlum out to snatch some media attention. A nobody trying to become somebody.

"That almost certainly was so in Cardinal Boyle's case.

"And, you see, Father, that sort of act very unfortunately has a way of building upon itself. Now, this morning, the dastardly act was repeated in the case of Cardinal Gattari. The only link I see is that with Cardinals Claret and Gattari, each of their assailants had dreadlocks. And dreadlocks are not that unusual. Do you see anything beyond that, Father?"

"I guess I'd have to grant you that the attack on Cardinal Boyle was—as you describe it—a solitary act. But there is something at work here, I think.

"There is, of course, no way of predicting with any certitude who the prime candidates for the Papacy are, let alone who will actually be the next Pope. But there is gossip and talk and news—and, gradually, a consensus builds.''

''Yes?'' Koznicki's interest was piqued.

''Well, according to nearly everyone, Cardinal Gattari was, by far, the front-runner, the top favorite to be elected the next Pope. Of course, that would depend on a lot of imponderables. Pope Leo XIV, of course, would have to die. And he would have to die while Cardinal Gattari was still young enough to continue to be the favorite.''

''What does that have to do with—''

''My next point. Next in line after Gattari was Cardinal Claret.''

''A Canadian?''

''The Italian succession has been interrupted. The Papacy, at least for the foreseeable future, should be internationally attainable.

''So you see, Inspector, that is my common denominator. The favorite to be the next Pope and the next favorite in line, both murdered. Both murdered by men in dreadlocks. It is not an indisputable hypothesis, but it is worth consideration, I think.

''And there is one more very peculiar similarity in the killings of the two Cardinals. When I attended Cardinal Claret's funeral, I was puzzled to see a black fist painted on the historical marker outside the cathedral. That same black fist was imposed on all the programs for the funeral rite.

''This morning, after the body was removed and things had quieted down, I went back to where Cardinal Gattari had fallen. The blood had been cleaned away. But there, where the body had lain, was the small image of a black fist.''

''A black fist! I must admit that is a most peculiar coincidence!''

They strolled on in silence.

''I would be glad to advance your hypothesis to the proper authorities for their consideration, Father. But what does it all have to do with us?''

''Just this: Not very far down that list of papal possibles is our own Cardinal Boyle.''

This observation literally stopped Koznicki in his tracks. He stood stock still. After a few moments, he moved a few steps to the low railing at the edge of the sidewalk. Koesler joined him. Silently they gazed at the ruins of the Forum.

"Each time I see the Forum, I am astonished again to think of the ideas that were born here," mused Koznicki.

Koesler was surprised at this turn in their conversation. Seemingly, Koznicki wished to put this possible threat to Cardinal Boyle's life on a mental back burner.

"Five hundred years before Christ," Koznicki continued, "Rome became a republic with a system of rights for its citizens. Much of our concept of justice, our legal system, was formed here in the Forum." He turned to Koesler. "Is it not impressive, Father?"

"Oh, yes, indeed." He would not press the point; he would go along with his friend's digression. "Rome is the fountainhead of our Western civilization. Even today, they still use that ancient inscription, SPQR—*Senatus Populusque Romanus*—The Senate and People of Rome. You look at these ruins of the Forum and the Colosseum across the street and you are impressed with how ancient traces of the twenty-seven-centuries-long history of Rome can be found all over the city. I can't think of any other place where the past and present seem to coexist more completely and comfortably than Rome."

There was another long silence. Koesler felt the verbal ball was definitely in Koznicki's court.

"So, Father," the Inspector still gazed at the Forum, "you believe there is a threat against the life of Cardinal Boyle because he is a recognized candidate for the Papacy."

"Yes, but I don't know why." Of course Koznicki was concerned. Perhaps he had temporarily changed the subject in order to clear his mind—as a gourmet savors a sorbet between courses to clear his palate. He should have had more faith in the Inspector's professionalism. "I mean, I don't know what the motive might be. I may be wrong, but I think both Cardinals Claret and Gattari were killed because they were top contenders for the Papacy. But I don't know who . . . or why anybody would do it."

"How many other Cardinals, would you say, fit into the category of papal candidates?"

Koesler thought briefly. "I would guess not more than

eight or nine serious candidates who would be pretty well universally acknowledged by students of this sort of thing."

"And the names of those Cardinals would also be generally acknowledged? I, for instance, am not specifically aware of them. And I consider myself to be well read."

"You *are* well read, Inspector. Your problem is that until now you were not specifically interested. For those who are interested, it is easy to work up a list. Why, a few years ago, a small publishing house in the midwest, Sheed Andrews and McMeel, published a book by Gary MacEoin on this very subject. If memory serves, it was titled, *The Inner Elite.*"

"I see. I would assume then, that uncompromising security for these men is called for. I shall be instrumental in informing the appropriate authorities."

"I think you've hit on it, Inspector. And I think a lot of added security is vital for many of the Cardinals in question. But I believe we've got a major problem when we get to the man we would most like to protect, Cardinal Boyle."

"Oh . . . and why is that?"

"Most of the Cardinals on the papal list are bureaucrats far removed from free association with common everyday people. It should not be terribly difficult to protect them. This is definitely not true of Cardinal Boyle. He leads a large and busy archdiocese. You know as well as I that he is no hothouse flower. He presides over confirmation ceremonies in parishes all over the six-county Archdiocese. Most of those parishes would present security problems. He attends open meetings. He frequently answers his own door.

"And to cap it all, most days you can find him walking down Washington Boulevard between his office and the Gabriel Richard Building, or to his automobile.

"And you know from past experience that he will not permit any major alteration in that open lifestyle. Both of us know Cardinal Boyle would never countenance walking about surrounded by a bunch of Swiss Guards."

Koznicki was silent for a few moments. "In which case, Father, Cardinal Boyle had better pray that he is not elected Pope . . . or he's going to be surrounded by Swiss Guards on top of Swiss Guards.

"Nonetheless, I think, Father, there are at least two ways to approach this problem: defensively or offensively. And, to use the familiar football metaphor, the best defense is a good offense.''

Koesler felt great relief that his friend finally seemed to be committing himself to an active role in the matter. "Then you agree there may be something to my hypothesis?"

"Father, in all the years I have been on the police force, especially those I have spent in the Homicide Division, I have learned one predominant lesson, and that is to keep an open mind on all possibilities.

"I could not tell you the number of times in an investigation that the least likely possible solution turned out to be the correct one. And I do not mean to denigrate your hypothesis. I only mean that to dismiss a tenable theory merely because it is not probable is to act the fool. My rule of thumb has become that memorable tune from *HMS Pinafore:*

> Things are seldom what they seem,
> Skim milk masquerades as cream;
> Highlows pass as patent leathers;
> Jackdaws strut in peacock's feathers.''

" 'Very true,' " Koesler responded in kind, " 'So they do.' " He smiled. "I would have thought your theme might have been 'A Policeman's Lot Is Not a Happy One.' "

Koznicki smiled back. "No; in point of fact, I have found this policeman's lot to be distinctly happy." He paused. "Well, Father, you are quite obviously somewhat in advance of me in thinking through all these possibilities. Before you draw me out any further, do you have anything else in mind?"

"Well, as a matter of fact, I have. I had thought of presenting this to you in the guise of a defense against the threat to Cardinal Boyle. But now that you have mentioned the possibility of going on the offense, I will suggest this man as our offensive weapon." An uncertain pause. "Ramon Toussaint."

Koznicki stiffened. Perceptibly.

"Ramon Toussaint? Yes, I would agree that could be a decidedly offensive weapon." He looked at Koesler fixedly. "I have by no means forgotten Ramon Toussaint, Father. The name conjures up a one-man vigilante force and a series of grotesque human heads found mounted on statues in Detroit churches. One head found stuffed inside the late Cardinal Mooney's ceremonial red hat in the cathedral, save the mark.

"Let's see, the victims were . . . oh, yes: the local Mafia don, Detroit's top pimp, Detroit's leading drug dealer, a particularly abhorrent abortionist, and then a roofer and an auto repairman who were unscrupulous and unprincipled workmen. Each of them escaped justice, as so many criminals do, until our unidentified vigilante administered his own peculiar brand of capital punishment.

"Our particular problem, as I recall—and believe me, I shall never forget it—was establishing the cause of death of those men. In the first five cases, all we were able to find were the victims' heads.

"Do I remember Ramon Toussaint! Lieutenant Ned Harris and the rest of us who worked on that case strongly suspected that our anonymous vigilante might well have been Ramon Toussaint!"

During this outburst, Koesler seemed to be recoiling as he withdrew deeper and deeper inside himself. "Those murders are still in your unsolved file," he said, almost in an undertone.

"That's true," Koznicki said, as if to himself.

"Does this mean, then," Koesler asked at length, "that you will not work with Toussaint?"

"I have been known to state that I would take a lead from the devil himself if it would help break a case."

"Then you will!" Koesler's relief was evident.

"But how is this possible? When last heard of, Toussaint was working in San Francisco."

"No, he's here. He's in Rome. I spoke with him earlier today. He is here to help. He is determined to help. The only question was our cooperation."

"I, too, have a question: This man was a suspect in an extraordinarily bizarre murder case. Do we count on him as our ally, or our enemy?"

"He is in our camp, Inspector. No doubt about it. He, as we, deeply admires Cardinal Boyle. It was Cardinal Boyle who ordained Toussaint a deacon. While he was in Detroit, Toussaint and the Cardinal were comparatively close." Koesler hesitated, then having obviously reached a decision, continued.

"I have not had an opportunity to speak with Toussaint at

any length, but he does agree with my hypothesis. I don't know how much he knows . . . or what exactly prompted him to come here . . . but he has come to Rome to try to protect the Cardinal and to stop whoever is responsible for all this. I assure you, Inspector, we will be far ahead of the game with Toussaint in our corner."

Koznicki looked searchingly at Koesler. "Then you feel that the Reverend Toussaint's presence in Rome and his reason for being here confirms your hypothesis?"

Koesler looked sheepish. "Yes. But I was afraid that if I led with Toussaint you might have rejected the whole idea out of hand. I felt that only if you reached the same conclusion in the same fashion I did—based on your own evaluation of the facts, possibilities, and coincidences—would you be amenable to Toussaint's collaboration."

"You were wrong."

"I'm glad," Koesler said simply.

"When can we get together?"

"Tomorrow. After the concelebrated Mass in St. Peter's."

"Not till then?"

"He told me he had to establish some contacts here. He said he should be able to do so by tomorrow afternoon."

"So be it, then. Tomorrow afternoon."

5

Irene Casey was by no means alone in finding St. Peter's Basilica incomprehensibly huge. This, the largest church in Christendom, is so big that it is difficult to believe that its dimensions are as colossal as they actually are.

Here, in St. Peter's Square, where Irene now stood contemplating the view, one-third of a million people regularly gather at one time to hear the Pope speak. In the center of the square stands the red granite obelisk that Caligula took from Heliopolis and Nero later had placed in the Circus Maximus.

Then there are Bernini's columns. The double colonnade surrounding the square consists of four rows of columns and spreads out from the Basilica, opening, as someone once said, "as in an ideal embrace from Christianity offered to the world."

The facade of St. Peter's alone is 374 feet long and 136 feet high. The famous central dome is 139 feet in diameter and 438 feet above ground.

Inside St. Peter's, the central aisle is an eighth of a mile in length; a seemingly infinite number of people can be packed into the church. For the usual papal functions, some 70,000 tickets are distributed.

As she rehashed these figures, Irene studied the ticket she held. It was a pass to this Friday morning's Mass to be concelebrated by Pope Leo XIV and the new Cardinals. A few thousand of the Cardinals' closest friends had been invited to attend. The service would include the ceremony of bestowing on each Cardinal his strikingly simple ring of office.

Irene's ticket did not disclose much. During this week of juggling tickets to various ceremonial events, Irene, as well as almost everyone else involved, discovered that identical information was printed on every ticket. An announcement of the event for which the ticket would gain admittance, the time, and the place of the event.

What mattered, everyone soon learned, was the color. Depending on one's ticket color, one saw, heard, or even participated in the event. Or, one became part of the great unwashed, stuck behind barricades so that if one's height were not well in excess of six feet, one had a magnificent view of chests, backs, and shoulders, depending on which way people were facing.

Or, one just might be stuck in Outer Darkness, where many had found themselves for the red hat ceremony, and where many had gnashed their teeth.

Irene's ticket to this event was gold. She wondered what that augured.

"Hi!" It was Pat Lennon. "What color do you have?"

"Oh!" Irene was startled. "Oh, it's gold. How about you?"

"Blue." Joe Cox did not attempt to conceal his disgust. "Blue has not been kind to us this week."

"Mine's blue, too," said Lennon, echoing Cox's tone. "Say," she continued, "I have an idea. How would it be, Irene, if Joe and I tag along with you? You show the official your gold ticket and we'll try to follow you in."

"It's all right with me. But do you think it'll work? Isn't it risky?"

Lennon laughed. "They're not going to throw us into the Sacred Penitentiary."

"And besides, if you're determined, they don't insist on perfect compliance," said Cox, missing Lennon's allusion to the former Vatican office that once dispensed, among other things, indulgences.

"O.K.," said Irene, "let's try it."

The three walked briskly toward the basilica.

As they walked, Irene's thoughts turned to yesterday's startling events. She had not been in the Sistine Chapel when Cardinal Gattari had been attacked. As far as her work for the *Detroit Catholic* was concerned, it didn't matter that she hadn't been there. Her paper was a weekly, and by the time it went to press, the world would know what had happened to the late Cardinal. She would cable color stories to her publication. But today, the Cardinal's death was on everyone's mind.

"Wasn't it terrible what happened yesterday?" Irene said. "Were you there?"

"Were we there? Joe, here, chased the killer!"

"No kidding!" Irene turned to look at Cox. "What happened? Did you catch him?"

"No, I didn't catch him. But I did learn what dreadlocks are." Cox threw an indignantly scornful glance at Lennon.

"Oh, you mean the way a black person's long hair hangs after it's washed," said Irene.

"How come everybody but me knows about dreadlocks?" Cox spread his hands wide.

"Oh, don't feel bad, Joe," said Irene. "We lived in a mixed neighborhood for years. So I know all about dreadlocks and dorags and so on."

"Look out!" Cox snapped.

Lennon was forced to literally jump to get out of the path of about fifteen nuns, swiftly advancing in close order drill, heads down and single-mindedly taking the shortest route between two points.

"Whatinhell was that?" asked Cox.

"I don't know their religious order," Irene smiled, "but those are Italian nuns."

"How do you know?"

"Partly intuition. Plus there aren't that many national groups that still have nuns dressed from head to toe in yards and yards of wool. And the Italian nuns have a habit of staying close to each other like that contingent."

"Like an army of red ants," Lennon commented. She was not all that happy at having been nearly run over.

The trio approached one of the officials who was scanning tickets, then sending people off in various directions. Irene flashed her gold ticket and was directed to the left. She was closely followed by Lennon and Cox, neither of whom so much as glanced at the official. No word was said, so they blithely continued on their way. Soon, following the crowd, they entered the right transept, off to one side from the main altar and to the right of the Chair of the Confession. Excellent. Pound for pound, the best seats in the house.

But the seats were going like hotcakes. With the exception of the first few rows, which were reserved for visiting dignitaries, it was first come first served. Fortunately, there were several chairs together in the third from the last row. Irene, Lennon, and Cox immediately staked their claim.

"I wonder where we'd be if we'd used our blue tickets," mused Lennon.

"Somewhere out there." Cox indicated the nave of the basilica where sawhorses had been placed to segregate and contain the crowd.

As Cox looked into the main section of the basilica, his attention was captured by something out of the ordinary in the second section from the front. Several officials were moving the crowd aside to allow a woman carrying a baby to stand at the very edge of the middle aisle. He pointed this maneuver out to Lennon. Neither could fathom what it signified.

Lennon looked at her watch. "It's 9:30! This thing was supposed to start at nine! And there's no sign it's about to start anytime in the near future."

Irene patted her hand. "Dear, tardiness is Continental. But in Italy, it's an art form. Maybe you've read in the past that there has been a good deal of rancor, insults, and even bottle-throwing on Christmas day at the Cave of the Incarnation in Bethlehem. It's because each of the Christian sects has its appointed hour to celebrate its Christmas liturgy there. The

Italians are always late starting and late finishing. Sometimes that becomes the final straw for the Armenian Christians. And then the bottles fly.''

"Sure," Cox affirmed, "you remember, honey, the other day when we were lunching with those Italian journalists at the cafe on the Via Veneto. We had to file our regular stories. That guy, what was his name, Valentine, kept saying, 'One more glass of wine.' We tried to tell him we had deadlines. As a journalist he certainly should have been able to understand that. Remember what he told us? 'If there's any story out there that's really big, it will find you!' ''

Perhaps it was a combination of the long delay in starting this ceremony, combined with a periodic fluttering of the curtain covering the entrance through which the procession would come. But every so often, with greater frequency as time passed, the crowd would come alive. Someone would shout, "He's coming!" and the cry would be picked up by others. Only to die away in disappointment.

Out of the corner of her eye, Lennon noticed unusual movement. Two of those small Italian nuns were inching their way down the steps toward the front row. For some reason, she could not take her eyes off them.

All these false starts were beginning to get on Cox's nerves. He had been jumpy anyway since yesterday's turmoil. It happened every time and any time he worked on a hot story as he was with this Gattari killing. He just couldn't come down quickly from his high. The adrenalin just continued to pump. This—working on a breaking story or uncovering an investigative story—was mother's milk to him. He could not believe that the death of Gattari was the end of it. There had to be more. And the sequel could come from anywhere. He had to be ready for it. And he was. His restless eyes roamed the basilica. With each false start, with each mistaken cry of anticipation, Cox's heartbeat accelerated. If only something—anything—would happen.

"Look! Down there!"

Cox's concentration was so intense that Lennon's screech almost catapulted him out of his chair. Neither Cox nor Irene immediately identified what Lennon wanted them to see even though she was pointing.

"Down there! The front row!"

Cox sighted down to the front row directly before them. He saw figure after figure of uniformed or grandly attired people. Heads of state, ambassadors, royalty, and other Very Important Persons. Then, in the midst of the august assemblage, he saw it: the sore thumb. Two, actually.

"How'd they get in there?" Cox exclaimed.

"Oh, my dear!" Irene spotted the two little Italian nuns sitting composedly among the VIPs.

"I've been watching them inch down to the first row," Lennon explained. "They moved in just behind the first row. Behind the very seats they're in now. When that last false alarm was sounded, the two men sitting there stood and stepped to the railing to see if the Pope was really coming. Now, I'm not kidding, those two crazy nuns vaulted over the backs of the chairs and sat in them! When the two men turned back to their seats, they found them taken. You could see it written all over their faces: What could they do—throw two sweet little old nuns out?"

By now, Cox and Irene focused on the two very dignified, lavishly bemedaled gentlemen shrugging and making their way out of the front row and moving up the aisle toward the rear of the section.

The three onlookers had a good laugh.

Suddenly, "This is it!" Cox heard himself exclaim, though he didn't quite know why.

In any case, there was no doubt the procession had indeed commenced. The noise began as with the previous false alarms. But instead of slowly dying out as had the earlier cheers, this one surged and swelled to a mighty roar.

Cries of "Viva il Papa!" rose from the throats of everyone, including those who did not understand Italian, as well as those who did not even know what they were yelling. As the Pope passed, borne aloft in his *sedia gestatoria*, flashbulbs and strobe lights exploded throughout the scene, creating the appearance of bolt after bolt of lightning crackling within the basilica.

Pope Leo XIV all the while beamed an ear-to-ear grin as his chair gracefully swayed from right to left, left to right, right hand tracing benedictions over the crowd, then alternating that gesture with a scooping motion of both hands. They were playing his song. And it went, "Viva il Papa!"

It was virtually impossible not to be caught up in the excitement. Even Joe Cox, nonpracticing unbeliever that he was, found himself on his feet applauding and popping in an occasional "Viva!"

Then without warning, the Pope's chair stopped while the procession of functionaries and prelates moved on toward the altar without him.

"Look!" cried Cox, with a note of triumph, "the woman with the baby! The woman with the baby! The Pope is kissing the baby! It's the Designated Baby!"

That was it. The woman whom Cox had earlier spied being moved to the edge of the middle aisle had lifted her child toward the pontiff. As if by prearrangement, the chair porters had halted before the exact spot where the woman stood. The Pope reached down and took her baby. He kissed the child and returned it to the mother.

The crowd loved it. There were mixed cries of "ooh!" and "aah!" and the good old faithful, "Viva il Papa!" by the unimaginative, and some explanation by Italians for the benefit of their foreign guests, "Da Papa, shesa lova da bambino!"

The Pope having demonstrated his love for little children, or at least for this designated baby, the procession moved on as cheers continued to ricochet through the basilica.

The *sedia gestatoria* was lowered when the Pope reached the main altar of St. Peter's. Leo XIV completed two circles around the fringe area of the altar, pressing the flesh of princes and princesses, heads of state, ambassadors, and two small Italian nuns. The strobes and flashbulbs continued to pop, even from the rear of the cathedral whence their light affected only the consolation of the amateur photographers who were popping them.

Once the actual Mass began, matters not only became more solemn, they grew in beauty. Amplified voices of the Sistine Choir proved this was one of the world's most exceptional singing groups.

But Joe Cox had a difficult time concentrating on a ceremony he neither understood nor believed in. His mind and his gaze wandered. He focused on the delegation of American Cardinals in attendance.

"Pat," he whispered, "look at the American Cardinals

over there." He gestured in their direction. "Do you notice anything out of the ordinary?"

"No, not really. Like what?"

"You were telling me how the vestments of the Cardinals had been simplified. How, instead of long red robes and ermine capes, they now wear just the red cassock and white surplice, right? Well, with that in mind, look again."

Lennon focused more seriously on the group. "Well, I'll be—that so-and-so from Los Angeles is wearing a gold surplice!"

"Just in case anyone forgets that California is the Golden State!"

It was time for bestowing the ceremonial ring of office, a surprisingly simple circle of silver with no stone, only an inscription.

Since the new Cardinals were in alphabetical order, Cardinal Mark Boyle was the first to be escorted up to Pope Leo XIV. Boyle knelt before the seated pontiff, who positioned the ring while intoning, "Receive the ring from the hand of Peter and know that your love for the Church will be reinforced by love for the prince of the Apostles."

Cox thought that a rather self-serving statement. He did not know that diocesan priests, when they are ordained, are not called upon to promise to serve the people to whom they will be sent. Rather, they promise reverence and obedience to their ordaining bishop and his successors.

Again Cox mentally wandered from the ceremony at hand.

"Hey, look over there!" He nudged Lennon.

"Where?"

"The Chicago Cardinal—what's his name?"

"Cardinal William Hitchcock."

"Yeah, Wild Bill Hitchcock. I think he's sitting on two chairs."

"Go on!" But as everyone, including Cardinal Hitchcock, stood, it was obvious he had, indeed, been sitting on two chairs. Cox snickered.

"Joe! Pay attention!" Lennon scolded.

But there was nothing further to which to pay attention. The ceremony was concluded. The ecclesial dignitaries formed in procession and began the long march out. Again the Pope was carried, surrounded by guards and accompanied by cheers and illuminated by flashbulbs and strobe lights.

As Irene, Lennon, and Cox turned to leave, they beheld a scene worthy of a De Mille epic. A sea of humanity was being funneled through what was in actuality a gigantic door space. But from their perspective it appeared to be that narrow gate Jesus spoke of through which the rich could not easily pass.

There was little choice. It was either wait at their places for an additional hour or so for the basilica to empty, or test their fate and put their lives on the line and join the exciting crowd.

"What the hell," Cox urged, "let's try it. You only live once."

"Yeah," Lennon agreed, "and this may be it!"

As they made their way down the steps they were quite literally swept up by the crowd. Cox was convinced that, were he to take both feet from the floor at once, he would be carried off by the press of the crowd. But he feared if he did he just might fall. And that would mean death by stampede.

Irene was sure she had been pinched—several times. But for now, her one thought was to escape this adventure alive. Later—if there were a later—would be time enough to check for bruises.

As he was vortexed through the doorway, Cox witnessed an almost unbelievable sight. A man was attempting to get back into the basilica. As he and Cox passed as buffeted ships in the night, the man was pulling himself from one shoulder to the next, as one literally swimming against the current. As far as Cox could tell, the man did well merely to remain *in situ* and not be swept backwards.

From time to time, in future years, Cox would wonder whatever had happened to that man and what he was trying to accomplish that had motivated him to such a bizarre form of suicide.

6

The tables sagged and the shelves drooped, so heavily laden were they with foods—all of them delectable.

Trays filled with rich varieties of antipasto alternated with

trays heaped with fresh figs, berries, cream puffs, salads.
Pans overflowed with red tomatoes, red peppers, green peppers,
clams, and melons. Cucumbers were fitted between stalks of
fresh asparagus that nestled among fruit-filled platters. On the
topmost shelf was an unprepared leg of calf. Peeking from
behind the leg were spinach and various kinds of lettuce. The
aromas mingled to whet the appetites of all who entered the
restaurant.

Gallucci's was located on a typically narrow Roman street
off the Via Merulana near the Church of Santa Maria Maggiore.

It was not one of Rome's more famous or popular restaurants.
But for the few cognoscenti it was among the very best Rome
had to offer. And Rome had some of the best in Europe.

One who knew of Gallucci's and frequented it when in
Rome was Inspector Walter Koznicki. He had chosen this
spot to meet Father Koesler and the deacon Ramon Toussaint
at 6:00 P.M. partly because he prized the place and partly
because he knew they could conduct a secluded meeting there
during dinner.

Koznicki arrived at Gallucci's several minutes before six.
Koesler and Toussaint arrived together promptly at six. The
two had spent much of this day together renewing their
friendship. In Detroit, Toussaint and his wife, Emerenciana,
had been extremely close friends of Koesler's. A friendship
that had survived even the Toussaints' embroilment in that
episode wherein violent justice was brought to those who
were escaping the punitive arm of the law. Shortly thereafter,
the Toussaints had left to relocate in San Francisco. Koesler
had not seen them since.

Koesler, in his half-Latin, half-quasi-Italian, informed the
maître d' that they were with the Koznicki party. They were
shown to a private booth in the rear of the restaurant, where
they sat and absorbed the sight and smell of tempting, tantaliz-
ing food.

Bottle after bottle of wine lined those shelves not piled with
food. Each table was topped by a white cloth over the traditional red and white checkered cloth. In sum, it resembled
most other authentic Roman restaurants. But Koznicki assured them it was far from merely average.

Although Koznicki had been well aware of Toussaint, had

seen photos of him, and had even seen the man at a distance, the two had never formally met.

As Koesler introduced them, the Inspector appraised the deacon.

Though in his middle years, Toussaint appeared to be an exceptionally strong and vigorous man. Koznicki also noted there seemed to be much going on behind Toussaint's lively brown eyes. The Inspector guessed Toussaint would be a worthy chess opponent; he was not likely to come in second in any game of wits.

Long, long ago, in his early days in Detroit, Toussaint had correctly appraised Koznicki as one of the most astute and effective detectives Toussaint had ever known.

"Since I am familiar with Gallucci's," said Koznicki, "perhaps you will permit me to make a few suggestions?"

"Of course. Take over," Koesler said.

Toussaint merely smiled and nodded.

Koznicki summoned the waiter. "I think a nice Chianti to begin," he turned to his guests, "and for the antipasto, I would suggest the *caponata* for both of you." He looked at the waiter, who nodded. "It is a cold salad of eggplant, celery, capers, tomatoes, olives, vinegar, and sugar," he explained to his friends. "For a first time at Gallucci's, it is a good, innocent way to begin. And," he turned again to the waiter, who realized he was dealing with one who was on easy terms with the menu, "I will have the *carpaccio*."

"Well, where to begin?" said Koesler, as the waiter went about bringing breadsticks and butter, followed by the requested Chianti for the Inspector's approval. "I guess since much of this is my idea, I'd better bring you up to date, Ramon, on what we suspect is going on."

Koesler, halting only to permit the waiter to serve the salad, then reviewed with Toussaint what was mostly his hypothesis on the possible connection between the murders of Cardinals Claret and Gattari. The fact that both killings seemed entirely unmotivated and unusual. Both murders were perpetrated by black men in dreadlocks. Both victims were prime candidates for the Papacy. And, finally, the strange appearance of a symbol of black power in the form of a black fist.

"And you are right, Bob, in connecting them, I believe," said Toussaint, as he set down his wine glass. "I heard some talk on the part of a small segment of the black community in San Francisco after the murder of Cardinal Claret. So I went to Toronto to see for myself. My contacts there corroborated the fact that there is a conspiracy of sorts, but they were not certain where it would lead. Then, at a meeting in San Francisco, my Haitian friends told me they had learned that this conspiracy would spread to Rome. And so it has.''

"But do you know who is responsible? And why?'' The questions were Koznicki's. Before Toussaint could reply, the waiter arrived to clear away the salad dishes.

Koznicki again consulted the menu. "I would recommend, again for a first visit, the *Stracciatella*. It is eggs, cheese, and nutmeg blended, then poured into boiling chicken broth.''

The waiter's eyes sparkled in the presence of a *bongustaio*.

"Fine,'' said Koesler.

"I believe I will skip the soup course, Inspector,'' said Toussaint.

"As you wish,'' said Koznicki. "For myself, I will have the *pasta e fagioli*.''

The waiter refilled their glasses with Chianti and departed.

Koznicki, eager for a reply to his questions, nodded at Toussaint.

"It is a long story that I shall try to make as short as possible without omitting any of the essential details,'' said Toussaint.

"Perhaps you are aware,'' he began, "of the dissatisfaction of many of the home-counties English with the people of many colors who now live in London and its environs—Indians, Africans, Pakistanis, Jamaicans, and so forth. These so-called native peoples have a difficult time making a living and conforming to English mores, particularly in so urban a setting. When the English become unnerved, the classic response from the erstwhile colonials, is 'We are here because you were there!' Which means, of course, that the problem is due solely to the fact that Great Britain's empire once included all its colonies. In making India a British colony, it made the Indians British subjects. If Britain had stayed at home, as it were, so would the Indians have remained in India.

"This concept is even more relevant when one considers Africa,'' Toussaint continued as Koznicki and Koesler began their soup. "Black Africans were taken prisoner and removed from their homeland and delivered to the West. To America, where, in the South, they were made slaves to King Cotton. And to island countries, like Haiti and Jamaica. But in those two countries, the Africans experienced vastly different treatment.

"In Haiti, their masters," Toussaint winced at the word, "were the French. The French considered their slaves to be human, if inferior. Ergo, they were souls to be saved. The slaves were required to be baptized and thus become Catholic. In a sense, I owe my Catholic heritage to Haiti's French slaveowners. Knowing what I do now, I would choose to be Catholic. But that does not blunt the fact that Catholicism was forced upon the slaves of Haiti.

"The slaves, of course, had little to say about this enforced religion. They simply mixed their new, alien religion with their own religious practice which Westerners know as 'voodoo.'

"In time, many of the slaves of Haiti either won their freedom or escaped and emigrated to many large cities in many countries. That is why you will find the descendants of former Haitian slaves in virtually all Western urban centers. And with them you will find this amalgam of Roman Catholicism and voodoo.

"The experience of the African slaves of Jamaica was quite different simply because they belonged to the English. And the English considered their slaves not as humans but as property. There were no forced conversions, thus their development was comparatively free from Western influence. But Jamaican slaves suffered one of the highest mortality rates of any of the islands. So the black population growth derived almost entirely from repeated importation of more blacks from many parts of Africa. The form of voodoo that developed in Jamaica was called 'pocomania,' or 'the little madness' or 'possession.' It evolved from a mixture of differing forms of voodoo brought from different parts of Africa.

"But because of the forced mixing of these differing African cultures, there were few shared traditions or experiences. So that different beliefs and different practices evolved in a variety of different groups."

Just then, their waiter returned, removed the empty dishes

and waited with polite curiosity for Koznicki's order for the next course.

Toussaint consulted his watch. It was growing late and he had much to do before this day was finished. He would have to hurry through this explication. But it was important—very important—that these two should understand.

"Inspector," said Toussaint, "I will eat no more. I hope you will make allowances. There is much I have yet to do. But please; order for yourself and Bob. I will talk. You will enjoy your meal. We never know how many more meals we have to enjoy before we will eat no more."

A strange statement, thought Koznicki.

"I will now order the pasta and the entrée for the Father and myself. Our friend will have no more," Koznicki said.

An expression of sadness passed over the waiter's features. He could not bear to think of anyone's being only a spectator at a Gallucci meal.

"Father will have the *fettuccine*." He turned to Koesler. "It will remind you of egg noodles, Father, only so much better." He turned again to the waiter. "And I will have your *gnocchi*. When we have finished, please serve the entrée. Father will have the red mullet—you will like that, Father. It is prepared right at the table. And I will have the *pollo scarpariello*. And bring us a bottle of your Orvieto." He glanced across at Toussaint. "Are you sure you want nothing more? Something to drink, perhaps?"

"Thank you, no, Inspector."

"Then please go on."

"I will not burden you with the history of the slave rebellions of Jamaica, the Maroons, or a long list of freedom fighters. For our purpose, I will merely mention Marcus Garvey and his prophecy to the slaves of Jamaica—the slaves who wanted nothing more than to escape what they saw as a massive conspiracy of Western civilization to keep them in bondage and away from their homeland—Africa.

"Garvey prophesied, 'Look to Africa, when a black king is crowned, for the day of deliverance is near.'

"The majority of Jamaican blacks believe that prophecy was fulfilled when an Ethiopian named Ras Tafari was crowned emperor in Ethiopia in 1930. Ras Tafari took the name Haile Selassie. From that moment on, Ethiopia became the longed-for homeland for a majority of Jamaican blacks; Haile Selassie became their savior, and they became, after his given name, Rastafarians.''

The pasta was served.

"Rastafarianism is not a religion or a government or a social order. It is a way of life and it is not understood in precisely the same way by all Rastafarians.

"Jah is God and he is black. The Bible, especially the Old Testament, is their textbook. But it must be appropriately interpreted. For instance, in the Book of Numbers it says,'' Toussaint quoted from memory, "'All the days of the vow of his separation, there shall be no razor come upon his head: until the days be fulfilled, in the which he separated himself unto the Lord, he shall be holy, and shall let the locks of his hair of his head grow.' All of which justifies the style called . . .'' Toussaint paused.

"Dreadlocks,'' Koznicki supplied.

"Exactly. Or this from Genesis: 'And God said, Let the earth bring forth grass, the herb yielding seed, and the fruit tree yielding fruit after his kind, whose seed is in itself, upon the earth; and it was so. And the earth brought forth grass, and herb yielding seed after his kind . . . and God saw that it was good.' And this Biblical passage legitimates . . .'' Toussaint paused again.

"Marijuana,'' supplied Koesler.

"Which they call ganja. And which, for them, is a sacrament.

"Their music is reggae. It was made popular by the late Bob Marley. Perhaps you are familiar with it?''

Koesler slowly swallowed some *fettucine* and shook his head.

"I must admit I was aware of both Mr. Marley and his music,'' said Koznicki, "but I have steadfastly avoided both.''

"It does not matter,'' said Toussaint, "'Reggae is not that germane to our present situation.

"What is of importance is to understand the Rastafarians, how they became what they are, and what their hope and aim is. Essentially, Jah is their black God; Haile Selassie—formerly Ras Tafari—is their savior . . .''

"But Selassie died years ago,'' Koesler protested.

"It does not matter. Many Rastafarians refuse to believe he is dead. To others, he has merely preceded them into heaven.

"But to go on with the essential Rastafarian creed: Ethiopia is the homeland; Addis Ababa is Zion; the Western world is Babylon, an enslaving, corrupt, selfish, persecuting society from which the black man must one day escape and return whence he came.

"Ganja they have adopted probably because the weed grows abundantly in Jamaica and also because the narcotic offers some release and escape from the poverty and degradation the black man in exile feels.

"Now, when we come to the way in which each Rastafarian reacts to these beliefs that structure his or her way of life, we find great diversity."

Toussaint's chronicle was interrupted by the waiter's return.

Before Koznicki, he placed a dish containing small sections of chicken which had been crisply fried, then sauced with garlic, rosemary, and white wine.

On a serving cart next to the table, the waiter prepared Koesler's fish. The mullet lay in a large pan. With a single stroke, the waiter split the large fish and then boned it. After squeezing half a lemon over it, he poured first wine, then the fish's own juices over its length. It appeared delicious, and it was.

"Most Rasta men," Toussaint proceeded, and then, as if interrupting himself, "despite the popular and current feminist movement, we might just as well dismiss the Rasta women because the Rasta men have dismissed them: Rasta women are respected, protected, supported, and appreciated; but, if something important is happening, Rasta females will not be there.

"Anyway, as I was saying, most Rasta men are peaceful, at least as long as they are not provoked. There are some, however, who are comfortable with violence. You can find ample evidence of this in your daily papers.

"There were, for example, the twelve Rasta men who kidnaped a young black woman and her son in the Bronx some years back. Rastas executed four of their fellow Rastas in New York City. There have been Rastas wounded and killed in gunfights with police. Rastas have been known to traffic in drugs and to commit robberies. So, for a group officially espousing peace and love, some of the Rastas can be and are very violent. And it is, quite evidently, these violent Rastas with whom we must now deal.''

"All of what you have told us is both interesting and informative," said Koznicki. "But why? Why should even a violent Rastafarian want to attack a Cardinal, a prince of the Catholic Church?"

"That is the fundamental question, is it not?" Toussaint said reflectively.

"Some years ago," he proceeded, "there was a segment of the popular Sunday evening television program, 'Sixty Minutes,' that dealt with the Rastafarians. It opened with a scene of a Rasta man, dreadlocks and all, beating on a small drum and chanting, 'Death to the Pope! Death to the Pope!' ''

"I must have missed that program, although I usually watch the series," said Koznicki.

"I remember it," said Koesler, "but I don't recall the scene you describe, Ramon. I must have missed the opening of that segment. Was any reference made to it later in the program?"

"No, oddly. But it was there in the beginning."

"But again," Koznicki touched napkin to his mouth, "why? Why 'Death to the Pope'?"

"The Rastafarians," Toussaint replied, "consider the Pope the most powerful and significant figure in Western civilization."

Koesler smiled. "There are those who would accord that description to the president of the United States, or, perhaps, to the Russian premier."

"Yes," said Toussaint, "but neither of them has had the supreme spiritual authority over the great number of centuries that is inherent in the Papacy.

"While the Rastas will grant that, here and there, individual whites may be able to reform and break the chains of their condemnation before Jah, generally they believe that the white race—the oppressor—is in conspiracy with Satan and the Pope, both of whom they equate."

There followed a relatively long period of silence while Koesler and Koznicki finished their entrées and carefully considered all Toussaint had said.

"All right, then," said Koznicki at length, "suppose for the sake of argument we say that not all, but certain Rastafarians wish to kill the Pope out of vengeance for all they have had to suffer in those centuries of slavery. Why have they killed Cardinals Claret and Gattari?''

''Bob supplied the answer when he grasped that the connection between the Cardinals was their position as probable papal candidates.

''You see, since the assassination attempts on Pope Leo XIV, the security surrounding the Pope has been intense. And even before this increased security, he was by no means an accessible man. Now, he is, as much as can be said for any public figure, almost beyond physical attack, particularly at close range.

''Since they perceive they cannot successfully assault the reigning Pope, this fanatic minority among the Rastafarians has decided to cut down the prime candidates for the Papacy. That is what I feared when Cardinal Claret was murdered. That is why I went to Toronto—to check with my sources there. What they had learned from infiltrating some Rasta meetings, and what my contacts here in Rome have told me, only reinforce my fears.''

''You have contacts both in Toronto and Rome.'' It was a question uttered as a statement by Inspector Koznicki.

''If you had not been in my land, I would not be in yours.'' Toussaint smiled. ''There are Jamaicans and Haitians all over the world whose ancestors were forcibly snatched from their homelands in Africa. So, there are networks of voodoo and pocomania and Rastafarians all over the world. Only a worldwide network could attempt a plot of this magnitude.''

There was another pause in the one-sided conversation during which their waiter cleared the table. Koznicki ordered a fruit and cheese plate, a bottle of Asti Spumante, and espresso for himself and Koesler.

''If I am to understand correctly,'' Koznicki said, ''the book you mentioned yesterday . . .'' he mentally groped for the title.

''*The Inner Elite,*'' Koesler prompted.

''Yes. Thank you. That is not a definitive listing of papal candidates?''

''Oh, no. There is no definitive list,'' Koesler replied. ''For one thing, any such list shortly becomes outdated. Cardinals grow old and die, new ones are appointed, and others are waiting in the wings. And, in any event, any listing of *papabili* has to be pure speculation, mixed with a few educated guesses. When the Cardinals enter the conclave in the Sistine Chapel, literally any one of them may emerge the next Pope. And frequently, the touts are wrong, hence the saying, 'He who enters the consistory a Pope comes out a Cardinal.' So much chemistry, even politics, is involved in the selection of a Pope.''

"Some would even claim there is the influence of the Holy Spirit,'' Toussaint said with a smile.

Koesler returned the smile. "Some might so claim. And I would not deny it.

"Let me put it this way, Inspector. In 1939, the Catholic world would have been very surprised if Eugenio Pacelli had not become Pope Pius XII. And in 1963, we would have been extremely surprised if Giovanni Battista Montini had not become Paul VI. On the other hand, in, let me see, I think 1903 or 1904, the Catholic world was stunned when Giuseppe Sarto became Pius X. And, in our own time, remember how astonished everyone was when in 1959 Angelo Roncalli became the great Pope John XXIII.

"So you see, Inspector, predicting who will be the next Pope is not an exact science. But there sometimes are strong possibilities. And, right or wrong, somebody always has a list of *papabili*, as they're called in Italian.''

"Yes, I see,'' said Koznicki. "But what I am driving at is that not only might the most informed list of papal candidates prove incorrect, but that there must be more than one list.''

"I'm sure there is,'' said Koesler. "I suppose the degree of probability would depend on the prognosticator's credentials and, conceivably even on his track record.''

"So,'' Koznicki concluded, "it is possible, even probable, that the listing found in *The Inner Elite* could well be different from that of the Rastafarians.''

"Yes, I'm sure that's true,'' said Koesler.

"Then we are left with the indeed literally vital question of which Cardinals are on the Rastafarians' list.''

"That is correct, Inspector,'' said Toussaint, helping himself to some cheese. "And that is my current undertaking: to try to get a copy of their list. And to discover, if at all possible, how, when, and where they intend to assassinate the men on that list.''

''Ah,'' Koznicki sat back in the booth. ''Now, short of having no problem at all, that knowledge would put us in a perfect position—what Red Barber would call the catbird seat. When do you expect to obtain that list?''

''I hope to get it sometime tonight or tomorrow,'' Toussaint replied, ''I pray I will have it before the new Cardinals take possession of their Roman parishes tomorrow evening. Until then, they have no scheduled public appearances. They should be in seclusion and relatively safe. But tomorrow evening, even those Cardinals ordinarily protected by their bureaucratic remoteness will be available to anyone who wishes access to them for whatever reason.''

''We shall join you in that prayer.'' said Koznicki.

''And now, if you'll excuse me,'' Toussaint eased out of the booth and stood, ''I will be on my way.'' He checked his watch. '':I must go now to meet my first contact.''

After a hasty farewell, Toussaint left the restaurant.

Koesler sipped the effervescent Asti.

''I don't suppose I ought, but somehow, after listening to Ramon, I feel sort of relieved. At least now we know who is responsible, as well as the motive.''

''That is,'' Koznicki responded, ''if all our theories are correct.''

''You doubt the conclusions Ramon reached?''

''Remember, Father, I have been in this business long enough so that I've learned to keep an open mind on everything. Everything! It was that open mind that led me to give ear to Toussaint in the first place. And it is that same open mind that will not close off other hypotheses that could be just as possible as the ones we have proposed.''

''Gee, I don't know. It all sounded very logical to me.'' Koznicki's skepticism was contagious. Koesler felt his sense of confidence waver. ''Whether or not he gets this list, I feel encouraged that Ramon will be with us and close to Cardinal Boyle.''

''And I will be right there beside him.''

Koesler turned to look directly at the Inspector. ''You don't trust Ramon!''

''Things are seldom what they seem.''

Once a Cardinal is created the Pope plants a metaphorical ecclesial magnet in the man. A magnet that keeps drawing that Cardinal back to Rome.

At the drop of a red hat, the Pope can call a consistory, which is a solemn meeting of Cardinals convoked and presided over by the pontiff. The death of a Pope, of course, summons the Cardinals into conclave to come up with a replacement.

And the Cardinal is symbolically given a Roman parish. He becomes titular pastor of said parish. From that point on, he may do as he wishes with said parish. He may treat it with benign neglect or take a paternal interest in it.

His Eminence Mark Cardinal Boyle was about to take symbolic possession of St. John XXIII parish near Monte Mario. It was Saturday, May 3, early evening of a soft Roman spring. At 6:00, there was still plenty of daylight.

This was to be the final ceremony of the ceremony-filled week. At the conclusion of this rite, all the newly created Cardinals would be free to leave Rome. If, indeed, as was the case with most, their actual assignment was somewhere in the world beside the Eternal City.

The usual buses that had ferried the tourists from one event to another had done it again. Except that now, for the first time, all the buses of all the tourists from all over the world were not all going to the same place. For the first time this week, each Cardinal was going his separate way. And wherever each Cardinal went, his entourage was sure to go.

Many in the Detroit contingent felt exposed to be alone with each other rather than rubbing shoulders with Germans, Dutch. Spanish, French, Portuguese, and even Californians, Missourians, and New Yorkers.

St. John XXIII was a comparatively recently constructed church, just as St. John XXIII was a recently canonized saint. But somehow, everything in Rome, even recently constructed buildings, seemed old. It was almost as if Rome's antiquity were infectious. As yet, St. John XXIII church had not fallen victim to Rome's communicable dry rot, but there was every indication that it would.

One lesson immediately learned was that the Detroit contingent by itself did not come close to filling this church. The second lesson was that either the parish had not properly publicized this ceremony or that its parishioners were not crazy about going to church more than once a week. It was clear from all the recognizable faces that no one was present but Detroiters.

Koesler and the Koznickis were seated about midway from the front of the church. Organ music was playing softly. Koesler was gazing absently at Joan Blackford Hayes. As he had already observed, she did resemble Elizabeth Taylor so it was pleasant gazing at her.

"How are you coping with our water shortage, Father?" Koznicki asked.

Koesler emerged from his daydream. "Not very well! When I saw that sign in the lobby this noon that due to construction work outside, the water would be turned off for a few hours, it never entered my head that by the time we left this evening, it still wouldn't have been turned back on.

"You have no idea of all the things you depend on water for until you lose it. Not only washing, showering, and drinking, and brushing your teeth—but flushing. I can't believe we're paying to stay there—they should be paying *us!* And as for our concierge, who up till now has been very helpful, once the water was turned off he caught our bus driver's disease and forgot how to speak English."

Koznicki, smiling, shook his head.

Funny, thought Koesler, how easy it is to get used to talking in church. In the good old days, talking in church had ranked as a very common venial or lesser sin. He could recall when, as a young boy, each of his confessions had included many disobediences and not a few talkings in church. Must be some sort of hangover from times past, he thought. It's still rare to see people talking in church. Generally, even when nothing is going on in a Catholic church, people—even whole families—just sit there, saying nothing.

But not in Rome. St. Peter's resembled more a noisy museum than a church. And even here, in the more typical setting of a parish church, nearly everyone was talking to someone—albeit softly. He wondered whether silence in church would be a thing of the past for these pilgrims once they returned home.

He looked at his watch. 6:20. Funny, too, how you could get used to things starting late. It had taken less than a week in Rome to be infected by that *domani* attitude. It must, he thought, be a variant of Murphy's Law. Something indigenous to Latinism, perhaps. If it's important, it will find you. If it's important, it will still be important tomorrow. If you don't do it, relax; neither will anyone else.

Koesler's stream of consciousness ran low and then out.

Suddenly, he was thrust back into reality. The soft dreamy organ music faded, to be replaced by strong, full-powered chords. Everyone was brought to his or her feet. It was the processional.

"Ecce sacerdos magnus, qui in diebus suis placuit Deo," the choir sang. "Behold the great high priest, who, in his days, pleased the Lord." The traditional choral greeting for a bishop.

All turned to the rear of the church to view the entrance of the procession. Instead of candle-bearing and cross-carrying acolytes, an elderly priest was jumping up and down, waving his arms frantically. Obviously a false start. But the choir sang on as the congregation had a good laugh.

"You were saying, Inspector, that Rome is a walking, talking cinéma verité?" said Koesler.

They chuckled.

Shortly, the choir director, who was himself searching for the missing procession, caught sight of the leaping monsignor. The singing stopped and the organ returned to soft, soporific music.

Gradually, lulled once more by the soft meandering organ music, Koesler's mind slipped into neutral. He had drifted even beyond the innocent contemplation of Joan Blackford Hayes into shimmering recollective montages of quiet, peaceful visits to various small churches of the past.

His head began to nod. He had almost dozed off when he was abruptly jarred wide awake. Someone had slipped into the pew and knelt next to him. It was Ramon Toussaint, in lightweight black suit and roman collar. An ordained deacon, Toussaint was as entitled to wear such clerical garb as was a priest.

At one time, not that many years before, Catholic clerics were seldom out of uniform. Many were uniformed at all times except bed, bath, beach, or golf course. With a few sensible exceptions. Koesler was of that school. Most current younger priests were seldom in uniform. Some, reportedly didn't even own a black suit, let alone a roman collar.

There was no doubt that Toussaint was a striking figure of a man. And that was especially true when in clerical garb. The black suit seemed to streamline his tightly muscled body. The immaculate roman collar was a narrow, neat band made whiter by being sandwiched between the black suit and his dark chocolate complexion. Close-cropped salt-and-pepper hair crowned his chiseled features.

Having made his prayer, Toussaint sat back in the pew next to Koesler. The priest introduced him to Wanda Koznicki. With Koesler and the Inspector between them, there was no point in attempting anything as physical as a handshake, so Wanda and Toussaint merely smiled and nodded at each other.

After a few moments, Koznicki leaned across Koesler and asked, "Were you able to get it? The list?"

Toussaint shook his head slowly. "No. It is a matter of timing. My sources assure me they will have it before we leave Rome tomorrow. Apparently, the Rastafarians involved in this plot have only one item that is their equivalent of our 'Top Secret,' and that is this list of *papabili*."

Koznicki sat back with a worried look. A criminal investigation, he had often thought, was somewhat comparable to a football game played in inclement weather. Coaches seemed to agree that competing on a wet or slippery field favored the offensive team over the defensive unit. Particularly on pass plays, the receivers knew which receiving routes they would run. The defenders, on the other hand, were forced to react to the receivers' moves. The unsure footing enhanced the odds the receiver would be able to outmaneuver the defender.

In the realm of crime, particularly in a premeditated attempt at homicide, the assailant knew well in advance of the event who the target would be. The law enforcement officer usually could only react to the assailant's action. In such a situation, ordinarily there could be comparatively little crime prevention. Only a great deal of post-factum crime investigation.

It was one thing to suspect that Cardinal Boyle was the

target of a murder plot, quite another to be certain of it. The measure of security that it would be possible to impose on a strong-willed Cardinal and possible to elicit from a limited number of *carabinieri* would be far different depending on the degree of certainty one could establish.

Koznicki wished he knew.

Koesler was about to divert Toussaint with an account of the previous false alarm that had triggered the nonprocession of dignitaries when, once again, the soft music tapered off and all the stops were opened.

"Ecce sacerdos magnus," the choir poured out in rich polyphony, *"qui in diebus suis placuit Deo. Ideo, jurejurando fecit illum Dominus crescere in plebem suam."*

Once again, the congregation stood and swiveled toward the rear of the church. There were indications this was no dry run.

Proof positive was the presence of television. Two camera crews were grinding away on the steps outside the church's front door.

This phenomenon quite naturally caused its concomitant phenomenon: the gathering of a crowd.

Drawn solely by the magnetic power of television, people began first to cluster on the street outside the church. If TV cameras were present, this must be an Event. Thus, as the cameras retreated into the church, covering the entering procession, so then did the crowds enter.

TV had a little crowd/Its mind was blank as snow/And everywhere that TV went/The crowd was sure to go.

There they were, the invited Detroit delegation, in full strength, such as it was. Yet it fell woefully short of filling the church.

Koesler was put in mind of the parable Jesus told of the large dinner feast that fell far short of standing room only. In that case, the master of the house sent his servant on a mission, bidding him, "Go out into the highways and along the hedgerows and force them to come in. I want my house to be full."

If Jesus were on earth today, Koesler thought, he would not use a servant in his story. He would more probably say, "Call a press conference, make sure the local TV channels show up. Then my house will be full."

As the bystanders filed in in a seemingly endless line, they all appeared to have the same expression: I don't know what's going on in here, but it must be important.

With the Rastafarian threat uppermost in their minds, Koesler, Koznicki, and Toussaint were alert to the presence of blacks in the crowd. There were, they were somewhat uneasy to note, quite a few black men in the congregation. Some were well-dressed. Some wore menial garb. Some, evidently African seminarians studying for the priesthood in Rome, wore cassocks in a variety of colors. None seemed overtly dangerous. But who could tell?

In any case, thanks to the miracle of television, a literally SRO crowd now filled all the pews, as well as the area along the back and side walls.

"Nel mone del Padre e del Figliolo e dello Spirito Santo. Cosa sia."

What was that? Koesler wondered. Certainly not English. Nor was it Latin.

It was Italian.

Funny how insular one could become. Automatically, Koesler had equated English with the vernacular. But of course when in Rome, the vernacular was Italian. In addition, he now recalled that Boyle was fluent in Italian.

Other than enjoying the sheer beauty of the Italian language when spoken gracefully, Koesler concluded he would not derive anything significant from this liturgy. The Cardinal did in Italian speak, thought Koesler, paraphrasing Shakespeare, and those who did understand did nod their heads. But as for me, it was Italian to me.

He began to mull over the relatively brief history of the contemporary vernacular liturgy. The first document to be approved by the Second Vatican Council reinstated the use of one's native tongue to the liturgy. It had been such a guarded step. Only a certain few parts of the Mass were to be celebrated in the vernacular. And those only after a nation's hierarchy had officially requested such a change. And with the approval of the hierarchies of every other nation that shared that language. And finally, only after Rome had approved the request.

At the time, at least as far as the impatient liberal liturgists were concerned, implementing the decree seemed a tortuous series of red tape-bound steps. And all just so people could understand in their own language what was happening liturgically.

Little did they know the far-reaching ramifications of that simple change.

Few could have guessed at that time that this at first insignificant step into a vernacular liturgy would eventually lead to the discarding and virtual desuetude of Gregorian Chant, as well as to the disappearance of Palestrina and most of the other religious classical music that had evolved so beautifully and lovingly down through the centuries.

Koesler smiled regretfully as he considered some of the lesser and more prosaic consequences of the seemingly innocent exchange of languages.

From the time of his ordination in 1954 until the mid-sixties, he had used as a language of worship a tongue that few, if any, of his parishioners knew. Which meant that when he spoke during services, almost no one understood him.

On the one hand, that had led to a nearly universal sloppiness on the part of a great number of priests. When dispensing sacraments or sacramentals to large numbers of people, slipshod elisions became common. And few, if any, were the wiser. On the other hand, constant repetition of a formula in a foreign language frequently engendered thoughtless, absent-minded mistakes. Neither of these occurrences could one get away with when speaking a language the listeners understood.

Koesler's mind turned to Ash Wednesday. For some reason he had never fathomed, on Ash Wednesday a priest would find attending services people he would see again only on Easter, Palm Sunday, and Christmas. Easter and Christmas attendance was easy enough to understand. Perhaps the popularity of Palm Sunday and Ash Wednesday was explicable since these were the two feasts when the Church gave something away . . . even if it was only a palm frond and a thumbful of ashes.

In days gone by, the manner of distributing ashes was that a priest would dip his thumb into a container of ashes (the residue of burning old unused palms from Palm Sunday of the previous year) and trace a sign of a cross on the recipient's forehead while saying, *"Memento homo, quia pulvis es et in pulverem reverteris."*

Confronted by a line of people that often extended clear out of the church, many a priest found a way to zip through that formula in record-breaking time. And no one was the wiser.

Such sloppiness could not work in the vernacular, Koesler thought sheepishly; he recalled any number of times he had caught himself tracing the forehead cross while saying distractedly, "Remember dust that thou art man . . ."

There was a stirring in the church of St. John XXIII as people sat down rather firmly. Those still standing on the periphery leaned heavily against the wall.

Koesler shook his head penitently. He had daydreamed through the Mass. Evidently, now Cardinal Boyle was about to address the congregation. He had removed his liturgical vestments and stood attired in black cassock with cardinal-red accessories: piping, buttons, combination cummerbund-sash, and zucchetto. Koesler was again made aware of what an eyepopping color cardinal red was. Its 3-D-like vividness was almost breathtaking.

The Cardinal approached the lectern, adjusted his glasses, and, without script or notes, began to speak. In Italian.

Lost again! Koesler tried to understand what the Cardinal was saying, but failed. This puzzled him somewhat. Throughout this week in Rome, Koesler had managed to communicate rather well with the locals by means of a combination Latin-English-Italian.

Suddenly, it dawned on him: He had gotten on so well only because the Italians had taken the trouble to try to understand him, while, at the same time, they had spoken very slowly, simply, and distinctly.

As he sat and listened to the Cardinal speak at a normal—and thus, to him, incomprehensible—pace, Koesler's appreciation of and gratitude to all these kind and considerate Italians grew.

Evidently, the Cardinal had completed his remarks, whatever they were, for he stepped back from the microphone.

The monsignor who had earlier been seen leaping near the front door as a dead giveaway that the procession was not coming, stepped forward to make an announcement.

The announcement was made first in Italian, then in English. The English version ran something like: "Anna now, Hissa

Eminenza Boyla, shesa gonna give-a hissa beneditzionay to-a
heverybody. You come-a hup to-a da communionay railing.''

At that, it was better than Koesler could have done in
Italian.

Those standing along the walls were first to form a line that
began in front of the altar dedicated to St. Joseph. In no time,
a double line stretched almost completely around the interior
of the church.

As far as Koesler could ascertain, no one from the Detroit
contingent had joined the line. The Detroiters seemed to be
remaining in their pews. After all, there was no hurry; the
buses would not be returning to their hotels until after the
ceremony. And they weren't going anywhere without their
buses.

But unexpectedly, there were two exceptions, both from
Koesler's pew.

First, Toussaint rose and quickly strode up the center aisle
to stand beside Cardinal Boyle. The clergy surrounding Boyle
would have prevented Toussaint from this approach except
for two considerations. Few people ever remained in Toussaint's
path when he was going somewhere. One would have been as
inclined to stand in the path of elephants en route to their
water hole. And secondly, Toussaint's clerical garb provided
him with entrée.

When he reached the Cardinal, who had not known of
Toussaint's presence in Rome, Boyle greeted him warmly.

Toussaint was followed like a shadow by Koznicki, who
had excused himself as he made his way around Koesler, then
purposefully continued up the aisle. Koznicki, in turn, might
not have been able to approach the Cardinal except that, like
Toussaint, and for the same reason, people seldom deliberately attempted to block the Inspector's trajectory. And, as he
approached the Cardinal, Boyle motioned him to come closer.

So, as Cardinal Boyle turned to welcome the lines awaiting
his blessing, he was flanked by Ramon Toussaint on one side
and Walter Koznicki on the other. Koesler could not imagine
a more dedicated brace of bodyguards.

As each person reached the head of the line, he or she knelt
before the Cardinal, who gave his blessing and might or
might not exchange a few words, depending on the initiative
of the recipient.

The line shuffled and moved slowly, almost imperceptibly. Noise in the church was at a low decibel count. It consisted of shoes shuffling along the tile floor, people shifting in pews, soft speech, and whispers. All in all, it was mesmerizing. Koesler had all but drifted off into a light nap when . . .

. . . all hell broke loose.

It began with a startlingly loud shout. Instantly, Koesler was on his feet heading toward the front of the church. In this endeavor he had little luck because as those in the rear seemed to be trying to approach the altar, those in the front seemed to be trying to escape it. Thus, a pile of humanity gridlocked the center aisle.

Koesler's height helped him see part of what was going on. As soon as he had heard the shout and stood, he saw Toussaint dive forward, taking someone to the floor with him. Not a second later, Koznicki followed Toussaint down.

Then, things became further jumbled. Several other people seemed to fall onto the squirming figures before the altar. Most likely they had been pushed on by those behind trying to see.

Pandemonium ensued. Women screamed, men shouted; most of the Detroiters tried to get closer to the action as most of the locals fought to get out.

Koesler noted that Joe Cox, Pat Lennon, and Irene Casey, who had been seated near the front of the church, had managed to get very close to the action. In fact, Koesler watched in bewilderment as Cox and Lennon were absorbed into the pileup. Irene undoubtedly would have suffered the same fate had not Cardinal Boyle stepped forward and assisted her up to the step next to himself.

Koesler looked every which way to find a passage to the altar. He spotted the by now familiar jumping jack figure of the small round pastor clambering along the rear section of the center aisle headed for the narthex. Once out of the melee, the monsignor began leaping up and down again, and shouting, this time for the police.

They came soon enough, and promptly, like an icebreaker, began clearing a path to the altar. Koesler followed in their wake.

He hadn't seen such a sight since the Super Bowl. And that had been via television, not on the spot.

Bodies were sprawled every which way. All one could see was arms and legs and heads and rumps, purses, hats, and shoes.

The police began righting people, starting at the top of the pile and moving downward. It reminded Koesler of a referee unstacking a pileup of football players to ascertain who has possession of the ball. From what he had seen, Koesler was positive that when the police got to the bottom of the pile, Toussaint would be on top of whomever was the cause of all this ruckus. And Koznicki would be on top of Toussaint. Koesler began to feel sorry for whomever was at the bottom of the pile.

The *carabinieri* peeled Cox off the pile. Making no move to smooth his rumpled jacket or pull his clothing together, he located his notepad and pen inside his jacket pocket and began taking notes. A reporter to the core.

Next up was the redoubtable Joan Blackford Hayes. Oddly, she seemed totally unmussed.

The police righted Lennon, who shook loose from their hands and began rearranging her clothing. "When I catch the sonofabitch who was pinching," she addressed the still squirming pile, "I'm going to make some human pasta!"

Then the *carabinieri* reached Koznicki, the Inspector got to his knees as he displayed his identification. They stepped back and allowed him to assist Toussaint.

The deacon very slowly and cautiously raised himself from the man he was covering. "I would appreciate it, Inspector, if you would take the weapon."

Koznicki painstakingly gripped the man's wrist. His arm had been twisted behind him by Toussaint. Koznicki removed a vicious looking knife from the man's hand. There was blood on the blade.

"Are you cut?" Koznicki asked anxiously.

"Just slightly, I think," Toussaint replied.

Together the deacon and the Inspector lifted the man to his feet. Immediately, the Italian police handcuffed him.

Koesler elbowed to his friends' sides. "Ramon, you're hurt!"

"It is not so much, Bob." There were several gashes on the back of Toussaint's right hand.

"We'll get you to a hospital immediately." Koznicki,

using his pen and his handkerchief, tied a tourniquet around Toussaint's arm.

Now that Toussaint had received first aid, all attention was focused on the assailant. He was a black man of moderate build, plainly dressed except for the scarf on his head. He had said nothing and appeared determined to say nothing.

"Another random attack?" Koesler's sardonic question was addressed to Koznicki.

But it was Toussaint who answered. "I think not." He jerked the scarf off the man's head. Long black ringlets sprang free.

"Dreadlocks!" said Cox in awe.

"How did you know?" Koznicki asked.

"Partly intuition," said Toussaint. "I was looking for *some*one. The scarf looked as if it was covering more than the ordinary amount of hair. But mostly it was his eyes."

Koznicki looked intently into the man's eyes, then nodded.

"His eyes are clouded," Toussaint continued. "He has the appearance of someone under the influence of some chemical substance. Probably marijuana—ganja."

"Wow!" was Cox's contribution.

By this time, Lennon, too, was taking notes. Irene Casey stood nearby garnering details for her second-day story.

"Look!" said Koesler. He pointed to a small image on the floor where the scuffle had taken place.

"The black fist!" said Koznicki.

"Can someone tell me just what the hell is going on here?" As the words left Lennon's mouth, she remembered where she was and immediately regretted the epithet. She caught a quick glimpse of Cardinal Boyle, still standing on the altar step looking concerned. She fervently hoped his preoccupation with what had just taken place precluded his being aware of her inappropriate language.

"In point of fact, yes, young lady," said Koznicki. "I believe enough pieces have fallen into place so that we can tell you the story. But first," he turned to the *carabinieri*, "someone see to this man's wounds!"

8

Even for Rome it was a tiny street, a cul-de-sac near the Aurelian Wall. And even though it was late Saturday night, very little was going on here. Every so often, a couple, arm-in-arm, would leave one of the flats, walk down the street, and disappear around the corner. Or a wage-earner would make his way home hurriedly. Or a wide, round wife and mother would stagger home under a load of groceries. At least the street itself was quiet.

In a basement flat in one of the buildings, a mournful and angry rite was taking place.

The windows of the flat had been boarded up and no sound escaped the room. Like everything else in Rome of any age whatsoever, the room seemed ancient. Here and there, niches that had once held small statues, busts, or urns were now empty. The room, bare except for a couple of long benches against the walls, was devoid of any decoration or appointment save for a large framed color portrait of a bushy-haired man in uniform with many medaled decorations on his chest: Haile Selassie I, late emperor of Ethiopia, Lion of Judah, and oblivious patron of the Rastafarians.

The small room was nearly filled with men, all of them black, most of them with dreadlocks, all of them smoking marijuana in one form or another—standard-sized cigarettes, gigantic spliffs, or chillum pipes.

One man was mournfully beating a single bongo-size drum at a funereal tempo.

"Hellfire and damnation!" shouted one man.

The drum continued to sound. Some of the men shuffled back and forth across the floor. Others slumped on the benches against the walls.

"We and we has failed Selassie I," another man bellowed.

"Shame on our house!" called out another.

"Bredren!" commanded one man, evidently the leader. "Jah not be happy with us and us. He put into our hands dem condemned tings. We and we failed to make da sacrifice. Jah not pleased!"

"Dread Rasta!"

"But der be peace!" the leader called out. "Selassie I bring peace to his Rastas!"

"Praises due Selassie I!"

"Our and our condemned ting goes now to Babylon England place where other condemned ting be! Our Rasta bredren make da sacrifice. Make a sacrifice of both condemned tings!"

"Dread Rasta! Praises due Selassie I!"

"Now, bredren," the leader continued, "it be time for our unityfication with da Rasta men in all of Babylon. First off, we and we make our sacrifice, we and we make da longing prayer to Addis Ababa and den we and we go way for tree days of grounation."

"Praises due Selassie I!"

Each of the men unsheathed his knife. One left the room to return with a small goat that had been tethered to an iron fence outside the basement landing. He led the goat to the room's northwest corner, the general direction in which lay England.

With a single stroke of his long knife, the leader slaughtered the goat.

The others approached the dead animal. One by one, each bathed his knife in the blood.

"Dread Rasta!" the shouts rose, "praises due Selassie I!"

9

"Good morning, ladies and gentlemen, this is Captain Kamego speaking. Welcome aboard our Trans World Airlines charter flight to London. The weather is clear all the way and we anticipate no turbulence. We will be cruising at an altitude of 25,000 feet. Our flying time is approximately two and a quarter hours. So we should be touching down at about 10:30 A.M. London time. Have a good flight."

The flight attendants began serving a brunch, with a beer, wine, and liquor lagniappe. However, few aboard desired any alcoholic beverage.

Cardinal Boyle turned in his seat to face Inspector Koznicki. "I'm sorry your wife was unable to continue this trip with us."

"It is all right; she understood," said Koznicki. "This is not the first time we have had to cancel or cut short a vacation."

"But my dear Inspector, you did not have to deprive yourselves of a well-deserved vacation on my account."

"With all due respect, your Eminence, we did. There is an unavoidable element of danger now until we can clear this matter up. And I think it is of vital importance for you to be aware of this danger. That is why I asked to be seated with you on this flight, so we could discuss this very matter."

"Oh, I'm afraid you may be mistaken, Inspector."

"Oh, I am afraid not, your Eminence. Would you mind taking a look at this list."

Koznicki handed the Cardinal a small piece of paper on which were written nine names.

Koznicki noted that while others on the plane had doffed jackets and coats to make themselves more comfortable, Boyle had retained his lightweight black suit coat and starched white linen roman collar. He never wore the voguish black shirt with the white plastic insert at the neck. Across his chest was stretched the gold chain that held his pectoral cross, now tucked into the inside pocket of his suit coat.

"Yes?" Boyle looked up, blue eyes inquisitive.

"That is the list the Reverend Toussaint acquired from his contacts in Rome. These are alleged to be the names of those who are intended victims of an extremist element of the Rastafarians."

Koznicki correctly anticipated that Boyle would be familiar with the Rastafarian movement. But the Inspector went on to explain what was now understood to be the intent and motive of this violent segment of the group.

"And so, your Eminence," Koznicki concluded, "I would be very much interested in your evaluation of these Cardinals."

"Well, of course, this list includes the names of Cardinals Claret and Gattari, both unfortunately slain."

"But the rest, your Eminence—would you not agree that they are—how is it you say it . . . *papabili?*"

Boyle smiled and waved a hand in dismissal of the idea. "Oh, no, my dear Inspector. That is an oversimplification that has been going on for centuries and, recently, has been taken over and amplified by the media.

"There is no such person as a *papabile*. Although, of course, I have not yet participated in one, I am sure the Cardinals enter a conclave as equals. Of course, since they bring with them different backgrounds, talents, ages, and philosophies, there is no way of predicting who will be elected Pope. That depends as much on the workings of the Cardinals as it does on the workings of the Holy Spirit.''

"I understand what you are saying, your Eminence. But even if this is no more than a game people play, you must admit there are those who believe in it. There is speculation about who might become the next Pope. Books are written about it. In all due reverence, your Eminence, there are even people who bet on it. To some people, the probability is a reality. And, you must admit, if there is such a group as the Rastafarians who, since they feel they cannot reach the Pope himself, intend to eliminate those who are next in line, it would be necessary for them to have a list of all who are in the running for the Papacy.''

"But why would they attempt such an undertaking? As long as there is one Catholic left in the world, there can be a Pope, I suppose—though I have never thought about it. In any case, with many more than a hundred Cardinals, and with the Pope's power to name as many more Cardinals as he wishes, eliminating all possible candidates to the Papacy is a veritable impossibility.''

"I cannot presume to interpret their drug-numbed minds, your Eminence. But I would guess they feel that if they can do away with everyone on that list, there would be no appropriate candidate left.

"Or, perhaps, more probably they feel that as they eliminate one after another of the most prominent Cardinals, the others will become so frightened of becoming victims, they will abolish the office of the Papacy. Thus, having accomplished the destruction of the Papacy, the Rastafarians could then in an indirect way feel they had achieved their aim of 'death to the Pope.' ''

Boyle toyed with the ring on the third finger of his right hand, as was his habit. "I suppose there is something in what you say," he admitted.

"Well, then, your Eminence, I would ask you once again to reflect upon the list I have given you.''

Boyle did.

"Now, your Eminence, granted the caveats and disclaimers we have already discussed, would you agree that this is at least a fairly comprehensive listing of those Cardinals who would be strong candidates for the Papacy? At least as appreciated by the students of this sort of thing?''

Boyle considered for a moment. ''Well, yes, I suppose so.''

''Do you know everyone on this list?''

''I know *of* all of them. Some are personally known by me, yes.''

''Then, tell me, your Eminence, if you feel we are correct in our somewhat hurried evaluations. With three exceptions, the men on this list all have bureaucratic positions in Rome.''

Boyle again considered briefly. ''Yes, I would agree.''

''Good. Now, those in such bureaucratic positions are generally removed from everyday contact with ordinary people, and thus can be protected rather easily. The sole exception would have been poor Cardinal Gattari. Yet, if we had known of the danger to him, we could have protected him until we got this situation under control. For one thing, we would never have let him go into the Sistine Chapel unaccompanied while this threat lasted.

''But now, we come to the other three. The three that would not be in such protected and protectable positions.''

''Yes,'' said Boyle, a new note of gravity in his voice, ''That would be Cardinal Claret, Cardinal Whealan, and,'' he paused, ''myself.''

''That is correct, your Eminence. Cardinal Claret is, unfortunately, already a victim. That leaves yourself and Cardinal Whealan, Archbishop of London. The two Cardinals most vulnerable . . . and you will both be in the same place for the next two days.''

''That is correct.'' He continued to finger his ring. ''But of course we did not have the slightest notion of such a bizarre plot when we made our plans to meet. We are old friends, you know.''

''Well, I do not think we should have too difficult a time providing security while both of you meet away from the public eye. Say, in Cardinal Whealan's quarters. Is there any plan for the two of you to be together in any public place?''

''Yes, there is.'' Boyle felt somehow apologetic about something over which he had neither foreknowledge nor control. ''Tomorrow evening there is to be an ecumenical service involving the Anglican Archbishop of Canterbury, Cardinal Whealan, and myself.''

"And where might this service be planned?'' Koznicki almost hated to ask.

"Westminster Abbey.''

Koznicki shut his eyes and tried to conjure up the Abbey from memory. He knew it was and had been for many centuries the site for coronations of British monarchs. He assumed it would be a devil of a place to make secure. Still, they must have provided a maximum type of security for the coronations.

Koznicki had been silent so long Boyle finally spoke up. "Is there something wrong, Inspector?''

"We will work it out.''

"I have one question, Inspector. You have been saying such things as, 'until we get this situation under control' and 'until we can clear this matter up.' Am I to take this to mean that you see an end to this threat at sometime in the near future?''

"Oh, yes. The danger comes from one small though aggressive segment of the Rastafarians. They are a splinter group of extremists—zealots, if you will. Just as many situations breed terrorist extremists, so their background and environment has spawned this unbalanced bunch of religious fanatics. It is merely a matter of finding them and apprehending them. And this, in time, will be done. We have contacted Interpol as well as the police forces of each city where any Cardinal on that list is located. In effect, your Eminence, in fictional parlance, we know whodunit; the question remaining is, can we stop them and catch them? I think the answer is most decidedly yes.''

Satisfied, Boyle nodded.

"Oh, and one last thing, your Eminence. With all due respect: not a word about that list to anyone. The news media do not have that information and we do not wish them to have it until this case is closed. We do not want the Rastafarians to know that we know who their targets are. This is the element of surprise that will be our ace of trump in foiling their plot. Only the police, the listed Cardinals, Father Koesler, and, of course, the Reverend Toussaint, through whose good offices we have the list, know about it. No one else is to know.''

Koznicki was torn between the enormous reverence he felt for a Cardinal of the Catholic Church and the necessity of stating his admonishment as forcefully as possible.

"Of course, Inspector."

"Ladies and gentlemen, this is the Captain. If you look out the windows on the right side of the plane, you'll get a good view of the Alps. It's a breathtaking sight this morning with the sun glancing off the snow cover."

"It never fails," said Joan Blackford Hayes to Irene Casey. "When one of those announcements is made, I am always on the wrong side of the plane."

Neither of them made a move to the other side of the cabin to take in the Alps.

"Anyway, as I was saying," Joan continued, "I just knew I shouldn't have been in that greeting line last night at St. John's. I mean, I looked around and saw that I was just about the only Detroiter in line and I said to myself, you shouldn't be here. And the next thing I knew I was on the floor in a heap of people."

Irene Casey studied Joan Hayes. There was not a hair out of place, including the white streak that ran through her otherwise black, perfectly groomed tresses. Irene had known Joan for a considerable number of years, going back to their days at Marygrove College. She had never known Joan to be less than perfectly put together, not even, she recalled, on the basketball court. Even last night, Irene, from her perch of safety near the Cardinal, had watched Joan topple into the pile and emerge somehow unscathed.

"Checking things over back at the hotel later," said Joan, "I found I did have a run in my stocking."

Poor dear, thought Irene.

"But it was exciting, wasn't it?" Joan continued. "The closest I'd ever gotten to a murder was reading about it. And there I was, as close to a real murderer—uh, I guess you call them assailants if they're unsuccessful—as I am to you."

"Yesterday," Irene commented, "I didn't even know what an eyewitness was, and today I are one."

"Exactly!"

"Is that why you're carrying your rosary?" Irene gestured at the rather ornate black rosary resting in Joan's lap. "Did the experience frighten you into getting religion?"

Joan glanced down at her all-but-forgotten rosary, and chuckled. "No, this was a last-minute purchase." She laughed again. "Actually, it was and it wasn't."

"Make up your mind, lady."

"Well, it started the first day we arrived. Remember when we were driven all over the countryside for hours because our rooms weren't ready?"

"I'll never forget! Nor will I forget that yesterday they told us the water would be turned off for a few hours, and we never saw it again . . . including this morning!"

"Yes, it was dreadful, wasn't it," Joan sympathized. "I do hope you had the foresight to fill your tub with water before they turned it off."

Ms. Perfect again, thought Irene.

"Well, anyway, no sooner did we get to the hotel than this peddler—you know, the one with a pushcart full of religious articles—came up to me and started rattling away in Italian. He saw that I admired this rosary, so he took it out of its box and showed it to me. I said—with gestures, 'How much?' He said—with gestures, '6500 lire.' I said—with a lot of gestures, 'Too much!' He just shrugged and walked away. I think he knew I was going to become a captive audience."

"Sixty-five hundred lire! Why that's . . . that's . . ."

"About five dollars."

"Robbery!"

"That's what I thought. But every day as I left or entered the hotel, there he would be. With the rosary. And every day the price would go down. And every day it was still too high.

"Well, this morning I took a short walk outside the hotel before breakfast and there he was. By now, the price was down to 2600 lire."

"About two dollars." Irene's arithmetic was improving.

"So I said, 'No, no,' and held up a one dollar bill, but he just shrugged and walked away again.

"Then, after breakfast, we were about to get on the bus, and I guess he could tell this was the end of our negotiations. He came over to me with the rosary, and said, sort of disgustedly, 'Hokay, una buck.' But I told him that was my offer *before* breakfast. Now I had only fifty cents left. And I showed him the two quarters.

"He shook his head and muttered something.

"Well, I got on the bus and sat down. Suddenly, there was a tapping at the window. There he stood, grimacing, but nodding, with the rosary held up in one hand and the other open palm outstretched.

"So I opened the window, took the rosary, put the two quarters in his hand, and he turned and walked away and that's the last I saw of him."

"Bet he'll never forget you!"

"I guess not. I really feel rather proud of myself." Joan held up the rosary rather like a trophy. "Oh, I forgot to get it blessed."

"I think you can probably find a clergyman not a hundred miles from here to do that."

"How about you?" Joan asked. "Did you get any souvenirs?"

Irene nodded, and smiled sheepishly. "Yes, but unlike you, I sort of got taken."

"Oh? How?"

"Well, I went on that bus trip—you know, Rome's version of the Grey Line Tour. We began and ended at St. Peter's. When we finished the tour, the guide touted us into a religious goods store right in the building. So I bought a bunch of stuff. Then I went up the stairs to the first roof of the basilica—you know, where all the tall statues are.

"And there, I discovered another religious goods shop run by a bunch of sweet little nuns. Their stuff was lots nicer than what was selling downstairs, and a fraction of the price."

"No!"

"Well, I went right back down and demanded my money back. I'll say this for them: they didn't bother pulling that 'no spika English' routine. They just told me that there were no refunds. I could see my traveler's check on top of a pile of others on the back counter, but I couldn't reach it, or I would've just taken it."

"How frustrating!"

"Yes. But the Irish kid doesn't quit when the score's one to nothing against her.

"I marched outside just as another tour bus was pulling up and the guide was giving the passengers the same pitch our guide gave us—all about this great shop where you could get all this great stuff at a great price. I'll bet every one of those guides gets a kickback from the shop owner.

"Anyway, before all those passengers could even go in, I stood at the door and told them all about the better, less expensive place upstairs."

"You didn't!"

"Yes, I did! And everybody marched up to the little sisters' shop. And you should have seen the salespeople from that ripoff shop: they weren't happy, any of them—including the bus driver and the tour guide. Oh, I'm sure they get some sort of rakeoff for touting the store.

"And none of them got any happier when I spent the entire afternoon standing there diverting tour passengers away from their store and upstairs to the nuns' shop."

"They let you get away with it?"

"Oh, they said a few things in Italian, English, and Profane. But I guess they decided it wasn't worth putting out a contract on me—although at one point they did call the police. And when I explained to the police that those people refused to give my money back, they told the police I was crazy in the head from standing in the sun all afternoon! By that time, it was late in the day, so I decided I'd made my point, and called a halt to my crusade."

"Well, good for you! That's showing them. I'm proud of you!"

"It was sort of a standoff. They didn't get any more customers that afternoon . . . but I didn't get my refund either."

"Excuse me, Irene . . ." Joan stood and stepped into the aisle. "While I'm thinking of it, I'm going to take this rosary to Bob Koesler for a blessing."

"Why stop with a lowly priest," Irene called after her, "when there's a Holy Roman Cardinal aboard?"

"Oh, I wouldn't bother the Cardinal just to bless a rosary!"

"Ladies and gentlemen, this is the Captain. We remain on schedule. We should be touching down at Heathrow Airport at 10:25 A.M. London time. The temperature in London is fifty-eight degrees Fahrenheit and the weather is—you guessed it—rainy.

"Ladies and gentlemen, if you look out the windows on the right side there you can just see Paris off in the distance. At least you should be able to make out the Eiffel Tower."

"It never fails," said Father Koesler to his row companion,

Ramon Toussaint, "when one of those announcements is made, I am always on the wrong side of the plane."

Neither man made a move to the other side of the cabin to see the Eiffel Tower.

"Oh, Bob," said Joan Blackford Hayes, "could I get you to bless this rosary for me?"

"Of course, Joan. But why pick on me when you've got a Cardinal on board?"

"Oh, I couldn't bother the Cardinal just to bless a rosary!"

"Well," Koesler grinned at Toussaint, "I guess that puts me in my place!"

Holding the rosary in his left palm, Koesler traced a cross over the beads with his right hand. Then he returned the rosary to Joan.

"That's it?" she said with a touch of incredulity.

"That's what you get for giving your rosary to a simple parish priest," Koesler responded. "Now, if you had tried the Cardinal, he probably would have used incense."

"Of course he would have, Bobby. But you're sure it's blessed?"

"It's blessed already."

"Then thank you."

Koesler watched Joan as she returned to her seat.

"Don't you wish you could do that?" Koesler said to his companion.

Toussaint smiled. "Make a pretty lady happy by blessing her rosary? That would indeed be nice. But I am only a deacon."

"You ought to be a priest."

"Have you forgotten that I am married?"

"Who could forget Emerenciana? Nevertheless, I'm convinced you'll be the first modern married Latin rite priest."

"And how will that come about, Bob?" Toussaint smiled again. In his soft, Haitian accent, 'Bob' rhymed with 'daub.'

"I'm not sure. But somehow you'll pull it off."

"That is probably true, Bob."

"Is your hand still troubling you?"

Toussaint touched the bandage exploratively. "No, not much, anymore. The cuts were not that deep."

"I can't get over how you were able to pick out that

assailant last night. There were quite a few black men in that line."

"Oh, it was not that much, Bob. It was just a feeling that grew stronger the closer he got. It started with the kerchief on his head. The feeling got stronger when I was able to see his eyes. They were sort of glazed. He seemed not to be focusing normally. Like someone who was at least partially under the influence of some kind of drug. And, finally, I saw the edge of the knife inside his sleeve. At that, I think I might have missed the knife if it had not been for the other indications."

"Amazing! But how did you happen to become an expert on Rastafarians?"

"I am not an expert." Toussaint chuckled. "I know something about them, of course. Most of the black community knows of them. But when I first suspected and then learned that some of them might be involved in this plot, I began to read everything I could put my hands on about them.

"The Rasta is a complex way of life, Bob. This could help you understand it." He removed a softcover book from his briefcase and showed it to Koesler. It was titled, *Rastafari: A Way of Life*, with a text by Tracy Nicholas and photographs by Bill Sparrow. Adorning the cover was the photo of a turbaned black man with a dreadlocked beard.

"Let me first tell you," said Toussaint, "that when the Rastafarians were first developing in 1933, their creed included hatred for the white race, which was considered by the Rastafarians to be inferior to the black race. Also among their tenets was the desire to seek revenge for what they considered the wickedness of the whites; the destruction, downfall, and abasement of the local forms of the white government of Jamaica; readying themselves for a return to Africa and, of course, affirming Haile Selassie as their divine deliverer, and the true sovereign of the black race.

"This was in 1933. Nothing has changed much in the fifty years since then," Toussaint continued. "The Rastafarians' current belief is still that Haile Selassie is 'the living God'; that whites are inferior to blacks—or that blacks are superior to whites; that the Jamaican establishment is hellish and the Jamaican existence is hopeless; that Ethiopia is Eden on earth; that the immortal and invulnerable Emperor of Ethiopia is even now arranging for disenfranchised blacks to be repatriated in Ethiopia, and that eventually, blacks will reign over all the earth.

"You see, Bob, they have not much altered their principles or goals over the years."

"But why marijuana? I mean, I know it's a popular drug, but, as far as I can tell, the Rastafarians are alone in adopting it as a group lifestyle—a sacrament, indeed."

"I think because it is there. It grows abundantly on the hills and in the Jamaican mountains. And, I think, because it helps blot out the harsh realities of their lives. With the possible exception of my own country, Haiti, the poor blacks of Jamaica exist in the most abysmal poverty of anyone in the Caribbean.

"The Rastafarian poet Sam Brown voiced the horror of his people's degradation and brutalizing poverty when he wrote of families—whole communites—forced to coexist with dogs and rats amidst unspeakable stench; of the old dying of despair and the young broken on the wheel of malnutrition, disease, and ignorance."

There followed a prolonged silence as each man sat lost in his thoughts.

"I remember one of my few surgical experiences." Koesler finally broke the silence. "They gave me a shot of Darvon. For a while there, everything looked pretty great: God was really in His heaven and all was really right with the world. I remember thinking at the time that if this was the kind of escape that drugs provide, I could understand why people who led utterly miserable lives could conceivably grow to depend on this kind of escape from reality.

"I guess I can begin to see why ganja has become a sacrament for the Rastafarians."

"Yes." Toussaint thought for a moment. "What with their peculiar beliefs and the constant use of ganja, they certainly march to their own drummer. It even reflects itself in their manner of speech."

"How's that?"

Toussaint thumbed through the book he had shown Koesler, and found the passage he was seeking.

"For one thing, Bob," he looked up from the open book, "there is the importance for Rastafarians of the number one, which they also identify by its other significance: the alphabet letter 'I'. Whether it appears as the roman numeral or the letter of the alphabet, they always pronounce it as the letter, 'eye'.

"It is as this book states," and Toussaint read, " 'I' is part of His Imperial Majesty's title—Haile Selassie *I*. It is the last letter in Rastafar*i*. 'I' is so important that a Rasta will never say 'I went home,' but would say instead, 'I and I went home,' to include the presence and divinity of the Almighty with himself everytime he speaks. 'I and I' also includes bredren who also say, 'I and I.' In this simple way, through language, Rastafari is a community of people all the time."

"That's beautiful," Koesler commented. "It's similar to the Christian ideal of identity with God and each other through Christ."

"Exactly," said Toussaint, and smiled. "And they certainly did not get any help forming this belief from the example of their 'Christian' masters.

"But see, the book goes on to explain how the Rastafarian importance of 'I' can influence their entire speech pattern," and again Toussaint read: " 'I' is also used in combination with other words, to glorify them: by substituting 'I' for a syllable, the Rastas create their own meanings. The word 'power' becomes 'I-ower,' 'thunder' 'I-under,' 'total' 'I-tal,' and so on. The word 'irie' (pronounced eye-ree), is an ultimate positive. 'All is irie' means nothing could be better; the 'irie heights' or 'ites,' in Rasta talk, are tantamount to heaven or a strongly uplifting spiritual feeling."

"Remarkable."

"Yes. Bob, I think you should read this book. It will give you a good basic grasp of what the Rastafarians are all about."

"I intend to. This afternoon after we check into our hotel. But you didn't mention: Does this book have anything to say about the black fist symbol that we've found at the scenes of these attacks?"

Toussaint frowned. "No; as far as I could see there was no mention of that. Of course, this book is about the basic Rastafarian movement in general. I do know that at least some, if not most, of the Rastafarians are of the opinion that the Pope is the Satan of Babylon. But there is no mention in this work—or any others I have read—of any segment of

Rastas who would want to kill the Pope, let alone any Cardinals.

"This smaller, almost isolated, group of Rastas are blazing a new trail, as it were. So, they are not in a position to rely on their own traditions as much as setting new courses. Very probably, they have borrowed the symbol of the fist from the Black Power movement in the States. There is every reason they should do so. Theirs is definitely, if peculiarly, a movement to establish Black Power over the white religious figure they perceive as the centuries-old oppressor of blacks all over the world."

"But," Koesler's brow furrowed in confusion, "from what you've read and explained about the Rastafarians, I don't understand how they could produce such violent members. Their whole creed would seem to lead toward and engender the formation of a peace-loving holy people!"

Toussaint smiled wryly. "Is that not the way of it, Bob? The Rastas—the Haitians, for that matter—might say the same about white Christians. Jesus taught only love. It was His one commandment. It was His teaching to turn the other cheek, to pray for one's persecutors, to identify with those most in need.

"If the white Christians had lived up to their faith; if they had been true products of the creed they profess, Africa would still be home for the forcibly transplanted black men and women. How could one enslave the very people one has been instructed to love and serve?

"Here and there, there are Christians who live up to the faith. Just as there are Rastas who live up to theirs. In a sense, the Rastas we are now involved with are, at worst, not the run-of-the-mill selfish sinner. As evil as is their purpose, they are only trying to wipe out their principal enemy . . . or those whom their confused minds perceive as their principal enemy.

"Which," Toussaint smiled again, "does not mean we must not prevent them from achieving their goal."

Koesler shook his head. "I'm going to have to mull this over." He wondered briefly if Toussaint was aware that he, the deacon, had just delivered a sermon on basic Christianity to a priest.

"Ladies and gentlemen, this is the Captain. We are still

right on schedule and will shortly be making our descent preparatory to landing at Heathrow. Just off to the right side of the plane, you may be able to make out the Cliffs of Dover as we complete our crossing of the English Channel.''

"It never fails," said Joe Cox to his everything companion Pat Lennon, "when one of those announcements is made, I am always on the wrong side of the plane."

Neither reporter made a move to try to behold the White Cliffs of Dover or the bluebirds that might be over them.

"Look at it this way, love," said Cox, "if that murder and attempted murder hadn't happened in Rome, you'd be winging your way back to Detroit with the rest of them."

"Joe!" Lennon turned toward him, "that's grotesque!"

"It's also true. Even with that attack on Boyle last night, poor old Nelson Kane had to roust Larry David and a slew of the other brass before he got an OK for my continuing on this story."

"No kidding! What possible argument could anyone make against your staying with this?"

"That the Boyle assault was a fluke. That it won't be repeated. That now that they've caught one of the assailants, the rest—if there are any more—will give up their plan. That they can save a lot of money if I get my tail back to Detroit."

"That's what you get for loyalty! You should have come over to the *News* when they invited you."

"What! And leave Nellie Kane? For the glory of the Freep, I'll live with my fate and be the only one aboard this plane who can't afford the trip."

"You're forgetting Irene Casey."

"What?" Cox craned to establish that Irene was aboard.

"What do you mean Irene can't afford the trip? She works for the Archdiocese, doesn't she?"

"I know." Lennon was laughing quietly. "That's what I thought, too, till I talked with her about it this morning. The *Detroit Catholic* is financially independent of the Archdiocese."

"No kidding! That little paper has to pay for this trip? I thought the *Detroit Catholic* was owned by the Archdiocese."

"In a way yes and in a way no. Technically, the Archbishop is president of the Detroit Catholic Company and publisher of the *Detroit Catholic* newspaper. But that's only a legal fiction. The paper stands—or falls—on its own."

"I never thought—"

"We're not the only ones who thought the paper was under the financial wing of the Archdiocese." Lennon smiled. "Irene told me everytime they enter negotiations with the Newspaper Guild—"

"They've got the union? That little paper?"

"I was surprised too. Anyway, she says the Guild always takes it for granted that, in a pinch, the Church will sell the Sistine ceiling to cover its demands."

"Well, as they used to say on 'Saturday Night Live': that's different; never mind." He shook his head. "I'll have to lay this on Nellie next time I see him: The little *Detroit Catholic* pays the freight for its editor to cover this story while the mighty and friendly *Free Press* equivocates.

"And, speaking of this story, where do you think it's going?"

"I'm not sure. I have a feeling there'll be another attempt on Cardinal Boyle's life."

Ordinarily, competing reporters would not discuss any story they were each developing, unless it were to subvert the other's coverage. But the relationship of Cox and Lennon was, in many ways, unusual if not unique. Each was at or near the top of their common field of print journalism. Each had the self-confidence such a position ought to engender. Beyond that, each was reasonably confident that neither would take undue advantage of the other. And, with most infrequent exception, neither did.

"Do you buy the motive?" Cox asked. "That this group of Rastafarians is after top-ranking Cardinals because they can't get at the Pope?"

"Makes as much sense as anything else, I suppose."

"How about if it's just a group that wants to gain publicity by knocking off some pretty important people?"

"I don't think so, Joe. This would be the first time in my memory that a world conspiracy of murder or terrorism was initiated solely to gain attention. Sure you'll get your Middle East group, for instance, claiming responsibility for some act of violence so they can call attention to themselves. But there's always some additional motive: They are nationalists seeking independence for their colonized country, or they are revolutionaries seeking to establish a new form of government in their country . . . something along those lines.

"Individuals might resort to violence to gain attention. But not groups. Groups always have an ulterior motive. Besides, no individual or group—no one, in fact—has publicly claimed responsibility for these acts of violence. Far from seeking the spotlight, they're lying low."

"I suppose you're right. At least they've got the guy who tried to kill Boyle last night. They're probably trying to sweat information out of him right now." Cox closed his mouth, pinched his nostrils together, and blew to clear his ears. "We must be descending."

"Ladies and gentlemen, we are now in our descent pattern. The Captain has asked that your seat belts be fastened and that you extinguish all smoking materials. Please remain in your seats until we have arrived at the gate and the plane has come to a complete stop."

"You're a prophet, Joe."

"On the other hand," Cox resumed his line of thought, "if they don't get the inside story from this guy, and if this theory is correct, then we're playing in a pretty big ballpark. I mean, there are a lot of Cardinals. Who's to say which one might be next?"

"That's right," Lennon agreed. "As far as which Cardinals might be favorites to win the next papal election, it all depends on whose lineup you're looking at."

Cox nodded, then his eyes narrowed as if struck by a new thought. "Pat . . . suppose—there's a list."

"A list?"

"Yeah. Look at it this way: These Rastafarians must know who they're going after. They must have some sort of list. Sort of a rotten parody of Gilbert & Sullivan—you know: They have a little list; they'll all of them be missed." He turned to her. "What do you think?"

Lennon slowly nodded. "I think you're right; they'd have to have a list."

"Okay; assuming there is one, do you think the cops know about it?"

Lennon shrugged. "Beats me. But," she tilted her head, "if *we* were smart enough to figure it out, the cops must have come to the same conclusion. The big question is: Do they know who's on such a list?"

It was Cox's turn to nod. "I think their best shot is that guy they apprehended in Rome. He could open a lot of doors is my guess." He pondered for a minute. "Boyle is making only one public appearance in London, isn't he?"

"Right: Westminster Abbey, tomorrow evening."

"What say we check it out, file our stories, and then get down to some serious investigation?"

"Sounds good to me."

"Your place or mine?"

"Mine, silly. You know the *News* provides better accommodations for its reporters than the Freep."

"Ladies and gentlemen, welcome to London. We hope you have an enjoyable time."

Cox squeezed Lennon's hand. "We intend to."

LONDON

The two friends were seated at a small table just inside the entrance to Beoty's, a Greek restaurant on St Martin's Lane adjacent to the theater district. They were about half an hour early for their 8:00 P.M. dinner date with Inspector Koznicki.

After landing at Heathrow earlier that day, Father Koesler had gone directly to the Hotel Carburton, grateful that the British, unlike the Italians, did not conduct prolonged sight-seeing tours of the countryside while the hotel rooms were being prepared. After a most welcome shower—he had been without running water for something more than twenty-four hours—he had napped and now felt refreshed.

Ramon Toussaint, on the other hand, after arriving at the hotel had left immediately to establish his mysterious contacts.

By prearrangement, they had met in the hotel lobby a little after seven and taken a taxi to Beoty's, Inspector Koznicki's suggested meeting ground.

"The Catholic Church of the future will be interesting. But I don't have the slightest clue what it will be like." Koesler rattled the ice in his bourbon manhattan.

"You mean the priesthood, whatever it will be, will have

changed?'' Toussaint sipped from his Myers's dark rum and soda.

"Yes, exactly. There are so very, very few seminarians! Somewhere down the line, it's got to show. The median age of active priests keeps going up. I just don't know where it's going to end!''

"The exodus from the priesthood seems to have decreased. Is that not a hopeful sign?''

"In a way, I suppose. But that decreasing number will be more than made up for by a recent phenomenon that hasn't drawn sufficient interest so far.''

"Let me guess, Bob. You must be referring to the retired priests.''

"Exactly. When I was ordained in 1954, a retired priest was most rare. And if and when retirement did take place, it was almost always caused by some sort of terminal or at least debilitating illness. Why, the pastor of my first parish had such poor blood circulation that one of his legs had been amputated. Of course, he used to claim that he had one foot in the grave. But what he most feared was that the bishop might put him on the shelf.

"No, the image then, and, as far as I know, for centuries, perhaps right back to the beginning of Christianity, was that the priest went on doing his sacerdotal work as best he could until death. Every older priest I knew, from the time I was ordained, feared most being forced to retire. The ideal was that you were to die in harness—with stole around your neck in midabsolution.

"Nowadays, retirement is taken for granted as much for priests as it is for those in secular jobs. In Detroit, they become 'senior priest' and move out to a rest home, or a private home—or, as pastor emeritus, they continue to live in a parish rectory and do what little they wish.

"The contrast is provocative: If, after twenty years of active priesthood, a priest opts for laicization—and possibly marriage—a certain stratum of the fraternity looks down on him; but if, after twenty years of active priesthood, he retires to Florida—with or without his housekeeper—that same stratum considers him a good ole boy.''

"To what do you attribute this phenomenon?''

"I don't really know. I suppose one of these days the

sociologists will get hold of it, spread out the statistics and enlighten us. In the meantime, I don't blame it on Vatican II, but I think it must be attributable to the Council.

"The after-effects of the Council appeared to change much of what many of us considered to be the heart of the religion we had been preaching and teaching. Some of us grew to understand that these reforms—and many more—were needed, indeed overdue. But others never made the adjustment. Their whole attitude changed and congealed. The green pups, as they saw the younger clergy, had managed to mutate the genuine Church and create an organization without rules and regulations, without all the convenient blacks and whites of the past. Very well, then; let them have it! Some of the older guys decided to mark time until they could fully bequeath this bastard Church to what they considered its progenitors.

"So now, even before clerical retirement, some priests resign the position of pastor—an office many of them spent fifteen or twenty years longingly preparing for. They voluntarily demote themselves to assistant pastors. Why should they take the heat of being in charge? The monetary income remains the same, while the responsibility diminishes."

"All of the bonus and none of the onus," Toussaint commented.

"Beg pardon," the waitress appeared beside the table, "would you like to order another drink?"

Toussaint glanced at Koesler and noted their accord. "No, thank you, miss. We will just wait for our companion, if you please."

"It's a good thing she stepped in," said Koesler, "I was getting carried away on a topic that not enough people are concerned about."

"Not at all, Bob; please go on."

"Well, priestly retirement is just a manifestation of our times.

"I know that may be too broad a statement, but consider how assignments—at least in Detroit—are made. In the good old days, whenever the chancery bureaucrats wanted to move a priest from one parish to another, you simply got a letter—not unlike the one the government used to send to military inductees—saying, 'For the care of souls, I have it in mind to send you to . . .' and then you'd be told at which parish you would spend the next several years of your life.

"No wonder that back then the Church was considered second in efficiency only to General Motors.

"By contrast, now, parish openings are listed in the priests' newsletter, and, in effect, parishes advertise for a pastor, an associate, a chaplain, or whatever. There's no doubt about it: it used to be a buyers' market and now it's a sellers' market.

"But, you see, that is pretty much the way it always was in the secular business world. Employees would apply for the jobs they wanted. And they went where they wanted to. Of course, their employers might transfer them elsewhere, in which case the employees had no choice—other than to quit and try to find another job.

"Actually," he paused for a moment, "it's ironic. With the current recession in the U.S., the priestly employee has met and passed the secular employee on the bridge. Now it is a buyers' market in the business world and their employees are hard put to find an alternate job—while the priest, whose services are very much in demand, can have his pick of clerical jobs.

"But back in the good old days, for us there was no practical recourse, no alternative. Quitting the priesthood was unthinkable.

"It is no longer unthinkable. And, in addition, there is a drastic shortage of priests. So, today's priest is free to apply or not for the parish or position of his choice. There is precious little pressure. There can't be; it is, as I said, a sellers' market.

"And, just as priests now apply for jobs as our secular counterparts do, so priests retire just as our secular counterparts do.

"Whatever, there is no doubt that retirement is a drain on the priesthood that hardly anyone considers. It's just, 'Father deserves his well-earned retirement.' Everyone takes it as a matter of course. But it remains a contemporary phenomenon that very definitely and substantially cuts down the number of active priests that are available.

"So, where do we go from here?"

Toussaint's fingers drummed the table top. "It would seem that an alert organization in a situation like this would take some drastic steps at recruiting. Otherwise it would be forced to face the very real possibility of self-destruction.''

"Ah, yes, Ramon. But you see, the bishops fall back on Biblical passages such as, 'You have not called me but I have called you.' And, 'Behold, I will be with you unto the consummation of the world.' So, they tend to look at this as *God's* problem. They will pray about it and God will solve it.'' Koesler spread his hands, palms up, as if indicating the solution had been miraculously found.

"But,'' said Toussaint, "perhaps God's solution is not theirs. Perhaps God's solution is that others be called to the ministry. Women. Laicized priests. Married men.''

"Aha! You see, Ramon,'' Koesler playfully nudged his friend's arm, "you thought I was joking when I said you would be the first married Latin rite priest in centuries.''

Toussaint laughed. He was joined in the laughter by Koesler. Then the two became conscious of another presence. They looked up to see Inspector Koznicki, bigger than life, smiling down at them.

"May I join the conclave?''

"Inspector!'' Koesler exclaimed, "we were just solving one of the major problems of the Church. On second thought,'' he added ruefully, "as a matter of fact, we weren't solving it, after all.''

"I hope you have some strength left in your fertile minds for the solution of an annoying residual problem of an attempt at murder,'' Koznicki said good-naturedly.

"I thought you had that fairly well under control.''

"Thanks to the Reverend Toussaint here, we have a leg up on it, at least. But please: take your glasses and let us go in to our dinner.'' The two had been so occupied with their discussion that they had not finished their drinks.

The maître d' led them to the rear of the relatively small, reasonably illuminated restaurant. Once again, they found themselves in a secluded booth. Koesler wondered how Koznicki could arrange such consistent seclusion in country after country.

"How do you do it, Inspector? How do you find these out-of-the-way places? And how do you get these secluded booths?''

"Experience. Asking advice. This was—would have been," he glumly corrected himself, "our fourth trip to Europe."

"I miss Wanda too," said Koesler, who knew that Mrs. Koznicki, sensing the Inspector's increasing interest and involvement in this affair, had returned to Detroit in order that her presence would not take time from or interfere with his professional plans.

"Well, in any case," Koznicki brightened; he was involved in an investigation and that helped fill the void, "we have our own list—of favorite eating places. And this happens to be one of them."

The waiter appeared. Koznicki ordered a glass of sherry. His companions declined another drink.

"I should tell you the specialties of the house," said Koznicki, as he opened his menu. "There's *Taramosalata, Arnaki Melitzanes,* and *Moussaka a Khirokitia.*"

"Order what you will, Inspector. Ramon and I have decided to stick as close to all-American food as possible."

"Then let me suggest the *tiropetes* as an appetizer—they're just cheese puffs. Then the *soupa avgolemeno;* the *salata Athenas;* as an entrêe, either the *keftedakia*—meatballs—or *kotopoulo riganato tis skaras*—chicken. Perhaps green beans oregano or tomato pilaf for a side dish. And maybe just baklava for dessert."

"The meatballs and green beans sound good," said Koesler, "but no tomato pilaf, please—and I'll pass on the dessert."

"I'll have the chicken and the pilaf—but, like Bob, I shall forgo dessert," said Toussaint.

When the waiter arrived with Koznicki's sherry, the Inspector ordered for the three and requested a bottle of *Marvo Naoussis*.

Once the waiter left the table, Toussaint leaned forward. "My sources tell me it is to be tomorrow evening at the ecumenical service in Westminster Abbey. They say both the British Cardinal and Cardinal Boyle are to be the targets. So we can anticipate more than one assailant."

Koznicki smiled broadly. "Very good! Excellent! That will work out magnificently. We have been able to persuade both Cardinals Boyle and Whealan to remain in seclusion today and tomorrow until the service. And believe me, that was not easy."

Koesler shook his head. "And all you're trying to do is save their lives."

"Well, they are strong-minded men," Koznicki stated. "After talking with the Cardinals, I spent the rest of the afternoon with two of my friends from Scotland Yard going over a scale model of Westminster Abbey to check security arrangements."

"Your friends, Inspector . . . ?" Toussaint made bold to inquire.

"Assistant Commissioner Henry Beauchamp of the Central Criminal Investigation Department, and his subordinate, Charlie Somerset, Detective Chief Superintendent of the Murder Squad."

"Is that S-o-m-e-r-s-e-t and B-e-e-c-h-a-m?" Koesler was writing the names on a small piece of paper.

"You have Somerset correct, Father. But the Commissioner's name is spelled B-e-a-u-c-h-a-m-p."

Koesler smiled. "He must have a problem like mine with people mispronouncing his surname."

"I'm afraid the Commissioner does not share your problem, Father. Beauchamp is a rather common name over here. The British are at home with its pronunciation, which is, to our ears at least, how shall I put it . . . compressed. Something akin to the treatment they give to Worcestershire . . . or Cholomondely." The Inspector gave the names their English due, which, to Koesler's ear resembled something akin to "Woustershirr" and "Chumley."

The priest almost blushed. "Uh . . . I thought that perhaps somewhere down the line I might be introduced to them, and I wanted to be familiar with their names."

"Quite so, Father. I would be most appreciative if both you and the Reverend Toussaint would join me and the London police tomorrow evening." Koznicki had sought Koesler's help in previous investigations, especially when a Catholic element was inextricably involved.

Koesler glanced at Toussaint and caught his look of concurrence.

"We'd be eager to be of any help possible, of course, Inspector. Would you like us to . . . uh, rehearse, or something, tomorrow? We were going to catch some of the sights of London. But that certainly can easily be put off—"

"No, no; that will not be necessary, Father. We will want the two of you at hand tomorrow evening, though. There are places reserved for you. We have planned more than adequate police protection. But it is quite possible that your eyes might pick up something ours might miss. Or pick it up more quickly. As, indeed, did occur in St. John's just last evening." Koznicki nodded appreciatively at Toussaint. "Meanwhile, do take in the sights of London. There is much to see and you have but one day. Make the most of it, by all means."

"Then, Inspector, you are satisfied with the security precautions?" Toussaint persevered.

Koznicki hesitated before replying.

"Of course one can never take too many precautions, nor have too much security, Reverend. If I had my preferences, I would prefer that the Cardinals not appear publicly, particularly not together. We will apprehend these conspirators, I am sure of it. In the meantime, it would be helpful if the targeted Cardinals could be persuaded not to expose themselves to danger."

"Is it not true, though, Inspector," said Toussaint, "that you might apprehend the conspirators more quickly if the Cardinals do turn out and are accessible to the general public?"

"Oh, much more quickly. But in that path lies the definite possibility, however slight, that the assailants might be successful and that their prospective victims may be injured . . . or worse."

"I suppose," Toussaint concluded, "it is a risk that one is either willing or not to take."

"Quite correct, Reverend. And the Cardinals, in this instance, have decided to take the risk. Which puts us on notice to do our very best to ensure that the assailants are unsuccessful."

Koesler looked from one to the other of his friends. He liked and respected each man so very much that he wished there were some magic by which he could render them friends with each other. There was no way, of course. Relatives one inherited. Friends were freely chosen.

At least, Koznicki now accorded Toussaint the title of Reverend. Until lately, the Inspector had not called the deacon anything. Not even, "hey, you." Koesler reckoned that as progress. He hoped that, little by little, Koznicki was beginning to invest a growing measure of trust in Toussaint.

That, Koesler knew, was progress. Initially, when asked if he would collaborate with Toussaint, Koznicki's only comment was that he would be willing to take a lead even from the devil to solve a case.

So, perhaps it was possible that the relationship between Koznicki and Toussaint might evolve from uneasy collaboration to friendship. Koesler knew only that each of them was a good and dear friend of his and that there was nothing he could do to accelerate this friendship into three-sidedness.

"I even find it strangely encouraging," Koznicki commented, "that we ourselves are in the very place where it all began."

"Where what began?" Koesler asked.

"The modern approach to crime prevention and detection," Koznicki replied.

Good, thought Koesler, as he chewed on his salad contentedly, the Inspector was about to launch into a lesson. Something he did very well and with self-satisfaction.

Koesler knew Koznicki to be not merely a police officer but also a most well-informed, well-read, and shrewd student of his profession.

Koesler had learned much about police work from Koznicki. He recalled particularly the Inspector's impromptu lecture on evidence at the scene of a crime. Koznicki had waxed near-reverential about the silent sign that would never lie or deceive. The sign that would be present only once, from the time the crime was committed until someone disturbed it. It could be a shell casing, a fingerprint, fibers from a coat or blanket, a strand of hair, a drop of blood. Investigators might fail to discern the message of the evidence at the scene of a crime. But the evidence would never mislead the alert investigator.

"As is the case with everything else in civilization," Koznicki continued, "police procedures developed very slowly. But it is interesting how many of these procedures, especially as we in the western world have adopted them, developed right here in England. Take, for example, the field of forensic science."

"Like Dr. Quincy on television?" Koesler interrupted.

Koznicki smiled. "No, more as in our own Dr. Wilhelm Moellmann, Chief Medical Examiner of Wayne County and one of the world's best forensic scientists. But, very good,

Father, that you draw our attention from the abstract to the concrete.

"Think of the expertise of a Dr. Moellmann and the exquisite tools of science he has to work with, and reflect that just little more than a century ago, the average physician's participation in police work consisted of advising the authorities as to how much torture the accused could absorb, and, ultimately, when the accused or convicted person was dead.

"With that in mind, consider that in just one year in the late 1970s, the seven British regional forensic science laboratories dealt with more than 50,000 major criminal cases, the majority of them successfully.

"Why, it was just at the turn of this century that one Professor Locord formed the principle behind all forensic science. That is, that 'every contact leaves a trace.' Which means that a criminal always leaves something at the scene of the crime and, on the other hand, always takes something away. He may, for instance, leave a dead body, but take away some of his victim's blood. Or leave a body and a hammer while taking away some tissue and hair.

"A hit-and-run driver may leave a scraping of paint at the scene of his crime while taking away a broken headlight or a peculiar type of soil or gravel in his tire tread. Do you see?" Koznicki clearly enjoyed lecturing even if the class size was, as in this case, minuscule.

"Something like what you once told me about evidence at the scene of a crime, isn't it, Inspector?" Koesler commented.

"Yes," said Koznicki brightly. He remembered well the lecture and was pleased his pupil had too. "The scene of a crime is a never-to-be-repeated prime clue. The silent evidence that does not deceive. Locord's formula adds a dimension in that in forensic science, one looks not only for what is present at the scene of the crime but also for what is missing. That which the criminal has taken with him. Once you find both what was left behind and what was taken, you have found the perpetrator of the crime." Koznicki concluded with a tone of finality.

"Now," he proceeded, "when you come to the field of crime in England, one finds that, much the same as in the field of forensic medicine, dramatic changes come about as the result of simple but radical ideas.

"In the fourteenth century, about the time of the Black Death, there was a veritable war going on between crime and civilization. You may think we have a problem with organized crime today. But back then, gangs of criminals would band together and descend on towns where festivals were being held. The people gathering to celebrate would be lulled into believing they had achieved safety in numbers, never suspecting that great hordes of criminals would fall upon them and commit almost every outrage imaginable.

"And there was not much going on in the way of detection. The conventional way the authorities would process an accused person—when they were fortunate enough to catch one—would be to torture him until he confessed—and, as we have seen, the 'physicians' were there to tell the officials how much torture the accused might be able to bear. Or the accused was bound and thrown in a lake; if he floated, he was innocent. Or he was brought into the presence of the corpse and if the deceased's eyes opened or wounds bled, the man was guilty.

"In the middle of the eighteenth century, Henry Fielding, the novelist—and author of *Tom Jones*—became a magistrate. The question in his mind was: Why not drop the emphasis on bizarre and barbaric punishments—gibbets, torture chambers, the rack, the iron maiden, and so forth—and attempt to *prevent* crime before it happened by creating an efficient police force?

"A simple concept like that of Professor Locord, but one whose time was long overdue.

"Fielding's idea led to the formation of the Bow Street Runners, the forerunners of the 'bobbies' of the nineteenth century."

Koznicki looked across at his two companions with a self-reproachful expression, as if suddenly realizing that he had talked throughout almost their entire dinner. Although, somehow, he had managed to finish his dinner while lecturing between bites.

"Oh, I do beg your pardon," he said, "I am afraid I have gone on far too long."

"Not at all, Inspector," said Toussaint, whose expression throughout had been, as usual, inscrutable. "Please continue."

"Well, there is little more to tell. Sir Robert Peel, after

whom the bobbies are named, organized the first professional police force for London, after trying out his theories in Dublin. He selected the building, which backed into an ancient court known as Scotland Yard, thus the name. The first commissioners laid down some guidelines that today, 150 years later, are still as significant and relevant to police work as they were then.

"I secured a copy of those guidelines this afternoon from my friend, Superintendent Charlie Somerset." He took a sheet of paper from his inside jacket pocket. "Let me just read them to you: 'The primary object of an efficient Police is the prevention of crime: the next that of detection and punishment of offenders if crime is committed. To these ends all the efforts of Police must be directed. The protection of life and property, the preservation of public tranquility, and the absence of crime will alone prove whether these efforts have been successful, and whether the objects for which the Police were appointed have been attained.' "

"And now," Koznicki summed up, "we find ourselves in London, determined to prevent a crime, in the very city where the notion of crime prevention came to full flower.

"But," he shrugged apologetically, "I have made a short story too, too long."

"Not at all, Inspector," reiterated Toussaint. "It was a very informative explanation. And interesting. One does not often think of the police in terms of crime prevention. The more popular image is that they are the ones who come to pick up the pieces and to catch the criminal."

"Now that you have brought it up," Koesler said, "I can think of many instances when the presence of the police can prevent crime: speeders on the highways, shoplifters in the stores, muggers in the streets—they all have to watch out for the police. And with the police around, the potential criminal undoubtedly is deterred from acting."

"Let us hope that the presence of the police in Westminster Abbey tomorrow evening will deter a couple of assailants," said Toussaint.

"From every indication we have so far," said Koznicki, "I fear that killers such as the ones we are dealing with are not the type to restrain themselves from acting even if they know the police are present. These give every evidence of being such fanatics. We will simply have to anticipate them and move faster than they do.''

"Let us pray you are able to," said Toussaint.

"Say," said Koesler, "maybe that's an answer to our vocation crisis: Maybe we should train seminarians to *prevent* heresies instead of reacting to them."

Toussaint laughed. "I do not think that approach will fill the seminaries, Bob."

"Well," said Koesler, "back to the drawing board."

"Oh, by the way, Inspector," said Toussaint, "our tour tomorrow will include Westminster Abbey. We can do a little reconnoitering ourselves."

"Very good," said Koznicki, "it is impossible to have too much security."

2

"I'm sure you've all seen blokes like these before," the guide said loudly. He was referring to the men dressed in the ancient livery of the English Yeomen of the Guard. "At least I'm sure you've seen outfits like these if you're a fancier of good gin."

The group tittered appreciatively.

Father Koesler regarded the yeomen more carefully than he first had. They looked ridiculous. Further, he thought, some of them seemed conscious of looking ridiculous, especially as the guide, like a circus barker, was calling the group's attention to them. But, Koesler concluded, if you could buy the uniform of the Swiss Guard, why not the Yeomen of the Guard? Besides, these men would get done with their day's work, change into modern-day civvies, and drop in at the neighborhood pub on the way home. Swiss Guards, on the other hand, he thought, quite possibly slept in their pantaloons.

"Well, now, folks," the guide continued in his semi-shout, "there's a bit of a story behind the moniker these chaps carry. They're called beefeaters, as you all very well know. There's them as says they're called beefeaters simply because they were given a lot of beef to eat. Now that's hardly a very romantic reason.

"No, I prefer the explanation that goes like this:

"Now, the king, God save him, has not always been the most popular personage in town."

Appreciative titter.

"So, when the king would go out among the people—rare as that was—he would be surrounded by his guard, attired in precisely the same manner as these blokes here who are wearing the authentic uniform of the time.

"And just in case there'd be an angry constituent or so as would try and smack His Royal Highness, who would take the blow but his ever-faithful guards, the ones who had surrounded him—the ones dressed exactly like these blokes here.

"Now the Norman French saw all this goin' on and they up and called the guards, 'buffetiers,' or those which took the buffets or the blows that was intended for the king. Don't ya see?"

The guide was a squat man whose face seemed to have been pushed in from a few too many fights and whose vein-discolored nose betrayed a habit of downing a few too many Beefeater gins. His accent was drifting in and out of very correct English, while angling into the vague fringes of cockney. Koesler assumed the man to be a born actor, if not an outright professional. He'd be willing to bet the guide could put on any accent that seemed appropriate.

"Now," the guide continued, "people began callin' these yeomen 'buffetiers,' according to this story. Except that the English simply didn't fancy tryin' to wrap their tongues around foreign soundin' words. So they very simply changed the pronunciation to 'beefeaters'. And that's what they've been called to this very day."

Oohs of comprehension and agreement.

"And a good thing, too, wouldn't you say, ladies and gents? For wouldn't it have been a God's awful pity for that loverly London drink to be called Buffetier's gin!"

More appreciative merriment.

"By the same token, the worl' famous bridle path in Hyde Park where the king was apt to go ridin' was known to the Normans as 'Route de Roi' —the king's road. So, a'course, our English tongues made their own sense of it, and converted it to . . ." He looked about. "Anyone have a guess?"

His audience was stumped.

"Believe it or not, we call it 'Rotten Row.' "

"That's what happened to that man's name!" exclaimed Koesler.

"What man's name?" Toussaint asked.

"That commissioner—Inspector Koznicki's friend from Scotland Yard. What was it . . . ?" Koesler removed from his coat pocket a small piece of paper and consulted it. "Beauchamp! Assistant Commissioner Henry Beauchamp of the C.I.D.

"It is, of course, a Norman French name. If I can trust my none-too-trustworthy French, 'beauchamp' means fine, or handsome, field. But the English, as our long-winded guide has just explained, are not only unwilling to admit that any other nation should have a mother tongue, they disdain even pronouncing words that seem foreign and therefore unpleasant to their ears. So, if circumstances force them into confronting a non-English word, they simply anglicize it.

"Thus, 'buffetier' becomes 'beefeater,' 'Route de Roi' becomes 'Rotten Row,' and 'Beauchamp' becomes 'Beecham.' It's a lucky thing for the linguistic world that, finally, the sun can set on the British Empire!" He shook his head. "But what a sun and what an empire!"

"Eh?"

For the past several minutes, Toussaint had been immersed in his own thoughts. He had been paying little attention to the guide, who was doing his best to educate his covey of sight-seers as he commenced to give them a capsulized history of the Tower of London, the first stop on their Frames Tour. Even Koesler's enthusiasm had fallen on all but deaf ears. Toussaint had heard only Koesler's last few words.

As if in apology, the deacon picked up his end of the discussion. "I know this strategic site goes back to Julius Caesar and the Roman Empire, and that it was at one time a fortress from which the city could be defended. And now, it houses, among other memorabilia, the crown jewels. But all I can think of it as is an infamous prison, a place of torture and execution."

"Yes, I know what you mean."

Koesler and Toussaint separated from the tour group and strolled to a nearby stark fence. A flight of steps led down to the moat, once filled with water from the Thames, but now dry. Several feet beyond the bottom step was an ancient portal. Above the portal was inscribed the words, "Traitor's Gate."

"Can you imagine the emotions of all those famous prisoners as they were ferried into this place through that?" Toussaint, in a sweeping gesture, indicated the gate.

Both were silent for a few moments.

"Yes," said Koesler, "when they heard that gate grate shut behind them, they must have known they had left freedom and now faced imprisonment, possible torture, and probable death. It must have been a terrifying moment."

"Anne Boleyn, Elizabeth I, Catherine Howard, and Sir Thomas More, among others." Toussaint enumerated some of the better known personalities who had at different times in history docked at these steps and climbed them to this very spot.

"And poor old Bishop John Fisher," said Koesler, consulting his *Guide to the Tower of London*.

"It says here, that both More and Bishop Fisher were imprisoned up there, in the Bell Tower. Of course, the skyline of London has completely changed. But just think: Basically, Fisher and More saw the same things we are now looking at. The same River Thames, the same shores, more or less, the same general land contours—and of course the same fortress prison."

"And they were here," Toussaint commented, "only because Henry VIII made himself head of the Church so he could marry the woman he would eventually have executed."

"Such a waste."

"You get the impression from reading the history of those times," said Toussaint, "that the doomed were made to feel grateful to the king for his commuting the manner of execution."

They began walking toward the site of the block where so many of the executions had taken place.

"Both More and Fisher," Toussaint sounded almost reminiscent, "had been condemned to be hung, drawn, and quartered. Barbaric! Then the king in his infinite mercy ruled that they simply be beheaded." He stopped and turned toward Koesler. "You know, the thought just occurred to me, Bob: I wonder how Thomas More would be regarded today if he had been successful in his strategy?"

Koesler thought for a moment. "You mean if he hadn't been executed? I never thought of that. We do tend to think of him in the role of a martyr. And as a martyr, we picture him marching quite deliberately off to his death for the sake of his faith. Which, of course, he literally did eventually, didn't he?"

"Yes," Toussaint replied, "but not before he defended himself as the brilliant lawyer he was. He did not want to die. But he refused to publicly commit himself to agreeing that the king was the head of the Church in England. On the other hand, he did not state that the king was *not* what His Majesty claimed to be. More maintained that his silence should be legally interpreted as consent to the king, even though he would not so state. And it was only because of perjured testimony that he was convicted. Do you know, Bob, he could be my patron."

"How's that?"

"I find that the longer I live, the more I have to live for. I do not know what I would have done had I been in the shoes of Sir Thomas More—none of us does, I suppose—but I believe I would have done the same thing: I would have fought to stay alive."

"But you brought up an interesting point, Ramon. How would he be regarded if he had succeeded in fighting off the death penalty? He probably would have remained imprisoned in one of these towers for the rest of his life. He would not have been a murdered martyr. I guess one could argue that he might never have been declared a saint. Yet, he would not have disappeared from history. He was too famous. Lord Chancellor of England, author of *Utopia*, and opponent, if not victim, of King Henry VIII."

"I think I could have lived with that." Toussaint smiled. In the distance they could see their guide gathering his group near the Bloody Tower. It was time to leave. Toussaint and Koesler hurried to join the others.

"We're going to have to stick with the group," said Koesler, "if we want to see everything on this tour. After all, we've got only the one day."

"At least until we reach Westminster Abbey. I am so eager to get there and do our reconnoitering, I would almost be willing to skip lunch and the visit to St. Paul's . . . but, all in good time," concluded Toussaint.

"I should say; especially St. Paul's. You wouldn't want to pass up the place where the Marriage of the Century between Prince Charlie and Lady Di took place, would you? Besides, before Henry decided to split with Rome, it used to be one of ours."

Koesler found that he was breathing heavily just from the rapid walking he'd been compelled to do to catch up with the group before it moved on. He was about to make a resolution to do some jogging when he returned to Detroit. However, he remembered that upon reaching his fortieth birthday he had resolved to stop making ridiculous resolutions.

"Hurry along, ladies and gents. Remember the motto of the Bloody Tower: If we don't hang together, we'll hang separately. Stay together now. Stay together. First, we'll visit St. Paul's, then we'll have a lovely luncheon, then the great one—Westminster Abbey—and, finally, the famous Madame Tussaud's, where, if we're in any luck at all, we'll see a likeness of yours truly."

An appreciative titter from the tourists.

3

"Now, ladies and gents, we've just come in the west entrance of Westminster Abbey. I'd like to call your attention to this plaque in the floor. It marks the grave of the unknown warrior. His body was brought over from France and laid to rest right here, in the presence of King George V himself, on 11 November 1920.

"And over there, you'll be able to see the memorial to Sir Winston Churchill."

"Do you get the impression," said Joe Cox, "that these places are more mausoleums than churches? I mean, those sarcophagi of Wellington and Lord Nelson in St. Paul's were humongous. And look at the statues in this place; two to one there's a body under damn near every one of them."

"Well," Pat Lennon responded, "if you go back to the beginning of Christianity, that's the way it was. Take Rome, for instance: not only were there no Christian churches, but the early Christians were forced to gather and worship underground in the catacombs. And the catacombs were burial places. So, I guess they've got the right idea burying people in churches.''

"I don't know why I let you talk me into this tour." Cox was on the verge of pouting.

"Quiet! It will broaden you. And besides, we don't have a story to file until after tonight's ceremony."

"Now, ladies and gents, you're lookin' at the old abbey in her best get-up. The nave roof, for instance, has just been cleaned extensively and is in its pristine splendor.

"Now, we're comin' to the south transept, where we'll find, among many other memorable relics, the Poets' Corner.

"You can just imagine, ladies and gents, a little more than a century ago, when the abbey was black with grime, and heavier stained glass windows obscured the light much more than now, it was Washington Irving who referred to this great abbey as 'the empire of Death; his great shadowy palace, where he sits in state, mocking at the relics of human glory, and spreading dust and forgetfulness on the monuments of princes.' ''

"Have you noticed," Joan Blackford Hayes remarked, "how much more reverential our guide's tone gets as soon as he finds himself in church?''

"Oh, yes, absolutely," Irene Casey replied. "He definitely is a man for a couple of seasons."

"Personally," said Joan, as the guide's rote recitation ran on, "I prefer St. Paul's; it is so much brighter and festive—"

"And bigger," Irene added.

"And bigger," Joan agreed. "But one cannot overlook the fact that the abbey is used for coronations. I suppose that's a factor in evaluating the two churches. One mustn't sneeze at a coronation.''

"Speaking of coronations," said Irene, "I meant to tell you what happened at lunch. Four of us were seated at a table set for five. When the waitress came to our table, it was ever so obvious that she had just come over from Ireland; you could cut her brogue with a knife."

"We must've had the same waitress. Didn't she have a beautiful complexion? And those rosy cheeks!''

"Yes, gorgeous. Well, anyway, when she noticed the extra

plate, she said, 'There'll be just the four of you, then? I'll just clean away this extra serving.' And one of the other diners remarked, 'Yes, we invited the Queen, but she couldn't make it.' And the waitress retorted. 'Well then, and aren't you the lucky ones!' "

The two women laughed.

"Now this, ladies and gents, is one of the two shrines within this magnificent church. Here, at the very heart of Westminster Abbey is a shrine that contains the body of its founder, Edward the Confessor. Henry III in his spankin' new abbey provided for Edward a much more gigantic and bejeweled tomb than the one you see before you. That tomb became a place of pilgrimage. The sick were often left at the tomb during the night hours, with all prayin' for a miracle. This shrine was despoiled at the time of the Reformation, as were so many other priceless treasures. So that which you now see is but a shadow of its former grandeur. But it does hold the remains of the saintly and revered King Edward the Confessor.

"Now, ladies and gents, if you'll follow me to the west of this shrine, we'll come to the next point of interest."

"Have you seen anything out of the ordinary or suspicious?" Father Koesler, unofficially commissioned to reconnoiter Westminster Abbey, and not at all sure what he should be looking for, was sticking close to the Reverend Toussaint. When Toussaint's attention was drawn to something in the abbey, so was Koesler's. What Toussaint overlooked, so did Koesler. As far as the priest was concerned, it was a foolproof little system.

"No, not really," Toussaint responded. "Just that the abbey is very beautiful and very rich in tradition. Even more so than I had expected."

"Well, let me ask you this," Koesler persisted, "do you have any idea what we're looking for?"

"I think we are looking for nothing in particular, nor do I anticipate that we will find anything untoward. As I see it, the Inspector wants us to familiarize ourselves with the abbey so that we might be alert to anything out of the ordinary tonight."

That sounded straightforward enough.

Koesler looked about as they moved to the west side of the

shrine. "Everything seems so tranquil, so settled, so lost in history, that it's hard to think there could be violence here."

"But," said Toussaint, "even as we talk, I am certain there are at least a couple of men who are preparing themselves to commit murder."

A tremor ran through Koesler.

Toussaint glanced about several times. "Bob, do you have the feeling we are being followed? That someone is watching us?"

Koesler reflected. "No, I don't. But that may be because, to my knowledge, I've never been followed. I don't think anyone ever thought I was worth following. I'm not sure I'd recognize the feeling if I were."

"Do not be concerned, Bob. I may very well be mistaken."

The guide cleared his throat, preliminary to continuing his spiel.

"Now this, ladies and gents, very ornate and obviously ancient wooden chair is the very throne used for the coronation of King Edward the First. And it has been used in the coronation of all subsequent English monarchs with the two exceptions of Edward V and Edward VIII. The coronation ritual has developed and changed over the centuries. But the coronation chair has remained the same over all.

"Now, you'll note the obvious presence of a large gray rock set right within the confines of the chair. That, ladies and gents, is the famed Stone of Scone. In 1296, Edward 'malleus Scotorum' captured the stone from the Scots, who had crowned most of their kings on their 'stone of destiny,' brought it to London and, at a cost of one hundred shillings, had this special oak chair made to contain it. Both the chair and the stone have been used at English coronations ever since.

"And now, ladies and gents, we'll just be movin' along." He checked his watch. "Time's gettin' short and we don't want you to miss Madame Tussaud's."

"What's this ceremony tonight supposed to be, anyway, another Mass?" Joe Cox asked.

"Not hardly," Pat Lennon replied. "It's some sort of ecumenical or intersectarian service. They can't hold a Mass. The Catholics and Anglicans don't agree with each other enough to hold a Mass. And the ceremony is going to have a couple of Catholic Cardinals along with the Anglican Arch-bishop of Canterbury.''

"Well, don't the Anglicans hold Masses in here?'' Cox persisted.

"They call them something like communion services.''

"Don't the Catholics have communion services?''

"Well, yes; but they're not the same.''

"What's the difference?''

Lennon sighed. It was all so complicated. And, in the final analysis, she wasn't all that interested in all this ecclesiastical red tape.

"Maybe it would help, Joe, if you thought of it in terms of an Australian tag wrestling match.''

"Now you're cooking.''

"The way Catholics view their Church is that Jesus Christ established it. He chose the Apostles to, in effect, be the first bishops, and gave the primacy—or 'the power of the keys'—to Peter. They, in turn, selected others to succeed them; those others selected others, who selected others, and so on. For instance, Peter became the first bishop of Rome. And he was succeeded by Linus, then Cletus, then Clement, and so on, down to the present Pope, Leo XIV.

"But, as far as Catholics are concerned, today's bishops of Christian sects are real bishops only if they can trace them-selves in a direct line from the Apostles.''

"And that means that only Catholic bishops qualify,'' Cox supplied.

"Not necessarily. The Orthodox bishops—Greek, Russian, and so forth—are also direct descendants of the Apostles, but they don't recognize the Pope as the supreme leader of Christianity, so they're not Catholic. But the Catholics recog-nize *them* as real bishops.''

"Then what's the matter with the Anglicans?''

"In the beginning, nothing. At the time of Henry VIII, all England was Catholic. When Henry decided to do it his way, the bishops were still kosher, to mix a metaphor. But then, somewhere along the line, the Catholics decided that the Anglicans had broken the chain. The rest, as they say, is history.''

"To return to your original metaphor,'' Cox was trying to clarify her explanation for his own comprehension, "just as in an Australian tag match, the partner in the ring has to touch his partner on the apron of the ring before the inactive one can take his place . . . so each prospective bishop has to be touched by a valid predecessor in order to be an authentic successor bishop. Right?"

"I think he's got it . . . by George, he's got it!"

"I have only one further question: What makes *you* so smart?"

"There are two kinds of people who go through a complete primary, secondary, and college Catholic education: those who pay attention, and those who don't. I belong to the former group."

They had to hurry. Lost in conversation, Cox and Lennon had fallen behind the group who had exited St. Edward's Chapel and reentered the main section of the abbey.

"Now, ladies and gents, I'll just call your attention to the high altar here. Isn't it a beauty! The high altar and that very ornate wooden screen behind it that runs along the whole wall were designed by Sir Gilbert Scott in 1867. The mosaic just above the altar, as you can well see, represents the Last Supper. It is at the high altar that the truly great services take place. The ecumenical service tonight, in fact, will take place right here. And that large golden cross you see over there on the left is the very processional cross that will be used in tonight's service.

"And now, ladies and gents, we'll just go on through the north transept here. And I'll just point out a few things to you as we continue on out through the north entrance and board our coach for the final leg of our tour."

As the group began moving out, Toussaint noticed that Koesler had remained behind just outside the sanctuary directly in front of the high altar. He was standing stock-still, looking intently at the floor.

Toussaint crossed to him. "What is it, my friend?"

"Ramon, I know we weren't supposed to be looking for anything in particular, but I think I found something anyway."

Toussaint followed Koesler's gaze to a spot on the floor. There, almost blending in with the Persian carpet, were two images of black fists, side by side.

The two stood motionless for a moment.

"My friend," said Toussaint, "I believe you have stumbled upon the very spot where the assault is planned to take place. Congratulations.''

"We have to get word of this to Inspector Koznicki!'' It was Koesler's first thought.

"Yes. But we cannot alarm or alert any of the others, especially those two reporters. It will be important that the police alone know about this.'' He thought for a moment. "You go now and inform the Inspector about what you have discovered. I will continue on with the group and conclude the tour. If anyone asks about you, I will make some excuse for your absence. Now go, my friend.''

Koesler hurried for the west entrance while Toussaint caught up with the tour group just as it was exiting the abbey.

As Toussaint boarded the bus he seemed lost in thought. Gradually, his thoughts were transformed into prayers; prayers of gratitude for the success they had so far enjoyed in protecting Cardinal Boyle, and prayers of petition for continued success.

4

"Now, ladies and gents, here we are at our last stop today, the very famous and, if I may say so, infamous, Madame Tussaud's Wax Museum.

"Be careful now, each of you, to take one of these passes as you leave the coach. With the pass, you won't be needin' to buy a ticket at the door.

"Now, ladies and gents, the exhibition takes up four floors of the museum. On the ground floor is the Battle of Trafalgar. On the first floor, you'll find the Grand Hall containin' kings and queens as well as the present royal family. On the upper floor will be the tableaux, the conservatory, and some of yer popular heroes. And, ladies and gents, below ground, and appropriately enough, I might add, is the Chamber of Horrors.

"We've only an hour, so step lively now. The next time I see you folks I won't be able to recognize you 'cause your hair'll be standin' on end after goin' through the Chamber of Horrors.''

An appreciative titter from the group.

To Toussaint, the building resembled an old theater slightly gone to seed. There was no one waiting to enter. This must be a slow time at Madame Tussaud's, he thought.

As he entered the museum, Toussaint became conscious that, even though he was a member of a tour group, he was quite alone; now that Koesler was no longer with him, he was with no one. The only person with whom he might have conversed was Irene Casey. And she was busy talking with Joan Blackford Hayes. Just as well, he concluded; his mind was busy with what they had just found in Westminster Abbey.

Thus distracted, Toussaint found himself staring at a pale, unblinking head. It was the wax image of Admiral Nelson as he lay dying aboard his ship at the climax of the Battle of Trafalgar. Toussaint read the description posted nearby. It stated that Nelson had signaled the beginning of that mighty sea battle by announcing, "England expects that every man will do his duty." And as he lay dying, he uttered the immortal words, "Thank God I have done my duty."

A smile crossed Toussaint's face as he contrasted the related statement of the late General George Patton: "Don't be a fool and die for your country. Let the other sonofabitch die for his."

Time certainly seemed to change the philosophy of war; Toussaint agreed wholeheartedly with Patton.

He climbed one flight and found himself among the kings and queens of history. Henry VIII and his wives! The last one, Catherine Parr—the only one of his wives with any luck at all—had been lucky enough to outlive Henry. Toussaint moved on and found himself passing American presidents, French, Russian, and Chinese leaders. Even a lifesize figure of Pope Leo XIV. Very realistically, the Pope looked tired. So tired he appeared ready to fall down and die.

Toussaint continued to stroll by the exhibits, but his final thought about the Pope triggered musings over the recent assaults against probable papal candidates. What a wild, rash plot! But a plot that had already produced two murders and one attempted murder. And, in all likelihood, another attempt at murder this evening.

Even with all their preparations, the police would have to be on their toes tonight. They simply couldn't disrupt a public religious service by detaining and interrogating each seemingly suspicious-looking person who entered the abbey. Besides, if they were to be totally and ultimately successful, it would be counterproductive to frighten away the perpetrators or alert them to the fact that they were walking into a trap.

No; tonight's operation must appear to be an ordinary ecumenical service. And this would immediately put the police at a disadvantage. It takes only a second for an assassin to strike. The police had only a fraction of a second to counterattack.

The police would need a lot of luck this evening.

No, not just luck; God's providential care.

Without quite being conscious of it, Toussaint had climbed another flight. He was now on the top floor amid the tableaux, the conservatory, and the heroes. Apparently, even with all his distractions, he was making better time than the others. He could, faintly, hear some of their voices from the floor below, but none of them was in sight.

In front of him was a mean-looking little wax man holding a sword and standing near a barrel of what appeared to be a keg of gunpowder. Toussaint checked the descriptive note. His guess was correct: it was Guy Fawkes, one of the leaders of the unsuccessful plot by a group of Catholics to blow up the Houses of Parliament.

How history might have been altered had Fawkes and his coconspirators succeeded, Toussaint thought. Then again, how history, in all probability, had already been altered by this weird plot of the Rastafarians. What if the aged and fragile Leo XIV were to die now? Two very promising candidates for the office had already been murdered. What would the Papacy have been under the reign of Cardinal Claret? Or Cardinal Gattari? The world would never know.

Toussaint strolled through the conservatory. The figures were so lifelike. Alfred Hitchcock, Agatha Christie, Jean Paul Getty; Telly Savalas in sunglasses, holding a cherry sucker in his role as Kojak; Larry Hagman in ten-gallon hat as JR in *Dallas*.

Now he was among the heroes. As he walked among the wax figures, Toussaint reflected that the choosing of a hero depended a great deal on who was doing the selecting. He, for one, would never have looked upon tennis player John

McEnroe as a hero. More a very spoiled but very wealthy brat.

Toussaint was quite sure—and his hunch was confirmed—that he would not find the Rastafarians' hero-god here. There was, however, one black man: Muhammad Ali. Strange that with all the achievements of blacks—Paul Robeson, Jackie Robinson, George Washington Carver, Ralph Bunche, Martin Luther King, Jr.—the only black hero was a prizefighter. Well, Ali had claimed to be the greatest. Perhaps he was right.

He had seen it all now except what many considered Madame Tussaud's pièce de résistance, the Chamber of Horrors. Appropriately, this was in the basement.

As Toussaint descended the stairs, he was unaware of the man who furtively removed a sign blocking the ground floor entrance to the chamber stairway. Nor, after Toussaint disappeared into the basement, did he see the man replace the sign in front of the stairway.

The sign read: Temporarily Closed.

The Chamber of Horrors was, quite deliberately, very dimly lit—one of those places wherein it requires several minutes for one's eyes to adjust to the near-darkness. Toussaint stood motionless at the landing until he could see more clearly. He was then able to discern the general design of the chamber.

It was laid out in a serpentine manner occasionally opening into larger compartments. Many of the exhibits had been set in large alcoves in the walls, the twisting nature of which tended to shield the displays, thus intensifying the viewer's shock.

He was greeted by the wax image of five human heads that had been severed by the guillotine during the French Revolution: Louis XVI, Marie Antoinette, Hebert, Carrier, and Fouquier-Tinville.

The heads were spattered with varying amounts of blood. Toussaint recalled the custom of the executioner's holding up a freshly severed head and exhibiting it to the crowd. There was no questioning this exhibit's stark realism.

Toussaint moved along the corridor. There was the Infamous Marat, murdered in his bath in 1793. And John Christie, his shirtsleeves rolled up as he busied himself in the kitchen of the house wherein he had concealed the bodies of his wife and five other women he had murdered. And there was Dr. Crippen in the dock with his paramour beside him. He had murdered his wife and attempted to flee England with his mistress disguised as a boy.

As he continued down the corridor, Toussaint heard noises intended to evoke a London street of the previous century. There was the sound of a horse-drawn carriage and the muffled speech of passersby. This was punctuated by the muted echo of a woman's scream. There was even a bit of fog. Toussaint peered into the exhibit. It was one of Jack the Ripper's disemboweled victims. Gruesomely graphic. He wondered if such depictions might not be nightmarish for impressionable children as well as for normally squeamish adults.

The thought of children and adults made him aware that he had seen no other living person in the Chamber of Horrors since he had entered. True, he had not encountered that many people on any of the floors above. But there had been some. And the chamber was supposed to be the most popular section in the museum. He thought it odd, but no more than odd, that he had encountered no one else down here. He shrugged; he would undoubtedly find someone else at the turn of one of these bends.

He recalled the story of the next exhibit clearly. It conjured up the interesting case of one George Joseph Smith. In 1915, Smith was arrested on a "holding charge" of suspected insurance fraud. The police strongly suspected he had murdered his wife, whose insurance he was trying to collect. One Inspector Neil was convinced that Smith, under three different aliases, had murdered three of his wives for their insurance.

Each woman had died in the same manner: by drowning in her bath. And in each case there were no marks of violence. Local doctors had listed the cause of death in each case as heart failure—in one case possibly due to epilepsy. One curious circumstance—again common to all—was that each was found lying with her head under the water at the sloping end of the tub with her legs sticking out the other end.

A pathologist later testified that an epileptic attack causes the body to first contract and then stretch out—which would have pushed the head out of the water. An ordinary faint would have allowed water to enter the mouth and nose and would have had a reviving effect. If the women had fallen forward and drowned, their bodies would have been found face downward, the pathologist concluded.

This same pathologist reexamined the bodies after evidence proved they were all connected to Smith. Still he could find no sign of foul play.

Neil solved the mystery. He experimented with a police-woman volunteer. After she got into a tub identical to those used by Smith, the inspector tried to force her under. Water splashed everywhere and, as she fought him off, it was obvious that if he were to be successful, her body would most certainly show signs of violence . . . which had not been the case with any of the wife-corpses.

Suddenly, he grabbed her feet and yanked upward. As her head went under water, she became unconscious almost immediately. Not until after half an hour's resuscitation efforts was she able to tell the inspector that the water unexpectedly rushing up her nose had rendered her unconscious.

Smith was hanged.

And now, here was Smith, in waxen form, firmly clutching the ankles of his naked wife as her head disappeared beneath the water, a shocked and horrified expression on her face.

He heard a sound. It wasn't much of a sound. But it was the first foreign sound, the first sound not suited to any of the exhibits. A clicking sound—like that made when a door is locked.

Toussaint was vividly aware of his solitude. He was alone—or worse, perhaps not alone. But he was isolated; no other tourist was down here, of that he was certain. And that was no longer merely odd, it was ominous.

Perspiration drew his shirt tightly to his back. He took out a clean white handkerchief and touched it to his brow. He sought to moisten his lips, but his mouth was very dry. Seldom had he felt so vulnerable, so impotent. He tried to see around the next bend but, seemingly, the already dim lights had been further turned down. He strained to see a mere few feet ahead of him.

One more step took him into a small, squarish room that seemed to contain five exhibits, though he could see none clearly.

He stepped closer to the nearest exhibit. It showed a man about to be guillotined. He was surrounded by guards. His arms were bound behind his body. His neck was on the block, his head turned slightly sideways. The blade was poised to fall. There was no mistaking it: The victim's face was that of Toussaint.

A chill knifed through him. Quickly he moved to the next exhibit. Here several men stood atop a gallows. Two guards stood at either arm of the condemned. A priest stood off to one side. The hangman was fitting a noose over the head of . . . Toussaint.

His breathing as well as his heartbeat had become rapid.

He moved to the next exhibit. A dingy Spanish prison cell. A man tied to a stake. An executioner was garroting . . . Toussaint.

To the next. An electric chair. Strapped into the chair was . . . Toussaint.

The final exhibit. A man strapped in a straight-back wooden chair. Pinned to the man's shirt was a target, the bull's-eye directly over his heart. The sound of rifles being cocked, fired. The figure in the chair appeared to slump in death. The figure was . . . Toussaint.

He turned and ran back through the narrow and now all-but-lightless corridor. He reached the entrance, but it was closed—locked. He rattled the door several times. He was about to call for help when he heard a voice behind him.

"Don't turn!" the voice ordered in an amused but mirthless tone. "We go."

Toussaint felt something hard and round pressed into the small of his back. It had to be a gun barrel. He felt the panic of a man trapped and, perhaps, doomed.

Before leaving the Chamber of Horrors, the gunman's companion affixed an image of a black hand to the floor just inside the exit door.

5

It was so senseless. That's what bothered him most.

Long ago, Boyle had come to grips with the inevitability of his own death. But he found himself thinking about it again as he vested with deliberation for the ecumenical prayer service in Westminster Abbey.

It was, as a friend had once observed, that everybody wanted to go to heaven but no one wanted to die. Boyle certainly was not eager to die but, at the same time, he did not inordinately fear death.

And, indeed, he was no stranger to the danger of death. As another of his friends had once remarked, if you stick your head up out of a crowd, someone is likely to want to use it as a golf ball.

Well, when the cause demanded it, he had been unafraid to stick his head up and take a public position on any number of controversial issues. And there had been no dearth of antagonists who had taken at least figurative swings at him. He had been picketed, jeered at, and even, as far as his annual archdiocesan collection was concerned, boycotted.

There was always the possibility that some of his adversaries might escalate their verbal or economic assaults into physical attack. And he was on public exhibition so often. If it was not services at the cathedral, it was innumerable services at the various parishes; confirmation ceremonies, chairing or attending public meetings . . . or just his frequent walks up and down Washington Boulevard. Anyone who wanted to attack him physically did not lack for opportunity. Indeed, there were countless opportunities.

From time to time, he would become conscious of this possibility at some public function, especially when, as not infrequently happened, tempers became intemperate.

But, usually, in such a situation, he would console himself with the conviction that should he have to suffer some physical abuse, even death, at least it would very probably be for a cause in which he believed.

Such was not the case now. Since being named a Cardinal, he had been attacked twice. The first time, as Inspector Koznicki had assured him, it was only a deranged man intent solely on gaining notoriety; the second time, as part of a bizarre plot to eliminate the more prominent *papabili*. In either instance, Boyle would have considered his death a waste.

And that was the reason he had consented to participate—no, insisted on participating—in tonight's service. All the principal participants, including Cardinal Whealan and the Most Reverend and Right Honorable Arthur Bell, Archbishop of

Canterbury—who was not considered to be in any danger—had been frankly warned, then thoroughly briefed by the authorities at Scotland Yard. All agreed the ceremony should go on.

As far as Cardinal Boyle was concerned, he wanted only to get it over with. He agreed entirely with Inspector Koznicki's assessment of the situation. The police could and would smoke out the conspirators, this splinter branch of the Rastafarians. But the task would get done far more quickly if the perpetrators were caught in the act than if they were run to earth only after a long, drawn-out investigation.

Why, only a few minutes ago, Inspector Koznicki had informed Boyle that the Italian police had apprehended what they believed to be the entire group of Rome Rastafarians suspected of involvement in this conspiracy. And the Toronto police had had similar success.

Even though Boyle and Whealan would be given the maximum possible security during the service, there was always the possibility that even the maximum might prove insufficient. Boyle was trying to get his thoughts in order for that possibility. He was preparing his mind and soul for death. His body, in an excellent state of health, all things considered, was not prepared for death.

But it was so senseless. That's what bothered him most.

"How do you get into one of these? Any idea?" Assistant Commissioner Henry Beauchamp asked as he struggled with a long, white alb.

"I would try to advise you, but first I must find one that fits." Inspector Koznicki was searching through the press for a vestment large enough for him. In trying several, he had ripped the stitching of a couple while trying to pull them over his head and shoulders.

" 'ere, 'enry," said Detective Chief Superintendent Charles Somerset, who had slid into his alb easily, one might even say professionally, "you pull it over yer 'ead. Did you never see yer wife pull over 'er bloomin' petticoat?"

"Oh, that's the way, then." Enlightened by Somerset's metaphor, Beauchamp managed to tug the vestment over his head and slide it down till it fell just short of his shoe tops. "I wonder how those unmarried, celibate chaps learn how to do it?"

"That's why they got their seminaries, 'enry. So they can learn important things like this."

"Oh, that's why, then," Beauchamp replied. "There must be better ways to learn, wouldn't you think, Charlie?"

"Oh, I quite agree, 'enry. And I allow as how we've found all of the better ways."

Koznicki finally found an alb that fit. He wondered which gorilla it might have been made for.

"Should not the Reverend Toussaint be here by now?" Koznicki asked Father Koesler, whose familiarity with the vestments had helped him finish vesting several minutes earlier.

"He certainly should. We were supposed to meet in the chapter house at 7:30, and here it is ten to eight. It's not like Ramon to be late."

"You say the last place he was seen was at Madame Tussaud's?" Koznicki slipped the alb on and fastened it tightly at the neck. Only the top portion of his white shirt collar showed.

"Yes; Irene Casey saw him enter the museum, but she lost track of him inside. And when it was time to leave, he wasn't on the bus, and the guide couldn't locate him."

Koznicki shook his head. "He may join us during the ceremony. I have instructed the sacristan to keep an eye out for him. If and when he arrives he will be shown to his place in the sanctuary."

Koesler noticed the two British detectives bunching up their albs under the cincture to cover the pistols attached to their belts. For the first time, he became conscious of the fact that Inspector Koznicki was not carrying a gun.

Any number of times in Detroit, Koesler had seen his friend in shirtsleeves with his revolver in a shoulder holster. Now that the priest became conscious of it, he wondered that he had not sooner been aware that Koznicki had been without a gun during this trip.

"Inspector," said Koesler, "what happened to your gun? I don't think I've seen you wearing it on this trip."

Koznicki smiled. "It is against the law, Father."

"But you *are* the law."

"Not here. It is against the law in both England and Ireland for anyone but a very few authorized police officers of these countries to carry firearms, except as they are issued in extreme situations."

"Even you?"

"Even I."

"Doesn't it make you feel . . . different? I mean, back in Detroit you wear your gun, well, practically . . ."

". . . in the shower. Yes, it does feel odd, when one is accustomed to the weight and cumbersomeness and significance of a weapon almost constantly, to be without it. But, after a while, one gets used to it. I, in fact, enjoy being without it."

"You do?"

"Yes. This is the way life should be. Many law enforcement people in the States wish our laws regarding firearms were the same as those in England and Ireland. It is only because almost anyone in the States is entitled to carry guns— and those who are not so entitled can secure them easily—that the police are armed. Life would be much better without firearms. One does not have to be a police officer very long before learning that many maimed people would be uninjured and many dead people would be alive if there were no guns available."

"That was always my feeling. But I didn't think gun control was that popular with the police."

"Oh, yes, indeed, Father. We are often called to the scene of disputes and violence of one sort or another. And all too often, one or more persons in those situations are armed. When the police arrive, those arms are turned on us. Or, at least, the probability of that happening is very high.

"So, I find it most pleasant to be unarmed for a couple of weeks. Although I must admit, in our present circumstances, dealing with probable assailants who are most likely armed, I do feel a bit underdressed."

The signal was given for the procession to begin. Koznicki took the ceremonial cross, while Beauchamp and Somerset carried the large candlesticks.

All in all, thought Koesler, they did not look unlike adult acolytes at an important ecclesiastical event such as the one about to begin.

Before they began the processional, Koznicki turned to Koesler and murmured, "Don't worry about the Reverend

Toussaint. If there is one thing he has demonstrated, it is that he can take care of himself.''

Koesler found the thought reassuring as well as time-proven. Yes, Ramon could take care of himself.

Besides, he had a good forty-five minutes to an hour before the open reception in the abbey. And that was the critical part of this service—when all present could approach the Cardinals and the Archbishop for their blessings.

As the procession reached the Poets' Corner in the south transept on its way to the high altar, the organ, which had been playing softly, boomed out the first majestic chords of "God of Our Fathers."

"Let's see if I've got it right," said Joe Cox. "The guys in the red and black are the authentic tag team members. But the guy in the silver robes is a fake."

"That's a little strong," Pat Lennon replied. "But, yes, that's about the way the Catholics look at it."

"Silly game."

"You're right."

Cox and Lennon had tickets to this service. And they had been pleased to discover that their tickets admitted them to excellent seats near the high altar.

Cox had concluded, correctly, that their good position in the abbey was the result of default. No royalty would be present.

Behind them, in front of the altar, as well as down the north and south aisles and in the rear of the nave were the great unwashed—those without tickets who had crowded into the abbey out of curiosity, devotion, general interest, or, perhaps, to commit murder.

"God of our fathers," the congregation sang lustily, "Whose almighty hand,/Leads forth in beauty all the starry band,/Of shining worlds in splendor thro' the skies,/Our grateful songs before Thy throne arise."

"One thing we must all admit about our 'separated brethren,' " said Irene Casey, "they do sing their hymns with vigor."

"And well, too," said Joan Blackford Hayes.

"Hey," said Irene, turning toward her companion, "is that supposed to be a reflection on *my* singing?"

If it were, it could come as no surprise to Irene. All felt free to remind her she sang terribly.

"Well, if the shoe fits . . ." Joan allowed her mixed metaphor to trail off.

"I like that! May I remind you that it was no less than St. Augustine who said, 'Who sings, prays twice.' " Irene could not hide her smile.

"That's, 'Who sings *well,* prays twice.' "

"Refresh Thy people on their toilsome way . . ." The congregation was on the final verse, singing with even more gusto than before. "Lead us from night to never-ending day;/Fill all our lives with love and grace divine,/And glory, laud, and praise be ever Thine."

The Most Reverend Arthur Bell, Archbishop of Canterbury, approached the standing microphone. Henry Beauchamp, in the role of acolyte, exactly as he had rehearsed it earlier in the day, held an open copy of *The Book of Common Prayer* before the Archbishop.

"O Almighty God," the Archbishop read, hands upraised in a prayerful gesture, "who pourest out on all who desire it, the spirit of grace and of supplication; Deliver us, when we draw nigh to thee, from coldness of heart and wanderings of mind . . ."

Right there, Koesler knew that for him this was going to be a useless prayer. His mind never stayed still. It raced constantly. Just as at age forty he had resolved not to make any more futile resolutions, he also knew he was doomed to make countless excursions in his stream of consciousness. He asked God to accept all his thoughts and deeds, even his distractions, as a prayer.

". . . that with steadfast thoughts and kindled affections, we may worship thee in spirit and in truth; through Jesus Christ our Lord."

From the congregation came a sturdy, "Amen."

And then followed that peculiar rustling sound that is heard almost exclusively in church as everyone tries to find a comfortable position in which to sit or, if unlucky, to stand.

Archbishop Bell, who remained at the microphone, began to speak. He spoke movingly, if predictably, of the longing in Christian hearts for the reunion of all Christianity.

As he had feared, Koesler's attention wandered, as past ecumenical experiences came to mind.

Archbishop Bell was speaking of the many recent attempts to tear down the barriers that still divided the various Christian sects.

At that point, Koesler recalled an Irish missionary priest, who had spent many years in Africa. Koesler could see him in memory: a large, white-haired, ruddy-faced man, who told countless stories about his years as a missionary. One of his stories he prefaced by explaining that he had received a rather liberal training in the seminary. Not, he stressed, like the training given priests just a generation older.

It was with just such an older priest he had been assigned to work in one of the more populous cities in what was now Tanzania. The older man, he explained, as a result of his uncompromising training, could not stand the sight of a Protestant missionary. "Why," he said, "when Father O'Brien would even catch sight of a Protestant missionary, the very hairs on the back of his neck would stand on end.

"It was not that way with me. I was never thus affected by the sight of a Protestant minister. Of course," he added, "I knew they were all goin' to hell . . ."

Koesler had laughed. But, on reflection, he had wondered why, in a small Third World country, missionaries representing various Christian sects and working more or less the same territory never considered their work redundant.

Here was an entire world, most of which was considered heathen, or at best not Christian, and the various sects spent their lives criss-crossing each others' paths, preaching roughly the same general doctrine with their peculiar sectarian shadings.

How much time, he thought, was wasted on sectarian idiosyncracies. He recalled a friend, a dedicated nun, who was returning to her mission in Japan in the company of a very elderly priest who was to become chaplain to her order.

The two had encountered a Japanese couple, who expressed surprise and sympathy to the nun, the only one of the two who understood Japanese. They assumed that the priest and nun were married—why else would a couple travel together? —and they also assumed the marriage had been "arranged"—why else would a pretty young lady marry an old man?

In the time it took for the nun to explain the concept of celibacy and virginity, she could have gotten in quite a few plugs for Christianity. As it was, the Japanese couple found the concept so incredible and mind-boggling that there was neither time to get into the matter of Christianity, nor any use in attempting to do so.

As Archbishop Bell continued to speak, he noted some of the differences between the Churches that realistically continued to delay the reunion that theoretically everyone desired.

Koesler's attention returned to the Archbishop's speech just long enough to note the topical turn he had taken. Then he was off again: Of course it was simplistic to overlook the significant differences that had accumulated over a 400-year separation between Protestantism and Catholicism. A thousand years, when one considered the separation between Catholicism and Orthodoxy. And when one considered the ultimate separation—for Christianity unquestionably flowed from Judaism—two thousand years.

Koesler recalled the night years before when he had gone to Mercy College to hear the rabbi who had been widely and wildly touted as "the rabbi who was only one step away from being Catholic."

Two very satisfied and relevant nuns had shared the stage with the rabbi. One introduced him. In his address, he touched on certain elements in both the Old and New Testaments. His main objective that evening had been to demythologize all the miraculous events of the New Testament. If it happened in the Old Testament, it *may* have been by divine intervention, he opined. If it happened in the New Testament, God had nothing to do with it.

With each destroyed miracle, the two nuns appeared more smug and more relevant. Koesler recalled thinking at the time that if this was the rabbi who was only one step removed from Catholicism, it had to be a giant step indeed.

Archbishop Bell had concluded his speech. Once again, Henry Beauchamp held the open book to enable the Archbishop to read the prayer.

The congregation stood.

"O God, the Father of Our Lord Jesus Christ, our only Savior, the Prince of Peace; give us grace seriously to lay to heart the great dangers we are in by our unhappy divisions.

Take away all hatred and prejudice, and whatsoever else may hinder us from goodly union and concord; that as there is but one Body and one Spirit, and one hope of our calling, one Lord, one Faith, one Baptism, one God and Father of us all, so we may be all of one heart and of one soul, united in one holy bond of truth and peace, of faith and charity, and may with one mind and one mouth glorify Thee; through Jesus Christ our Lord.''

Again, the congregation responded with a hearty "Amen."

Both Cardinals Whealan and Boyle were scheduled to respond to the Archbishop's remarks. Whealan was first.

By and large, Koesler thought, it was not the people in the pews who formed the barriers to reunion. It was the people at the top. It was as Pope John XXIII once noted: As much as he desired and prayed for Christian unity, he recognized that it was he and his position in the Catholic Church that was most responsible for the continued separation.

Koesler recalled ecumenical services he had attended. One, in particular, during a Lenten season in St. Anselm's, his own parish.

A number of neighboring ministers had joined Koesler in the sanctuary; the congregation comprised a mixture of their parishioners as well as some from St. Anselm's. All of those in the sanctuary were men, which in itself was a statement, while, as was usual during a weekday, the congregation was composed entirely of women.

In the sanctuary, there was an almost palpable feeling that everyone there was most conscious of the identity of each and every doctrine and principle that separated each from the other. In the congregation, on the other hand, was an equally palpable yearning for reunion.

And when, during that service, the time came to solicit prayers led by volunteering individuals from the congregation, the Catholics, if they did not already know it, learned that their Protestant counterparts were extremely skilled in informal public prayer.

One other, but one very pleasant thing Catholics would learn from their Protestant neighbors when unity became a reality—how to pray extemporaneously. As one Catholic lady had remarked after that service, when each Protestant lady launched in prayer, it seemed that she would never see shore again.

Both Whealan and Boyle had concluded their remarks and still Toussaint had not arrived. There was very little time now before the reception. Koesler was definitely and extremely worried. Only a meditation hymn was left to precede the reception. Hymn announced, the congregation stood.

> And did those feet in ancient time,
> Walk upon England's mountains green?
> And was the holy Lamb of God,
> On England's pleasant pastures seen?

Irene Casey raised her chin and vocalized very loudly. Joan Blackford Hayes stepped as far away as possible.

> Bring me my bow of burning gold!
> Bring me my arrows of desire!
> Bring me my spear! O clouds, unfold!
> Bring me my chariot of fire!

In the sanctuary, preparations were being made for the reception.

One of the ushers, in reality a police officer, or bobby, as were most of the plainclothes attendants and ushers, approached Henry Beauchamp. "There's a bit of a run on coloureds out there," he said directly into Beauchamp's ear, though he had to almost shout rather than whisper. "But not a bloody one of 'em is wearin' dreadlocks."

"Not going to make it easy for us then, are they?" Beauchamp passed the news to the other officers in the sanctuary.

The tableau began to be formed by the Master of Ceremony. Beginning at the pulpit and extending across the sanctuary just above the step leading to the chancel the lineup was as follows: a C.I.D. officer, Archbishop Bell, a C.I.D. officer, Commissioner Beauchamp, Cardinal Whealan, Superintendent Somerset, a C.I.D. officer, Cardinal Boyle, Inspector Koznicki, Father Koesler. All the police were disguised as acolytes.

The two images of black fists had been left where Koesler

had discovered them so that whoever had put them there would not become leery.

Koesler looked again at the two impressions. They were imposed one directly in front of where Whealan now stood, the other before Boyle.

Some clue! Koesler thought. All they prove is that someone had advance knowledge of the ceremonial setup.

In retrospect, it had not been worth it; bringing the information to Inspector Koznicki had meant leaving Toussaint. If they had not gone their separate ways, he would at least know what had happened to Ramon as well as his whereabouts. Koesler glanced at the doorway leading to St. Faith Chapel. Not a sign of Toussaint. Koesler forced himself to pay attention to the proceedings. Events now could take on literally vital importance.

While the choir sang softly, most of the congregation, in turn, began forming lines leading to the three prelates. Once they arrived, each person paused a moment in silence before his or her bishop, who would trace a sign of the cross over the worshiper's head. Then, each would either return to his or her place or exit the abbey.

"How about it," said Joan Blackford Hayes, "want to go get an ecumenical blessing?"

"I think I'll just pass this time," said Irene Casey. "These feet are tired from having walked all over London." Joan's feet are probably in excellent shape, thought Irene.

"Well, I think I'll get one," said Joan. "You only go around once, you know."

And few of us go around flawlessly, thought Irene.

Koesler carefully watched each person who approached each Cardinal for a blessing. It was not that he was uninterested in the Archbishop of Canterbury, only that he considered Archbishop Bell to be not in harm's way.

The congregation certainly was a mixed bag. Wealthy, poor, black, white, British, American, African, Indian; Koesler thought he could even distinguish some Pakistanis. As they approached the prelates for a blessing, there was no uniformity whatever in the formula. Some stood, some knelt, some genuflected, some curtsied, some bowed, some stood upright.

It put Koesler in mind of his seminary days many years before. One of the Michigan bishops had come to St. John's for an ordination ceremony. Back then, to receive communion, one was expected to kneel. When the priest arrived with the consecrated wafer, one tilted one's head back and extended one's tongue whereon the priest placed the wafer. Except when the priest happened to be a bishop. Which happened rarely if ever in the lifetime of most Catholics.

With a bishop as the minister of communion, one was to kneel, as usual, and when the bishop arrived, one was expected first to kiss the bishop's ring, which he wore on the third finger, right hand. Only then' did one extend one's tongue for the wafer.

The bishop as minister then, occasioned a considerable change in the Catholic's familiar communion routine. Seminarians would rehearse the variation the day before, be very conscious of it during the ceremony and, usually, carry it off quite well. Not so the lay relatives who were guests at the ordination. After long lines of seminarians had successfully consummated this altered form of communion, it was amusing to watch the laity, most of whom had no idea what was going on except for what they had witnessed the seminarians doing.

Having had no instruction or rehearsal, most of the laity did not do well. And so what usually resulted was a convoluted mishmash of bishop presenting ring to communicant who had tongue out, followed by bishop presenting wafer to communicant who now had lips pursed to kiss ring. And so on.

Koesler recalled with especial glee that day's final lay communicant. It was a young girl, who, as was the case with almost all the laity, went through the mixed-up tongue/lips routine, until, in final frustration, she licked the bishop's ring, then extended her tongue. The bishop gave her communion, then, in manifest disgust, spent several minutes wiping off his ring.

But enough of that. Koesler forced his ever wandering attention back to the business at hand.

"How about it, lover," said Pat Lennon, "do you want to accompany me up there and get your agnostic self blessed?"

"Let me clarify this before I get into a situation I can't get out of," Joe Cox responded. "If I get in this line with you, there's no way I can get out of being blessed, right?"

"Right."

"Then I'll just sit here and watch you. I could do worse . . . lots worse."

"You may be making a mistake. It couldn't hurt."

But Cox maintained his seat while Joan Blackford Hayes stepped back to allow Lennon into the line.

Koesler was trying to be vigilant, but it was not easy. The combination of the soft choral singing, the endless shuffling of the crowds approaching and leaving the chancel, the soporific heat generated by all those bodies had a tendency to dull the senses. Still, he tried to pay close attention.

If only Toussaint were here! Ramon would have been single-minded in his concentration. And his reflexes were still fast and keen. He had proven that in the Rome confrontation.

Koesler's preoccupations swept him back to the occasion when he had first become aware that he was slowing down, even if barely perceptibly. It had been during a make-up touch football game. Koesler had been an average to slightly-better-than-average athlete. At least he had loved to participate in almost all sports.

But the game he was now recalling had occurred almost five years after his ordination. It had been played on the football field at the seminary between some seminarians and some priests. Koesler had been in the priestly defensive backfield and, on a pass, his mind had told him where the play was heading—but his legs had refused to take him there.

It was a peculiar experience he had never forgotten: there he was, not yet thirty, on the verge of being forced to take golf more seriously.

"Death—!"

The assailant had been cut off in mid-shout.

Koesler looked over in time to see the flash of an upraised knife poised to strike Cardinal Boyle. Before the weapon could descend, Koznicki's bulk lunged over the assailant, and the two men, as well as nearly everyone else in the vicinity, were tumbled into a pile of struggling, panicky humanity.

A fraction of a second after Koznicki's lunge, Beauchamp and Somerset had tackled and overwhelmed the assailant who loomed up before Cardinal Whealan.

Cardinal Boyle had reeled backward unharmed. Cardinal Whealan had not been as fortunate. He was bleeding. Koesler could not tell where the blow had struck, but the Cardinal's hand was covered with blood.

Koesler considered it vital that he somehow get involved, although by now the police had things pretty much under control. However, he could not see what was happening at the bottom of the pile for all the squirming humanity at the top of the pile. So he stepped down from the sanctuary and bent over to help sort out the mess. Instantly, his feet were swept out from under him and Koesler joined the pile.

The choir had stopped singing; many of its members were shouting and shrieking. The congregation was a mass of pandemonium. The organist, thinking that music might soothe the savage beast, opened up the sforzando and added to the din.

Irene Casey hopped onto her chair. She wanted to be able to report this for the *Detroit Catholic,* but there was no way she was going to get close to that pile.

Her first concern was Cardinal Boyle. She was greatly relieved to see that he appeared to be all right, albeit apparently dazed. His eyes were opened wide and his mouth agape as he regarded the tangled mass before him.

Then she saw her. Joan Blackford Hayes being assisted to her feet by one of the acolytes. Not a hair mussed. She didn't even have to readjust her clothing; it hung perfectly. She looked about with only the slightest air of involvement, as if watching a movie.

Irene seldom used the word, but it seemed appropriate. "Damn!" she muttered. She wished Joan no harm. Only that for once in her life, just one hair might be out of place.

Joe Cox, reportorial senses aquiver, pushed to the edge of the pile. Like a hockey referee, he was determined to stay close to the action so he could assess it without becoming enmeshed in it.

He noted that Cardinal Boyle appeared unhurt. But Cardinal Whealan, obviously shaken, was ashen-faced. A clergyman was wrapping a cloth of some sort around the Cardinal's hand. The cloth was already sodden with blood.

Then Cox heard a familiar voice. Even above the full organ and the tumult of the congregation, Cox clearly heard a most familiar voice.

"Let go of me, goddammit! You goddamn sonofabitch

mother! Take your filthy rotten hands off me, you male chauvinist pig!''

Pat Lennon was struggling to get to her feet from roughly midpile. A hairy male hand was firmly grasping her bottom.

6

"Didja telex your story?"

"Uh-huh. 'you?"

"Yeah," said Joe Cox, "I suppose *you* wrote it as an eyewitness."

"Eyewitness, my rear! I wrote it as a victim."

"Victim! Hell, you were just closer to the action than I was."

"What do you mean 'closer'? I was *attacked*!"

"So the *News* will award you the Medal of the Purple Butt.

"That English Cardinal was lucky," Cox continued, returning to the point. "If those cops hadn't been as fast as they were—"

"Not as fast as Koznicki," Lennon said. "I didn't think a man that big could move that fast. And he's no spring chicken, either."

"I guess I'd like to have him on my side in a fight. I'd sure as hell hate to see him among the opposition . . ."

"By the way, did you tumble that all those altar servers were British cops?"

"Nope," Lennon admitted. "It got by me completely. Turns out the place was crawling with constables." She looked thoughtful. "Wouldn't you say they were providing a little more than ordinary security tonight?"

"Yup!" Cox emphasized. "Tonight's protection was just about maximum security. They couldn't have provided better protection for their queen." He paused. "What do you make of it?"

Lennon ran her index finger across her upper lip. "You want to know what I think? I think they know! Somehow they *know* who's on this crazy Rastafarian hit list. That's the only thing that could possibly explain all those cops in the abbey tonight."

"But how? How could they know? They couldn't have gotten it from the Rastafarians . . . could they?"

Lennon pondered. "What about that black deacon . . . what's his name, Toussaint?"

It was as if a bulb lit above Cox's head. "Yeah, Toussaint. Of course! Remember when he was in Detroit? He had connections all through the black community. I never saw anyone to beat him—not even Mayor Cobb."

"Yes, and remember his contacts with fellow Haitians . . . and what I've always suspected was a voodoo network."

"Voodoo!" Cox sounded incredulous. "Come on, Pat; this is the twentieth century and we're smack in the middle of Western civilization. Voodoo's part of the past."

"Don't kid yourself, Joe. You and I may not be invited to any voodoo rites; honkies seldom are. But the African slaves brought their religion, which happened to be voodoo, with them. And although it may have changed a bit and blended with some of our culture, it's still alive and healthy. And I'll just bet that you could find voodoo cults in any metropolitan area where there's a large concentration of blacks."

"Maybe so, but I doubt it. Anyway, for the sake of discussion, let's say Toussaint *did* somehow come up with this hypothetical Rastafarian hit list. So if he is the police source, wouldn't you think he'd have been there tonight? I didn't see him . . . did you?"

"No . . . no, I didn't. And that's odd: Now that I think of it, Toussaint is the one who nailed the Rastafarian who tried to knife Boyle in Rome. Which just reinforces my feeling that he did latch onto that list."

"All that proves is that he's a little faster than the amazingly quick Koznicki. But, where was he tonight?"

"I haven't a clue. Maybe we can look into that tomorrow."

"You're so right." Cox reached up and turned off the light. He pulled up the covers and snuggled closer to Lennon.

"You know, you're right about something else, too," said Cox.

"And that is . . . ?"

"That the *News* provides better accommodations than the *Free Press*. But isn't it nice that the *News* reporters are so generous."

"We are generous only to the deserving poor."

"And am I deserving?"

"Joe, you always deserve everything you get."

Cox raised himself up on one elbow and kissed her tenderly. It was not the end of the day, only the beginning of the night.

7

It was almost impossible to see, the smoke was so thick in the small downstairs room of a tenement apartment in the Brixton district of London. It was a stark room, with no furniture but a small wooden desk with a straightback chair behind it.

On one wall hung a large, framed, color portrait of a swarthy, bushy-haired man in uniform with a chestful of ribbons and decorations. Haile Selassie I, late Emperor of Ethiopia, King of Kings, Lord of Lords, Conquering Lion of the Tribe of Judah, and unwitting patron of the Rastafarians, was so honored.

Eight men had crowded into the room; none was moving about. Some sat on the floor, others leaned against the wall. Heavy ganja smoke poured from their mouths and nostrils, filling the room.

An air of discouragement, dejection, depression, and gloom was almost tangible.

Occasionally, one or another would speak, though without enthusiasm or spirit.

"Damnation! Hellfire!"

"We and we has failed Selassie I!"

"Shame on our house!"

Finally, one man rose from the floor. In each hand, he bore an imposing, unsheathed knife.

He lurched to the desk, on which rested two effigies, each swathed in cardinal red. He raised both knives over his head and with manifest concentration, drove both into the effigies simultaneously.

"Dread Rasta no dread," he called out with some air of ritual. "It be de end!"

8

"Seems t' me, Charlie, that you're a fraction away from it, what with the years getting on," said Commissioner Beauchamp, a bit impishly.

"Oh, I don't know, guv'nor," Superintendent Somerset shot back in a combative tone, "I believe I was on our man quick as anyone. Surely, as any man in this room."

"Maybe, but then neither of us got to him with the speed of lightning like our Inspector friend here."

"Now, now," retorted Inspector Koznicki, waving a large paw reprovingly, "free me from the middle of this, if you will. We did our job. We protected our charges."

Beefeater gin to the contrary notwithstanding, they were sipping Dewar's White Label Blended Scotch.

Beauchamp, Somerset, Koznicki, and Father Koesler had gathered in Koznicki's room at the Carburton to celebrate their victory earlier that evening over the Rasta forces. The two assailants had been taken into custody and were presently being interrogated by Scotland Yard specialists.

"Blimey," Somerset commented, "but I've never seen anyone move any faster'n you did tonight, Inspector. Maybe as fast, but no faster. And none of us is of the spring chicken variety, I'd say!"

Koznicki shrugged. "The circumstances were just different. My man raised his knife above his head, and, of course, he was the one who shouted. It was enough of an invitation to act as any I have ever experienced. Your man, on the other hand, brought his knife up from his side directly. You both acted as quickly as could be expected. As it is, it was fortunate that Cardinal Whealan received only a hand wound. It could easily have been much worse."

"Well, in any case," said Beauchamp, "we've wrapped it up, I'd say, really. And your party will be movin' on tomorrow then?" It was a statement, but expressed as a question.

"Yes," said Koznicki, "our next stop is Dublin. But do you really think it is 'wrapped up,' as you say? According to our list, Cardinal Whealan is one of the targets of this conspiracy. Will that not remain so?"

"For the time being, it will be very true, indeed," Somerset replied. "But we've got two of 'em, and like as not we'll find the rest. Should push come to shove, I'll wager one or another of 'em will tell us anything we'll want to know just for a puff on their precious ganja weed.''

"Oh, yes," Beauchamp agreed, "we'll round 'em up. And in the meantime, we'll take special care of His Eminence, indeed."

The two British detectives moved to the table for a dash more of Scotch.

As they did so, Koznicki turned to Koesler. "Speaking of that list, Father, have you heard yet from the Reverend Toussaint?"

"Not a word—and I told the hotel operator I'd be in your room in case there were any calls." Koesler had been silent partly because he was hesitant to join in a conversation between police professionals and partly because there was something about this entire case that he found puzzling.

"Is that what is troubling you?" Koznicki was sensitive to his friend's moods and to him it was evident that something was bothering Koesler.

"Partly. It's been too long since I've heard from Ramon. I just feel that even if he'd been occupied with something that came up suddenly, he would have phoned. After all, he was supposed to be at that service this evening."

Koznicki turned up his palms in a gesture of helplessness. "All I can say to reassure you is what I said before: Your friend can take care of himself." After a pause, he asked, "Is there something else?"

"Well, as a matter of fact, yes . . . but I find it difficult to express. It's as if something else is missing, but I can't quite get a handle on it or identify it." He looked from Koznicki to the two officers as if hopeful they might identify his problem.

"Well, sir," Beauchamp fielded the lead, "I think your trouble might just be that you think everything is too simple to be true."

"Yes, that's it all right," said Somerset with even more assurance than Beauchamp. " 'ere we know 'oo we're lookin' for, so to speak. And we even know where the bally blighters are gonna be standin' so we can 'ave a go at 'em. It's just too cut and dried to be real. Isn't that it, sir?" He didn't pause for a reply. "You assume, from all your readin' and the films and the telly, that police procedure, even a murder case, God save us all, is a complex puzzle requirin' the fine detective work of a Mr. 'olmes! Well, in all truth, many of 'em are. But every once in a while, you come across a case that is, as the crime writers would 'ave it, open and shut. Such a case, I do believe, we 'ave on our 'ands this very minute.''

"Yes," Beauchamp continued, "as the Superintendent has very rightly put it, some cases are simpler than others. It is all up to the perpetrator. Some criminals are deucedly clever, while others are incredibly stupid. Reminds me of one we had not long ago. Remember, Charlie," he directed at Somerset, "remember Alfred Kirkus?''

"Dummy Alfie? 'oo could forget 'im?''

"Was a clot," Beauchamp continued, "who was a contract killer. What is it you call such a fellow in the States?''

"A hit man," Koznicki supplied.

"The very thing," Beauchamp confirmed. "Now, Alfie was given a contract to kill one Arthur F. Knoff, an industrialist makes one of his homes in London.

"Well, the first time ol' Dummy Alfie tried was in Mr. Knoff's parking garage.''

"Right," said Somerset, eager to get in on the storytelling, " 'e 'id in the garage, and when Mr. Knoff arrived at 'is Bentley, the car 'e was goin' to use that particular day, they start to scuffle. Alfie's gun falls to the floor and Mr. Knoff kicks it under a vehicle several cars removed. So Alfie beats an 'asty retreat.''

"The second time he had a go," Beauchamp resumed possession of the verbal ball, "Alfie very carefully reconnoitered Mr. Knoff's private club, learned the whole layout, where the gentleman took his lunch, the usual time—a very thorough job, if I may say—''

"And then," Somerset interrupted, "Alfie goes and shows up to shoot Mr. Knoff on the very day 'is backgammon group meets.''

"The third time he tried to fulfill his contract was in Harrods—crowded Harrods, God save us all. Well, this time, Alfie does get off a shot and wings Mr. Knoff pretty good.''

"But then," said Somerset, continuing the antiphony, "Alfie tries to make 'is escape in the tube!''

Koesler looked puzzled.

"The subway," Koznicki translated.

"Not only did 'e try to get away in the tube," Somerset continued, "but Dummy Alfie tells everyone on board 'oo'll listen what 'e just did. One of the passengers gets off, tells a constable, 'oo gets back on board and takes Dummy Alfie into custody."

Everyone laughed. As the laughter subsided, the phone rang. Koznicki answered it. "Yes, he is here." He beckoned Koesler to the phone.

"This a Mr. Robert Koesler?"

"Yes." He decided to overlook the absence of title.

"Would you know a Mr. Ramon Toussaint?"

"Yes, why do you ask?" Koesler felt a foreboding.

"We found your name and your hotel on a piece of paper in his pocket. And since we did not know who to notify, we thought we should tell you—"

"Tell me what?" Koesler's knees were turning to jelly.

"Mr. Toussaint is dead."

9

"If you would prefer, Father," Koznicki said, "you can remain here in the car. I can go in and make the identification and the arrangements. I knew Ramon Toussaint well enough to do that and I am used to the procedure. It is really not very pleasant—and he was your good friend."

"No, thank you very much, Inspector. I think I can do it. But," he added, looking in turn at each of his companions, "I would be grateful for your presence."

None of the four had said much since the phone call. The others had expressed their sympathy briefly to Koesler. Then Somerset had driven them to the hospital.

Now, all four exited the car and entered the hospital. Locating a nurse in the casualty department, Koznicki explained why they were there. She asked them to wait, then went for the doctor. When he entered the waiting area, the doctor seemed a bit surprised. Apparently, he had not expected four people.

"Which of you is Koesler?"

"I am."

Again the doctor exhibited mild surprise. "You're a priest?"

Koesler nodded, as the others identified themselves.

"Sorry, Father. I wasn't expecting a member of the clergy. The attendant failed to mention that."

"The attendant?"

"Yes. The one who phoned you. He was only doing his job, of course, but . . ." He shook his head, then looked at Koesler with an odd expression. "You see, Mr. Toussaint is not dead.

"Not dead!" Koesler felt a sudden exuberance, then a weakness brought on by relief.

"No. Though I must say that for all intents and purposes, he might as well have been. He certainly appeared so when he was brought in. If our attendant hadn't rung you so soon . . ."

The other three offered congratulations to Koesler. Beauchamp and Somerset each took out a notepad. Obviously, they felt this could become a matter for police investigation.

"What happened?" Koesler asked.

"Well, Mr. Toussaint's body was discovered in Regent's Park. It was most fortunate he was found so soon, really. A romantic young couple strolling by the lake almost literally stumbled upon him. Otherwise, I fear he wouldn't have been found till daylight . . . and I very much doubt he would have been alive at that point.

"In any case, he was brought in here at," the doctor consulted his chart, "2230 . . . no, 2235, to be precise. At first blush he was thought to be dead." He looked up. "That's when our attendant called you. But then, one of our people thought she heard a sigh escape from Mr. Toussaint. She checked and got a pupil reaction and then we all began to work very quickly indeed."

"Is he conscious?" Beauchamp inquired.

The doctor shook his head. "He was comatose when we first examined him and that condition has remained unchanged."

"Then what exactly is 'is condition?" Somerset asked.

"Critical. Extremely critical."

"And you can't tell yet what happened to him?" Koznicki asked.

"A beating, I should think. A beating the likes of which, I'm glad to say, we don't see often." Again, the doctor referred to his chart. "So far, we've found the following fractures: frontal," he looked up from the chart, "that's his

forehead.'' Then, ''right and left zygomatic.'' Again he looked
up. ''That's both cheekbones. Right mandible . . . that's the
lower jaw; nose; clavicle . . . that's the collarbone; right and
left humerus, radius, and ulna . . . that's both upper and
lower arms; all ten fingers; ribs—seven fractures to the
ribs . . .''

As the doctor proceeded through his medical litany, Koesler
first flinched, then felt his stomach turn. He feared he was
going to be physically ill. His companions were taking notes
very professionally.

''. . . right femur . . . that's the thigh; and tibia . . . that's
the lower leg; both patellae . . . that's the kneecaps, several
metatarsi in each foot. Then dislocations: one hip and one
shoulder.''

''That it?'' asked Somerset.

''That's all we have found so far.'' He stopped, suddenly
aware of Koesler's wanness, and looked at the priest with
professional concern. ''Are you all right, Father?''

Koesler half-nodded in a peremptory manner, while his
right hand made an impatient I'm-all-right-please-go-on gesture.

The doctor looked at him doubtfully, but resumed. ''The
good side of it is that, as far as we can tell, incredibly—
miraculously—there's been no internal bleeding, and no collapsed lung. With all those fractured ribs, you fear a thing
like that.''

''Well, then,'' said Beauchamp, ''it's a professional job,
no doubt of that. But tell us: What is the prognosis?''

''Too soon to say, actually. I'd guess his age to be in the
late forties, early fifties—''

''He's fifty-six,'' Koesler said quietly.

''Really! He does appear younger. But even at fifty-six
. . . now that's a fairly young age when one speaks of
recovery from a thing like this. And, outside of the massive
multiple injuries, he seems in excellent physical condition.
All in all, I would guess there to be something like a 40
percent chance of survival.''

''That's all?'' Koesler, newfound hope ebbing, seemed
stunned.

''Father,'' the doctor replied, ''let me assure you: for the
severity of the beating your friend received, he is very, *very*
fortunate merely to be alive. From the extent of his injuries, I

do not believe his assailant or assailants meant for him to survive. And now, we are faced with, in effect, trying to put Humpty Dumpty together again.

"And even if he survives, we cannot be sure he will suffer no permanent physical or neurological after-effects."

Koesler fought waves of nausea. "Then I'll stay here."

"What? Here at the hospital?" asked the doctor.

"No, here in London."

"You're on holiday then?"

"A charter," said Koznicki. "We were scheduled to leave tomorrow for Ireland."

"Then, by all means, go. Believe me, Father," said the doctor earnestly, "your staying in London can serve no useful purpose whatever. There is nothing you can do for Mr. Toussaint. He will, believe me, not be at all conscious of your presence . . . or your absence. I do not even expect that he will regain consciousness for several days—if at all. And when and if he does, we will then have to ascertain to what extent, if any, he has sustained brain damage. Although, it *is* odd . . ." His brow furrowed and his voice trailed off in puzzlement.

"What is odd?" pressed Koznicki.

"Oh, only that with what seems to have been a brutally methodical shattering of most of the bones in this man's body, there is no damage to the cranial bones—as if whoever did this deliberately left that part of his skull uninjured.

"Well, in any event," he looked again at Koesler, "after we get done patching him as best we can now, he'll be in an intensive care unit, with virtually all visitors barred. After that—IF he survives to that point—it will be a long period of bed rest while we hope and pray no blood clots form.

"So, truly, Father, there is absolutely nothing you can accomplish for your friend by remaining in London."

"But—"

"The doctor is correct, Father," said Koznicki. "You should go on with us. Don't forget: We still have Cardinal Boyle to protect. If there is any dramatic change in Reverend Toussaint's condition—for better or worse—we'll be only an hour away by plane in Ireland."

"I suppose you're right," said Koesler, without a great deal of conviction.

"Meanwhile, we'll notify Mrs. Toussaint, and make arrangements for her to come and be with her husband," Koznicki added.

"That very thought was just crossing my mind." Koesler sounded slightly heartened.

"Oh, and by the by, doctor," said Somerset, "the blackguards who did this aren't likely to be delighted when they discover he's still alive. So we'll be keepin' security on him around the clock."

The doctor nodded.

Koznicki smiled. "That is very good of you, Superintendent."

"Not at all. That's perfectly all right, Inspector. And not to worry: we'll get 'em. We'll get 'em as have done this to your friend. And you can put your bottom dollar on that!"

10

"Good afternoon, ladies and gentlemen, this is Captain Kamego. Welcome aboard for this little hop over the Irish Sea. Our flying time will be approximately fifty minutes. I'm afraid our altitude will not be sufficient to climb out of these clouds. So, while it was raining in London as we departed, it will be raining in Dublin when we arrive. But, as they say in Ireland, it is a soft day. If you've never experienced it, take my word, you're in for a treat. I just want to assure you, there is a sun up above these clouds. Take it on faith."

"And you must take what I am saying on faith also, your Eminence," said Inspector Koznicki. "You still need every bit as much protection and security as you have needed since we uncovered this plot."

Boyle loosened his safety belt and turned partly toward Koznicki. "You don't believe the danger is over . . . or at least diminished?"

"No, I know it is not, your Eminence. With all due reverence, you are still alive."

Boyle thoughtfully ran an index finger across his lips.

"Their plan is to do away with you," Koznicki continued. "They have attempted twice to do just that. They failed the first time and tried again. They failed the second time. We have every reason to believe they will try again."

"I suppose you are correct."

"I know these precautions we urge on you are irritating and that they restrict your movements on what was planned as your vacation, but you must understand their necessity."

Boyle gestured broadly, indicating his numerous relatives aboard the chartered plane. "Neither are they amused."

For Boyle's brothers, sisters, nieces, nephews, and cousins, this trip had been planned as an unalloyed vacation. The reality of being involved in a murder plot, even superficially, had dampened their enthusiasm appreciably.

"It cannot be helped," said Koznicki. "We can be sure that for Reverend Toussaint there is also little amusement."

"Poor man." Boyle shook his head slowly. "That poor, poor man! When I heard what happened to him, as you know, I would have canceled the tour at that point if you had not convinced me that we must continue on as scheduled."

"As I said last night, Eminence, this is turning out to be like an unpleasant but unfortunately necessary operation. We will expose those who are responsible for this plot by luring them to the surface and flushing them out, as was done in Rome and is being done in London."

"And I am the bait."

"Unfortunately, Eminence. But we are closing in; we're getting to the root of it.

"And now, if you will excuse me, I must go speak with Father Koesler."

As Koznicki rose and left him, Boyle picked up his breviary. Many priests, particularly the younger ones, had discarded this collection of daily prayers which was, technically, obligatory. And though most of those who read it did so from an English translation, Boyle continued to read it in Latin. He turned to his favorite psalm and prayed it: *"Etsi incedam in valle tenebrosa, non timebo mala, quia tu mecum es. Virga tua et baculus tuus: haec me consolantur."*

"Yea, though I walk through the valley of the shadow of death, I will fear no evil: for thou art with me; thy rod and thy staff they comfort me."

"Ladies and gentlemen, we're going to experience a bit of

turbulence for a little while. So, as much as possible, please stay in your seats. And buckle up.'' The seat belt sign lit up.

"Do you think he'll recover?'' Pat Lennon asked.

"Geez, I don't know,'' Joe Cox replied. "The list of his injuries reads like an anatomy lesson. Just about every bone in his body is broken and the ones that aren't broken are dislocated. And on top of that, he's an old geezer—somewhere in his fifties.''

Lennon laughed aloud. "I'll have to remind you of that when you reach your fifties, lover.''

Cox reddened. He seldom blushed. But his statement had been foolish and he, to his credit, immediately realized that. "I'll never be fifty. Peter Pan and I, we're never going to grow up.''

Privately, Lennon would have agreed that in some ways Cox probably would never grow up. She was willing to live with that, though not marry it.

"This trip hasn't turned out at all the way **we** planned it,'' Cox observed.

"If it had,'' Lennon responded, "we'd be back in Detroit now. I'd be pounding my CRT and you'd be laboring over your VDT. Our story would have concluded in Rome.''

"Yeah. I must admit I thought this was just going to be a few predictable, dusty ceremonies that you could just as well cover by Italian TV from a friendly bar. It's lucky I didn't try that.''

"You're damn right it's lucky. Pull a stunt like that and can you imagine what Nelson Kane would have done to you?''

"Yeah . . . but I'd rather not.''

"Speaking of how our tour has expanded, did you get a handout on the Irish itinerary?''

"Yeah, Boyle's secretary was giving them out as we boarded. You didn't get one? Here, take mine. There's only one major public appearance—at a cathedral in Dublin. The rest of the time, Boyle and his relatives will be sightseeing and visiting other relatives.''

"Which cathedral? Are you sure it's a cathedral?'' Lennon quickly scanned the sheet.

"What difference does it make?''

"You're not paying very close attention, Joe. There are

two cathedrals in Dublin; but neither is Catholic—they're both Church of Ireland. Then there's what they call the procathedral—St. Mary's. *That's* Catholic.''

"I thought everything in Ireland was Catholic.''

"It was until a Pope gave Ireland to England.''

"Huh?''

"Nicholas Breakspear, the one and only English Pope, in effect gave Ireland to England.''

"I didn't know that.''

"You will also be surprised to know that after the Republic of Ireland freed itself from English rule, it didn't repossess all the churches that had been taken from them by their English conquerors. So,'' she located on the information sheet the site for the public ceremony, "the cathedral in question will be St. Patrick's. Now you would think that would have to be a Catholic church, wouldn't you?''

Cox nodded. "But I'd be wrong, right?''

"Right. It's Church of Ireland and the resting place of one Jonathan Swift. But there isn't much more by way of public appearances on the agenda. Looks like we can do some sightseeing ourselves.''

"Great.''

"They've got a nifty series of nice, cozy bed-and-breakfast places over here.''

"Sounds exactly like the kind of vacation that was planned for me. Bed and breakfast. We just get out of bed for breakfast and then hop right back in.''

Lennon smiled. "What about the sightseeing?''

"I would be seeing a lot of my favorite sight.''

"Joe, you have put an entirely new light on the maxim that travel is broadening.''

"Ladies and gentlemen, this is the Captain. We'll be touching down at Dublin International Airport in approximately twenty minutes. The temperature is fifty-seven degrees Fahrenheit. It is overcast and, of course, raining. But it is a soft rain.''

"So you think it was the Rastafarians who abducted and beat Ramon?'' Koesler asked.

"I do indeed,'' said Koznicki. "Who else? Besides, Father, they left their calling card.''

"That's right; they did.'' Koesler reflected for a moment.

"What do you make of the fact that the symbol was an open hand instead of a fist?"

"At this juncture, Father, we can only speculate. Either could be symbolic of the black power movement. Perhaps our Rastafarian splinter party uses the symbols interchangeably.

"As a matter of fact, the Rastafarians being held by Scotland Yard in connection with the attack on Cardinals Boyle and Whealan deny any knowledge of the attack on Toussaint and also of any symbols. However, it is quite common for accused persons, just arrested, to deny everything. And, it is helpful to realize that we are not dealing here with a rational or well-coordinated group. Don't forget, these are largely unlettered men whose incense is marijuana! And who may be lucky if they can remember anything they've done, much less why they've done it."

"But why would they attack Ramon? He is, by no stretch of the imagination, in the running for the Papacy."

"No, of course not." Koznicki was letting out his seat belt, giving himself plenty of room prior to buckling it. "But he has proved very successful in frustrating their efforts to do away with Cardinal Boyle. It was the Reverend Toussaint, you will recall, who prevented the assailant in Rome from harming the Cardinal. I would suggest the Rastafarians simply decided to eliminate their antagonist."

"You think, then, that they meant to kill him?"

"Oh, yes. That beating was certainly intended to be fatal. The only reason it was not, I believe, was because they underestimated the Reverend's strong constitution. Even the doctor at Hammersmith was amazed at the Reverend's stamina."

"But why the beating?" Koesler almost instinctively gripped the armrests as the plane began its gradual descent. "If they wanted to kill him, why didn't they just do it and get it over? Their attacks on Cardinals Claret and Gattari—on Cardinal Boyle, for that matter—show they are not strangers to good-sized knives. And they seem to have no hesitancy in using them. Why not just kill Ramon outright?"

"That," Koznicki responded, "must remain another matter for speculation until such time as those responsible are apprehended or until, perhaps, the Reverend recovers."

"Any theories?"

"Oh, I would imagine they were trying to make an example of him. Their raison d'être, as blacks in exile, is to return to their homeland, which they recognize, for reasons of their own, as Ethiopia. Some few of them, again for reasons of their own, believe the figure of the Pope to be the 'Satan of Babylon,' and as such, much responsible for their enslaved condition.

"Now in their campaign to eliminate candidates for the Papacy, to be effectively stopped by another black man perhaps is just too great an affront. They wish to make an example of this black 'renegade,' so they decide not only to kill him, but (a) to beat him to death, and (b) to leave his body where it will be found and thus, in effect, send a message—a warning—to others who might have thoughts of getting in their way."

Koesler shuddered. "I guess I just don't understand how anyone could do that to another human. I find such violence simply incredible."

"It is a violent world, Father. In police work, especially in homicide, one unfortunately becomes quite accustomed to this sort of thing. For some it is not enough to commit the ultimate act of violence—the taking of a human life; for such types, total satisfaction comes only through inflicting preliminary agony as well."

The plane touched down smoothly and taxied toward the terminal.

"So," said Koesler, relaxing his grip on the armrest, "what's on your agenda for Ireland?"

"Actually," Koznicki replied, "I believe I will have the opportunity to enjoy a few days of recreation before the religious ceremony on Saturday evening at St. Patrick's."

"Really? I didn't think you would be able to relax until we get back to Detroit."

"There is very little else to do for the next few days. There are no public ceremonies scheduled until Saturday evening. The Boyle clan will be traveling around the various counties sightseeing and visiting relatives."

"Won't there be danger even in that?"

"A minimal amount at most. There are no publicized itineraries or agendas. Even if an assailant wanted to attack the Cardinal, there would be no way of figuring out where he was going to be in time to plan an attack. And since many of the Cardinal's relatives live in villages where everyone knows everyone else, the unexplained presence of a stranger would be immediately taken note of. Plus the fact that if one wanted an accessible target, the Cardinal will be at his most vulnerable at the ecumenical ceremony in St. Patrick's.

"However, I have been in touch with Liam O'Connor, who is Commissioner of Police for the Republic of Ireland. He fully understands the situation and will take every precaution to provide security for the Cardinal, not only at the public ceremony but also throughout his stay in Ireland.

"All in all, I feel reasonably confident about the Cardinal's safety, at least until the Saturday evening at St. Patrick's."

The plane rolled to a stop at the terminal gate.

"Well, then," Koesler unfastened his seat belt, "do you have any plans between now and Saturday evening?"

"None to speak of." Koznicki snapped open his seat belt but did not rise. He was in no hurry to deplane. Or rather he was in no hurry to stand crouched over while a motionless line of passengers blocked the aisle.

"What would you think of joining me?"

"Of course. If it is not troublesome, I would be pleased to join you." After a pause, "What did you have in mind?"

"Well, this afternoon I plan to visit Trinity College Library, mostly to see the Book of Kells, and then I was going to see about tickets for a play this evening."

"That sounds excellent."

"You may not think the rest of my plans are as enjoyable."

"Oh?"

"Tomorrow, I plan to rent a car and drive up to Boyle to see the town, the river, and the old abbey. My maternal grandfather came from there. A friend of mine is part owner of a pub in the neighboring village of Gurteen. Before we left Detroit, he urged me to spend the night there if I got as far as Boyle. How does that sound to you?"

"Just different enough to be very interesting. Are you sure there will be room for two at the pub?"

"Reasonably. But I'll reconfirm that before we leave Dublin."

"Strange," the aisle cleared, Koznicki stood, "I have

known you so long and so well. Yet I did not know of your Irish ancestry. Irish and German, are you?''

''Afraid so.''

''And not a drop of Polish?''

''No.''

''A pity. You might have had a bright future in the Church.''

IRELAND

By prearrangement, Koesler and Koznicki met at 3:00 P.M. in the lobby of their hotel, the Royal Dublin on O'Connell Street.

"How is your room, Inspector?"

"Fine; first-rate. And yours?"

"The best so far on this trip."

"Now, where was it you said we were going first?"

"Trinity College."

"Ah, yes: the Book of Kells."

"Exactly."

They took a few steps through the lobby. It was a relatively small, functional area with a convenient registration desk at the rear and just enough room for a small crowd to gather.

Seated at the left on banquettes against the wall were several nuns in the modified blue habit of the Religious Sisters of Mercy. And appropriately so, thought Koesler, since the order had been founded in Ireland, and the foundress, Mother McAuley, was buried here at the Mother House in Dublin.

The nuns were alike in their uniforms, their milk-white, rosy-cheeked complexions, and in the beatific smiles that appeared when they spotted Koesler's clerical collar. Like a row of sailors sounding off, each sister in turn nodded happily in Koesler's direction while mouthing, "Good afternoon, Father."

Koesler smiled and nodded back.

Koznicki stopped just short of the revolving doors and looked about. "Father," he said to Koesler, who had halted beside him, "since we arrived in Dublin—I know it has been only a short while—but have you had the impression of being watched . . . or followed?"

Koesler thought for a moment, but was unaware of any such perception. "I can't say that I have."

Koznicki glanced about again, then shrugged. "It is probably nothing. Perhaps I have been overly apprehensive lately."

"That's probably it, Inspector. You need to relax."

They exited the hotel through the revolving doors, then stopped in the middle of a busy sidewalk on the very wide, historically significant, and statue-punctuated O'Connell Street.

"I know it's within easy walking distance," said Koesler, "but I'm not certain which way."

A gentle—or soft—rain was falling steadily. If one stood in it long enough one would be soaked. But for the moment, the drops splattered off their hats and raincoats.

Koesler approached a passerby, a medium-sized man perhaps in his mid-forties. "I beg your pardon, sir, but could you tell us the way to Trinity College?"

The man squinted up at him through the rain. Spying the clerical collar, he whipped off his cap and stood at a sort of awkward attention.

"Well, Father, is it Trinity College you're wanting? Actually, it's not a hundred miles from here!"

"We suspected it was nearby." Koesler, as he noted that the man rolled his r's, wished he wouldn't stand at attention bareheaded in the rain. "But we wondered in which direction. Could you tell us?"

"I could."

There was a pause. Then, "Yes?"

"Well, now, Father, you'd be going down O'Connell Street here, the very street we're on. Is that clear so far?"

"As a bell."

"Well, then, Father, you'd be crossing the Liffey at the

O'Connell Bridge. Are you acquainted with the Liffey then, Father?''

"Yes.''

"Of course you are. What could I be thinking of? Well, then, Father, you'll be crossing the Liffey, as I've said, by the O'Connell Street Bridge. You'll keep on going—a slight jog to your right it is, on Westmoreland Street. And then, Father, ahead on your right you'll be seeing Dame Street. And right on the corner, on your abrupt right, you'll see a large, white building.'' He paused.

"And that's Trinity College?''

"It is not.''

Throughout this one-sided colloquy Koznicki's smile continued to widen.

"That would be the Bank of Ireland. Actually, directly across the street—there's some vicious traffic and many's the crash on that very corner—as I was saying, directly across the street would be Trinity College itself. Is that clear now, Father?''

"Crystal.''

His face radiated triumph. "Is it books you'd be looking for?''

"That's right.''

The triumph glowed more brightly. "It's the Book of Kells, then?''

"You're very perceptive, sir.''

Raindrops trickled into the upraised corners of the man's mouth.

Koesler hesitated, but finally decided, against his better judgment, to essay one more step. "Now, from Trinity, could you tell me how we get to the Dublin Gate Theatre?''

"I can. But you'll never make it. Begging your pardon, Father, but follow me.''

He pulled on his cap and led Father Koesler and Inspector Koznicki down O'Connell Street. Starting with the General Post Office Building, which was bombarded half to shreds during the Easter Uprising of 1916, their self-appointed guide gave them a running commentary on the historicity of nearly every building they passed . . . including the McDonald's hamburger emporium.

2

"Joe!" Pat Lennon admonished, "if we're going to spend our declining years together in Sun City, you're just going to have to remember to drive on the left side of the road."

"Oh, yeah." Cox eased the rented Toyota from the right to the left side of the road. "It's hard enough getting used to a manual gearshift again—plus, it's on the wrong side of the steering wheel—without having to remember to drive on the wrong side of the road. But you're right: going over one of these hills on the right side of the road could lead to the closest encounter of the worst kind."

"I love it!" Pat shrieked. "Because we in the States drive on the right side of the road, everybody who drives on the left drives on the 'wrong' side. Boy! Talk about your ugly American!"

They drove on in silence for a brief time, while Cox concentrated on a reversed style of driving.

"I can certainly see why they call this the Emerald Isle," said Cox, glancing at the verdant fields and green shadings of the bogs.

"Wait till you get a look at the Burren to the south—or worse, at Connaught, up a bit north of here. It was Cromwell, that clone of Attila, who vowed to drive the Irish to hell or Connaught."

Cox shook his head. "You are a source of constant amazement. How do you know so much about this place?"

"Well, for one thing, for such a small island, it has a fascinating history. It was known as the Land of Saints and Scholars and—watch it, Joe! We're getting into Claregalway; there's a thirty-mile speed limit up ahead."

Cox touched the brake and slowed the car. They glided easily through the quiet streets, encountering hardly any traffic.

As they left Claregalway behind, they saw on the road ahead an elderly woman laboriously pedaling her bicycle uphill.

"Joe, pull over. Maybe she could use a lift."

"But she's got a bike."

"Joe, there's a rack on the roof. You can put the bike up there."

"But—"

"Joe, she's an old lady."

"Right."

They slowed to a stop several yards ahead of the cyclist. Lennon got out and turned to face the woman, who had slowed to a stop. "May we give you a lift?"

After some protestations that the trip had been made many times before and would be again, the woman finally allowed Cox to heft her light, well-worn bicycle atop the car. Then she climbed into the back and settled in as the journey resumed.

Pat turned to smile at the woman gently fanning herself in the back seat. "My name is Pat Lennon."

"Oh, then, and mine would be Conlon, Mrs. Mary Ellen Conlon." Eyes crinkling and face creasing into well-worn laugh lines, she returned Lennon's smile. There was indeed, thought Pat, a world of truth in the old song about when Irish eyes are smiling. Mary Ellen Conlon must have been a real beauty as a young woman.

"And this," Lennon indicated her companion, "is Joseph Cox. We're newspaper reporters from Detroit, Michigan."

"Ah, and that would be where they make all those automobiles, now, wouldn't it?"

"Among a few other things, yes," said Cox, keeping his eyes on the road.

Suddenly, doubt touched Mrs. Conlon's face. "Lennon and Cox," she repeated. "And were your people from England, then?"

Lennon chuckled. She wondered whether Mrs. Conlon had visions of being kidnapped by the English. "I'm afraid Joe has English ancestory, but Lennon is my married name. My maiden name was Cahill."

Mrs. Conlon's furrowed brow smoothed. The score read Irish-2, English-1.

It was Cox's turn to chuckle. "Of course; why didn't I think of it? No wonder you know so much about Irish history."

"It's a proud history, Mr. Cox." Their passenger's tone was at once defensive and assertive.

"I'm sure it is, Mrs. Conlon," Cox replied. "We were just talking about Connaught and Cromwell."

"Ah, the divil himself. He wanted to rid the world of the Irish, but we outlasted him, we did."

"Not only him," Lennon agreed, "but everyone and everything that, barring near miracles, should have destroyed the Irish.''

"You mean the Famine?'' Cox asked.

"Oh, much more than the Famine—though that alone could have done it,'' Lennon replied. "The first Celtic tribes came here a few centuries before Christ, and their battles among themselves might have become a sort of suicidal genocide. But, regardless, they enjoyed a golden age of their culture until the late eighth century. Despite all the wars and fighting, poetry and art flourished. And each of the Celtic kings kept a bard, a poet-in-residence, and of course each village had its *seanachie*, the storyteller who passed on the oral traditions of the people.

"Then came St. Patrick and Christianity, which produced a lot of scholars, saints, and missionaries.''

"And the Book of Kells,'' Cox supplied.

"The Book of Kells,'' Lennon agreed, "the illuminated manuscripts of the Gospels. But then the country was invaded by the Norsemen who, again, might have destroyed everything if it hadn't been for the great king, Brian Boru.

"Boru broke the strength of the invaders at the Battle of Clontarf and established a peace that lasted 150 years, during which Ireland was free of all foreign influences.

"And then, along came Adrian IV.''

"The English Pope you mentioned on the plane?''

"The same: Nicholas Breakspear. He gave overlordship of Ireland to Henry II of England. After that, things went steadily downhill and continued in that direction for roughly 800 years.

"Gradually, the English took possession of the land and the Irish were lucky to have enough room for a hovel and a little earth in which to grow their precious potatoes.

"Then, when Henry VIII broke with the Church, he feared a Catholic invasion. So he stepped even harder on Catholic Ireland and established as his own the 'Church of Ireland.' Which didn't daunt the Irish Catholics; it just drove the wedge between Ireland and England deeper.

"The Irish rebellion in the mid-seventeenth century was the one crushed by our genocidal friend Cromwell. It cost hundreds of thousands of Irish lives and, once again, nearly destroyed the race.''

At this point, Mrs. Conlon began to hum softly. Cox wasn't sure, but he thought he caught a tune that sounded like "Wearin' of the Green."

"And on and on it went from uprising to uprising, until 1846 and 1847, when the potato crops failed. For the majority of the Irish, the potato was their sole source of nourishment. And, while the English did little to help, and even continued to export Irish produce to England, two million Irish men, women, and children starved to death over a two-year period, or died of disease brought on by starvation.

"Add to that all the Irish who fled on what came to be called 'coffin ships' to North America, and you've got to wonder how the Irish race survived!"

"But for the Grace of God!" Mrs. Conlon said, almost as a prayer.

"That's about as complete a thumbnail sketch of a nation's history as I've ever heard," Cox commended.

"Once I get started on Ireland, it's hard to stop."

"We're coming into Galway, Mrs. Conlon," Cox announced needlessly, as signs were everywhere. "Is this as far as you go?"

"It is not," she said. "But I'll not be troubling you two young people any further. This is fine, just fine."

"No, no," Lennon protested, "we're in no hurry. Besides, we want to drive out on the peninsula and get a look at the shore and the bay."

"Well, if that's the case," said Mrs. Conlon, "I'll just stay with you until you get to Barna, if it's all the same."

"Sure," said Cox, "no trouble at all."

As they left Galway, to the left they could see the bay. A few minutes later, as they neared Barna, far out, they could make out the Aran Islands.

"This will be fine," said Mrs. Conlon, "just fine."

"There's a pub up just a few more feet," said Cox. "How about joining us for a little drink?"

"Well, if it's no trouble," said Mrs. Conlon, "I don't mind if I do."

Cox pulled the car off the road into the small parking lot that fronted the pub.

There were a few elderly men and one middle-aged woman inside. After waiting several seconds for their eyes to become accustomed to the dim interior, Cox and Lennon and their passenger took a table near the middle of the rectangular room.

Lennon and Cox each ordered a Guinness. Mrs. Conlon's order was, "a half one," which, to Cox and Lennon's interest, turned out to be a whiskey, neat. Lennon and Cox began sipping their stout while Mrs. Conlon merely contemplated the amber liquid that rested quietly in her glass without benefit of ice or water.

"And where will you two young people be going from here?"

"We're going to try to make the Connemara circle," said Lennon.

"Ah, that would be ambitious," Mrs. Conlon observed. "But you'll love the Twelve Bens, as well as Killary Harbor. And then of course there's Croagh Patrick. It's a grand sight, all in all."

Cox stared out a side window. Nearly sotto voce, he sang, "And watch the suds flow down by Galway Bay . . ."

"I think you'll find that's '. . . and watch the sun go down on Galway Bay,' Mr. Cox," said Mrs. Conlon.

"Not according to the Clancy Brothers," said Cox.

"But come now," he continued raising his glass, "all those things the English—my people—did to the Irish—your people—took place long ago. The Republic of Ireland is free and, I'm told, forgiving. So, how about a farewell, a parting toast? How about it?"

Lennon and Mrs. Conlon obligingly raised their glasses.

"The Queen!" Cox tipped his glass to his lips.

"Up her kilt!" Mrs. Conlon added, and downed her whiskey in a swallow.

As Mrs. Conlon was leaving the pub, she paused to look back. Joe Cox was still choking and Pat Lennon was still pounding him on the back.

3

"I had intended to tell you before the play began, Father, but, as it turned out, there simply was no time."

"What is it, Inspector?"

Koznicki and Koesler had met at the Dublin Gate Theatre just as the performance was about to begin. They had had time only to find their places and be seated as the curtain rose on Act One.

Koesler had had in tow one Daren Ahern, the helpful gentleman who earlier in the day had led them to Trinity College and the theater box office. As a reward, over Ahern's protests, Koesler had bought him a ticket too.

It was now intermission and the three men were standing in a tightly packed crowd on the sidewalk just outside the theater.

"Mr. Ahern," said Koznicki, "would you mind very much getting the three of us some orange juice at the stand in the lobby?"

"I would not mind at all," said Ahern, almost snapping to attention. "It would be a privilege and a pleasure."

As Ahern plowed back through the crowd, Koznicki said, "What I have to say is for your ears alone, Father. Just before leaving for the theater tonight, I phoned Hammersmith Hospital in London."

"You did?" Koesler asked anxiously. "How is Ramon?"

"In a word, better. The doctors, of course, continue to marvel . . . and to be most guarded in their prognosis. But the Reverend Toussaint has been removed from the intensive care unit."

"He has? That's wonderful!"

"I thought so also. But the doctors continue to caution that the possibility of complications from any number of sources is very great. The Reverend remains on the critical list."

So far so good, thought Koesler. But what was there in what Koznicki had said that couldn't have been said in front of anyone, including a stranger such as Ahern?

Koznicki was about to address the point. "This is what I wanted to tell you alone: I asked the doctors to release the information that their prognosis of the Reverend Toussaint's condition is such that they do not expect him to regain consciousness—ever—even if he should happen to recover physically."

Koesler's mouth dropped open. "But you just said the doctors believe he is improved and they've removed him from intensive care!"

"That is correct. But the people who beat the Reverend

wanted not only his suffering but his death. The fact that he is not dead must be a source of frustration—and concern—to them.

"It is the same with Cardinal Boyle: There are those who want him dead. That he has survived two assaults is undoubtedly galling to his would-be assassins. We must assume they will continue to try to achieve their ultimate aim . . . and that is why we continue to guard him."

"And you feel the same may happen to Ramon."

"He is still alive and his enemies want him dead, certainly. But, added to that, there is always the possibility that if the Reverend should regain consciousness he might be able to identify his assailants."

"And consider this, Father: Whoever attacked the Reverend seemed determined to exact revenge not only by taking his life but also by brutalizing him in the process. A publicized prognosis of a permanent coma—pray God it does not prove true—should more than satisfy his enemies. If in some way they could have transformed him into a vegetable, they surely would have. With this information released, they should be content that he is condemned to this living death . . . sufficiently content not to again attempt his actual extinction."

"How shrewd, Inspector. An excellent plan!"

"The Polish mind never rests." Koznicki could not resist a grin.

Koesler grinned back, but stopped suddenly. "Oh, I almost forgot: What about Emerenciana?"

"His wife is at the Reverend's bedside. She arrived today and will remain with him."

"I'm glad. I'll phone her tomorrow."

"Now then, isn't it a grand play, though?" Ahern returned, on cue as it were, bearing three paper cups of orange juice. He had all he could do to avoid spilling them as he elbowed his way through the crowd.

"Yes," Koesler agreed, "I'm so glad they're having this revival of Brian Friel's *Translations*. I read some reviews of it when it premiered here in 1980 but I never thought I'd get a chance to see it. It is so inventively done, don't you think?"

"Oh, yes, definitely," said Koznicki. "I admire the device of having everyone in the cast speaking English while the interpreter pretends he is translating for the Irish, who are supposed to be speaking in their native tongue, unable to understand English.'' He shook his head. ''It's hard to comprehend the English taking over Irish life to such a degree that they would insist on the Irish abandoning their native tongue, and then go on to change the names of places in Ireland so they would sound more natural to the English ear!''

''Arra, but that was how it was just the same.'' Ahern sucked in his breath sharply.

Koesler was jolted. He recalled from his childhood, members of his mother's family, the Irish side of his ancestry, making the same sound. He hadn't heard it from the time the last of the elderly Boyle clan had passed away until now.

''The hedge schools they have in this play,'' Ahern went on, ''used to be the only way the Irish traditions and language could be passed on. Not to mention havin' to hold the Holy Mass with the English in hot pursuit, and havin' to hide the holy priest of God from them too. Both priests and schoolmasters were banned and hunted with bloodhounds . . . the English paid a bounty of five pounds for the head of a wolf . . . or the head of a priest. Not meanin' any irreverence, Father, but that's the way it was.''

''It's a wonder any of you Irish survived,'' Koznicki observed, empathetic from the awareness of centuries of persecution of his own Catholic ancestors in Poland.

''That is so,'' said Ahern, ''we're only a tiny island, but look, we've populated half the United States.''

Koesler and Koznicki laughed.

''Well, that may be a slight exaggeration,'' Ahern admitted, ''but only slight.''

The marquee lights flashed on and off several times.

''I think that's management's way of telling us it's time for Act Two,'' said Koesler.

At that instant, several things happened almost simultaneously. Someone jogged Ahern's elbow, causing him to spill some orange juice in Koesler's direction. Koesler, in turn, in an attempt to avoid the juice, jumped back, bumping forcibly into someone behind him.

''Excu—'' Koesler was almost deafened by a loud roar immediately behind him. Instinctively, he threw his arm up protectively, and turned. As he did, he saw Koznicki slump to the pavement.

Koesler was so stunned, as were the other bystanders, that no one got a good look at the gunman, who immediately on firing had turned and run swiftly into the night.

Koesler, whose spirits had been buoyed by the news of Toussaint's improvement, now felt drained. He did not know who had fired the shot or why. All he knew was that his dear friend, Inspector Koznicki, was lying on the sidewalk, very, very still.

Koesler dropped to his knees beside his friend. He hesitated to touch the Inspector before medical help arrived. Whispering, Koesler gave conditional absolution—conditioned by whether there were any sins to be forgiven; by whether, indeed, there was still life.

Then Koesler noticed, on the sidewalk, at the very spot where the assailant had stood, the imprint of a black hand.

4

It was not a small room, as hospital rooms go, but it was crowded. Besides the large patient in the bed, the room held a nurse, a doctor, a police officer, and a priest.

"You're a lucky man, Inspector," said the doctor, "a very lucky man."

"And there," said Inspector Koznicki, indicating Father Koesler, "is my lucky charm."

Koesler came near to blushing. "I think you're mistaken Inspector; your lucky charm is a self-effacing Irishman named Daren Ahern. If he hadn't spilled a cup of orange juice in my direction, I would never have jumped backward into the gunman and diverted his shot."

"Wherever the bit of luck came from," said the doctor, "you are the beneficiary, Inspector. There's no doubt about that at all. The gun was fired at point-blank range. It could easily have killed you on the spot if it had hit you in a vital area. And we must assume whoever fired that shot knew what he was aiming at.

"As it is, the bullet is lying up against your spine in the lumbar region. And there it just might remain for good."

"You're not going to remove it then?" asked Garda Superintendent Thomas J. O'Reardon, who was head of the Republic's Murder Squad.

"'fraid I can't answer that one just yet, Superintendent. It's in a surgically hazardous area. We've just got to watch it for the next little while. But if the Inspector here experiences no symptoms such as numbness or excessive pain, and if there's no infection or bleeding, we may just leave bad enough alone."

"That would suit me fine," said the Inspector, who was in no hurry for an operation. "There are many, indeed, who, from a war, an assault, or an accident, are walking around healthy with lead still in them."

The doctor sucked in his breath sharply.

There it is again, thought Koesler, that same sound. It must be endemic to the Irish.

"That's God's truth, Inspector," the doctor said. "There's many a patient walks out of this hospital carrying inside him the same bullet he came in with. And most of them, over the years, are none the worse for it. We'll just be keeping compression dressings on the wound, like the one the nurse is putting on just now, and pumping antibiotics into you, against any kind of infection. And now, if the nurse is done . . ."

"Yes, that I am, doctor."

". . . then we'll just be leaving these good men alone to carry on their business."

The doctor and nurse exited the room.

"I've set up two Gardai outside your door, Inspector," said Superintendent O'Reardon, "there'll be twenty-four-hour security on this room."

"I thank you," said Koznicki.

"Two Gardai!" Koesler marveled.

"Yes, indeed, Father," said O'Reardon. "Someone out there wants the Inspector here dead and we very much intend that they shall not succeed. We generally have fewer than fifty murders per annum here. And we very much object to the killing of a fellow officer."

"It is just as in the case of Cardinal Boyle and the Reverend Toussaint, Father," said Koznicki. "Someone wants them dead, but they are still alive, so we must protect them, just as the Irish police will protect me while we try to apprehend those involved in this whole plot."

"But why shoot you?" Koesler asked.

"If we were back in Detroit, Father," Koznicki replied, "I am sure I could find many criminals with whom I have dealt who could find reasons for bearing a grudge against me. But," he exchanged glances with O'Reardon, "I fear I was asleep at the switch here. It seems quite clear that those who wish to get at Cardinal Boyle have now retrenched and are determined to eliminate any and all obstacles. That would explain why they attempted to kill the Reverend Toussaint as well as why they attempted to kill me.

"The Reverend foiled their attempt on the life of the Cardinal once, as have I. With the two of us out of the way, I assume they feel they will have easier access to the Cardinal. But they have failed to take into account the Gardai of Ireland."

"Indeed!" said O'Reardon. "We plan to be more than ready for them. We have both the Crime Task Force and the Security Task Force with His Eminence now as he tours the country. And even Sir Robert Peel himself would be amazed at the number of Gardai we'll have in St. Patrick's Cathedral Saturday evening.

"But now, Inspector," O'Reardon turned toward the patient, "you shouldn't be blaming yourself so much for being caught off guard last night. We had as much information about these crimes as you. We should have anticipated this. And on top of it all, we're the very ones whose job it is to protect our good visitors as well as our citizens. We should have had some plainclothes with you. But you can bet your bottom dollar that we'll be taking better care of you from now on."

"All is well that ends well." Koznicki smiled wanly. "And let us hope this will end well."

"We'll not only hope, we'll pray," Koesler affirmed.

"I'll be leaving you two now," said O'Reardon, retrieving his hat. "I'll just give you my card."

The card carried his name, rank, and the address: Garda Siochana, Phoenix Park, Dublin 8, and the phone: 771156.

"And let me just scribble on here my home phone number." He laid the card on the bedside stand. "Please, Inspector, feel free to ring me up anytime, should you have any need or wish to communicate with me."

With that and parting handshakes for Koznicki and Koesler, O'Reardon left the room.

"Are you comfortable, Inspector?" Koesler seated himself in the room's single chair. "I mean, you don't appear to be in pain."

"How does the expression go: But for the honor of it, I would just as soon be in Philadelphia. This is the first time I have been shot, and it is damned uncomfortable, not to mention painful. But," Koznicki shrugged, "there is nothing for it. In my profession, one learns to live with the knowledge that you can be hurt or even killed. It is a dangerous and violent world, as I have said . . . and the police officer lives at the very focal point of this violence."

"Why do I feel so guilty?" Koesler looked up with a half grin, half grimace. "It's as if somehow I were responsible. If I hadn't invited you and gotten tickets to the theater, you wouldn't have been there and, perhaps, wouldn't have been shot."

Koznicki started to chuckle, then stopped, wincing. "Oh! Now I know what people mean when they say it only hurts when they laugh.

"But please, Father, do not think those thoughts. Whoever did this to me would have done it whether I had gone to the theater or not. He probably had been keeping me under surveillance ever since we arrived in Ireland, waiting for his opportunity. And when he saw us purchasing tickets, his plan took shape.

"But the same thing would have happened had I gone to a pub or a restaurant or even merely for a walk. Actually, despite what the Superintendent said, *I* was the one who was negligent. I should have perceived that with the Reverend Toussaint out of the way I was the one remaining obstacle who had a track record of thwarting their plans. I should have been more vigilant.

"As for your feeling guilty—not a moment of it! No, on the contrary, Father, being with you in those circumstances was undoubtedly what saved my life. If you hadn't jarred the gunman's arm, he would have accomplished what he set out to do, and you would now be busy arranging to ship my body back to Detroit for burial." Koznicki shuddered as he verbalized, for the first time in his life, a scenario that might follow his death.

"But," he said more brightly, "now for your tour, Father. Where are you going and when do you begin?"

"Oh, I'm canceling that. I'm going to stay here and keep you company."

"Nonsense! There is nothing you can do for me here. I will be well taken care of by the medical staff and I have every confidence in the Gardai. Besides, short of killing me, the Rastafarians have accomplished their immediate purpose: to prevent me from attending Saturday's service at St. Patrick's. So, perhaps they will not bother with me again.

"You see, there is a difference between my situation and that of the Reverend Toussaint. They not only determined to kill him; obviously, they wished to inflict agony on him as well. There was none of that in their plans for me. They meant to dispatch me quickly with a single fatal bullet. And the Reverend remains in peril since, if he recovers sufficiently, he may be able to identify one or more of his assailants. Not only did I not see my attacker, none of the eyewitnesses was able to give a description of him. So, I should be safe for now.

"But yes, Father, there is one thing you can do for me before you go off on your tour. I have already spoken to Wanda by phone. But if you would just call and reassure her that I am all right. I told her I was, but," he smiled, "she may believe it better coming from you."

Koesler smiled back. "Of course. I'll be glad to call Wanda and tell her that you are doing very well in an Irish hospital surrounded by Sisters of Mercy who are tending to all your needs and fulfilling your every whim. And then I'll just start on my tour."

"Good. And when you return from the hinterlands, you can tell me all about the bogs."

"You really think I should go?"

"Absolutely. No question about it."

Koesler brightened. "Well, if you're sure—"

"I'm sure."

"Then I guess I will—through I do wish you were coming."

"Well, as I've said, you can tell me stories. When do you leave?"

Koesler glanced at his watch. "I'd better get going soon. I'll drive into Boyle this afternoon and look around for my roots, as it were, and then drive on to Gurteen. It's just a few miles beyond. Then I'll stay there one or two nights. Tomorrow, I'd like to just do a little sightseeing. Maybe drive down through Connaught to the Burren."

"That sounds like a most relaxing trip. And you still intend to stay at that pub in Gurteen?" The Inspector was smiling.

Koesler nodded.

"A priest in a pub!" He wouldn't laugh outright; he didn't want to hurt himself again. "That should shake the faith of the Irish."

"Perhaps. But my friend in Detroit insisted. On the one hand, I wouldn't want to offend him by not accepting his hospitality. And, on the other, it will be very convenient.

"Here . . ." Koesler searched his pockets until he found a small box of matches, "there's a picture of the pub on this matchbox."

Koznicki examined the box. The picture showed a large, two-story brick and wood building with the words, "Teach Murray" across its front.

" 'Teach Murray'? What in the world does that mean?"

"The very question I asked Chris Murray back in Detroit. It's Irish and it's pronounced 'Chalk Murray.' Chris explained 'Teach' as the equivalent of 'Chez' in French. I guess the closest we can come to it in English is 'Murray's Place.' Doesn't it look interesting?"

"Yes. So you will be staying there . . . oh, yes," he smiled again, "by all means do tell me all about it when you come back.

"But for now," his face took on a serious aspect, "will you give me your blessing, Father, please."

Koesler traced the sign of the cross over Koznicki. "May the blessing of Almighty God, the Father, the Son, and the Holy Spirit descend upon you and remain with you. Amen."

The two shook hands and Koesler left the hospital.

As he walked toward his rented car, a bright yellow late-model Ford Escort, he thought he heard someone call his name. Turning, he saw a well-dressed black man walking rapidly toward him. A gold watch chain was stretched across

the vest of his gray, pin-striped suit. His hair was closely
cropped. Koesler took him to be a professional man.

"It is Father Koesler, is it not?"

"Yes. And you are . . . ?"

"My name does not matter. I am a friend of Ramon
Toussaint."

Even if he had not said this, Koesler would have guessed
there might be some connection. The man spoke with the
Haitian accent that characterized Ramon's speech.

"He sent a message," the man said, without further
preamble, "asking us to look into a matter. We know of his
condition. We know also of his friendship with you. Since we
cannot give the information to him, we give it to you: The
Rastafarians are not in Ireland so they will make no attempt
here on the life of Cardinal Boyle."

He turned and walked quickly away.

"Wait!" Koesler called. "Who are you? How do I know—"
He stopped, sensing it would be futile to try to catch up with
the man or to expect any further discourse from him.

The priest stood motionless for some time, pondering the
stranger's message.

5

Talk about serpentine! Father Koesler thought as he left
Dublin and drove toward Boyle; the roads of Ireland seemed
to weave in and out and up and down more than any other
place he could recall. In addition, it had been many years
since he had driven a stick-shift automobile. Also, the gearshift was to the left of the steering wheel instead of to the
right.

And, to cap the climax, he had to remember to drive on the
left side of the road. It seemed that no sooner did he allow
himself the luxury of thinking things over than his car would
begin to slow down going up a hill and he would be forced to
shift down into third. He wondered how long it would be
before he would become accustomed to this car and the
driving procedures of this country. Ah, there seemed to be a
fairly long stretch of unswerving, flat road coming up. He

leaned back in the bucket seat and aimed the car down the straight and narrow.

What a strange message! And delivered by a stranger! After he had recovered from his surprise, he had returned to Koznicki's room and related his strange meeting to the Inspector.

Koznicki's initial reaction had been to doubt the authenticity of the message. They had no idea of the identity of the messenger nor any way of verifying the message. Just as easily as being true, it might as well have been a ploy to lull them into lowering their guard. After all, *somebody* had shot Koznicki.

Still, Koesler leaned toward belief. He was not a particularly intuitive person, but he had a strong feeling the message had been genuine.

He also had been perturbed since leaving the outskirts of Dublin by a strange but definite feeling that he was being followed. As often as he was able, what with all the uncommon distractions of driving this strange car in this foreign land, he glanced into the rearview mirror. But he saw nothing that he could in any way describe as unusual or untoward. Finally, he dismissed the possibility of being followed, and ascribed the sensation to tension or stress.

He returned to his consideration of the stranger and his message. If it was the truth—and Koesler strongly believed it was—the Detroit contingent could relax . . . at least during their Ireland stay.

Which was precisely what he intended to do. He deserved three days of rest and relaxation, he assured himself; he had paid his dues.

And, regardless of whether the message had been calculated to put them off their guard, he was positive the Irish police would be out in full complement and with intense vigilance at the single public ceremony on Cardinal Boyle's schedule. Sufficient unto that day was the possible evil thereof. Now, for some relaxation.

He had no sooner determined to relax when he spied coming toward him, over the crest of a hill not less than fifty yards ahead, a compact car about the same size as his Escort, but a foreign model. The oncoming vehicle was traveling at high speed on a collision course with Koesler's car.

The adrenalin began pumping. Did the Irish enjoy playing chicken? What should he do? Pull off the road to the left into a bog? Pull over to the right and chance a collision with some other driver who might come over the hill in the correct lane?

In the seconds that had passed since the car had appeared, typically, Koesler had come to no decision.

Suddenly, the other vehicle swerved to Koesler's right and, to his great relief, continued past him on the other side of the road. As it whizzed by, Koesler took considerable interest in the driver and passenger. Unless he was badly mistaken, the driver was Joe Cox and the passenger Patricia Lennon—who appeared to be giving Cox what-for. If Koesler was correct in his identification, they must be returning to Dublin after learning of the attempt on Inspector Koznicki's life.

He chuckled. Their excursion had been ended abruptly by a news story that needed reporting. While, with everything in as good order as possible in Dublin, and with the promise of no further trouble during their stay, *his* excursion was just beginning.

The engine seemed to be laboring. He looked down at the gearshift. It was still in third, where he had shoved it after slowing for Cox's near-miss. Koesler depressed the clutch and shifted into overdrive.

There appeared to be another fairly straight, flat stretch ahead. Gazing down the asphalt highway of indifference, Koesler mused, his mind turning to reminiscences with Irish overtones.

He recalled, and laughed aloud at the memory, the time in the seminary when some patriots, to celebrate St. Patrick's Day, had painted all the toilet seats green. In apparent response then, some others, to commemorate the Feast of the Circumcision, had painted them red.

His mind wandered on to Irish jokes. The one about Mrs. McGillicuddy, whose thirteen children all were in a peck of trouble in various precincts throughout greater New York. She was being consoled as well as admonished by her friendly parish priest.

"Ah, now, Mrs. McGillicuddy," said Father Murphy, "you must look for your inspiration, as well as your consolation, to the Holy Family. And particularly the Blessed Mother: think of her trials and tribulations, her sorrows, her afflictions—"

"Oh, yes," says Mrs. McGillicuddy bitterly. "Her and her *One*!"

He shifted as he drove through Carrick-on-Shannon, which he knew was the home of Nelson Kane's mother, one of Ireland's grandest and most delightful gifts to the City of Detroit.

Koesler smiled, depressed the clutch, and shifted to third for a brief but steep hill. Then, back in overdrive, he relaxed again and returned his thoughts to Irish humor.

He remembered the one Arthur Godfrey liked to tell about the small-town girl who became a dancer in New York City. Back home on a visit, she went to confession one Saturday at the parish church.

As luck would have it, she was the last one in line. So, after she had gone to confession, the priest left his confessional, and the two of them began to talk about her life as a dancer. "Now, isn't that wonderful," said the priest, "and why don't you just show me a bit of your routine?" So the girl did a couple of time steps and turned a cartwheel.

Just at that moment, Mrs. Murphy and Mrs. O'Toole entered the church to go to confession. Taking a look at what was going on outside Father McKiernan's confessional, Mrs. Murphy nudged Mrs. O'Toole: "Glory be to God, would you look at what Father is givin' out for penance, and me with me patched-up bloomers on!"

Koesler smiled again, as he shifted for another hill. He momentarily considered building up speed as he approached each hill so he wouldn't have to shift, but in, for him, a rare moment of prescience he also considered the odds of traveling up the hill at considerable velocity only to reach the crest and encounter another Joe Cox coming at him on the wrong side of the road. All things considered, he decided it would be less risky to continue shifting.

Then, he recalled, letting his mind shift back into neutral, there was the time one of his classmates was being measured for a pair of trousers by an Irish tailor, who announced quite loudly, "He's farty in the seat."

But, Koesler reflected, that was missing the point. Those were not genuine Irish jokes, not authentic Irish humor. They were the transplanted Irish-American, Pat-and-Mike humor.

He recalled hearing Liam Clancy offer a taste of genuine Irish humor. Now, how had it gone?

Oh, yes; it was coming back.

It had happened in a small Irish village, where, one rainy day, the parish priest came to the Maloney house to anoint the ailing grandmother. Over his head, he held an open umbrella. Now, it was the only, and, in fact, the first umbrella the villagers had ever seen. They couldn't get over it: a man carrying his own cloud over his head.

The priest entered the house and laid the big black umbrella, still open, on the hearth to dry.

All during the ceremony of the anointing, there were sidelong glances cast, as the eyes of all present kept wandering back to the Thing. None had seen such a sight ever.

By the time the anointing was over, the rain had stopped, and the old pastor forgot about his umbrella, leaving it on the hearth, and returning to the parish house without it.

Then, the woman of the house said to her husband, "I'll not have that *Thing*," jerking her head sidewise at it, "in my house." And she kept it up and wouldn't let the matter rest.

Well, they couldn't get the umbrella out of the door no matter which way they turned or twisted it. So the husband gathered the men of the village in for a consultation. They put their heads together and tried to figure out how to make the door wider without ruining the foundation, so they could get rid of the Thing.

Meanwhile, it began to rain again. The priest, recalling his umbrella, returned to the house, was admitted, picked up the umbrella, and walked to the door, the eyes of all upon him. He stopped, closed the umbrella, exited, and opened it, lifting it protectively over his head as he strode off.

Silence. Finally, the woman turned to her husband, nudged him, and said solemnly, "There's no doubt about it: *they've* got the power!"

Koesler laughed aloud, resolving to tell that to Inspector Koznicki when next they met.

His attention to the present returned as he entered a small town. So preoccupied had he been with his Irish humor that he had forgotten to look for a sign. But it was about the right distance from Dublin and there were some railroad tracks nearby.

He stopped, rolled down his window, and called to a passerby, "I beg your pardon, but could you tell me, is this Boyle?"

"It is that," said the man, who then noticed Koesler's clerical collar. Promptly, he whipped off his cap and stood bareheaded. "Is it the parish house you'd be wantin', Father?"

Most of the Irish, Koesler was learning, pronounced 'Father' as if it rhymed with 'lather.' He was also being made ever more aware that the Irish never used a simple yes or no in answer to a question.

"No, not really. I just sort of wanted to look around. My maternal grandfather came from this town." Koesler surprised himself by laying such ancestral claim with a touch of pride.

"Did he now? And would he have been a Boyle, by any chance?"

"Yes. Kevin Boyle."

"Ah, well, then, Father, have ya given any thought that some of yer relatives might still be here?"

"No, I haven't," Koesler admitted.

"Well, it's just possible, definitely possible, you know. The place is crawlin' with Boyles," the man exaggerated. "Beggin' yer pardon, Father, and meanin' no irreverence, but ya might just want to reconsider yer decision not to visit the parish house. Father'd know which among them might be yer kin. And he'd be pleased to be tellin' ya."

"Well, maybe," Koesler responded hesitantly.

"The parish house would be right down at the end of the street, Father. Ya can't miss it."

Koesler thanked him and drove on. He had no intention of calling at the local rectory or searching out any possible relatives. He wanted only to absorb some of the atmosphere and see for himself some of the things that his Irish ancestors had grown up and lived among.

He turned off before he reached the end of the street and drove through what seemed to be the center of town. Almost every parking space on the main thoroughfare was taken. That surprised him. Without quite knowing why, he had assumed that not many in a small Irish town would have cars. But there they were in a variety of vintages and makes, all compact or subcompact.

Eventually, he found a space at what seemed to be about midway down the main street. He pulled in, set the brake, and got out of the car. It was good to stretch his legs after a long drive. He began walking at a leisurely pace.

The people he encountered seemed genuinely pleased to see him. They were accustomed to seeing no priest but their own. So a stranger in clerical garb was a pleasant surprise, and there weren't that many surprises in Boyle. Since he was a priest, it was a pleasure for the deeply reverent Irish to greet him. All along his walk, men tipped their hats and women performed an abbreviated curtsy. All wore ear-to-ear grins, and the greeting, "Good afternoon to you, Father," was heard in the land.

He certainly hadn't received this sort of heartfelt welcome in Rome, London, or, for that matter, anywhere else—other than from the Sisters of Mercy in Dublin.

Ordinarily, Koesler yearned to be greeted in a neutral, matter-of-fact manner. His complaint was that people met him as a priest prejudiced either for or against him. And he considered either premature judgment unfair. But he had never been greeted with such evident warmth and almost childlike openness. And, he had to admit, he liked it. He remembered overhearing two Irishmen talking. "They don't apologize for bein' priests in this country!" one had said with vigor. Now, he understood.

Turning left at the corner, he found himself walking toward a bridge over what had to be the Boyle River. He reached the bridge and stood looking around at the town.

For its size, it held quite a few stores and shops. He wondered how many, if any, had been standing when his grandfather had left for the States little more than a century before.

More probably, this had been farm country owned by absentee landlords in England. The native Irish would have been fortunate indeed if they had been allowed to work the fields. And, in those years, they would have been lucky to harvest enough from the tortured land of that time for them to survive.

But the Boyle River, now boiling away in a swift current beneath him, would have been flowing. His grandfather had possibly fished the river from this very spot. In his imagination, he began to anthropomorphize the river as Hammerstein had done with the Mississippi.

He walked back to the main street and set off for the other end of town. It was there he came upon Boyle Abbey, or more properly, the ruins. The outer and some of the inner walls were standing, but that was about all that was left of it. That and the memories that were inseparable from it. It would have been no more than a remnant even in his grandfather's day. Cromwell or someone of his ilk undoubtedly would have made sure that no more prayers were offered within it.

But, as Koesler stood at the outer wall looking in, he could easily picture the monks walking reflectively through its corridors while meditating. He could almost hear the swells and diminuendos of Gregorian Chant. The people who lived in this area centuries ago must have heard those chants and felt comforted that while they were toiling for their very existence, there were dedicated men interceding with God on everyone's behalf.

Years before, Koesler had visited the Trappist Abbey of Gethsemani in Kentucky, where silence enjoyed a sacredness that may never be recaptured. He remembered being deeply impressed, especially by the silence. All those men going about performing their chores and duties and no one saying a word. One could almost slice the silence with a knife.

It must have been like that here . . .

Now that he had recalled Gethsemani's monastery, Koesler recalled also his first evening there. He had been ordained a priest only a few weeks earlier. One of the monks asked if he wished to say Mass. When Koesler answered in the affirmative, the monk asked what size alb he needed. Already aware that most albs were too small for him and further that there was no way of adjusting a vestment that was not large enough, Koesler had confidently said, "The biggest one you've got."

Next morning, he would have sworn the monks had spent most of the night making that alb. It had been at least a foot too long for him and he had spent several minutes rolling up the sleeves. The monks must have decided to fix that wise guy. After all, there was such a thing as silent laughter.

All in all, this was becoming a most satisfying trip down Nostalgia Lane. Koesler decided he just might follow the ad-

vice of his nameless tour director and call on the local parish
priest sometime before returning to Dublin.

But not now. He wanted to get settled in at Teach Murray
and begin to start experiencing what it was like to live in an
Irish pub.

6

If Koesler thought Boyle was a small town—and he did—
he was quite unprepared for Gurteen. The name, his friend
had informed him, meant "small, tilled field." And that
pretty well described Gurteen.

First there was a cemetery—a rather imposing one if he
could trust the glance he was able to steal as he drove by.
Then a string of small homes and a few shops on either side
of the only street in sight—a little less than a mile in length.
Aside from that street with its modest houses, shops, and
establishments, all else, as far as Koesler could see, consisted
of little plowed fields. Whoever had named Gurteen had been
proven inspired.

He drove as slowly as possible, looking attentively at each
edifice on the north side of the street, for that was the side on
which Chris Murray had told him the pub was located.

Approximately halfway through the village, he came upon
Teach Murray. The large letters identifying the pub extended
across the front of the building, which looked exactly as it
had in the picture—neat and well-kept. There was something
to be said for truth in advertising, even if one rarely encountered it.

Koesler stopped the car in front of the pub and looked
about for a parking place. Only then did he notice the lot on
the pub's east side. He depressed the gearshift, enabling him
to put the car in reverse, as he breathed a prayer of thanks
that the young lady who had delivered this rental car had
informed him of this operational necessity. Otherwise, he
would have made innumerable U-turns.

He parked, took his suitcase from the trunk, and entered
the pub through the front door. Once inside, he stood
motionless, trying to give his eyes a chance to adjust to the
dim interior. The only light in the pub came through several

side windows, but the day had turned overcast, and it was no longer all that bright outside—which meant it was even less bright inside.

"Father Koesler?"

"Yes?" He peered through the gloom. "Tom?"

"That's right."

Koesler had been informed by Chris Murray that his son Tom would be caring for the pub, taking time off from his spring term at Henry Ford Community College to do so.

"Right this way," Tom invited.

"Right which way?" People whose eyes were accustomed to the dark seldom empathized with those who were going through the adjustment process. Koesler instantly recalled the occasion when he had gone into a darkened church to lock it for the night. He had lingered in the sanctuary, praying. Meanwhile, the pastor, not realizing his assistant was locking up, sent a young man over to do so. When the man entered the rear of the church, he could not see well in the dark, so he groped his way toward the front. As he reached the communion railing, Koesler, who could see quite well, reached out to grasp his hand in guidance—and scared him half out of his wits.

The recollection took only a split second to pass through Koesler's mind. The next, related memory was that of an old joke. A priest, figuring he has finished hearing confessions of a Saturday evening, turns out most of the lights and returns to the confessional to complete his prayers. At which point, a teaching nun enters the near-dark church, kicks aside a misplaced priedieu, then stumbles over several kneelers, all of which makes quite a racket.

Finally making her way to the confessional, she begins by saying, "Bless me, Father, for I have sinned. It's two weeks since my last confession and I have been angry with my children several times—"

"How many children do you have?" the priest interrupts.

"Sixty-two," she answers.

"Get the hell out of here," says he, "I knew you were drunk the minute you came in!"

"Oh, all right; I can see you now," said Koesler, as Tom materialized before him.

"Sorry, Father; I keep forgetting: My eyes are accustomed

to this place and yours aren't. I was just stocking the bar. Would you like something to drink, or would you like me to show you to your room?"

"Well, I would like to get settled in."

Tom nodded, and gestured toward an open door behind the bar. "Follow me." He led Koesler through the door and up a flight of stairs.

"This is the bathroom." Tom indicated a room to the left of the landing at the top of the stairs.

Koesler looked in. A rather large room, painted blue, with a washstand, toilet, and tub. No shower, Koesler noted.

"And this is your room down at the other end of the hall, Father."

Koesler stepped into an adequately furnished room. A chest of drawers and mirror, a large closet, and what appeared to be a queen-sized bed. He set down his suitcase, then pulled the light curtain aside from the room's only window. "What's that?"

Tom stepped to the window and followed Koesler's finger.

"That's the church . . . St. Patrick's, what else?" Tom said, smiling. "Or, at least it's the bell tower."

"Kind of close, isn't it?"

"Four or five buildings away . . . but they're all jammed together."

Koesler nodded. "Thanks, Tom. I'll just get cleaned up and be down in a little while."

Tom left, closing the door behind him. Koesler seated himself on the bed and began to wonder if this had been such a hot idea after all. This place seemed to be further out than the proverbial boondocks. And, from experience, he knew himself to be urban . . . very urban.

But, he reassured himself, he did have wheels. So, in case he started feeling too isolated from civilization, he could always move on.

Besides, this had been such an unexpectedly hectic trip, he thought he might be in actual need of some measure of tranquility. And this certainly looked like the place to get it.

After freshening up, Koesler returned to the bar, where Tom was still occupied in setting up shop for the expected late afternoon and evening business. Tom was looking at Koesler while arranging bottles of Guinness. He was smiling.

"Sorry to be grinning at you, Father, but it does seem funny to have a priest in the pub."

"Doesn't the parish priest come in?"

Tom shook his head vigorously. "Not that he doesn't have his private stock, but, no, he doesn't come in here . . . or in any pub for that matter."

Koesler suddenly felt self-conscious. "I suppose I shouldn't be wearing my roman collar."

"Why not?" Tom continued to smile. "It gives the place some added class."

For the first time, Koesler's eyes had adjusted to the dimness and he was able to more carefully inspect the pub.

The section in which he was standing was long and narrow and dark. The traditional bar with stools on the patrons' side ran the length of this section where there were also tables and chairs available. In one corner, on a wall-hung platform, was a TV set—not operating at the moment. This section opened upon a much larger area with a small stage and a huge fireplace, also not operating.

Then, Koesler saw him. A small man at one of the tables near the wall in the semidarkness. He sat motionless, a cap on his head, a pipe in his mouth, and one hand wrapped around a shooper of Guinness. But for the wisp of smoke drifting upward from the bowl of his pipe, he might have been a statue.

"Who's that?"

Tom followed his glance. "Oh, that's Paddy O'Flynn. He's usually here as soon as we open. Then he stays with us much of the day and is usually with us when we close."

Koesler decided to go over and introduce himself.

"Excuse me," he said as he neared the man, "I'm Father Koesler, Father Robert Koesler. And you, I'm told, are Mr. O'Flynn."

"I am." Patrick Joseph O'Flynn snapped to his feet and whipped off his cap, but did not release his grip on either pipe or shooper.

He could have been a clone of Barry Fitzgerald. The contrast between his five-foot-five and Koesler's six-foot-three was pronounced.

"Please sit down, Mr. O'Flynn. I just came over to visit, if you don't mind."

"It'll be Paddy to you, Father."

Somehow, Koesler knew better than to invite O'Flynn to get reciprocal and call him Bob.

"Very well, Paddy." Koesler sat down at O'Flynn's table. Sitting did not prove much of a help. There was still a significant difference in size between the two men.

"Would ya be givin' me the honor as well as the pleasure of buying yer Reverence a pint, perhaps?"

"Thank you."

With a large smile, O'Flynn rapped the table a couple of times. Then, having gained Tom's attention, he pointed to his glass and held up two fingers.

"Have you been here long, Paddy?"

O'Flynn consulted the clock. "Oh, I'd say since about noon."

"No, I meant in Gurteen."

"All my life."

"You're a native then."

"I am."

Koesler wondered again that no one had ever introduced the Irish to a simple yes or no.

"Then maybe you'd know how big the town is? How many inhabitants?"

"One hundred sixty-seven souls."

"One hundred sixty-seven? That's a pretty exact figure."

"It is. People die; people are born. People marry. Some move away. It's not all that much trouble to mind who's doin' what. The 167 souls would include five Protestant families, poor dears! They had a church for themselves, but sometime back in the fifties it fell into disuse. Now, it's just a ruins out in the cemetery. An appropriate place for it, all things considered." O'Flynn sucked in his breath sharply.

Tom delivered the Guinness and departed wordlessly.

"One hundred sixty-seven," Koesler repeated, and thoughtfully sipped his Guinness. "That would make a pretty respectable clientele for this pub, I take it."

"It would, but it's not."

"Not what?"

"The only pub."

"It's not?"

"It's not! There are seven pubs in Gurteen."

"Seven pubs in this little town?"

"Seven pubs. That would make it, in case yer doin' yer arithmetic, 23.55 souls per pub." O'Flynn paused a moment. "But it doesn't work out that way." He paused again. "This one's the most popular. Because of the stage up there, more than likely. People like their music these days, ah, yes, they do."

Koesler gestured toward the mute TV mounted high up on the wall. "Back in the States," he said, "it's hard to get people to go out at night for live entertainment. They all seem to want to stay home and watch the tube."

"Ah, yes, Father. But then y've got all those channels, haven't ya?"

"Well, yes, quite a few, especially with cable TV."

"We've got two."

"Just two?"

"On one of 'em," O'Flynn glanced at the clock, "in just an hour and a half, they'll be havin' the Angelus."

"No!"

"They will!"

"Well," Koesler was impressed, "what do people do besides come to one of the pubs?"

"There's the parish mission."

"What?"

"The parish mission is goin' on all this week. Mornin' Mass at seven; evenin' services at half seven."

Koesler thought about that. "That's interesting. I think I'll go visit the cemetery for a while to get ready for the mission."

"Ah, now wouldn't that be right grand, Father." O'Flynn, taking him quite seriously, added a Biblical quote: " 'tis a holy and wholesome thought to pray for the dead."

They spent a silent moment contemplating their glasses.

"But tell me, Father, if it's not altogether too impertinent, what's a fine, upstandin' priest like yerself doin' stayin' in a pub? I assume," he added in a conspiratorial tone, "that after yer cartin' yer bag up the stairs and all, that ya are stayin' here?"

"I'm a friend of Chris Murray's; he invited me to stay here."

"You know old Chris!" For the first time since Koesler had encountered this elfish man, O'Flynn removed his left hand from the shooper that held his Guinness. He rubbed both hands together. "A fine man, Chris! A *fine* man! Comes back regular. Oh, he's made it in the States, he has. But still, his heart is here."

"True," Koesler agreed. "Besides, it's not all that new an experience for me. I may not know what it's like to live over an Irish pub, but I certainly know what it's like living over an American bar."

"Do ya, now?"

"Indeed. When I was a young lad we lived over a bar, the Tamiami, on the corner of West Vernor and Ferdinand in Detroit. I can remember trying to go to sleep every night with the juke box pounding away under my ear. That's how I got to know all the words to all the popular music of the time. Like 'Sentimental Journey' and 'Flat Foot Floogie with the Floy Floy' and 'Mairzy Doats and Dozy Doats' . . .'" Koesler allowed the familiar titles to drift away. It was evident from his expression that O'Flynn's musical appreciation stopped at the Irish harp and the tin whistle.

"But then, Father, if you'll forgive my pryin' a tad further, how did it happen that a fine young Catholic boy as you must have been; how did it happen that you were livin' over an American pub. Was it during your troubles?"

"Troubles?"

"The Great Depression, I mean to say."

Koesler chuckled. "No, it wasn't the Depression. Our family owned a grocery store adjacent to the bar, in the same building, you see, and the two families—my parents and my mother's sisters and their mother—lived in the two flats. One above the store, the other above the bar. Actually, my mother and her sisters owned the store, so it was called Boyle's Market."

Again, O'Flynn brightened, almost as much as he had at the mention of Chris Murray. "Boyle, ya say? Boyle! It couldn't be that yer mother's people were Boyles, could it now?"

"It could," said Koesler, attempting a Gaelic-style response, "although originally I believe it was O'Boyle; they lost the 'O' somewhere along the way."

"Boyle! Boyle! Boyle! I knew there was somethin' I liked about you from the first I set eyes on ya, Father. Apart, that is, from yer bein' a holy priest of God. And where is it yer folks would be comin' from?''

"Right down the road, in Boyle."

"They didn't!"

"They did!"

"Well, then, Father, let me just tell ya a little bit about the village of Boyle and the Boyles who lived there."

O'Flynn rapped on the table again until he attracted Tom's attention. Again he pointed to the Guinness and held up two fingers.

He turned back to Koesler with a sprightly look. "Then, Father, after I tell ya all about Boyle, we can skedaddle over to St. Pat's and catch the parish mission before tonight's music at Teach Murray."

"I don't know about the parish mission, Paddy. That would sort of be a busman's holiday. What's on TV tonight?"

"Well, there's always the Angelus at six."

7

What with one thing and another, an evening of dreary TV programming, together with cold and rainy weather, 7:30 found Father Koesler at St. Patrick's Church for the parish mission.

Following Paddy O'Flynn's advice, Koesler did not wear his clerical collar. "There'd be altogether too much adulation over it. Father. Sure, they'd be pullin' ya up to the altar to preside. Best go as an ordinary human."

Koesler was astonished at the size of the crowd. This was a good-sized church. Still, it was SRO—standing room only—this evening. Koesler had gotten one of the last seats available—and he was surprised that they were in the rear of the church.

The whole thing was foreign to his experience. In the States, parishes were lucky to get a crowd like this on any of the big three: Christmas, Easter, or Palm Sunday. And this was not a large community such as you'd find in the States. This was a small, a very small, village.

In addition, people filling the church from the rear forward was a clichéd event in the States. So much so that Koesler could recall a Detroit bus driver admonishing the passengers crowding about him in the front of the bus, "Pretend you're in church, folks, and move to the rear of the bus." Here, however, people evidently sought the front of the church first.

Koesler looked around. No one seemed to be talking. All were either sitting or standing against one of the walls in silence. Gradually it came to him that although he was undoubtedly the sole stranger in this tight-knit community, no one was gawking—or even looking in his direction. Incredibly polite and gracious people, these Irish.

In the front of the church, in the sanctuary at the left, or pulpit side, the visiting priest, who was conducting this week-long mission, was handing out hymn cards to the ushers, who were, in turn, distributing them to the congregation. On the other side of the sanctuary were the two men—one young, one middle-aged—who would lead *a cappella* singing.

The priest was vested in cassock, surplice, and stole. From the style of his clerical collar, Koesler recognized him as belonging to the Redemptorists, the religious order founded by St. Alphonsus. Koesler recalled the analysis of a Detroit seminary professor, one Father Sklarski: "Alphonsus," he had said, "yes, Alphonsus, boys; great man, great man. But if you read him too long, you'll be putting on your pants with a shoehorn!"

Koesler tried not to laugh. The citizens of Gurteen obviously took their parish mission seriously.

There was no sign of the pastor, whoever he was. Koesler assumed that at least the tradition of the missing pastor was common to both the States and Ireland. Most parishes seemed to schedule a mission every other year or so, concomitant with which the pastor almost invariably went off on a "well-deserved vacation."

Things gave every sign of getting underway. The Redemptorist was needlessly tapping the microphone to make sure it was on. People winced at the machine-gun-like clatter. On the other side of the sanctuary, the two singers were pulling at their ties preparatory to warbling.

"O.K. now, folks," the priest announced, "we'll just begin with our opening hymn." Everyone fiddled with the hymn cards. "We'll start by singin' 'Holy God,' cause everyone knows 'Holy God.' "

People were still juggling their hymn cards while, on the

other side of the sanctuary, the two hymn leaders were alternately looking from the priest to each other to their hymn
cards. But nothing was happening.

After a few moments, the priest quite patiently announced,
"Now, we're goin' to start with number one on our hymn
cards—'Holy God'—'cause everybody knows 'Holy God.' ''

Again, the two singers frantically looked from the priest to
their hymn cards to each other. Again, nothing happened.

Ever so patiently, the priest announced in his broad brogue,
"We're goin' to begin with hymn number one, 'Holy God'
—'cause everybody knows 'Holy God.' ''

It was obvious, at least to Koesler, that the song leaders did
not have the same hymn card as everyone else had. On
Koesler's card, "Holy God" was, indeed, hymn number one.

This time, the two singers consulted with each other, turned
to their microphone, and began loudly and confidently to
sing: "Amazing grace, how sweet the sound,/That saved a
wretch like me . . .''

And everyone joined in—'cause everyone knew "Amazing
Grace."

The hymn was followed by a lengthy sermon, during which
Koesler suffered one of his patented distractions. He couldn't
recall whether the account was fact or fiction. But one Detroit
parish was reported to have held a mission during which, on
the final day, the visiting priest preached on Mary, the mother
of Jesus. Reportedly, the priest got carried away and told the
congregation that Mary was so powerful with God that at the
end of the world, she would swoop even into hell and rescue
the souls there.

Understandably, this caused considerable consternation among
the parishioners. When the pastor returned from his well-
deserved vacation, and was told what the missionary had
supposedly said, he determined to clear up the matter.

So, the following Sunday, the pastor told his flock that the
visiting missionary had been zealously carried away . . . that
he had not intended to imply that at the end of the world
Mary would rescue all the souls in hell . . . but only those
who had been unjustly condemned.

Once again, Koesler barely succeeded in not smiling. St.
Patrick's people gave every evidence of taking seriously whatever their missionary was saying.

After the homily, a family group was called to the sanctuary, where they gave a demonstration of how to recite the family rosary. A simple maneuver that required minimal instruction. This was followed by a benediction and that evening's mission celebration was concluded.

There followed a virtual stampede to Teach Murray, where the Wolfe Tones, an internationally famous and extremely popular group of Irish male singers and musicians, were scheduled to perform. Citizens of many neighboring towns had joined those of Gurteen for this concert.

When Koesler reached the pub, he could scarcely shoulder his way in. In fact, he would have been discouraged from trying to enter, except that, for the nonce, he lived there. Once inside, he found that Paddy O'Flynn had miraculously managed to save a seat for him in the rear near the stage.

"You'll like 'em," O'Flynn said. "The boys are among Ireland's finest, especially when it comes to the rebel songs!"

Ordinarily, the Irish were so polite that even with a crowd this large, one still could converse in a normal tone. However, repeated testing proved the amplification system to be at peak decibel emission. As a result, people had to raise their voices to order drinks. O'Flynn, however, already had a Guinness on the table for himself and one for Koesler.

Most enthusiastic applause greeted the Tones, who plunged immediately into their first offering:

> There was a wild colonial boy;
>   Jack Duggan was his name.
> He was born and bred in Ireland,
>   In a place called Castlemain.
> He was his father's only son;
>   His mother's pride and joy.
> And dearly did his parents love
>   The Wild Colonial Boy.

"Is that a rebel song?" asked Koesler.

O'Flynn shook his head and grinned. "Ya haven't heard anything yet."

And he had not.

Next came the rakish "Rockon Rockall." Everyone was invited to—and everyone did join in the chorus, which concluded, "The natural gas will burn your ass, and blow you all to hell." Then followed, in rapid succession, "The Boys of the Old Brigade," "My Highland Paddy," "Bold Robert Emmet," "We're on the One Road," "James Connolly," "God Save Ireland," and on and on.

Three Guinnesses later, Koesler turned to his companion. "Paddy," he said, "it's been a long day for me. And I hope for some sightseeing tomorrow. So, I think I'll just call it a night. But I thank you for making this day so memorable."

O'Flynn raised his glass in salute. "God rest ya, Father. May ya be asleep half an hour before the divil knows y'er in bed."

Koesler squeezed through the crowd to the stairs and went up to his room.

He couldn't get over how cold it was. It had been cold ever since he had arrived in Gurteen, a damp cold. Was it the Irish weather in general—or a geographic peculiarity of this village in particular? Whatever, he was *cold*.

He had brought two pairs of pajamas . . . and decided to wear them both to bed. Even so, he shivered under the covers. And in his head beat the inexorable rhythms from the pub below. He tried to recall how it had been when he had been a young lad going to sleep upstairs over the juke box in the Tamiami, with the Baker streetcar clanging and heavy trucks rumbling up and down Vernor. He had been able to sleep then; why not now?

He tried very hard. But, even so, shortly after the 11:00 P.M. closing time, he could hear young Tom Murray alternately shouting and pleading into the microphone downstairs: "Time, now lads! Are you right there now, lads? It's way past the time! Time, please! We gotta go now, lads! You, there, Paddy; are you right there, now? It's way past time!"

And on and on.

Finally, Koesler did fall asleep. But before he did, he concluded that his ease in sleeping through the din of Vernor had been attributable to young ears.

It made as much sense as anything.

8

His eyes snapped open as if waking from a nightmare. Astonishment fought with drowsiness for dominance.

The heavy bell sounded as if it were in his room. It almost was.

Koesler looked at his watch. 6:30. The bell kept ringing. Although he had no hangover, he knew he was about to get a headache. He caught up with the clangs at five, and then continued to count. The bell tolled an incredible twenty-four times, his head reverberating at each ding and dong. He was willing to bet the parish mission would have a grand attendance for morning Mass. If nothing else, the entire village of Gurteen was either wide awake or deaf.

Gradually, he tried to organize his thoughts.

Thursday.

Three days till his return to Dublin and the ecumenical service and the subsequent return to Detroit.

Three days of relaxation.

Last night, he had planned not to rise before nine. However, St. Patrick's bell had proven to be modified rapture. The rapture was that he now had more of the day to enjoy. The modification was provided by that infernal noise. His ears were still ringing from the din.

As he began to shiver his way out of bed—what made Gurteen so *blasted* cold!—the clanging put him in mind of an incident many years before, when he had been assigned to an inner-city parish.

It was Holy Saturday, the day before Easter. The pastor had excused him from the vigil service scheduled to begin at 11:00 P.M. He was grateful. He was tired from hearing all the confessions, and wanted to turn in early. He read till nearly eleven.

The ushers at this parish had been instructed to ring the church bell at the moment Mass began on Sundays and Holy days. No one had ever informed them that if Mass began at midnight—as it would in the Easter Vigil—they should not ring the bell. One would have assumed that to be common sense.

However, one would have been wrong. At midnight that Saturday night, or Sunday morning, the vigil service ended and the first Mass of Easter began. And some usher laid on the bell.

Koesler had awakened in much the same emotionally shattered state as he had this morning. And then the phone had begun to ring. The first caller had given Koesler the unexpected opportunity of using a minstrel joke he had almost forgotten.

"Why is the bell ringing?"

"Because someone is pulling on the rope."

"Oh."

She had seemed satisfied.

Perhaps Gurteen lay in some geological fault. There must be some reason why it was so bone-numbingly cold in early May.

By this time, Koesler had shaved and was looking with misgivings at the bathtub. No shower. And this had to be the coldest bathroom in Western civilization. He filled the tub with the hottest water he could tolerate, shed his two pairs of pajamas, and hopped into and under the water.

The problem was that he had to lift parts of himself out of the water in order to wash. The hot water evaporating from his body simply made him colder. Now he understood why the bathroom was painted blue: It matched the color of any naked body trapped within its confines.

Coffee and toast and aspirin in the pub's ample kitchen got things off on a more equable footing. Tom Murray was not yet up and about. So Koesler leisurely and quietly pondered the day. He was getting an earlier start than he had originally intended. Why not, then, take a slightly longer trip?

He consulted his map and traced the route that led south of Galway Bay to the Burren, to where, as well as to barren Connemara, the English had herded huge clusters of the Irish to survive if they could, but more likely to die.

Koesler had long wished to see for himself this starcrossed region. And, since St. Patrick's bell had gifted him with an unexpectedly elongated day, and since the sun was warming this into a more conventional spring morning, he decided to do it. Figuring the distance between Gurteen and the Burren, he concluded the trip would require no more than two-and-a-half hours. Which should bring him to the Burren before noon.

Driving was simpler today. There was very little traffic, especially on these back roads. There was little need to shift gears except between third and fourth on the hills, and Koesler was beginning to get accustomed to driving on the left. He thought he might even have some initial difficulty making the switch back to the right when he returned to the States. Nevertheless, he hoped he would not get caught in any heavy or problematic traffic today. After only a couple of days of Irish-style driving, he did not feel all that comfortable with it.

Still slightly ill-at-ease with his turned-about Escort, his mind wandered back to auto problems he had experienced in the distant past.

He winced as he recalled the time he had hit a parked car—the stupidest thing, he thought, a driver could do. That he could remember it so clearly made it the more painful. There had been nothing wrong with the weather; it had been a bright, clear summer day. The culprit, he defensively rationalized, had been his breviary, which he had that morning placed on the passenger side of the front seat. The breviary was, as usual, packed with notes, phone messages, and clippings—his office away from home. As he made a left turn, the prayer book began to slide off the seat. Horrified to think of the mess of papers that would litter the floor if the breviary fell, he reached for it.

When he was able to look up, the parked car was only a few feet away, too close to stop in time.

Nobody had been injured, but the front of his car looked like a pug dog, while the rear of the other car resembled an accordion. And he had spent the next several weeks getting the mess straightened out.

Ballyhaunis. A jog to Highway N83, a trunk road, better than the one that had led here from Gurteen.

Then there was the time he had attended an evening movie, leaving his car parked on Michigan Avenue in Dearborn. When he came out of the movie house, his car was nowhere in sight. The Dearborn police, however, knew where it was. They took him to visit his car as it lay dormant in the fenced-in lot of a service station.

This time it was his fate to be the victim of a driver who had run into a parked car. And this time it was the rear of his car that was accordion-pleated.

The irony was that the lady who had driven her car into his had done so deliberately—in an attempt to commit suicide. She had done a very good job of wrecking both cars, but a very poor job of suicide. A few bandages had repaired her. His car had been laid up for months.

Claregalway. He had to be careful now to leave N17 and move to N18.

Koesler, by long-established habit, kept his head in constant if imperceptible movement. Years ago, he had read that such motion, in addition to providing a more panoramic view of the terrain, helped the driver's concentration.

He was reminded of Johnny Cash's song about Ireland, "The Forty Shades of Green." Koesler had not been keeping count, but there surely were more than a few verdant nuances to this land. And yet, considering the incredible number of violent deaths in Ireland's history, and the amount of blood this ground had absorbed from the wars among the ancient kings to the battles with the Viking invaders to the seemingly endless British occupation, it was somehow odd that the land had not turned red.

Kilcolgan. It was time to turn down a secondary road that would lead along the circle of Galway Bay to the Burren.

He was now approaching an area of Ireland about which he had heard a great deal, but had never seen, not even on a picture postcard.

He had found it difficult to believe some of the descriptions he had heard. The Burren, after all, was a part of this lush, fertile island. And, of course, the Irish were known to exaggerate now and again.

He came to the crest of the hill he'd been climbing for the past several miles. And there it was. There had been no exaggeration in its description. It was awesome.

Layer after layer of limestone, stacked like shelves, going down one hill and rising in the next. He had never seen, much less imagined, anything like this. This, then, was the Burren.

He would not describe the scene as desolate. No; a moonscape would be his idea of desolation. At least in the Burren there were tufts of grass growing between the limestone slabs. And he had heard that cattle could and did feed on this grass and, indeed, that they gave good milk.

No water to drown a man. No tree to hang him from. And no earth to bury him in. So said one of Cromwell's men. It was both an accurate delineation as well as an exact description of the fate Cromwell intended for the Irish. Koesler was beginning to understand why, to the Irish, compared with Cromwell, Hitler had many redeeming features.

As he drove slowly down a hill, he tried to comprehend what it must have been like to be forced to try to eke out a bare existence from this land. To be forced to live here with the responsibility of nurturing a family. Again, it was a wonder there were any Irish left in Ireland, let alone on earth.

It happened suddenly, without warning. The shock of the impact made it seem unreal. Something had slammed into his car from the rear. The jolt snapped his head backward, then forward, then back hard against the headrest. His car shot forward as he fought to regain control of it.

In panic, he glanced for a fraction of a second in the rearview mirror. He saw a car, a large black sedan—he did not know what kind, perhaps a Mercury. He had not seen it before. He had been unaware of its presence. But it was behind him now. And it was bearing down on him again.

There was no place for him to go, no place for him to move. The road was so narrow, there was barely room for two cars to pass each other. And on either side was the Burren.

He tried to speed up. But his compact was no match for the larger vehicle.

He was hit again. Harder. Again his car shot forward. Again he fought for control. As he wondered vaguely what in hell was going on, he could focus on nothing but trying to survive.

It couldn't be—but it was: gunshots! Three of them. My God, now they were shooting at him!

He tried to swerve from one side of the road to the other in evasive action. It only made it more difficult to keep the car under control.

Suddenly, he was conscious of something pulling alongside him. He could afford only a brief glance to his right. The black car had moved even with him.

The crash was cataclysmic. The huge sedan hit his car alongside, knocking it from the road.

With his vehicle now totally out of control, Koesler could do nothing but hang on as the small Escort bounced and careened from one limestone shelf to another.

As it neared the bottom of the hillside, the car was virtually catapulted from a slab of limestone. Then, as if in slow motion, it nosed over. As Koesler saw the ground coming to meet him, his only thought was to wonder if, when next he opened his eyes, he would see his parents, departed friends, Jesus, or what . . .

9

"What's your name?"

A pause.

"Koesler. Robert Koesler."

"What do you do?"

Another pause.

"I'm a priest."

"That's a good sign."

A lot of Koesler's general education had come through the school of hard knocks. He'd been through this one before. Once, in the recovery room, he had just come to after an operation. A nurse's head had appeared over the side of his bed. "What is your name?" she had asked. Recalling a comedy routine of Bill Dana's, Koesler had replied, "My name José Jimenez." The nurse walked away, saying to another nurse, "He doesn't know who he is yet."

Koesler, too weak and groggy to summon her back, had been forced to lie there another half-hour until she returned to again check on his condition. Thus, he had learned the consequences of recovery room humor. He had resolved at the time never to try it again. And he had just kept that resolution.

"Does it hurt here?" asked the man in the white coat.

"No."

"Here?"

"No."

"How about there?"

"No."

"Would you sit up for us now, please, Father?"

It wasn't a recovery room. It was some sort of medical

office. At least there were medical instruments all around. The white-coated man poking and prodding and asking if it hurt appeared to be a doctor. There was another man in the room. Koesler had met him, knew who he was, but could not recall his name. If he had thought the clanging bell of St. Patrick's had given him a headache, he had not been prepared for this. This was Big Ben, the granddaddy of all headaches.

"Remarkable . . . truly remarkable." The doctor sucked in his breath sharply. "I'd almost say it was a bit of miraculous."

"That may be," said the other man, "and the luck of the Irish rubbin' off on him, as well as a nice solid buckled seat belt."

"Just the remote possibility of a very mild concussion," said the doctor, "and of course the external abrasions, contusions, and hematomas."

"The goods are all right, only the package is damaged?" the other man asked.

"Quite."

"What day is this?" Koesler decided to ask a few questions of his own.

"Thursday," said the doctor.

Ah, yes. Koesler nodded. Thursday. But what week? What month? "What's the date?"

The doctor, who had seemed affable, appeared to grow concerned. "What date do you remember?"

Koesler thought for some moments. "The eighth of May."

Satisfied, the doctor glanced at the other man, then nodded. "He's all right."

Thank God. At least it was still the same day. "Where am I?"

"Regional Hospital in Galway."

"How did I get here?"

"Superintendent O'Reardon here," the doctor indicated the other man, "had us send an ambulance for you."

That's who he was. Koesler had met him in Inspector Koznicki's hospital room. Superintendent O'Reardon must be spending a lot of time in hospital rooms lately.

"Do you know what happened to you, Father?" asked O'Reardon.

"The Burren . . . the car . . . out of control . . ." Koesler shook his head as if to clear the cobwebs. "But . . . how did you happen along?"

"Oh, Inspector Koznicki asked me to keep an eye on you."

Koesler's brow furrowed. "You mean you followed me all the way to Gurteen . . . and to the Burren?"

"I did."

"But you're the Superintendent. Why wouldn't you just send one of your men?"

"I felt I owed it to the Inspector. We didn't do much of a job making him secure now, did we? I sort of did it as a penance." It was said with a twinkle.

"And you followed me all the way from Dublin? I didn't see you."

"Well, now, that's the idea, isn't it? If I'm going to keep an eye on you, you shouldn't see me doing it, should you now? Otherwise, I might just as well ride in your car with you and save the petrol. It's a knack. But if I haven't learned it after all these years I would be a sad excuse for a saint now, wouldn't I?"

Koesler thought about this. There really was something to the feeling that one was being followed. It had happened to Toussaint and Koznicki and now to him. At least from now on, if someone asked what it felt like to be followed, he would be able to tell them. Suddenly, another thought occurred.

"Wait a minute: If you've been following me all this time, where were you when I was getting shot at?"

O'Reardon shook his head. "It was I was doing the shooting. Even on the road at that speed, I put a bullet or two in their car. If I hadn't been there, saints preserve us, after they forced you off the road, you can be sure they would have inspected their job and when they found you alive, they would have finished you off, there can be no doubt.

"But don't worry, we'll get 'em. And we'll get 'em soon."

"Well," Koesler extended his hand, "thanks is a poor word. I owe my life to you."

"Think nothing of it, Father." They shook hands. "But for the rest of the time you're in the Republic, there'll be a Garda nearby. I don't expect any more shenanigans, but we can't be too careful." O'Reardon rose. "I'll be leaving now, Father. Take care. And keep us in your good prayers."

Koesler turned to the doctor. "How about it? Can I—may I—leave now?"

"Whoa now, Father. You seem to be all right internally. But especially in view of your head injury, we'll be wanting to detain you at least overnight for observation. It's the very least, you know. Then we'll just see how you are tomorrow."

"O.K." He wasn't going to argue.

"Here, let me help you, Father. Can you just step down from the examination table and sit in this wheelchair?"

"I think so."

Koesler stood gingerly and felt pain in muscles he hadn't known he had. "Oh, yes; I think a little rest might do me a lot of good."

The doctor was alert. "And we'll give you something for that pain, too."

As Koesler took the couple of steps to the wheelchair, he caught sight of himself in a mirror. Then he knew the ugly reality of those euphemisms: abrasions, contusions, and hematomas. He looked as if he had been the big loser in a very tough fight.

"Oh, yes," he eased himself carefully into the wheelchair, "a little rest is definitely called for."

10

Patrick Joseph O'Flynn tipped his head to one side. He gave every indication of seeing something he found difficult to believe. He watched wordlessly as a uniformed Garda assisted an obviously battered Father Koesler into Teach Murray.

Until the arrival of the walking wounded, O'Flynn had had the pub to himself. Tom Murray was out back hanging up some bar cloths. O'Flynn was patiently awaiting the hour of ten, when he would start nursing his first pint of the day.

On catching sight of Koesler, O'Flynn had respectfully snapped to his feet, meanwhile snatching his cap from his head, leaving his fine brown hair pointing in every direction.

Then he noticed Koesler's obvious distress and was unsure whether to go to the priest's aid or await developments. He decided to remain at the table, especially since Koesler and his human crutch seemed headed in O'Flynn's direction.

Koesler lowered himself gingerly, wincing as his back met the unpadded chair. The Garda tipped his cap, excused himself, and retreated to the rear of the pub whence, on earlier orders from Superintendent O'Reardon, he continued to watch over Koesler. O'Flynn sat down opposite the priest.

"I suppose you're wondering what happened," said Koesler, after a brief but pregnant silence.

"Well, now, the thought did occur." O'Flynn jammed the cap back on his head. "Y've been gone only a day! Meanin' no irreverence."

"My car . . . that is, the car I was driving, was forced off the road. In the Burren. I crashed. The car's a total wreck."

Pause.

"Well," said O'Flynn, "ya might try lookin' at the bright side of it."

"The bright side of it?" Koesler fixed O'Flynn with a quizzical gaze. "What could possibly be the bright side of this?"

"Arra," O'Flynn stuck pipe in mouth, "it could have happened to ya in England." It was said with great conviction.

Koesler made no reply. His mind, recovering from a goodly amount of pain-killing drugs administered yesterday and this morning, attempted to compare the benefit of being nearly killed in Ireland with suffering the same fate in England. He was not doing well.

"Wait now!" O'Flynn almost shouted. "Was it forced off the road ya were?"

"That's right."

"Now who would do a shameful thing like that? To a priest! In Ireland!"

"I don't know. But it's the same one who shot a policeman from Detroit and one of the ones who will try to murder the Archbishop of Detroit this Saturday in St. Patrick's in Dublin."

Normally, though gregarious, Koesler was not garrulous. However, the combination of the events of the preceding week and the cumulative affect of the drugs caused him to be more talkative than usual.

O'Flynn sucked in his breath sharply. "Ya don't say! Arra,

the wonder of it! Why, nothin' in Ireland's happened the likes of that since . . . well, since the days of the Tans.''

"The Tans?"

"Surely, y've heard of the Black and Tans, Father."

"Well, yes, but I don't know much about them."

"Much about them, is it? My, oh my, oh my!" O'Flynn had worked a wad of tobacco into the bowl of his pipe and began the ritual of lighting it. Between efforts to draw the flame into the tobacco, O'Flynn reminisced about the Black and Tans. For he had lived through those days, though he had been a young boy at the time.

"It was back in '20 and '21 when the Brits tried one more time to wipe from the face of the map the IRA—that'd be the Irish Republican Army."

"I know."

"Well, the Tans were recruited from many of the British troops as had just finished combat in World War One, and then, later, from among the dregs of England—criminals, thugs, and hoodlums. They were called Black and Tans because they were such a ragtag bunch they had to wear make-shift uniforms of khaki tunics and trousers of the military, with the black-green caps and belts of the police." O'Flynn paused to puff on his pipe in an attempt to waken the embers.

"Black and Tan," Koesler mused. "Speaking of black and tan, that black man was lying after all. I wonder what he hoped to gain? He couldn't have thought we would drop all security just on his word that there were no Rastafarians in Ireland so there'd be no attack on the Cardinal. And if they weren't going to make an attempt on the Cardinal's life, then why bother taking Inspector Koznicki off the board? Strange . . ."

Koesler drifted off into his own reverie which would continue undisturbed by O'Flynn's continued commentary.

"They were sent here in '20 with orders to 'make Ireland hell for the rebels.' Well, what with one thing and another, they did their damndest—if you'll pardon the irreverence, Father—to make Ireland hell for all the Irish.

"Arra," O'Flynn sucked in his breath, "those were the days, and especially the nights, of terror. Ye'd hear the rumble of the lorry, racin' as fast as the horses could carry it. Then when the lorry stopped, ye'd hold yer breath. Especially if it stopped near yer own house. Then there'd be the bangin' on the door. And the Tans'd go runnin' through the house lookin' for a rebel but mad enough so's they wouldn't leave empty-handed. There was times a man'd be shot dead before the eyes of his missus and the little ones.''

He puffed again on his pipe. ''One night, they made a surprise attack: surrounded the barracks just up the street there.'' He tilted his head toward the east. ''Well, the lads weren't goin' to take that lyin' down, so a shootin' match started.'' He looked at Koesler. ''It isn't a barracks now; it's the doctor's house . . . but you can still see the bullet marks.''

''There's something wrong,'' said Koesler, continuing his soliloquy, now more audibly.

''Wrong?'' O'Flynn, concerned, looked at the priest intently. ''What's wrong, Father? Are ya not feelin' all that well? Would ya like to lie down or somethin'? Is there anything I can get fer ya?''

O'Flynn started to stand, but Koesler almost absentmindedly waved him back in his chair.

''. . . something wrong with the scenario. It doesn't fit . . . assumption is it's a Rastafarian plot to eliminate the *papabili* . . . discourage them all from becoming Pope . . . and thus do away with the Papacy itself.

''All well and good, as bizarre as the scheme is, when they actually attack prominent Cardinals. But then they attack Ramon and then the Inspector.

''Still all well and good . . . since those two have proven themselves effective guardians of Cardinal Boyle.

''But why me? How do I possibly fit into this scenario? Can they possibly believe I could be a hindrance? If so, then how? And then there were the black fists that changed to black hands . . .''

Koesler returned to his mulling. O'Flynn had listened politely to the priest's ramblings, while understanding none of them.

After what he felt was an appropriate period of silence, O'Flynn resumed. ''Arra, it was the Tans all right! They're the ones who shot prisoners, destroyed property, burned creameries. A bad lot altogether. Young Kevin Barry, saints preserve us, they tortured the lad and then hanged him—and he no more than eighteen years!" O'Flynn sucked in his breath sharply.

"And who could forget Terence MacSwiney? Died after seventy-four days on hunger strike in an English prison, he did. 'It's not those who can inflict the most, but those who can suffer the most who will conquer,' he said. Brings to mind Jaysus' sermons: 'The meek shall inherit the earth,' doesn't it? Arra, but then," he looked at Koesler with sly eyes, "Jaysus didn't have to contend with the Black and Tans, did he?"

Seemingly satisfied that his rhetorical question neither called for nor was about to receive a reply from his preoccupied tablemate, Patrick Joseph O'Flynn went on. "Then there was the time they caught the six Volunteers near Cork and when the bodies were found, the heart had been cut from one, the tongue from another, the nose from another, the skull of another had been battered in, and the bodies of the other two were identifiable only by their clothing. And in the west," O'Flynn jabbed the air with his pipe stem, as he gathered verbal momentum, "the bodies of two brothers were found in a bog, tied together and their legs partially roasted away." And thus O'Flynn continued his gory litany as he had so many times in the past. It was not often these days that he found fresh ears for his resolute recital.

"So, is it yer opinion, Father, that it was the Tans come back? Who else, I ask ya, would do such a thing to a holy priest of God?" He looked at Koesler quizzically.

"But what if it's the wrong grouping?" Koesler's question was right in line with his thoughts, though a non sequitur to O'Flynn's. "*I* certainly don't fit in with the Cardinals—for any reason." His voice rose and fell in correspondence with the strength of his conclusions. "But then, the link between the Cardinals and Toussaint isn't that strong either. And what connection could Ramon and the Inspector possibly have with me? That doesn't seem to make much sense either."

O'Flynn decided to go with the flow. If Koesler would not participate in O'Flynn's monologue, then courtesy demanded that the little Irishman join Koesler's stream of consciousness.

"Well, now," said O'Flynn, "not knowin' the other two gentlemen y've mentioned, I must admit I'm hard put to draw a connection between them and yerself."

"But then" —Koesler obviously needed to develop his hypothesis aloud— "it may be, as my dentist once put it, that we have more than one thing going on here. Of course he was referring to an abscess along with a root canal. Here we would have two things going on that would be related in only one direction. Is that possible?"

"Oh, indeed it is," O'Flynn responded. "I well remember old Tillie O'Flynn, my sainted aunt, a maiden lady her whole life long. How she suffered the heart palpitations in her later years from the stress of bein' impoverished. Bad off, she was! Worried constantly about endin' up in the poorhouse. Which, as it turns out, was a worthy worry, for it was just there that she did indeed end. But, in any case, that is what the doctor said took her—the stress of worryin' about bein' poor. And bein' poor caused the dear woman's stress. So, ya see, it was all connected up."

"Of course!" Koesler slapped the tabletop. "That would explain the sequence of events! It would explain the illusive symbolism. It would explain the whole thing!

"Paddy!" For the first time, he focused on O'Flynn. "I've got to get home!"

"Home, is it?"

"To Detroit!"

"Ya can't get there from here."

"Can you help me get back to Dublin?" Koesler started to rise from his chair. He was joined in this maneuver by O'Flynn, as well as the Garda who had accompanied Koesler on his return to Gurteen.

"Sure and it'll be a pleasure, Father. Meself and, I expect, this fine young Garda here, 'll get ya back to Dublin's fair city, alive, alive-o." And, offering some measure of support to the battered priest, escort Patrick Joseph O'Flynn convoyed Koesler off to the strains of "Molly Malone."

DETROIT

"Don Louis," the petite, attractive receptionist spoke into
the intercom, "there is a gentleman—a priest—to see you.
His name is," she glanced at her notepad, "Father Robert
Koesler. He does not have an appointment."

Silence.

"In a moment," came a sepulchral voice.

"It'll be a little while, Father," the receptionist relayed.
"Do you wish to be seated?"

"I think," said Koesler, "I'll take a chance on your being
right about that 'little while' and stay standing. I don't want
to move needlessly."

The receptionist noted several nasty bruises on Koesler's face
and hands. The rest of him was covered by a black suit and
clerical collar. But from the stiff and awkward way in which
he had entered the office and, indeed, was now standing, she
surmised that much of the rest of his body was similarly bruised.

In the inner office, a smallish dapper man sat behind an
extremely large desk. Perhaps in his late fifties or early
sixties, with salt-and-pepper hair and bushy black eyebrows,
the man, in immaculate blue pinstripe, with contrasting tie
and pocket kerchief, was clearly a very important person.

He smiled, revealing perfect teeth, as he turned to the two rather large men seated to the right of the desk. "The fly comes to be caught in the spider's web." He spoke in Italian.

The two chuckled, but not pleasantly.

The man pressed a button on the intercom. "Angela, show the good Father in.

As Koesler came through the door, on which was affixed the sign, "Louis Licata, President," the two large men were there to intercept him. One began to check the priest for weapons. As his sides were being patted down, Koesler winced noticeably, and let out a barely audible groan.

"Go easy," Licata directed, "the good Father seems to have had an accident recently."

The two laughed again, mirthlessly.

"*Vacante,* " announced the searcher.

"Very well," said Licata. "Leave us."

The two exited, leaving Licata and Koesler alone. Licata motioned Koesler to a comfortably upholstered chair in front of the desk. The priest gingerly eased himself into it.

"What brings you to me, Padre?" Licata leaned back and gazed at Koesler through the upper half of bifocals.

"I thought I'd better pay you a visit before you paid me another one."

"You are mistaken, Padre." There was a hint of amused smile. "In my memory, we have never met before this day."

"Perhaps not you personally, Don Louis. Perhaps it was your men, your *friends,*" Koesler emphasized the word to indicate he understood its Mafia connotation, "or those you hired. But it was at your command we were visited."

" 'We'?"

"My friends—Ramon Toussaint and Inspector Koznicki—and myself."

"Interesting." Licata's fingers formed a steeple touching his lips. "I did not know a simple parish priest could have such an overactive imagination. Tell me, how did you arrive at this preposterous conclusion."

His smile told Koesler that Licata was toying with him. Nevertheless, the priest persisted.

"I had no trouble believing the Rastafarian plot to kill *papabili,* bizarre as it was. But I began having doubts when the black fist symbol was found at each location where a

Cardinal was attacked. The Rastafarians have no history or reputation of leaving a symbolic calling card.

"But we were dealing, quite obviously, with a group that must have almost worldwide capabilities of action. This was a plot, after all, that demanded the capability of striking against Princes of the Church in widely scattered areas of the world. Among those organizations that have that sort of capability is the Mafia. Wherever the Mafia is not present in force, they have sufficient contacts to issue . . . I believe it is called a contract. In addition, one of the early symbols used by the Mafia was the black hand."

"Fascinating." Licata's smile had narrowed and frozen. "But very—how is it called in the courts?—circumstantial. The Mafia has no . . . uh . . . patent on any symbol. A black fist is the symbol of the Black Power movement. There is every reason to expect a group like the Rastafarians to adopt it. What are they if not believers in black power? Besides, what reason would the Mafia have to be involved in a plot against the Princes of the Church? Sicilians, after all," he spread his arms wide, "are Catholics."

"Precisely." Koesler, so absorbed in his exposition that he had, in effect, self-hypnotized himself against his pain, leaned forward. "But what if, with your excellent contacts, you learned of the Rastafarian plot early on? Learned that one of their targets was a man—a Cardinal—from whose assassination you could spin off and, under the guise of an attack against him, be able to settle an old score."

"An old score?" The smile had vanished.

"Yes, an old score. I may have had my doubts when it came to linking the clenched black hand with the Rastafarians, but I could have lived with those doubts. Then, attempts were made on Ramon and the Inspector . . . and my doubts grew. Up till then, only Cardinals had been attacked. Now a deacon? And a police officer? The only explanation was that they had been attacked because they were protecting the established target. Cardinal Boyle. Still, I thought it a pretty thin explanation.

"But once I was attacked, that explanation evaporated. *I* didn't fit into this picture—unless the scenario was divided differently. What if I were to group Cardinals Claret, Gattari, and Boyle together as targets of the Rastafarians? Targets in whose attacks *you* participated by placing the symbolic black fist at the scene of the crime, so the police would think all the attacks were linked.

"But, suppose I group Toussaint, Koznicki, and myself in a separate bracket. What is it that could possibly link the three of us, I asked myself. Only the incident several years ago, when some of Detroit's crime figures were murdered and their heads found on statues in Catholic churches. The first and most notorious of those victims was Rudy Ruggiero, the reputed Detroit Mafia leader.

"And, among those suspected of involvement in those killings was one Ramon Toussaint—although he was never charged with the crimes. Responsible for the homicide investigation, which concluded with the matter being placed in the unsolved cases file, was Walter Koznicki. Also involved—and perhaps the closest confidante of Toussaint— was myself.

"I put all this together and arrived at the successor of Mr. Ruggiero: the reputed present head of Detroit's Mafia family, Don Louis Licata.

"Also, in the assaults against Toussaint and Koznicki, the calling card changed ever so slightly. From a black fist to an open black hand, the celebrated symbol of the Mafia. The Mafia had made its statement. As the Rastafarians attempted to carry out their clumsy plans, the Mafia, with characteristic cleverness, was there even in advance of the Rastas. And the Mafia, with characteristic bravado, supplied a calling card that could easily be associated with the Rastas and the Black Power movement. The Rastas would not even tumble to what was going on.

"Then, with the Rastas discouraged and ready to abandon their grand scheme, the Mafia proceeded on its original plan to settle that old score. And, along the line, the calling card is changed ever so subtly into the notorious black hand."

Koesler looked at Licata expectantly. "Have I left anything out?"

"Nothing of any consequence." The smile reappeared. "You have only one problem—but it is a big one: You have no proof. There are no witnesses except those who will protect me with the *omertà*, their silence. Nothing you have said would stand up in court. That is your problem—and it is a formidable one."

"That may be my problem, but it is not my question. My question is why? There was no trial. No one was even arrested in the death of Mr. Ruggiero. Why would you take it upon yourself to attempt to kill three people, none of whom was charged with any crime . . . all of whom must be presumed to be innocent of any crime.

"Why, Mr. Licata . . . why? I just don't understand."

Licata spread his hands flat on the desk top. "You do not understand because you do not understand *us*.

"We Sicilians are most concerned about reputation, about saving face. An insult or a killing must be avenged. We cannot live with it; it *must* be avenged. We have an expression: *Livarisi na petra di la scarpa* . . to take a stone out of one's shoe.

"With some who are united in 'our cause,' this revenge must be taken by ourselves. We care nothing for the authorities. The authorities care nothing for us. We are our police. We are our banks. We dispense justice. We have to—because nobody else ever gave a fig for us, nobody else cared about us, nobody else helped us or defended us—or even knew we were alive, except to look down on us.

"Now, especially when outsiders dare to strike at us, they must know that we will not be satisfied even if they are punished by the authorities with merely a few years in prison. No; they must—and they will—receive our justice . . . and our cause is avenged.

"You three, Toussaint, Koznicki, and yourself, you were tried in our court, a court where I am judge and jury. I have no need of your 'due process.' I have no need of your meticulous evidence. I have need only of vengeance. I hold the three of you responsible for the death of Don Ruggiero. One of you has paid his debt in full. The others will pay. I have so judged. It is inevitable."

"But it's been so long! So many years!"

Licata shook his head. "We are always willing to postpone revenge if necessary. We will wait until the proper time and the proper place. This insane plot to kill Cardinals became the proper time, and England and Ireland became the proper place.

"You would have no way of knowing this if I did not tell you. Since Don Ruggiero had been badly frightened, perhaps even frightened to death before he was decapitated, we arranged a special surprise for your friend Toussaint before his beating. With the aid of some papier-mâché and a clever artist, we set up a special Chamber of Horrors at Madame Tussaud's just for him.

"You look surprised. You shouldn't be. After all, if we could discover the Rastafarians' assassination schedule, it was nothing for us to obtain your group's tour bus schedule.

"I promise you, he was frightened—just as Don Ruggiero was—before your friend became unconscious for the rest of his life. We deliberately left his cranium untouched to assure he would remain conscious long enough to experience the maximum of pain and fear.

"And you would have been able to see his fear, if you had accompanied him as you had planned."

"And if I had been there?"

Licata spread his hands wide. "What can I say? You would not now be here."

"But, at most," Koesler said, "Toussaint was considered merely a suspect in those killings—and that by a very few people. And on those grounds, you would have killed him . . . and Koznicki . . . and myself?"

"I told you, we dispense our own justice. The Jews have a saying, 'If I am not for myself, who will be for me?' No one of us is attacked without our vengeance. All must know there is no escape from our vengeance. And now your Reverend Toussaint is enjoying a living death. Don't you think that a most fitting revenge?

"But enough. Now that I have told you all this, I will tell you something else: You were very foolish, Padre, to come to me. You should have known that if your theory is correct, you—and Inspector Koznicki—represent unfinished business for us. We will bide our time, but eventually, we will take care of the Inspector.

"But for now, our business will be finished as far as you are concerned . . . once and for all."

He pressed a button on his intercom.

The door opened.

But instead of his henchmen, two homicide detectives entered, guns drawn.

"Louis Licata, you are under arrest for the attempted murders of Ramon Toussaint, Walter Koznicki, and Father Robert Koesler. You have the right to remain silent . . ."

2

"No doubt about it, it was a real coup," said Father Koesler.

"I mean, everybody wanted the Cardinal as a guest speaker the minute he returned from Ireland. Not only was he a new Cardinal, but there was all that publicity about those attempts on his life and all. But it was old Eddie Breslin who got him first as guest of the Detroit Economic Club."

"You don't suppose," said Wanda Koznicki, "that could be because Mr. Breslin is Chairman of the Board of General Motors, and is, with bonuses and stock options, perhaps the wealthiest man in town, do you?"

"Wanda," Koesler replied, "I would wager that Mr. Breslin is at least the wealthiest *Catholic* in town. And yes, I imagine that might have had something to do with it."

Mary O'Connor brought in a fresh pitcher of iced tea. Ordinarily, she would not have been at St. Anselm's on a Sunday afternoon. But, since Koesler was entertaining special visitors, the parish secretary had volunteered to return after the morning Masses to serve refreshments. And the refreshments were welcomed by all on this sunny afternoon in late July.

"What surprises me, Bob," said Emerenciana Toussaint, "is that *you* were at an Economic Club luncheon. Economics was never your strong suit. Why, if it were not for Mrs. O'Connor here, you wouldn't know whether you were within or without a budget. You have said so yourself."

Mary O'Connor blushed.

"You're so right, 'Ciane," said Koesler. "And in fact, I wasn't there. But a friend in PR at GM told me about it. Mr. Breslin had reserved a table for six. And after the luncheon and the speeches, Mr. Breslin signaled his people to come up and meet the Cardinal.

"Well, it turned out that the first five in line happened to be Catholic and the sixth was not. So each of the five tried to genuflect and kiss the Cardinal's ring—which, as you all know, the Cardinal would rather people didn't do. So, each one ended up going halfway down toward the floor with his right knee before the Cardinal gave his hand a tug. It looked as if they were doing a sort of half-curtsy, my friend said.

"And then he said that when they had all gone through the line, the non-Catholic came up to the others and said, 'What in hell were you guys trying to do?'

" 'We were trying to kiss the Cardinal's ring,' one said.

" 'That's crazy,' the man said, 'I kissed Breslin's!' "

Everyone laughed.

"The Cardinal . . . and how *is* the Cardinal?" asked Ramon Toussaint. He winced as he shifted slightly in the upholstered chair. Even after a convalescence of two months, he was still partially crippled . . . and would be for some time to come. But the doctors in London had decided—and Toussaint had concurred—that the rest of his healing could be better done at his home. Now, on their way back to San Francisco, the Toussaints had stopped off to visit Koesler and the Koznickis.

"He's fine, as far as I know," said Koesler. "Busy as ever, they tell me. Though some say he's a bit more reflective. But, I suppose that's to be expected after what he's been through."

"After what *he's* been through!" exclaimed Wanda.

Koesler chuckled. "On second thought, I don't suppose what he's been through could hold a candle to what we've been through."

"If what *he* has experienced has rendered *him* more reflective," Toussaint commented, "the three of us ought to be in a Cistercian monastery!"

"The three of us," said Inspector Koznicki solemnly, "are very fortunate that we are not in a cemetery."

His comment transformed what had been a lighthearted gathering into a serious group forced to face the sobering, recent proximity of death.

"The Inspector is correct," said Toussaint, after a brief silence. "If you had not found the real cause of our being attacked, Bob, we would most certainly have continued to watch out for Rastafarians while we would have been picked off from an entirely different direction. How did you figure it out?''

''Several suspicious incidents and a healthy dose of luck.'' Koesler picked up the pitcher of iced tea and offered refills to his guests.

''First of all, the Haitian who spoke to me in Dublin—the one who claimed to be your friend, Ramon. When he told me there would be no Rastafarian attack in Ireland, he was either telling the truth or lying. If he were lying, the only possible reason would be to lull us into lowering our guard during that ecumenical service in St. Patrick's. Such a lie would certainly not be aimed at lowering *my* guard as far as my own safety was concerned; none of us had any reason to expect me to be attacked, in any case. But it was, indeed, I who was attacked.

''So, in retrospect, I was willing to assume he was telling the truth. But if my assailants were not Rastafarians, then who? And why?''

''The Rastafarians definitely were involved in the attacks against the Cardinals. And—presumably—the attacks against the two of you. But now me. Why?

''Well, what if we crossed out the 'possibles' and counted only on the 'certains'? This point of view was strengthened by the changing of the symbol from a fist to an open hand. That would put the Cardinals in one category and the three of us in another. And, it could mean that none of the three of us had been assaulted by the Rastafarians. But, again, by whom? And why?

''The only time I could think of that all three of us were linked was during the investigation of that series of beheadings on Detroit criminals. Inspector Koznicki was in charge of the investigation and''—he hesitated a split second, then chose his words carefully— ''you, Ramon, were under suspicion of being somehow involved. While I, in addition to taking some small part in the investigation, am a very close friend to both of you.''

The faces of Koesler's friends were a study. Wanda Koznicki seemed engrossed; her husband professionally interested. Toussaint's expression was unfathomable, while, strangely, Emerenciana seemed almost detached. Her face reminded Koesler of the statues of the far-seeing sibyls of old; it was as if she were listening to a tale she not only knew but had always known.

Koesler picked up the thread of his explanation.

"If that *was* the connection, then whoever was after us had to have some connection with someone associated with that series of murders—the most logical someone being one of the victims. But which one? A Mafia chieftain, a head pimp, an unconscionable abortionist, a bilking auto mechanic, a similar construction man, or the kingpin of a drug ring?

"Then I thought back to when, on our flight to London, Ramon, you told me you were not sure where that black fist symbol had come from, but that it possibly had been adapted by the Rastafarian militants from the Black Power movement in the States.

"It was the weak link. It was the only 'probable,' the only '*un*certain.' So then, what if it were not a Rastafarian symbol? After all, they had no known sign or symbol other than their dreadlocks.

"I pursued that line of reasoning: If it was not Rastafarian, then what? Was there another group that used the symbol of a black hand?"

All present seemed to grasp Koesler's explanation. Indeed, several of his listeners appeared to be ahead of the explanation. They were, of course, familiar with the notorious Black Hand Society, which had been one of the pseudonyms of the Mafia, or Cosa Nostra, in earlier days. The black hand had become an almost universal symbol of terror as people had first become aware of it and then instilled with the fear of it.

"The Black Hand, of course," said Koznicki. "If only we had thought of that possibility early on. The whole concept is perfect for an organization such as the Mafia. The purpose of a syndicate murder is not profit—although that occasionally may be a byproduct. And such killings are frequently meant as a message, not just of revenge, but of punishment and intimidation.

"No, the syndicate cannot chance the possibility that such an execution might be mistaken as an accident or as a murder perpetrated by anyone else for any other purpose; they must make their message clear, or else the revenge, the punishment and the intimidation would be missing or overlooked.

"In addition, with the Mafia, we are dealing with a group

among whom symbols are of specific importance. When we find ritual victims of the Mafia, we can tell what syndicate crime the victim had been guilty of from the appearance of the corpse. Begging the pardon of you ladies, but a man whose tongue has been cut off has violated the *omertà*, the silence. He was a stool pigeon. Hands amputated indicates a thief. Genitals stuffed in the victim's mouth shows the victim offended another member's woman. A dead fish sent from one Mafia family to another means the recipient's messenger has been drowned."

As the Inspector went on, Koesler smiled to himself; his friend was never so happy as in his role as educator.

"Now the black fist—or the clenched black hand, however he wishes to describe it—was found at the scene of each attack against a Cardinal. Then, at Madame Tussaud's, after Toussaint's disappearance, we found another black hand. Only now, for the first time, it was not clenched, but open. And after the sidewalk was cleared, at the spot where I was shot . . . another open black hand. And had not Superintendent O'Reardon been on the job, there would have been a black hand to mark the spot on the Burren where the killing of Father Koesler would have taken place.

"These black hands served two primary purposes: first, as a red herring for the police, who were meant to—and did— assume that these attacks were all being committed by the Rastafarians. After all; all other evidence aside, wasn't there an imprint of a black hand at the scene of each attack to tie them all together?

"And second, to focus further attention more closely on the Rastafarians and divert any thought of investigation in any other direction.

"But there was a third purpose—and this was why the signature was changed from a fist to an open hand. When all was said and done, and all three of us had been disposed of, it was imperative—almost mandatory—that certain people get the word: This is what happens to our enemies. This is what happens to those who would strike against us. This is our revenge. This is our justice.

"And so the ancient symbol of the Mafia—the black hand— was resurrected to deliver a message to any who might think they could strike against today's Mafia with impunity.

"It was suggested that the Mafia chieftain killed in that series of 'unsolved' murders," the Inspector glanced at Ramon Toussaint, "had been frightened to death. If you will recall," the Inspector looked meaningfully at Toussaint, "this was the conclusion reached by Dr. Moellmann, our esteemed medical examiner.

"So, Reverend Toussaint, since the Mafia had convicted you in absentia in its own kangaroo court, it was obligatory to terrorize you before their very brutal attempt at murdering you. Not only was the symbolism to be carried forward, but, in effect, the murder was to be the message."

The Inspector paused, glancing at Father Koesler and then returning his gaze to Toussaint. "By their standards—b anyone's standards—that deadly beating settled a few debts

Koesler's eyes flickered; Toussaint's face remained impas

The Inspector sipped his tea and then resumed. "Ther no doubt whatsoever that they would have pursued their pl until it was successfully concluded. They have a phrase for their concept of revenge . . ." Koznicki searched his mind.

"Like taking a stone out of one's shoe," Koesler supplied. "Mr. Licata mentioned it during our conversation."

"Exactly. Once Father Koesler and I were away from police protection—as one day we surely would have been— they would have struck again. And the same would have been true in your case, Reverend Toussaint. Once they realized the report was false, that you were not in a lifelong coma, they would have come for you.

"As it was, instead of remaining in a coma, you were able to pick Licata out of a photographic lineup as the man who was not only present at your clubbing, but, indeed, as the one who ordered it. Licata thought you were in a permanent limbo, whereas actually you were gathering the strength necessary to testify against him."

"Yes, but that brings up another question," said Toussaint. "I was able to make a positive identification of Licata and I was able to testify against him. Why then, did Bob have to visit Licata? Was that not taking a foolish and unnecessary risk?"

"I think—I hope—I can answer that to your satisfaction, Reverend," said Koznicki, "since it was mostly my idea.

"You see, when Father Koesler returned to Dublin from